What peop

The Gathering Place

A gripping story that could take place anywhere the leadership of the Holy Spirit is replaced by men and women with unholy motives and followers who are not discerning. The Gathering Place *is a book you won't be able to put down or forget! I highly recommend it.*

—MARLENE BAGNULL, LITT. D.
DIRECTOR, COLORADO CHRISTIAN WRITERS CONFERENCE

The spiritual journey of Casey Ellis is an all-too-frequent experience in American Christianity. Many Christians are similarly enticed only to find themselves on the exit ramp to a spiritual dead-end street.... Casey's story is a page-turner. But it is also very instructive in how people find themselves entrapped in spiritual counterfeits.

—DAVID HENKE
FOUNDER, WATCHMAN FELLOWSHIP, INC.
(A MINISTRY OF SPIRITUAL DISCERNMENT)

Haunting, intriguing, eerily close to reality ... these are just a few words to describe Becca Anderson's intricately woven tale. Pull out your discernment antennae, folks, and prepare yourself for a journey into the twisted underworld of twenty-first-century religious manipulation at its finest.

—JANICE THOMPSON
AUTHOR, *HURRICANE*

The Gathering Place

THE
GATHERING
PLACE

BECCA ANDERSON

RIVEROAK®
Good News in Fiction

COOK COMMUNICATIONS MINISTRIES
Colorado Springs, Colorado • Paris, Ontario
KINGSWAY COMMUNICATIONS LTD
Eastbourne, England

RiverOak® is an imprint of
Cook Communications Ministries, Colorado Springs, CO 80918
Cook Communications, Paris, Ontario
Kingsway Communications, Eastbourne, England

THE GATHERING PLACE
© 2006 by Becca Anderson

This story is a work of fiction. All characters and events are the product of the author's imagination. Any resemblance to any person, living or dead, is coincidental.

Cover Design: BMB Design

First Printing, 2006
Printed in the United States of America

1 2 3 4 5 6 7 8 9 Printing/Year 10 09 08 07 06

ISBN-13: 978-1-58919-055-9
ISBN-10: 1-58919-055-6

LCCN: 200533718

Dedicated to
my husband, Bob Anderson,
who urged me to finish this book—for years

And to Wilma Carr,
for her eagle eyes and encouraging spirit
no matter how many drafts it took

PART I

I know that after my departure savage wolves will come in among you, not sparing the flock; and from among your own selves men will arise, speaking perverse things, to draw away the disciples after them.

—PAUL TO THE EPHESIANS, ACTS 20:29–30

1

The traffic light cycled red-green-yellow and back to red as Casey Ellis felt her irritation rise. The drivers around her seemed equally annoyed, some blaring horns in frustration. A wail of approaching emergency vehicles shamed them into silence and explained the delay. Casey drummed her fingers on a denim-clad leg and took stock of her surroundings. A grateful sigh escaped her, and she inched into the shopping center parking lot on her right, intent on waiting out the gridlock in her favorite bookstore. She winced as two wheels jounced heavily over the curb.

She stepped from the street's blaring confusion into the soft illumination of the shop. Sunlight shone between window posters to form patterns on the carpet and book stacks. As always, the smell of paper and binding quickened her pulse.

She wished the books she edited appeared on the shelves in this cozy place, with its drifting strains of contemporary Christian music. The air was punctuated by the scent of leather and dazzling rainbow colors from window-mounted sun catchers. She pressed past the bright covers on the current bestsellers and moved deeper into the store to her favorite corner, and combed a practiced hand through her short brown hair to brush away the tension of the interrupted morning of errands.

Another woman browsed through books halfway down the cramped aisle. Casey stood at the end of the shelves, picked up a book by a favorite author, and began to scan pages, losing herself in the ideas they captured. The deep, challenging thoughts claimed her attention and soothed the awkwardness of having to share her corner with a stranger. Several peaceful minutes passed as the traffic tension faded from her mind.

"I read that one about six years ago," a quiet voice said. "It's very good, as far as it goes."

Casey glanced up. The other customer, petite with pale blonde hair that made her look younger than her softly middle-aged face revealed, gave her a gray-eyed gaze and a flicker of a smile. Casey glanced at her own book, then turned to the other woman.

"What do you mean?"

The woman put back the volume she had been examining. "Well, the author is right about freedom in Christ, but he doesn't take the picture of the church far enough. There's so much richness he left unexplored, and so it's a bit disappointing if you've had a fuller experience."

Casey frowned and fiddled uneasily with the tie at the neckline of her peasant blouse. "I always find him challenging and a bit radical." She dropped her eyes back to the book she was examining.

"Oh, I know what you mean. I used to feel the same way." The woman laughed as she turned to face Casey. "I began my search with him and similar authors. Then I met people who seemed to live on a whole different level, and I had to rethink much of what I'd read." The woman's soft eyes danced with excitement. "The books I'd read gave me a good foundation, but that's merely a place to build on."

Casey studied the eager-faced woman, then extended her hand. "My name is Casey," she said, blushing.

The woman put her soft, pale hand into Casey's. "Lydia Steele. I've been on my feet all day and could use a break. Would you like to go next door and get coffee or something?"

Casey hesitated, then smiled. "A cup of something sounds great."

The two left the store. After a dozen steps Lydia held the door to the café for Casey. They entered, their eyes adjusting to the subdued light inside. Groups of young people sipped cold drinks.

Single individuals perched storklike on tall iron stools, as they bent over books or magazines.

The two women ordered iced cappuccinos and carried them to comfortable chairs in the corner. Casey dropped into her chair with a sigh, slouching down and propping her feet on an enormous footstool.

"Oh, this is marvelous. The perfect thing for a Saturday afternoon."

"I'm glad you agreed." Lydia arranged the skirt of her denim jumper over her legs and extended them onto the shared footstool. "I thought I'd drop if I had to stand another minute." Her sneakered feet looked delicate next to Casey's chunky athletic shoes, particularly with the dainty anklet that peeped from beneath the long skirt.

"I don't usually do things like this on the spur of the moment, but I want to understand what you meant. It's rare to see anyone back in the … well, I call it the 'serious corner.'" Casey laughed. "And when I talk about what I read, people's eyes glaze over."

"I remember feeling so desperate to get closer to God—and not finding another living soul who wanted to go with me." Lydia reached for her drink and took a small sip.

"Sometimes I feel like I'm crazy," Casey said, "or I expect too much from God."

"Don't lower your expectations of God because people around you do."

Casey marveled. Talking to Lydia was like reading one of her beloved serious books. "Did you finally find others who wanted to go with you, as you put it, to find God?"

"Oh, my, yes. It's made all the difference in the world to me." Lydia's eyes held an image of something beyond the coffee shop, and Casey wished she could see it too.

"Did you find them all in my 'serious corner'?" she asked, to bring Lydia back to the present conversation.

Lydia's laugh was musical. "In a way, yes." She grinned. "I come here about once a month and pick out some books to go into our own bookstore for the Saints to buy after our Gatherings."

"Saints? Gatherings? I don't understand."

Lydia waved her hand in apology. "The Bible calls believers 'saints,' doesn't it?" Casey nodded. "Well, we call each other by that term to remind us of our position in Christ and our relationship to each other; and we don't hold services, we 'gather.' So we call the times we get together 'Gatherings.' We enjoy the Word, discuss the depths of Christ, and relish being together." Lydia took a sip and put her glass down.

"Do you get together on Sunday, or is this a midweek Bible study?"

"There's a Gathering on Sunday, and we often have prayer together at about six each morning, with home fellowships once a week, and sometimes special Gatherings on other nights when the Spirit moves." Lydia's eyes gleamed, and she leaned forward as she spoke.

"Every day? How do you get anything else done?" Casey was aghast and wondered if constant meeting with other believers was what it took to be more spiritual.

"You know, when I first came to the Bodylife, I feared it would be boring and—"

"Bodylife?" Casey's brows inched together in her confusion, and she pushed her glasses up more tightly onto her nose, as she always did when trying to understand something new to her.

"We're the Body, enjoying life together, so we call it the Bodylife," Lydia said, a smile tugging at the corners of her expressive mouth. "Anyway, I found that when I attended a Gathering I had more energy, and I got more done when I involved myself in Gatherings several times a week than when I took time off to do chores."

Casey shook her head, repelled by the thought of spending so much time with other people.

"There's nothing like sharing a Gathering," Lydia went on. "We have such an incredible corporate worship experience, I feel lifted out of myself and into the very presence of God as soon as I hear the singing."

Casey wondered what it would be like to anticipate worship like that. She sank deeper into her chair and let the smooth, flavorful drink and Lydia's soft voice lull her, as she wondered about her new acquaintance and her strange church. When Lydia looked at her watch, Casey did the same, stunned to see that an hour had passed.

"Just like in a Gathering, time seems to fly. I'm afraid I have to go get my books and get back to my errands."

"I can't believe we've been here so long. I'll turn our glasses in." Casey rose from the enveloping chair. Traffic seemed to be moving smoothly again, she noted. They left the shop and turned back toward the bookstore, but she was filled with new ideas, and no longer wanted a new book. Her steps slowed.

Lydia turned to her. "Have you ever felt that you've arrived suddenly at a moment you've been waiting for a long, long time? I experienced that feeling in the bookstore when you came in. I sense we're going to become good friends." She hugged Casey, then pulled back and looked at her. "I'm glad we met today. I'm sorry I talked your ears off." She laughed. "But you asked me about what means more to me than anything, so what did you expect?"

Casey smiled. Despite her innate love of solitude, she wanted to talk to Lydia again. She adjusted her glasses and pondered whether to offer her phone number. Lydia solved the problem for her.

"I know you're seeking a deeper spiritual life. I want to encourage you to keep seeking until you have found what you were created for." Lydia rummaged in the deep pocket of her jumper and came up with a small notepad, with a tiny pen clipped to it. She scribbled her name and phone number and an address on the pad as she spoke. "Why don't you drop in and Gather with us sometime?" She tore off the page and handed it to Casey. "Or call me. I'd be happy to chat on the phone or meet you for coffee somewhere." Lydia put the pad and pen back into her pocket, squeezed Casey's arm, and turned to go.

"I enjoyed meeting you," Casey called after Lydia. "Thanks for the talk." Lydia waved and disappeared into the bookstore.

A half hour later, Casey pulled into her driveway still turning Lydia's words over in her mind. When she entered the house, her large, orange-striped cat stretched on the windowsill. He gave her a sleepy blink of recognition and then slumped back into peaceful sleep.

"Effusive as always, Andrew." She scratched him under the chin, and he purred and licked her hand with scratchy affection.

She took in the airy neatness of the house with the rush of pleasure it always gave her. As she climbed the staircase, ideas swirled in her head. She entered her room and flopped on the bed to consider them. She heard Andrew hop from the windowsill below. He padded up the stairs and curled into his accustomed place a whisker's distance from her face.

The paper with Lydia's phone number on it crackled in her pocket as she curled on her side. She patted the denim that housed it and wondered if she'd ever call.

2

Sunday morning's soft peach glow crept through Casey's window. She rolled over, buried her face in Andrew's soft fur, and listened to his contented rumble as she stroked him. She fought to throw off her sleepy lethargy, determined to get to church on time. In the end the cat goaded her from the bed when he demanded to be fed. Casey talked to him throughout her preparations for his breakfast and her own. She patted him as he went outside to hop onto his favorite lawn chair for an extended wash session.

An hour later she slid into her usual pew. She opened her Bible and tried to overcome her feeling of emptiness. She sang without spirit and nodded with others as the pastor spoke about the need for help in the Sunday school classes.

When he opened his sermon with jokes, Casey tried to focus on the Scripture text. It irked her that he apparently felt the Bible needed a humorous monologue to warm up the congregation to study it. The chosen text dealt with spiritual duty, but somehow he turned it into an exhortation for everyone to get involved in the churchwide yard sale later in the month.

Casey wondered whether she was being critical or discerning as she picked the sermon apart. She looked around at people she'd worshiped with for three years and realized that all she knew about most of them was what they revealed in their prayer requests. She found little depth when one woman asked for prayer so she and her husband could get a good price for their used car, and a man said his swimming pool might be leaking. Since the annual church party was held at his home, this became a matter for truly serious prayer. Relieved when the service ended, Casey shook the pastor's hand and walked back to her car to return home.

As she drove, her mind wandered to the strange encounter with Lydia, and the church she had described. It had sounded exciting yet unsettling. She lingered on her sense of uneasiness and wondered what prompted it. She yearned to be closer to God. There had to be more than the lightweight sermon she had heard and the vague sense of guilt she always felt when leaving her church. She pulled into the garage and listened to the metallic clicks of the cooling engine. "Oh, God," she prayed, sagging back into her seat, "is this what you meant when you commanded us to gather together? There has to be more to life in you than this. Help me to find it."

After a quick lunch of apple slices spread liberally with peanut butter, Casey felt restless. She couldn't seem to settle down to work on chores, nor did she have the energy to launch into a creative project. She sat in the recliner and debated whether to go for a drive or take a nap. Andrew stretched and crossed the carpet to jump into her lap. He settled down with his head on one of her hands. Casey stroked him, contented by the unexpected feline affection.

The telephone on the small table at her elbow shattered the calm. Andrew bolted from her lap and returned to his window perch. After debating whether to answer, Casey lifted the receiver on the fourth ring.

"Casey, I missed you this morning," an exuberant voice trilled from the receiver. "Did you stay home?"

"I'm fine, thanks, and how are you?"

"Oh, sorry." A pause. "Well, where were you?" Casey knew Gretchen's dark brows would be knitted together over her close-set tan eyes as she tucked a dark lock of disobedient hair behind one ear.

"I was there. I sat three rows behind you." Casey wasn't sure she had the energy for a conversation with Gretchen.

"I guess I never turned all the way around, because I didn't think you were there. Anyway, I wondered if you wanted to go shopping with me this afternoon. I have a list of things I need to get for the baby's room."

Gretchen's little shopping trips were legendary. She rarely came home without spending hundreds of dollars.

Casey had never quite understood what drew the two of them together. They were so different in their tastes and lifestyles. Sometimes it seemed that most of the drawing was on Gretchen's part. Gretchen cared about Casey in ways other people didn't, always trying to bring her out of her shell and get her involved in things. Irritating though the attempts sometimes were, Casey appreciated the spirit behind them, and sometimes gave in.

"I don't have any spare cash and—"

"I'm not asking you to spend money, just spend time with me. Just the two of us ... and Jennifer."

The thought of spending the remainder of her Sunday afternoon with a shop-happy pregnant woman and a two-year-old decided the issue for Casey. She envied Gretchen's outgoing manner; sometimes it brought out the best in her, too. On days like today, however, it was more than she could handle. "No, I can't. I've got some things I need to think about."

"Think, think, think. That's all you do in that house all by yourself! You need to get out, mingle a little. If you won't go with me today, then at least say you'll come to my new Bible study. It's your kind of crowd—lots of deep thinkers and serious people."

Casey rolled her eyes. Gretchen was always discovering someone or something and was excited about each new acquisition—at least for a few weeks.

"So I asked them what their church was called." Casey tried to focus. She had missed several seconds of monologue while her mind wandered. With Gretchen that could mean hundreds of words. "And the leader of the study said they just call themselves the Body."

Casey clicked into the conversation. "I met someone at the

bookstore yesterday who belonged to a group called Body-something. What was it? Bodylife?" she managed to insert into a short pause.

"That's it, Bodylife. I knew I had it muddled. Funny you should meet someone from the same group. What was her name? Or, better yet, was it a he?" Gretchen giggled.

"No, a woman. I met her at King's, back in my corner."

"That's where these people would be if they turned up any-where. I must admit a lot of the teaching goes right over my head, but oh, what singing and what sharing. Why don't you come with me? I'll go for the singing, you can go for the teaching, and we'll both be happy."

Casey played with a loose button on the chair arm as she con-sidered. "I thought their church was clear over in Crescent Hills."

"They have outreach Bible studies in different areas. The one here meets at the home of the morning deejay on the Christian radio station. Some people come the first time because he's a celebrity, but they come back for the teaching."

"Or the singing," Casey teased.

"Well, there's nothing wrong with going where the worship is as inspiring as the talking—especially when the talking gets a bit deep and overwhelming."

Casey was intrigued. It might be fun to check out the group, and to be able to do so closer to home lessened some of her uneasi-ness. "I'll go with you," she said at last.

"Really? I never thought you'd go. I've been talking myself blue in the face about this for weeks, and—"

"Hey, don't talk me out of it. I'll pick you up so you can show me where it is. Now it sounds like you need to go, by the noises I'm hearing." A wailing crescendo heralded Jennie's approach.

"Here she comes—like a fire engine. I think she gets those lungs from her dad," Gretchen said.

Casey put down the phone and turned to Andrew. "From her father, indeed." Andrew raised his eyelids halfway, cocked an ear, then tucked a paw over his nose as if to shut out the light and stop his mistress's unwanted conversation.

Casey gazed out the window and ran a slim finger back and forth along her lower lip as she felt a rising sense of anticipation.

3

asey arrived early on Thursday evening. Gretchen had just come in from speed-walking the dog and did not notice. Casey was glad; Gretchen could be a merciless tease about the stupidest things.

They navigated a maze of streets to a small cul-de-sac. Four cars were already crowded two abreast in the driveway, and four more of varying sizes pulled in and parked around the broad cul-de-sac. Gretchen bounded from the car with loud exclamations of welcome. It allowed Casey to study the house, the other guests, and the overall layout.

The house was flanked by other prosperous homes, their windows gazing toward the street. The windows of this particular house framed glimpses of high ceilings, soft colors, and at least a dozen people moving about inside. Casey could see Gretchen's head bobbing among others as she moved toward the house, apparently forgetting her for the moment. She got out, locked the car, and moved in Gretchen's direction. As they made their way up the walk, her friend introduced her to a blur of faces.

Inside, people conversed in exuberant tones. The large, open house had a room off the entryway cleared of all furniture except an upright piano and wall-to-wall colorful plastic lawn chairs. A stiff wooden chair faced the plastic chairs, and a floor lamp shone on it. The people in the house all seemed to know each other well enough to exchange liberal hugs, yet Casey heard more than one person ask the person hugged what his or her name was. She shrank back, not ready for such familiarity.

Gretchen reappeared, swooped Casey up, and hustled her off to the kitchen. "Hurry, let's get something to drink and maybe something to munch on. They'll start in a minute." She poured lemonade from a pitcher, grabbed crackers, and dropped them into the front pockets of her maternity smock. Casey put ice into a glass and selected a can of diet soda.

"Oh, let me introduce you around," Gretchen said. Casey's heart beat faster. She disliked feeling overwhelmed and out of control, but it was impossible to stop Hurricane Gretchen once she got going.

"This is Nancy, and this is Jeff. They host the Gatherings here." Gretchen turned Casey toward a couple busy with food and drink.

The two handsome people smiled and went on with their work. "We're glad you could come tonight," Jeff said. "There's nothing like a Gathering to light up the week."

Casey nodded, though she began to flinch at the repetitive use of the word *Gathering*. Gretchen, ever the chameleon, had picked up the lingo.

"Let's see, who else can I introduce you to?" Gretchen cast around in the crowd and beamed with excitement. "Oh, here's someone you must meet. This is—"

"Lydia Steele," Casey interrupted, glad to see the blonde hair and pleasant face of her bookstore acquaintance as she came through the crowd.

"Oh, you said you'd met someone at the bookstore. Was that Lydia?" Gretchen sounded miffed. Lydia approached and gave Casey a warm hug. Casey, set to resist such advances, felt unexpectedly comforted by it as she remembered the calm that surrounded Lydia when she had met her last. Lydia's face was lit with pleasure.

"Casey, what a surprise. I didn't know you lived in Grovers or I would have invited you here." As Gretchen turned to greet someone else, Casey let herself be led away from the noise and laughter toward the room with the plastic chairs.

She let out a relieved breath. "Whew. It was a little tight in there." She and Lydia sank into seats at the far edge of the chair-filled room. "This is better."

Lydia laughed. "I know what you mean, and sometimes Gretchen can be … too much."

It was Casey's turn to laugh. "I've never heard it put better." Casey began to relax and took a sip of her drink. "How long have you had this Bible study?"

"I think we started about eight months ago. Webster—Webster Forsythe, our leading Brother—wants to plant a Body here, and this Gathering is the beginning of that."

She appeared ready to say more, but the crowd surged into the room and the chairs filled. Electricity and anticipation emanated from the group. Casey studied the middle-aged man who took the wooden chair. His crisp, prematurely white hair shone in the light. He was dressed in a dark charcoal suit, and his cream-colored dress shirt was buttoned all the way up despite the warmth of the evening. He had the thinnest wrists Casey had ever seen. When she looked at them, she sensed a fragility that aroused her empathy. However, when she looked at his piercing eyes, she glimpsed unyielding resolution.

A young woman moved to the piano with confidence and familiarity. Songbooks circulated through the crowd, and Casey took one. The dark-haired girl at the piano began to play. Casey flipped through the book—there was not a single song she recognized. She grimaced.

"Number seventy-two," a young man behind Casey called out. "Amen," several people in the group exclaimed.

The girl at the piano plunged into a bright tune. Lydia turned to the back of her own songbook, and Casey hurried to catch up. She found her place and followed the unfamiliar words. The room filled with soaring voices to accompany the loud piano. Casey felt overwhelmed by the volume.

Lydia's high, clear, sweet voice caught Casey's attention. She tried to focus on the words but had already let the singing get past her. Lydia put her finger on a verse, still singing. Casey began to catch the simple, lovely tune and sang along. The group sang four verses and had just two more to get through. Casey began to think the singing wouldn't be so bad after all.

"Verse two again!" an enthusiastic voice cried from the back corner. The group finished the verse in progress and then began to sing the second verse again, with even greater volume than before.

The noise assaulted Casey. No song was sung all the way through before someone called for a reprise of part or all of it. She began to fidget. Her ears burned from the prolonged, loud singing. Her throat felt raw. She enjoyed a few songs, but most had lyrics that were a mystery to her. Her discomfort increased when, in the midst of the most obscure verses, someone would call out a lusty amen. She wondered what the others understood that she did not.

Between songs different people spoke in turn. Some spoke of what they had learned in the Bible recently. Others spoke candidly of struggles they were having. Casey liked these relatively quiet interludes before the musical storm broke again. However, at the end of each song and during and after each testimony, people would burst out with a loud amen. The unified, repetitive voicing of this one word began to grate on Casey's nerves.

With no warning all the songbooks were closed and put aside. She closed her book, put it under her chair, and picked up her Bible. She looked toward the man seated in the wooden chair with anticipation and some trepidation.

"Amen!" cried the man. He beamed as he looked out on the people assembled before him. The group echoed back noisily. "Oh, what glorious singing!" he shouted. "Amen," others in the group again exclaimed. "Oh, what a foretaste of what is to come," he said with a mighty shake of his head. The group replied with gusto.

Casey realized that the man's eyes were closed. She shut her eyes, but did not join the others in their outbursts.

"Oh, Lord, what a release to praise you!" *Amen!* "Oh, what freedom we find in your Body!" he intoned, as his voice broke on the final word. *Amen!*

From the middle of the room another voice took up the prayer. "Oh, Lord, we taste the sweetness!" *Amen!* the group punctuated, unimpeded by the change in prayer leader. "Oh, the sweetness of being in the Body!"

Another voice, a woman's this time, took the lead. "Oh, the
sweetness!" *Amen!* "Oh, there is no other such sweetness!"
Amen! "Oh, no other sweetness like being in the Body!" she
cried.

Casey sat still as a stone as the prayer leadership rotated among
many in the room. The format was new to her, but she struggled
to keep an open mind. The repetitive amen divided the short
prayers, structured into ten words or less at a burst. Speakers
extolled the Body and their joy in being together.

As she listened, Casey wondered if her negative reaction
involved the content of the prayer, which seemed quite refreshing,
or the different style in which it was offered. She enjoyed listening
to the words being shouted because they were so different from the
ones spoken during the prayer time at her own church, with the
pastor's dull, emotionless monologue of petition to God.

The quality of this prayer time also differed. Nowhere did she
hear a personal request. Gone were the stilted phrases she heard
each week at her church, many of which slipped into King James
English. These people took pleasure in praying. They went on for
several minutes with their lavish compliments to God, their thanks
for the saints, their deep enjoyment of salvation. As she got used to
the cadence they used, Casey's ears perked up with each change in
leader, and she wondered what else there was to praise.

At last, the whole group repeated "amen" several times. This
seemed to signal the end, and the people around Casey relaxed
back into their chairs. She saw them shake themselves back to reality, as though they had been far away and had to reawaken. All eyes
turned to the man in the wooden chair as he picked up a well-
thumbed Bible. The gold trim had been worn off the edges of most
of the pages, and the book flopped open on his knees.

"I see we have many guests this week, so I'll introduce myself.
My name is Webster Forsythe. In case you've stumbled in by mistake, we're here to study God's Word." Delighted laughter rippled
from the group. "Tonight I thought we'd backtrack a bit," he
began, "since there are so many new faces among us." Casey feared

he would make all the newcomers stand and introduce themselves. However, he continued to speak without even glancing around.

"About nine months ago the Lord laid on my heart the need for more Bodylife here in this area. We've been Gathering in Crescent Hills for six years, and we almost have the Gathering Place finished. For now we meet at the high school each Lord's Day, but by Christmas we'll be in our own Gathering Place." Many of the listeners inclined their heads, and from this action Casey deduced which of them were regular attendees at the Crescent Hills Gathering.

"When we first started a gathering here, it was wonderful to watch the Spirit draw in like-minded believers—and look how big we've grown!" Again many heads nodded, and a soft amen sounded. "But what is the basis of our Gathering? Why do we gather at all? To increase our number?" A sprinkle of chuckles. "No, we gather according to the Word." Webster held his Bible aloft. "We gather according to the desire the Spirit gives us, and we step in the direction in which the Spirit gives us peace and life. If the Spirit gives life, we go." Webster smiled, then opened his Bible, but his eyes were fixed on the group as he apparently quoted from memory, "And they were gathering house to house, sharing all things in common, and serving one another, and all those around them saw and gave glory to God."

Casey glanced over, saw where Lydia had her finger in her Bible, and turned hers to the same chapter in the book of Acts that described the early disciples' activities after the ascension of Jesus into heaven. Although the words Webster had spoken did not exactly match her version, she paid close attention to him as he continued.

"That's what we do also. We gather in house fellowships; we assemble at our Gathering Place to serve each other. We help each other every weekend. We eat together in house Gatherings, and we get together every opportunity we have to drink in the wonder of the Word and enjoy the Bodylife."

Casey did not have to wonder if there would be a hearty amen to that, and she wasn't disappointed. As the evening wore on, she began to dislike the simple word less as she anticipated it with better accuracy.

"We're commanded in the Word to love the believers, first and foremost," Webster continued, his voice intense. His dark blue eyes swept the room and fixed on each person in turn. "We're commanded to be the church, with all that name implies. The Bodylife is filled with seven-day-a-week believers and doesn't make room for Sunday Christians."

Casey blinked. Her heart skipped a beat as she wondered if she had finally found what she had sought so long.

"As we've met here in Grovers," Webster said, "we've found people who believe as we do, and who can be a Gathering of the church in Grovers—and one day I'm confident that will come about through God raising up a shepherd for this area."

More than a few people glanced at Jeff. He held Nancy's hand and listened, seemingly oblivious to the looks from the others.

"In the New Testament we see the apostles and others writing letters to churches to commend, reprimand, and correct," Webster said. "The church was very new in those days, and there was lots of shepherding to do. Today the world encroaches on us, presses on our spirits, gobbles up our time, tries to expunge all goodness from our minds through television and other entertainment media, and does its level best to press the church into its own faithless image. Often it succeeds."

Casey nodded. She had thought the same thing for many years.

"We've strayed from the path, and we've let the world infringe upon our territory. We fool ourselves when we think the church is still pure. If you have a plot of land and you keep ninety-nine percent for yourself, it is ninety-nine percent pure. If the one percent you give away happens to be in the center, your enemy walks all over you as he comes and goes to his own piece of the property. The purity and integrity of the land drop to almost zero. This is what the church has done."

Webster paused, bent to pick up his glass, and sipped from it. "No matter how many times I read the Bible, the message is clear.

The Body must be united, and believers must be involved in active Bodylife to keep the world and the Devil at bay."

"Amen!" The exclamation made Casey jump. She looked down at her Bible, and a blush flooded across her cheeks. She also began to wonder if Webster was leading up to a doctrine advocating "everybody just needs to get along." She had not come to hear about watered-down Christianity, and somehow she didn't think she would. The enthusiasm was too great for that.

"The apostles wrote to the church in each city, implying there was one Gathering of the church in each area. There were house fellowships to make things manageable, but the church was the church," Webster said. "It had no name, no denomination, and no designation. Its foundation was Jesus Christ, as it is for us today. We don't gather around a doctrine of baptism or speaking in tongues or speaking high-church English. Instead we gather on the solid ground of Jesus Christ and nothing else. Tonight we are the Body gathered in Grovers. When we are in our new Gathering Place, we'll be the same Body. However, we'll be gathering in Crescent Hills. Location makes no difference!"

The simplicity of what Webster said swept over Casey. Here was something that made sense to her. There was no need for denominationalism. There was only a need for the church to gather as the church. It was, indeed, a proposal for unity—but not blending differing doctrines into a meaningless stew. Instead it swept away the divisions until the essential remained.

When the amen burst from the people in the room, the word spilled out of Casey's mouth as well. Joy she had never known welled up from deep within her.

Amen! they cried again, and Casey joined them in full voice. Webster continued in the same vein for a while longer, and her pen flew as she scribbled her thoughts and kept half an ear on what he said to be sure she did not miss anything.

"I hope that felt as good to your spirit as it did to mine," Webster said with a laugh when he had finished speaking. The amen that thundered back was enthusiastic. "We'll talk more on this subject on Sunday." Casey felt eager to hear more.

As the group relaxed, and the young woman returned to the piano, Casey picked up her songbook with more interest. When the first song was called out, she heard familiar music and felt more at home. She turned to the page and found that the words were different from those she had learned years earlier. The words fit with the message Webster had given, however, and she liked the novelty of them. Between songs people again spoke from their hearts.

"When I first came to the Bodylife, I was so tired of playing church," said a tall, handsome man. "I had tried every way I could to get closer to God. I taught Sunday school, I worked with the youth group, I visited new people in the church—I even sang in the choir. I was busy seven days a week, and I thought I would get closer to God." He looked around at the group, and then a brilliant smile illuminated his rugged features. "All I got was tired." They all chuckled with him. "In the Bodylife, I'm busy every day of the week too—but there's a difference. I serve with joy, not with a sense of drudgery, and I meet God at every turn."

Several testimonies followed, echoing the same thoughts. Some were humorous, some brought tears, and all were punctuated with the ever-present amen.

A peal of laughter came from a pert redhead. Casey saw that she wore a denim jumper and pastel T-shirt. In fact, as she looked around the room, she counted no fewer than five women who were attired the same way. The woman's headband restrained her brassy curls and matched the green T-shirt.

"My first time at a Gathering, I sat in the back and thought, 'This is a cult!'" she said. There was a burst of laughter from the group, but Casey felt a cold shock. "How else could all these people be so happy unless it were some kind of conspiracy?" More laughter. "I even checked the ceiling for something to amplify the singing. There were microphones hung from the rafters, but they were for recording, not amplifying."

Lydia bent closer to murmur in Casey's ear. "You can get tapes of the messages or the singing at any Gathering. I love to take the

whole Body with me in the car. It helps me learn the songs as well."
She smiled.

Casey noticed a thin young woman seated at a table in the
entryway. She had headphones on her lap. On the table an open
suitcase held recording equipment, apparently for copying tapes.
She was impressed by the efficiency of the operation.

"Then I felt my spirit wake up," the redhead continued as she
gestured to her chest with a delicate hand. "And I knew I was home.
I hadn't known how homesick I was until that moment, but I didn't
even want to leave the building when the Gathering was over. Lucky
for me, someone asked me to lunch, or I would have sat there all day
and night, waiting for the next Gathering." Good-natured laughter
erupted at the end of her testimony, accompanied by gentle applause.

After a few more testimonies and more singing, Webster
rubbed his hands together and said, "Amen! Let's go and see what
Nancy's cooked up this week, shall we?" He rose to his feet as the
other people began to stretch the kinks out of their backs and rise
with him. There was a general exodus toward the kitchen again.
Lydia took Casey's arm as she stood.

"Nancy always makes homemade soup each Gathering night.
She's a fabulous cook, and she makes enough for everybody to have
seconds and thirds. Are you hungry?"

Casey put her Bible and notebook back on her chair and smiled
at Lydia. "I'm hungry for more of what I heard tonight, I'm hungry for meaning in my life—and yes, I'm hungry for Nancy's
soup!" She surprised herself with the forthrightness of her answer.

"Well, soup first, then we can talk more. Maybe you'd like to
come to the Sunday Gathering in Crescent Hills. I know it sounds
like a long way to drive, but it's more than worth it, and you can
come to our house for lunch afterward to make it last longer.
How's that?" Lydia squeezed Casey's arm.

Casey hesitated.

"Please say you'll come." Lydia waited as Casey debated with
herself. The sense of pleasant discovery swept her again, and she
put aside her usual reticence.

"All right, I'll come."

Lydia's blazing smile and warm hug were all the reward she needed to affirm the decision. They turned and, arm in arm, headed toward the kitchen with its enticing smell of soup and the warm noise of happy people in a confined space.

Webster Forsythe waved a last time to Jeff and Nancy as the van rounded the cul-de-sac and headed back to Crescent Hills. He adjusted the rearview mirror and watched them join hands and stroll back toward their front door. All the other cars had gone, and neighbors pushed garbage cans to the curb or trailed dogs taking a last walk before bedtime.

The van was filled with faithful Bodylife members who made the weekly trek to Grovers. The emaciated young woman who had operated the recording equipment throughout the evening readjusted the rearview mirror for driving. She fished a cassette tape from the pocket of her windbreaker and slid it part way into the player mounted in the dashboard.

"I thought it went well," Webster said, and half turned in his seat toward those in the back.

"Much better than the last few Gatherings," said Dominic, square-jawed, handsome, and immaculately groomed. "I think the back-to-basics approach did it."

"Yeah, you'd begun to lose a few of them, and with so many new ones each week it's hard to reach all levels at one time," said Audrey, her fingers still moving as though at the piano.

"It's good to see the new ones, even though they make it more difficult," Webster said. "They're harder to read than the ones who've come for a while. Did we seem to make any progress?"

"We did," the driver said, her voice husky. "Want to hear it?"

Stephanie extended her narrow finger and pressed the cassette tape home. The van filled with the sound of laughter, and they heard Webster's voice echo from the immediate past.

"Amen! Let's go and see what Nancy's cooked up this week, shall we?" his voice boomed. They heard loud scratchy sounds as Webster fumbled with his microphone and unclipped it from his tie, then a sharp clunk as he dropped it on the chair. The noise level decreased as the crowd moved away from the chair toward the kitchen. Webster and the others in the van waited. As distinct voices became clearer amid the receding chatter, everyone in the van leaned forward to catch the words. Webster noted that the volume, which had been too high before, was just right. Stephanie could bring out the most intricate sounds in any recording with a skill that bordered on magic.

Lydia's voice filled the van with a gentle, musical sound. "Nancy always makes homemade soup each Gathering night. She's a fabulous cook, and she makes enough for everybody to have seconds and thirds. Are you hungry?"

A pause. Then an unfamiliar voice responded. "I'm hungry for more of what I heard tonight, I'm hungry for meaning in my life— and yes, I'm hungry for Nancy's soup!"

They listened as Lydia offered her invitation and the other woman hesitated. Webster strained to hear the nuances in the voices.

"Please say you'll come." Lydia's voice sounded perfect, he decided. There was a long, thoughtful pause before the other woman spoke again.

"All right, I'll come."

After the exchange, the two moved away from the open microphone, and no more distinct words could be heard. Stephanie ejected the cassette.

"I'd say that tells it all, doesn't it?" Webster said. The others in the van murmured their assent.

"Lydia's wonderful. She seems so natural in her approaches," Audrey said. "She's a real asset to the house, isn't she?" She turned to redheaded Carol for information.

"From what I understand it was touch and go at the beginning, but you'd never know it." Carol tugged on an auburn lock wound around her left ear.

"I'll be sure to talk more about our living situations on Sunday," Webster said. "We don't want this new prospect to walk into the house and feel any uneasiness. She needs to see the love and the cooperation. Be sure she does, Carol."

"Oh, she will. I've already begun to plan both the food and the talk with her in mind."

"Good," Webster said. They sped through the night and exited the freeway.

"I'd begun to think it was time to call a halt to the Grovers Gatherings," said Dominic, his chiseled profile accentuated by the oncoming headlights. "It seemed we weren't getting anyone new there, other than Gretchen. Does she have any potential?"

"She's a bit flighty. I'm not sure she'd make a good candidate," Audrey said.

"Now that may not be true," Webster objected. "Some of our best candidates have been impulsive."

"Her impulsiveness is tempered by her husband's cool head," Stephanie said as she maneuvered the van through a turn onto a broad avenue. "He's out of town on business a lot, and he'll never go for a radical change. She's not a candidate."

"I hadn't realized that," Webster said. "You're right. That kind of situation has worked against us in the past."

"But this new person, what's her name?" The query came from the back, from a young man who was a technical genius-in-residence at a chemical lab in neighboring Harrisville.

"Her name's Casey something," Carol said. "Why, Kurt, you interested?" Good-natured laughter flowed from all as they turned to watch a blush wash across his features. The fact that the blush was predictable made it all the more amusing.

"I just wanted to know. She is nice looking, though."

"We're going to have to get you a wife, and soon," Webster joked. "Have patience, Kurt. Soon, I promise."

"We have to discuss these trips to Grovers one of these days," Dominic said after an expansive yawn. Many heads nodded, some with imminent sleep.

"I know," Webster said. "Just when I think it's time to roll up the carpet, someone like this Casey comes along, but this may serve a dual purpose to begin to encourage Jeff and Nancy to move closer to the Gathering Place. That would increase their commitment and force those who've been fringe candidates for so long to make a choice. If they don't have the Gathering at Jeff and Nancy's to attend anymore, they'll have to quit altogether or start attending the regular Gatherings."

"I'm dead on my feet the day after these things," Carol said. "It would be so much easier to centralize for a while."

"I'll start testing the water with Jeff at work," Kurt said, his voice soft from the rear seat. "I can talk to him tomorrow when he comes to do an interview with our new CEO."

"Okay, but be gentle," Webster warned. "Let me know how it goes, and I'll work on it from there."

The journey almost at its end, they all settled into a comfortable silence. Webster decided that the strategy session had been as good as the Gathering. There was still plenty of work before them, but then, there always was.

4

W ell, what did you think?" Casey held the receiver away from her ear. "I thought it was one of the best Gatherings yet!" Gretchen crowed.

"It was different," Casey said, not ready to admit to Gretchen that she had been right about something.

"Is that all you can say?"

Suddenly, it didn't matter to Casey what Gretchen thought. "I'm teasing you. It was wonderful. I had a great time, and I plan to go back. Enough for you?"

There was silence for a full three seconds. "Really? That's great. I was afraid you'd say I'd gone off the deep end again."

"This time you've gone off the *right* deep end," Casey said. "You and your passions. You're the kind of person Baskin-Robbins was made for; you love something for about thirty days. I'm amazed sometimes that you and Gerry have stayed together all this time."

"I have a longer attention span than you give me credit for," Gretchen protested. "Besides, Gerry's gone on business most of the time. When he comes home, it's like we're starting all over again every time."

Casey laughed. "That explains it. You think he's a new man every couple of weeks."

"How did we get on this subject?" Gretchen wailed. "We were talking about the Gathering. Didn't you love the singing and the fellowship afterward? I thought it was glorious."

"No, I didn't like the singing. You know I hate to learn new songs, and even with the ones I thought I knew they'd changed the

36

words. But the message was very different. I think I caught a glimpse of the vision Webster described, and it was incredible."

"He loses me pretty fast most of the time, but last night he seemed clearer. I bought the tape so Gerry could hear it. Did you?"

"No, I took notes." Casey watched Andrew stretch in the sun and begin his grooming process.

"You and your notes. Do you ever read those things after you've written them?"

"If I don't take notes, I don't listen. It's the way I am. But most aren't worth reviewing. The ones from last night will be."

"I love Jeff and Nancy." Gretchen's voice rose with new enthusiasm. "Their house always smells so nice, and they love to have people over. You know, a few months ago Gerry and Jennie and I went to their house for dinner. There must have been thirty people there. I don't know how Nancy does it, preparing for such crowds all the time."

"Were they all from the Bible study?"

"Some, but lots came down from Crescent Hills. We sang and shared, and someone gave a message, even though Webster wasn't there." Gretchen's smile was audible. "You know, that's one neat thing about this church. If Webster is out of town or doesn't have anything to say one Sunday, another Brother will stand up and speak instead. It's fun to see him sit there like all the rest of us and listen to another Brother preach."

Casey didn't like the hero worship in Gretchen's voice when she spoke about Webster. And the lingo hit her like a slap. Rather than argue, she changed the subject.

"Are you going to Crescent Hills on Sunday?"

Gretchen groaned. "I can't. Gerry's plane comes in at ten forty-five—right in the middle of the Gathering." Casey tried to picture a plane landing down an aisle during a church service, and she grinned.

"I suppose we could go for the first half hour or so, then leave, go get Gerry, double back, and catch the last bit too," Gretchen said, and her voice accelerated as the idea unfolded.

Casey laughed outright. "You're incapable of entering or leaving a room quietly with Jennie in tow. You'd disrupt everything—twice. Besides, Gerry will be tired when he gets off the plane. He probably won't want to head off to church."

"You're right. I guess Jennie and I will go to the old church here. It lets out a lot earlier. What about you?"

"I think I'll try the Crescent Hills church. Lydia asked me to come and to join her for lunch afterward."

"Oh, you're so lucky. Their house is great. They make a wonderful lunch." Casey could hear that Gretchen had settled into the dishes as well as the conversation. She was about to ask who "they" were, since Lydia had not mentioned having a husband or family. Just then Gretchen went on to explain. "A lot of the Saints live together in Crescent Hills," she added. "I think it's because it's so expensive to live there."

"What do you mean, 'live together'?" Casey felt her heart drop. Did Gretchen mean unmarried couples sharing the same house? That wasn't right, even if the church was incredible.

"If a family has an extra room, they'll have a single Brother or Sister move in. It makes for better fellowship and can be very helpful in getting chores done." The sound of banging pots and pans almost drowned out Gretchen's words. "Boy, I could use a few spare Sisters myself."

"So Lydia lives with another family?" Casey felt uneasy. She had been invited to lunch, but what did the other people in the house think about it?

"No, Lydia lives in the Sisters House." Casey heard water spraying loudly in the background. "It's a house where single Sisters live. There's also a Brothers House, but it's run by a married couple, because you know what Brothers are like." Gretchen laughed, and Casey joined her.

Casey heard a doorbell ring, a dog bark, and Jennie's voice receding saying, "I open door."

"Oh, no, the UPS guy is here. I have to go or Jennie will have him watching cartoons with her in fifteen seconds flat. I'll talk to you later." The last words faded away as Gretchen replaced the receiver.

"Have a nice day," Casey said to the silent telephone. She wondered what Gretchen had ordered this time. Once it had been an inflatable raft, complete with oars, life jackets, and coupons for snacks appropriate to the boating life. Gerry had never been able to take them out on the lake, but a detail like that wouldn't stop Gretchen's spending splurges. It was possible that this delivery was more practical, but Casey doubted it.

5

With guilty excitement Casey backed out of her garage Sunday morning. She wondered if people at her church would notice her absence. Several families had left recently when the pastor began to speak of a building program, and she feared he would think she'd done the same.

But her overriding emotion was that of spine-tingling adventure. The night before, she had reviewed her notes from the Bible study and was eager to hear more about the concepts Webster had shared. A long drive ahead added to the novelty.

Crescent Hills carried an unspoken cachet of class and snobbishness that both irritated and intimidated her. However, as she remembered the warmth of Lydia's smile, and the enthusiastic way other people had responded to the message, her concern receded. She rummaged in the armrest for a music tape, popped it into the cassette player, and settled more comfortably in her seat.

Audrey adjusted the miniblinds in the exercise room, which reduced the glare from the outdoor pool. She grimaced and longed for the day the Gathering Place would be completed and they could meet somewhere that didn't smell like chlorine and sweat. Brothers bustled to bring chairs from the storage room and set them up. The arranging of two hundred chairs made considerable noise and took a concerted effort to organize.

Two Brothers pushed the upright piano to its customary place, and another followed with the piano bench. As soon as it was in place, Audrey sat down and began playing, as much to settle her own spirit as to cheer the Brothers while they worked.

"Amen!" came a hearty cry from a Brother as he deposited chairs and waved an enthusiastic hand in her direction. Another Brother began to sing the song she played, and soon the whole room was filled with voices and smiles. Audrey began to relax, and she felt her mood begin to meld with theirs. For a while she could forget the smell, forget the inconvenience, and focus on the Gathering. She moved from one song to another, and the Brothers followed her as she led them down a musical path. Webster wandered in and put his Bible and songbook down on his chosen seat.

A chalkboard was rolled in, and one Brother was designated to keep up with the song numbers and post them throughout the Gathering. He stepped forward now and wrote #108 on the board, and Audrey moved into the song. Her practiced fingers flew and left her mind and eyes free to wander. She saw the Brothers at the door greet newcomers and watched the small signals among the women in the room. Once strangers were inside the door to stay, someone moved to greet them and guide them to seats that appeared to have been saved for them. The universal look of surprise and enjoyment on the faces of those who had expected to feel like outsiders was as constant as the smell of the locker rooms down the hall.

Lydia hovered just outside the door. Audrey knew the other woman sought the source of the voice they had listened to a few nights earlier. When Lydia's face lit with welcome, Audrey followed her gaze and recognized the brunette who approached. Audrey nodded to Carol, who turned for the door to add to the welcome.

Casey wrinkled her nose at the chlorine and locker-room aroma that pervaded the air. She saw a confusing swirl of people move through side hallways, in and out of the main door, and through double doors into a large room.

"You made it," Lydia exclaimed as she rushed to Casey's side. "I was afraid you'd decide the drive was too long."

"I thought it was farther than it turned out to be," Casey said, then added, "I didn't realize there'd be so many people here." Lydia drew her hand through Casey's arm as if to guide and comfort all in one gesture.

"This must be Casey," a woman's voice said. Both turned to see Carol, her hair a flame of russet and a smile dancing across her creamy face.

"Casey, you remember Carol, don't you?"

Casey put her hand out to shake Carol's. Carol looked at it and finally slid a soft, boneless hand into it. Casey relaxed her usual businesslike grip to accommodate the other woman's reluctant clasp. These people didn't shake hands in greeting, she realized; she had already made a mistake. She felt a wave of color creep up her neck.

"Yes, I remember you," she said. "I enjoyed your comments." From the looks on the two women's faces, she had saved the handshake situation. Perhaps she should leave now so she wouldn't do anything else stupid. Before she could act on the thought, Lydia guided her toward a large room set up for the service with concentric rings of chairs fanning out from a small, empty circle.

"Come on in, and I'll introduce you to the rest of my housemates. They're very excited that you're coming for lunch after the Gathering. They've cooked up something special in your honor."

Casey's feeble idea to plead a headache to escape evaporated when she heard that someone had gone to special trouble on her behalf. She wondered at her seesawing feelings. She had been eager to get here this morning, but now all she could think about was how to get away. The piano soared above the chatter, and Casey was guided to a chair in the middle of a row of women. Lydia sat on her right, Carol on her left.

"Let's start with number one-oh-eight, if your spirit feels like mine does," Webster called out.

Casey felt a hymnal slipped into her hands, already opened to the right page. She was overwhelmed by the sound that exploded as the song began. She had expected it to be loud from her experience at the Bible study, but the din was almost physical. The Brothers and Sisters sang at the top of their voices. Casey couldn't hear herself. By the middle of the first song, her ears were ringing and her throat felt raw.

As at the Bible study, there were frequent calls to take verses out of order in every song. In between songs individuals stood, and all eyes turned to them as they spoke of their love for God, their enjoyment of the Bodylife, and their appreciation for services that other Saints had performed for them in the past week. There was laughter, there were tears, and the music wove in and out and held it all together. Casey felt battered, yet exhilarated.

In the midst of the singing, two men rose and did something in the small circle at the center of the room. Casey strained to see. They appeared to crush something beneath a snowy handkerchief. Other men rose, and plates circulated through the crowd. Trays with tiny cups of grape juice followed a few minutes later. Casey noticed that Communion didn't stop the singing and sharing. Rather, each person partook, then returned to whatever was going on.

The plate came to her, and she saw that one large crackerlike wafer had been shattered. She took a small piece and watched Lydia, who held the piece she had taken and closed her eyes. A small smile appeared on her face as she prayed. Then, with no fuss but with infinite attention, she raised the piece of wafer to her lips. When the grape juice was passed to her, she repeated the process with the same quiet, reverent attitude. When she opened her eyes, they fell to the hymnal on her lap. She began to sing again. Following her example, Casey made a hasty but respectful Communion of her own.

When Webster rose to speak, it was as if a bubble of anticipation surrounded him and pushed him to his feet almost against his will. Casey glanced at her watch; an hour had passed since the singing and sharing had begun. Lydia caught her glance and winked.

Pages rustled as people opened Bibles and notebooks. Casey did the same, conscious that she always seemed to be alone in taking notes at other church services. The shuffle of papers was augmented by a flow of small pages passed from the end of each row, which turned out to be outlines and lists of verses from which Webster would speak. Casey glanced at the outline, but fixed her eyes on Webster before she took in a word.

"Amen!" he shouted. There rose a commensurate thunder of amens from the group. He grinned at them. "My spirit is so full it's about to explode. How's yours?" An amen louder than the previous one burst from the congregation. "I thought so. Today I want to do something the patriarchs were expert at doing. We've lost the art of this in our culture today. It was given to them by God as a touchstone of faith, and we would do well to revive it." He wiped his upper lip and stowed his handkerchief in his jacket pocket.

"I'm talking about the practice of revisiting small heaps of stones that dotted the landscape, piled up by faithful men when God did something incredible in their midst. Whenever people in the Bible came across these cairns, the stones acted as a remembrance of God's faithfulness, and they'd sit and ponder that act of God all over again."

Casey wrote *cairns* atop a fresh page in her notebook.

"In a few months our own cairn will be completed. Most cairns in the Bible have a name. We'll call ours the Gathering Place. It will serve as our touchstone of God's faithfulness to us as his people. It will be a visible reminder that he selected this place as one where he can rest the soles of his feet on this earth, for around it he will find faithful people."

Casey frowned, wondering if Webster thought there were no other faithful people but these. She scratched the question on the page in her notebook and hoped to hear the answer.

"We arrived here with nothing to our names but our hearts for the Lord. The dear Saints here took us in, helped us get established, and have been part of us ever since. As believers we banded together, not so much against the rest of the world, but for the

Lord and his kingdom. We live today as a continuation of that tradition and commitment."

Webster took a drink from a glass on a small table where he rested his Bible and notes. There was no pulpit; he had risen to his feet to speak much as the others in the room had done. His seat was near the center of the room, and he turned and gestured to all sides as he spoke, holding their attention with ease.

"I talked to a Brother the other day as we worked outside the Gathering Place digging holes for trees we were planting. He told me of his first impressions when he came to the Saints, and it was quite comical. He said, 'When I first came to the Bodylife, I thought this was a cult!'" Webster laughed, and the entire congregation joined him and rocked in their chairs. Casey felt a fresh jolt as she heard the startling statement for a second time. She didn't understand what was funny about it.

"I asked the Brother why he thought that. He said, 'Well, this has all the classic signs. You all came here together from somewhere else, lots of people live together in the same houses, and you don't seem to mix with other people very much. I've studied cults, and that's pretty much the checklist for identifying one.'" Webster wiped his upper lip and forehead with the handkerchief again.

"I was intrigued and concerned," he said. "After all, if people came to the Bodylife and were misled, that would be a bad thing. So, after we'd dug a bit more, I asked him why he remained with us and why he was standing in the hot sun digging a hole with me. Maybe I hoped if it was all for naught, I could stop digging—it was a very hot day!" Webster's laugh carried over the guffaws of his audience. Casey found herself smiling at the picture herself.

"I think I'll call upon this Brother to repeat what he replied. Brother Darren, will you give us your testimony?"

Webster turned toward the large muscular man who kept track of the song numbers on the board. He looked down as if in pain, then rose. He stood on the balls of his large feet, balanced as if in a stiff wind.

"The only reason I'll add to what Brother Webster has said is that it needs to be cleared up. I'm ashamed I ever thought this group was in any way a cult, and it's from my shame I speak, because I know that to do so is to die to a part of myself." Casey turned her gaze from Darren and jotted in her notebook, *Die to a part of myself?* Then she returned her attention to the uncomfortable man who stood in their midst.

"I've found when Satan wants to mislead people, he has a very simple strategy. He looks for the truth, and then he twists it a tiny bit. The books I'd read about cults were descriptions of his work, but his work was a twist of the true Bodylife."

Casey watched Darren's face. He had full lips, bright eyes, and a charmingly crooked nose. A close-cropped beard ringed his features and lent an air of competence and sobriety. His voice vibrated in a soothing middle register, and his honest words drew her into his story.

"When I first came here, I couldn't get over the love I saw. I came from a worldly background. A woman I hoped to marry had broken up with me because I wanted our spiritual lives to be paramount in our life together. She wanted a home and children and two cars and two careers and the American Dream. I wanted Jesus."

"Amen," whispered listeners all over the room.

"I worked at the same company as one of the Brothers, and he saw I was hurting. He brought me to this place, and it was like cool, refreshing water that washed me and soothed my pain. What I saw here was total love, total commitment, and total cohesion. I thought there had to be a catch, so I started to run through my cult checklist. I watched the people interacting, I listened to the way people talked, and it fit the list—so I began to watch my wallet!" Amusement sparkled in many eyes, and laughter swept over the crowd.

"I figured the wallet would be the key." Darren gestured to his back pocket. "Cults are always after money, so I paid particular attention to the offering time in the service. There wasn't one. People put their offerings in little containers in the back of the room. No appeals for a building fund, even though there's a building in progress. It's not even mentioned."

Casey glanced behind her and saw small wooden boxes near the exits.

"I decided the acid test would be what they did with Jesus." Darren smiled. "They lifted him higher than I'd ever heard him praised before. Their vision of the church was so much higher than anything I'd ever encountered that I decided at that point I had choices I needed to make." The sparkling sunlight on the swimming pool outside filtered through miniblinds and shimmered behind Darren.

"I went back to my Bible and read the description of the early Christians. Much of what was being done here is listed there: sharing things in common, helping one another, loving one another, building the Body. There were no fence-sitters in the early church. Everyone was sold out to Jesus. They put their lives, their material goods, and their futures on the line with each other.

"Jesus said not to put our hand to the plow and look back. I knew I needed to come alongside you, plow the fields he's given us to plow, and give my life to him in the most complete manner I could." There was soft sniffling from various areas in the room.

"I have to say when I told my family I wanted to break my lease and move in with people I didn't know, I almost turned back. I think my sister wanted to have me committed to a mental hospital. I see the hand of God in it all, because they've been here to visit this place since I moved and couldn't get over what they saw either." Darren looked at his feet and slid his big hands into his pockets.

"I have to make sure you understand that my attitude was dead wrong when I came here, and I've never been so happy as I am now as part of the Bodylife. I would do it all over again in a heartbeat—even if my family never came around to my point of view." Darren's voice broke. "I love all of you more than life itself, and I know in eternity I'll be able to look the Lord in the face and say, 'I took the right path,' and I'll see him smile." Tears shone in his eyes as he sat down.

Webster rose to his feet again. He raised the outline page above his head and smiled. "As you can see, I didn't complete the outline—again!" The room filled with laughter at what was obviously a normal situation. "But I can't continue after the sermon Brother Darren just preached. I'll sit down, and let's go back to praising the Lord and speaking from our hearts on this topic."

Audrey moved to the piano, and her fingers began to roam the keys. "Number seventy-three has been running through my head for the last several minutes. Can we sing it?" Pages turned quickly throughout the room. The singing began at a subdued volume, then built until the very rafters of the room seemed to shiver as the congregation repeated the chorus again and again.

> *I'm home in the Body, I'll never go out,*
> *For the hand of the Lord led me near.*
> *I'm home in the Body, there's never a doubt,*
> *My heart, my service is here.*

Casey read the words of the unfamiliar song, feeling the tune work its way into her heart. She pondered the quiet man who had given up everything to gain the one thing he wanted most: closeness to God and God's people. Wasn't there something in the Bible that urged believers to give up what they cannot keep in order to gain what they cannot lose? She thought of her home, her job, her solitude. She wondered if those things could keep her from someday making the kind of headlong dive into a committed community of believers that Darren had made. Had she finally found a place to take such a plunge?

Casey sang with her eyes closed, her hands gripped around the songbook. Her heart lifted to the Lord to seek her answers, and she felt moisture on her cheek. Lydia's arm stole around her and gave her a squeeze.

The rest of the Gathering passed in a blur. Person after person rose and told stories similar to Darren's. The joy on each face was like a blinding light to Casey. As each new speaker stood, she turned and waited to hear the words that spilled from enthusiastic lips.

When the stream of testimonies stopped, and the last song had been repeated a final time, Casey felt bereft, as if she had reached the end of a delicious chocolate confection and wanted more. She remained seated as the congregation headed for the doors laughing, chatting, and punctuating conversation with the ever-present amen.

Lydia put her hand on Casey's and smiled. "I sometimes want to stay and wait for the next Gathering, but they'd pick me up, chair and all, and put me into the storage closet if I did."

"I don't want it to end. Is it always like this?"

"Well, in some ways all Gatherings are like this, and in other ways they're all different. Webster never gets through his outline, so that's the same every time. The singing and sharing are the same too. We don't always hear a long testimony like Darren's, but when the Spirit leads, we could hear anything."

Casey felt something inside her relax. It would be possible to recapture it all again another day.

"Why don't we go to lunch? You'll see that a Gathering doesn't stop at the doors. We love to continue it over good food."

As they moved toward the door, Casey saw a knot of people surrounding a table. When they passed the group, Carol extracted herself from it and flashed a brilliant smile. She held out a cassette tape.

"I thought you'd like to have a copy of the tape from your first big Gathering. It means a lot the first time you hear about the Bodylife the way it was described today. Please take it as my gift." Casey accepted the clear plastic box.

"Thank you," she said. "I didn't realize they'd be ready so soon."

"Stephanie runs off the copies during the last part of the testimonies and singing," Lydia said. "So the last half hour or so won't be on there. Do you have a cassette player in your car?"

"Yes, I do." Casey yearned to go and put in the tape.

"Well, now you can take the Body with you wherever you go," Lydia said. "I couldn't get through my daily chores and errands without it."

The three moved through the doors. Casey's stomach growled loudly. Her idea to plead a headache was forgotten.

"It's easier for me to show you where we live than to draw you a map, since you're not familiar with Crescent Hills," Lydia said as they burst into the warm sunshine. The first breath of nonathletic air was a blessing.

"I'd hate to get lost. I'm too hungry to last long on my own." Casey laughed with an abandon she hadn't felt in many months.

"The others from our house have already left. By the time we get there, lunch will be ready."

The road raced beneath the wheels of Casey's small Toyota. The shadows of overhanging trees appeared on the hood, dashed up the windshield, and caught her eye in the rearview mirror as she drove past them on her way back home. The tires clicked over cracks in the roadway and seemed to whisper over and over, "amen, amen, amen!" The word wrapped itself around her as she digested the wonderful lunch and the warm fellowship that had accompanied and spiced it to perfection.

When she and Lydia had arrived at the Sisters House, the other young women were already hard at work in the kitchen and dining room. Someone sliced bread, spread butter on it, and sprinkled it with garlic powder before popping it into the oven to warm. Another tossed a salad and combined ingredients to make salad dressing. Carol, swathed in hot mitts to her thin elbows, removed aromatic lasagna from the oven. Lydia jumped in to fill glasses with ice and lemonade and put the final touches on the table settings.

A small cassette player perched on the pass-through from the kitchen to the dining area, and the sound of hundreds of people singing in a Gathering brought the morning's experience back to Casey. The women sang along with the tape and echoed each amen when it came.

Within minutes Casey was ushered to the table. The prayer went on longer than Casey would have thought possible before a meal, punctuated with the ever-present amen, and concluded with an impromptu rendering of the chorus that had so captured her heart at the Gathering.

From the lifting of the first fork off the pristine white tablecloth until the gathering of all the women around her car to see her off at the end of the afternoon, all conversation had focused on the Bodylife and the sermon they had heard. As she drove toward home, Casey savored the joy of deep conversation without a hint of small talk. It struck her that no one had asked what she did for a living, where she had grown up, or even what church she had attended. Facts that bracketed her life but did so little to define it didn't seem important in the face of the greater issues they discussed.

As Casey drove farther and farther away from the Sisters House, she sensed the warmth ebbing, replaced by the emptiness she had been feeling for months. Tears pricked at the back of her eyes, but she fought them off. What did today's experience matter? She had visited a different church and had lunch with people who seemed content and at peace with themselves and with each other, and who had a goal and direction in their lives she had never achieved. With a sigh she shook her head and realized that it mattered very much indeed.

She lifted the flap of her purse while she kept her eyes on the road, worked the cassette free, and inserted it into the tape player. The sound of many voices beginning the opening song from the morning's service filled the little car. As the singing continued, she felt her tension begin to melt.

She pictured the women who made up the special personality of the Sisters House, and she wondered what it must be like to live in such close proximity to other people. As an only child Casey never had to put her wants and needs aside when it came to her personal space. In college she had elected to rent an apartment off campus rather than live in a dorm with other students her age. The thought of the friction that must develop when several women shared bathrooms, kitchen space, a living room, and household chores tempered the soft image of the Sisters House in her mind. Yet there had been no evidence of friction. In such a situation she was sure she could put up a good front, for a while, at least. On the other hand, after spending just one afternoon with several women, Casey was exhausted.

That she even tried to picture herself living in such conditions shocked her and snapped her attention back to the traffic around her. She would never give up her home—her Jewel, as she called it. Nonetheless, the image of her own hands chopping the salad ingredients; standing at the immaculate, tiled kitchen counter; folding the napkins in creative and decorative shapes; or welcoming a new visitor to the Sisters House remained.

6

Casey disliked proofreading days. At Sandiford & Sons Publishing, the many scholarly works in progress followed a circuitous path through the system, but they all eventually came back to her desk for intense proofing.

Her eyes ached from scanning the long, complex sentences of Dr. Wendell Lorrimer on the String Theory. By ten o'clock Casey would have settled for a long look through a telescope and a nap. She craved a diversion. She was happy to see a flash of vivid yellow headed in her direction, knowing it was her favorite office compatriot.

"My, don't you look bleary-eyed," Jessie said. "What's the matter, seen too many black holes this morning?" Casey snorted and filled her eyes with the bright colors her friend wore. A glowing yellow jacket topped a pair of tropical print slacks and a fuchsia silk blouse. The earrings clinched it. Each large gold hoop served as the perch for an elaborate, multicolored papier-mâché macaw. The birds looked real enough to burst into raucous cries. Jessie dressed like a fashion plate, except she skewed the colors to the highest possible end of the spectrum. With her light coffee-colored skin and tightly curled black hair, she looked stunning. On anyone else it would have been vulgar.

"I'd give anything to gaze into a black hole for a while," Casey said. "Have you got one to spare? I've still got over a hundred pages to go."

"You need a break. Let's get some coffee and forget the universe for a few minutes. I'm sure it can run itself without your supervision."

Casey unbent from her chair with a groan and followed Jessie. Her mood lightened as she moved farther from the avalanche of work on her desk.

They entered the kitchen and waited while coworkers rinsed cups and dried hands on paper towels. There was fresh coffee. Even more amazing, there were clean cups and plenty of cream and sugar. But, Casey noted, the stir sticks were nowhere to be seen. Jessie, ever creative and flexible in such situations, fished in the oversized pockets of her jacket and found a large paper clip. She straightened it and left a loop at one end, then swirled her own coffee and Casey's with the makeshift spoon. They laughed, and Casey felt the day's tensions lessening.

"I haven't seen much of you," Jessie said as they settled on the battered couch at one end of the kitchen.

"I've been busy with this new church." Casey rested her head on the back of the couch. "It's up in Crescent Hills, so I have to leave right after work to get there in time."

"What denomination did you say it is?" Jessie sipped, her eyes on her friend.

"It doesn't have a denomination. It's called the Gathering of the church, and everyone there is serious about getting to know Jesus better. It's so refreshing—but kind of intimidating. I seem to have a long way to go to catch up."

"Catch up? God has a timetable for each of us. That's part of his love for us. We're never given more than we can bear, either in circumstances or in what we need to learn."

Casey thought about the many talks she and Jessie had had in this very room on the subject. Their special friendship began when they realized they shared a similar sense of humor and a deep love for Jesus.

"Well, when I'm around people who have mastered so much more of the mystery than I can even begin to grasp, I feel like I need to apply myself more," she explained. "I want to be around them more, read the Bible more, and put in the extra time necessary to be what God wants me to be." She took a sip and set the mug on a side table to let the liquid cool further.

"I'll say it again," Jessie said. "His agenda for you isn't something you should be sweating over. You sound like you've decided to take personal control of your growth. You know that won't work."

Casey's voice and her chin both rose a notch. "Maybe his agenda for me is to do what I'm doing. Maybe he's decided to send me to graduate school."

"I know you're excited about this church, and I've seen tremendous growth in your interest in the Bible and in the Lord since you've been involved there," Jessie said. "It's like you got a jump-start after you had stalled out for a while. I don't take any of that away from you. Just keep your discernment cap on and look at things through God's eyes. Have the courage to take a step backward if you have to."

Casey finished her coffee. "I'm sorry I got upset. It's just that I feel love and acceptance like never before. I wake up in the morning singing hymns; I go through the day eager for the Gathering after work. I feel drawn as if by a magnet. I forget you've never been to a Gathering. I wish you could come to one. Then you'd understand."

"I may surprise you some Sunday when Claude and I don't have to teach Sunday school. I must admit I'd feel easier in my mind if I knew what you're getting involved in so deeply."

"I hope you do come."

They refilled their cups and headed back to their desks. Casey thought about the Gathering she would attend in the evening. She hummed a chorus a group member had written a few weeks before and she had committed to memory. Somehow she would have to show Jessie what a great church was really like, and how much it could mean in her life too.

7

The house hummed with activity. Furniture and boxes surrounded a large rental truck that Casey could see through the open front door. Men lifted items to Stephanie as she indicated them, and she organized them in the metal-skinned space.

A boom box emitted the singing captured at a Gathering the week before. Everyone said this particular Gathering was one of the best, with many old favorite songs sung; the tape was an instant classic. People moved from room to room and packed remaining items to its accompaniment.

Casey straightened from taping a box. A parade of Bodylife members moved past her carrying boxes, bags, and leafy silk plants. She bent again to her task.

Hours later the entire home had been packed up, loaded on the truck, and the serious business of cleaning began. Sisters wielded mops, sponges, and vacuum cleaners while the Brothers left to follow the truck to its destination and unload it for Nancy and Jeff.

Nancy looked both radiant and shell-shocked. The decision to move to Crescent Hills had solidified in recent weeks, and a buyer had snapped up their beautiful home before the sign could be planted in the yard. There was no going back.

Casey slipped on rubber gloves and fell in beside the other women. She was surprised by the intensity of their efforts. She imagined that most people just ran the carpet sweeper over the rug and locked the door when they moved. Here, everything sparkled, and the whole house smelled fragrant and inviting. She was proud to have been part of it all.

"There's nothing like working with Sisters," Lydia said as she headed for the backyard to shake out her dust mop. She added with a soft chuckle, "It's even nicer when the Brothers leave."

Casey nodded. Even though everyone got along well, there was a certain tension in any job when the Brothers and Sisters worked together. As she had come to know from Webster, it was a situation of the Sisters dying to themselves a bit each time a Brother asked them to do something outside their personal agendas. It was good to be free to decide whether to dust or mop, to sit and take a break or go hug another Sister, without interference or suggestion.

As she worked, Casey envied Jeff and Nancy. They had bought their new home next to the Gathering place from another family in the church, and that family had moved one block over. She still questioned the clannishness of the Body, but after more than seven months, some things that had seemed odd in the beginning bothered her less. She heard many times that after a few moves people felt no more attachment to places. It was considered a real victory to those who experienced such freedom.

Casey felt guilty each time she heard the recital of this revelation in Gatherings. She had scrimped and worked to accumulate enough money for a down payment on her house, then had tastefully decorated it on a budget to express her personality. She loved her home and couldn't imagine ever leaving it. It was conveniently near her job, but to get to a Gathering meant additional hours on the road, and she pined for the warm fellowship everyone in Crescent Hills continued to share after she left. She scrubbed harder at a lingering, red fruit-punch circle on the counter top, as though getting the spot off would clear her turmoil. It didn't.

"Thank you so much, Sisters." Nancy entered the kitchen for the last time. "I couldn't have done it without you, and I wouldn't have wanted to." She hugged each woman in turn.

"Shall we go to the new house?" Carol, her bright curls escaping the bandanna tied around her head, turned from the sink and dried her hands. "We need to make sure you and Jeff are settled before your heads hit the pillows tonight."

Casey chafed at the thought of going with these exuberant and cheerful women, helping unload the boxes she had just taped shut, then driving back to Grovers, alone. In an instant she couldn't stand the thought of ever driving to Crescent Hills again. Or rather, driving *back* from Crescent Hills.

She moved next to Lydia as the other women decided who would go in which cars. "Lydia," she whispered, "I can't go and help." Her eyes met Lydia's smoky gray ones clouded with concern.

"Have we tired you too much?" Lydia moved her away from the others. "You haven't done this before, and I know it can be exhausting the first few times." Lydia had given her an easy way out, and Casey was tempted to take it, but her friend had led her to the most wonderful experience of her Christian life. She owed her the truth.

"I feel like I'm being ripped in two. I can't move into the Bodylife, yet nibbling at the edges is more unsatisfying than not tasting it at all. I have hard choices to make, and I guess I'd better start making them now."

Lydia's eyes filled with compassion. She squeezed Casey's arm.

"I'm both sorry and elated you feel that way." She hurried on before a surprised Casey could respond. "I've seen lots of Saints with the same struggle. Some came through the wall of fire and are now strong in the Bodylife. But I won't kid you, some felt the fire, smelled the smoke, and retreated to more familiar territory. We still see a few from time to time, but they'll never take the plunge."

Casey pictured a roaring wall of fire, with the Body on one side and herself and her home on the other. The wall was thick; it would take many steps to get from one side to the other, not a quick dash and a jump.

"I want to help you, if you want to be helped," Lydia continued. "A few Saints have been carried through the fire when they didn't want to be, and they're still torn in their hearts even in the midst of the Bodylife. Their pain is, if anything, greater than yours, and I won't have that for you."

"What should I do?" Casey whispered more to herself than to Lydia.

"May I make a suggestion?"

Casey nodded.

"Go home," Lydia said. "Rest, pray, read your notes from the last few Gatherings. Let me come and stay with you next weekend. We never have enough time to talk."

"I don't want to interrupt your weekend."

"I wouldn't have offered if I couldn't fulfill my promise. You need time to yourself. Then you need time with a Sister. I want to tell you how I came to the Body, and the story takes time. I'll be honest with you," Lydia cautioned. "I want you to become more a part of the Bodylife. You have something to contribute to the Body, and we won't be the same without it. I'm very selfish about wanting the Body to be all it should be. When it's strong, I'm also strong. I don't want to do without you, but I want you to be joyful and peaceful, not reluctant and unsure."

Casey pictured the Body as a jigsaw puzzle. Webster was a central piece. Darren was a big, quiet piece. Lydia was a shining border piece that hemmed in other pieces, and there was a hole in the puzzle, right near Lydia. It was Casey-shaped, and the whole puzzle, the whole Body, seemed to be weaker without it locked into place. Still she hesitated.

"I understand what you're saying, but I'm not sure I'm ready to hear it. I agree though that I need to go home now, to sleep, pray, and think."

"And next weekend?" Lydia prompted her.

"Yes, do come. Let me draw you a map."

Lydia reached into the voluminous pocket of her denim smock dress and pulled out the ubiquitous pad and pen. Casey scrawled a quick map, and Lydia looked it over to be sure it was clear to her. Casey felt infinitely fragile when her friend hugged her, then took her arm and led her to the back door.

"Don't come to the Gathering tomorrow," Lydia suggested. "You need to have time for you and Jesus. Don't let our clamor interfere." The tension in Casey eased. She nodded and slipped out the door.

A raspy sensation scratched against Casey's cheek in the night, and she cried out. The sound woke her and sent Andrew scooting into the walk-in closet. She brought her hand to her face and recognized the sensation; Andrew must have sensed her dreaming fear and attempted to comfort her. Her breathing slowed, and her pulse ceased racing. She flexed her hands to get rid of the odd warmth she always felt on the back of them when adrenaline released into her bloodstream. Andrew poked his head around the closet door.

"Yeowwww?" His eyes shone in the darkness.

"Oh, sweetie," she cried, and jerked back the covers. She crossed the room, scooped up the cat, and cradled him, his head tucked under her chin. She wasn't sure who comforted whom, but it made them both happier. Andrew began to rumble and licked her hand. She walked back to the bed and turned on a soft bedside light, then slid back under the warm covers, bringing the cat with her. He settled next to her, and she leaned back against the pillows.

"I'm glad you rescued me," she told Andrew, stroking his silky head and running her hand all the way down his body, out to the end of his bushy tail. He looked up at her, purred louder, and began to wash his front paws. Casey looked around, and her eyes fell on her Bible and notebook on the bedside table. She reached for them, and as she did, it occurred to her she had not prayed alone for some time. She always seemed to be too busy.

"I'm sorry I've been negligent, Jesus," she said, and then stopped. She was the furthest thing from negligent. Wasn't she in every Gathering she could get to? Didn't she work to learn the songs and read the books she bought at the book table every week? Hadn't she been at Jeff and Nancy's every chance she got for the last half year? She considered her prayer and tried again. "I don't know why I'm so scattered right now. I'm trying to do what you want. I know I told Lydia I'd read and pray and think all week, but it's Thursday, and this is the first time I've even come to you. I'm a jerk." As soon as she said the words, she felt a contradiction rise up in her heart. Though she didn't usually hear the Lord speak to her, she often had impressions of him in her mind—and this one was strong. He held out his hands to her, and she saw the nail prints. He gestured to his side and his brow, and she saw more wounds. They were there for her. She began to cry.

"In myself there's no value, but in you I'm priceless. Thank you for reminding me." She stroked the cat as she turned the pages in her Bible with a soft rustle. Her eyes lit on a well-thumbed page where the words of Jesus stood out boldly: "If you ask Me anything in My name, I will do it."

"Lord, I have such heavy things on my mind," she prayed. "I feel like I'm going to be pressed right through the floor and find myself downstairs in the kitchen. Please, Jesus, make things clear to me."

She fiddled with the Bible ribbon marker. As she moved it, Andrew put out a paw and tried to catch hold of it. She smiled, flicked the ribbon, and watched his lightning-fast reflexes as he tried to capture it. She tucked the ribbon back into the book and kissed the top of Andrew's head.

"Lord, I feel you led me to this house and provided the means for me to get it and keep it," she said. "So how could it be your will for me to give it up and walk away for an uncertain future?"

In the silence she again turned pages in her Bible. Once more the words of Jesus leaped off the page to her: "Truly I say to you, there is no one who has left house or wife or brothers or parents or children, for the sake of the kingdom of God, who will not receive many times as much at this time and in the age to come, eternal life." She stared at the words. She had read them many times before but never with a question like the one that was now uppermost in her mind.

She asked herself frankly if her house was holding her prisoner. No, she realized, the house represented freedom, independence, and individuality. She feared she would lose them in the Bodylife. Here in the night she could face the issue at last. She wanted to hold on to what she had.

She turned on the tape player and two hundred voices burst from the speakers. She lowered the volume and slid down in bed as she listened. She could pick out individual voices she had come to know as they called out songs or requested a reprise of a particular verse. She turned off the light and adjusted the covers. Andrew snuggled next to her pillow, lifted one paw, and brushed her jaw-line. The gentle touch made her grin in the dark.

The tape played on and filled the room with song, praise, and harmony. She sank into sleep and didn't stir when the player turned itself off with a soft click.

"The Bodylife is strong. I feel it coursing through my veins, don't you?" Webster sat back, thrust his legs out in front of him, and crossed them at the ankles.

Lydia nodded with the others and echoed their amen. She covertly studied the members of the small, early-morning group that shared the center circle of the Gathering Place's main hall. Stephanie fiddled with the zipper on her sweatshirt. Her housemate Carol stifled a yawn at the early hour. Webster's wife, Grace, wore a characteristic sour look. Kurt glanced at his watch, probably calculating the time it would take him to get to work. Handsome Dominic was immaculately groomed despite the hour. Lydia hoped that over time her steady commitment would make her more a part of this special circle.

"We've seen much growth lately, but not all of it for the best," Webster said. "I've seen four families move in, then move out in the last year. Why?" His piercing eyes glowered under protruding eyebrows and flashed from person to person in the circle.

"It wasn't like we didn't do all we could to make sure they were settled into the right places," Grace said as she shifted in her chair. "Everybody rallied around them and moved them in without a hitch, but from the beginning each of those four seemed to pull back. We could all see it was only a matter of time before they left again." She frowned.

"We've got to figure out what's going wrong," Stephanie said. "Were those four all escorted by the same person or people?"

"They came in under different mentors, but something went wrong." Kurt nibbled the skin around his thumbnail nervously.

"Maybe they weren't ready yet," Lydia said. She looked at the others and saw disbelief on their faces. Webster's features sharpened. She felt him probe her with his look.

"Are you saying we should discourage people from joining the Bodylife?" His voice was quiet and almost menacing. Lydia went numb, then felt strength rise in her. She knew she was right; she just needed to help the others understand.

"Sometimes," she said. "For a while, yes. Just until they're ready." She let apology creep into her voice. "Perhaps some Saints who have been here for many years have forgotten how hard the first steps into the Bodylife can be." She appealed to them with her eyes. "Even I have a hard time remembering the period of my decision, because the joy I've experienced since then has erased the pain and confusion."

"So what are you saying?" Stephanie cut in.

"Even though we forget the pain, it's a very real experience when tearing oneself away from the world to join the Bodylife. We need to recognize that the process takes time. It can't be hurried."

"How do you recommend we do that?" Grace asked, her tone crisp, her posture stiff.

"Let me give you an example," Lydia said. "You've all met Casey Ellis, haven't you? She lives in Grovers, near where Jeff and Nancy used to live." She saw their nods. "She told me she's torn between remaining in the life she knows and going all out to join us. I've sensed it for a while. She's made a life for herself, learned to be independent, and isn't yet accustomed to the idea of working with others to achieve a goal as great as the Bodylife. I encouraged her to pull back and think it over."

Before she could finish, the others burst in.

"You told her to stay away?" Carol threw her hands in the air in a gesture of defeat.

"Well, there's one more we lost." Stephanie's monotone was eloquent. "At least we didn't have to move her first."

"I think you've overstepped your authority as a Sister and a member of this Body." Grace sniffed and jerked her chin away from them all.

Lydia again felt the strength to straighten her backbone and increase the volume of her soft voice. "Excuse me, I haven't finished yet." They all looked at her. "I told her not to attend the Gathering yesterday." Lydia held them with her eyes. "I'm going to go to Grovers and stay with her for the weekend. By Sunday I think she'll be hungry to come back. I can't control her decision, though I've told her what I hope she will decide. I want her to have the freedom to consider it and the silence to hear the message Jesus has for her with clarity. We need to give people room to make an intelligent and Spirit-led choice. I think those who do so will stay." She clasped her hands in her lap to hide their shaking.

Webster let out a long breath. "There's always the outside chance this might work." He nodded reluctantly; the others appeared to adopt his wait-and-see attitude.

Lydia prayed as never before that her intuition about Casey was right and that the leaders would be pleased with her. It bothered her, though, that she worried so much about their opinion.

8

Casey lingered at the door to the break room unsure whether to go in. She watched as Jessie gazed into her coffee cup, afraid to step in lest they get into yet another discussion about the Bodylife. It seemed to be their sole topic of conversation these days. But Jessie looked up and saw her, and she knew she would appear rude if she didn't at least refill her cup before she headed back to her desk.

"Long time, no see." Jessie's warm voice pulled her into the room. Casey moved to pump the coffee dispenser.

"I feel like I live in meetings these days," she said. Jessie drifted toward the couches, and Casey followed, needing a break despite worrying how the conversation would unfold.

"I don't mean to add to your troubles today, but you look awful. What's wrong?"

"Gee, thanks. You look marvelous yourself." Casey ducked her head in the hope that Jessie would take the hint and let the subject drop.

"I'm serious. There are raccoon rings around your eyes, and your makeup looks stale. You usually wear that scarf with the African animals on it with this outfit, and you're not wearing it today."

"And your conclusions, Ms. Sherlock Holmes?"

"You aren't sleeping. You're worried about something, and you got up too late this morning to dress with your usual care," Jessie said.

Casey sipped the tepid coffee. "You've missed your calling. You should give up editing and become a private eye." Jessie let the remark pass and waited her out. Casey cleared her throat. "I've had nightmares all week," she confessed. "It's beginning to wear me down, but it'll pass. I have a few things on my mind, and I can't seem to make decisions. Thanks for caring."

"What's the problem? Sometimes another pair of ears can be a great way to help reason things out."

"I have a friend from church coming to spend the weekend with me. We'll drink pots of coffee and talk each other's ears off, and I'll be a new person on Monday," Casey said.

"Are you sure?"

Casey held up three fingers. "Girl Scout's honor. I promise."

Jessie snorted. "When were you ever a Girl Scout?"

Casey grinned. "Okay, you win. My aunt was a Cub Scout den mother, and the boys adopted me as their mascot."

They rose, washed out their cups, and left the break room. When they reached Casey's desk, Jessie rested her delicate fingers on the partition and captured Casey's eyes with her own.

"If you ever need to talk, you know I'll listen." Her soft words were nearly lost in other voices around them.

Casey dropped her eyes and nodded. She knew her friend would pray for her the rest of the day, and was suddenly confused to realize that since she had gotten involved in the Bodylife, it seemed as if the two of them prayed on opposite sides when it came to her life.

Andrew exited the kitchen at a trot and jumped to his special lookout place at the front window. Casey went to the front door and opened it just as Lydia put her finger to the doorbell, causing her to jump and give a nervous giggle.

"You scared me!"

Casey gestured her in, shut the door, and patted Andrew. "My guest announcer told me you were here. Andrew, this is Lydia. Lydia, my roommate Andrew." The cat sniffed the overnight case and looked up at Lydia with a massive blink. Then he sat, washed his left paw, and wiped it over his face.

"What does that mean?" Lydia whispered.

"It means he likes you," Casey whispered back, enjoying the game. "If he didn't, he'd have done something embarrassing like walk away or wash under his tail."

"Well, I'm glad I passed the cat test anyway."

After the expected chitchat about whether Lydia had any trouble finding the house and her compliments on Casey's decorating skills, there came an uneasy pause.

"If you don't want me here, say so," Lydia said bluntly. "I'll go straight back home if you aren't comfortable."

"Please stay." Casey fought panic. "It's been a long, quiet week, and I've looked forward to your arrival. No one has ever stayed here with me, so I'm not a very good hostess. I'm sorry." She felt silly, unsure what to do next.

"Then that's the problem. You look at me as a guest, not as a Sister. Do you have any real sisters?"

"No. I always wanted one," Casey said. "It might be nice to have one other female around for life."

"I know all the women in the Body are your spiritual Sisters, but I'd like to be your special Sister. I need a Sister like you."

"That would be great." Casey's eyes glistened, and for the first time she reached out to hug Lydia. She felt the other woman's surprise and knew everything would be all right. Then Lydia held Casey at arm's length and adopted a playful, stern tone.

"Well, Sister, where's my room?"

Casey bent and reached for Lydia's bag.

"Follow me, Sister, but don't leave your towels on the floor, and no hogging the bathroom."

Casey led the way, and Andrew brought up the rear. His whiskers twitched, and his tail formed a furry flag at full mast.

She had taken great care with the things she had hung on the walls to make sure the view changed with each rise in elevation in the open house. It was very different from the homes of others in the Body. She sensed Lydia looking at it, enjoying it, and measuring her by it. Had it been any Sister but Lydia, Casey would have felt the scrutiny threatening. She put the odd thought firmly aside, determined to enjoy the weekend.

"So, what did you do?" Casey opened her eyes wide, even as she felt a smile tease the corners of her mouth.

"What any self-respecting, independent woman would do. I slapped him!" Lydia crumpled on the sofa in laughter, and Casey whooped in delight. Andrew examined a cobweb in a vaulted corner twenty feet above their heads.

"I'm sure that helped the situation." Casey giggled and broke off as the telephone rang. She moved from the soft, cushioned couch to the kitchen and lifted the receiver from the wall unit, still savoring Lydia's story.

"Hello?" she said around a snicker.

"I think I might have the wrong number."

"Gretchen, it's me—unless you didn't want to talk to me, in which case you do have the wrong number."

A pause. "Are you sick?"

"I'm fine. What's up?"

"Did I interrupt something?" Gretchen's voice took on a shade of jealousy and a touch of gossipy inquisitiveness.

"You interrupted an entire life." Casey looked across the living room at Lydia making silly faces at Andrew and began to laugh again.

"I don't understand."

"You had to be here to get it." Casey turned her back to Lydia and focused on Gretchen. "Lydia is spending the weekend, and we were sharing life stories. We'd gotten to first-date scenarios when you called."

"I should come over and tell you about how Gerry and I met. So romantic and funny at the same time." Casey sensed Gretchen winding up for a full-blown story and knew she had to divert her.

"How was your trip? You've been gone for three weeks, and I didn't get one single postcard."

"Wonderful, of course. I see more of Gerry on a business trip than when we're home, but I also see far more tacky hotel rooms than I care to remember, and I missed the kids."

"Are you going to the Gathering tomorrow morning?" Casey tried to avert another story.

"Wild horses couldn't keep me away. How was last week?"

It would be too difficult to explain to Gretchen what had gone on in her life in the last seven days.

"I didn't go. I guess I got burned out when Jeff and Nancy moved. I helped with the packing, then collapsed for a week."

"I wish I'd been there. All those Sisters working together. Now Jeff and Nancy live right in the Bodylife. I wish I could." Gretchen picked up steam. "Think of throwing open the window and calling out across the lawn, 'Praise the Lord, Sister!' and have her answer, 'Amen!' What a great place to live!"

"I've got to go," Casey interrupted. "Lydia is trying to hold a conversation with Andrew. It doesn't look like she's being too successful." She felt another bubble of laughter start in her throat.

Gretchen's sense of being left out rang clear in her voice. "Oh. Well, maybe I'll see you at the Gathering tomorrow. Would that be okay?"

Casey knew that to many in the Body, Gretchen came across as a self-assured, noisy woman. However, there was a little girl inside her who longed to be loved. "Of course it's okay—and maybe we can get together for lunch one day this week?" She offered the olive branch and hoped Gretchen would take it.

"That would be great. Let's do it Thursday. My mother will have the kids for the day."

"Good. See you tomorrow." Casey hung up the phone and turned back to Lydia.

"Gretchen."

"So I gathered." In the pause the awkwardness Casey dreaded returned. Again, Lydia drove it away with her soft-spoken directness. "You didn't tell her what you've gone through this week."

"I couldn't." She settled back on the couch.

"It's hard to talk to someone outside the Bodylife—or at least on the periphery—about your struggle."

"Right." Casey automatically ran her fingers through her short hair.

"I'm what people like Gretchen call an insider. So why don't we talk about it?" Lydia kept her eyes on Casey and stroked the large warm cat in her lap.

"Okay, I guess I'm ready."

"Let me fast-forward to my experience with the Bodylife." Lydia twisted one ear like the knob on a VCR and crossed her eyes. Casey relaxed a fraction. "I met a Sister from the Bodylife at a tire repair shop. I went into the lounge, and there she was, reading a Bible." Lydia brushed a strand of hair from the corner of her mouth. "As we chatted, she asked me where I went to church, how long I'd been a Christian—the usual questions. I'd moved here from back East when midlife made me restless with everything that had come before. I was settled in a church but not happy with the worship experience or the continuous squabbling among the women. They'd fight over who would donate flowers for the ladies' luncheon or what color the napkins should be at the fall festival potluck. I was hungry for real Christianity, deep worship, meaty Bible study."

She smiled at the memory. "When I left the shop, I had new tires, a new friend, and the address for the Bodylife Gatherings. I went to visit the next Sunday." Lydia sipped her lemonade and stroked Andrew, who purred like a lawn mower.

"I didn't expect to be blown out of my socks by the Gathering, but I was. The message, the singing, the sharing, the atmosphere— it was more than I could handle the first few times. I would go back to the well, drink as much as I could, dash away again, and feel my thirst build until I had to take another drink." Lydia shook her head. "I finally realized I could go on trudging through the desert, dashing for water holes whenever I could find them, or I could pull up my tent and go live at the oasis. I felt physical pain as I wrestled with the decision. The war going on in my body reflected the one wrenching my soul. I hurt from the roots of my hair to my pedicure. I couldn't eat or sleep. I was a wreck."

"I can't picture you in such a state. You're always so calm and self-possessed," Casey said. Lydia's laugh was tinged with pain.

"It was the most horrible time in my entire life. I wanted to pack my bags and move to Argentina or sign up to be an astronaut—anything to escape the decision and the turmoil. Deep inside I knew that after I had made my decision, whichever way it went, my life would never be the same. Everything in me fought against making the decision."

"So what did you do?" Casey laughed at herself. "Well, I know what you did, but how did you get past that point?"

"I called the same Sister I had met at the tire shop and asked her to come and pray with me. She came at once, and we prayed for hours. The pain diminished while we prayed, but it would start up again when we stopped. She said that sometimes in a spiritual battle it's helpful to take one decisive step to show the enemy you're serious. I was ready to try anything. She said, 'Do you want to go on with the Lord in a deeper way?' I said I did. She said, 'Then let's start filling suitcases.'"

"Did the spiritual attack stop then?"

"Not with the first suitcase. Nor with the second or even the third, but by the time we got to the fourth one, I felt better. We packed until we ran out of containers. By then we were laughing and hugging, and I called another Sister to tell her what was happening. She came over and brought more boxes. It turned into a party, with other Sisters stopping by to bring boxes, sometimes staying to help pack, sometimes leaving encouragement. I knew then I had made the right choice, and I have never looked back. I've also never had an attack like that again, and I don't expect to."

Casey felt cut off and alone, wondering if anyone would help her if she ever moved. The thought of even beginning the process was like a cold slap that sobered her.

As though she had read Casey's mind, Lydia leaned forward and touched her hand. "The same Bodylife that waited for me, standing on tiptoe with anticipation of my arrival, waits for you too. I want you to recognize what's in front of you, so you can make an intelligent choice. The Body longs for all of its members to come home. We're incomplete without you. I have a hunch you believe the Body won't be any different whether you come or go, but don't let your feelings get in the way of the facts."

Sudden compression in her chest caught Casey off guard, as if Andrew had jumped on her from the window ledge above the bed when she didn't expect it. A stifling panic followed. Her palms felt slick. She placed them face down on her jeans and hoped Lydia wouldn't notice.

"I've said enough about this for the weekend."

Casey was surprised, expecting the discussion to continue until she made a choice.

"The Spirit is marvelous," Lydia reassured her. "When he moves, it's a powerful sensation, but he's a lot like the Saint Bernard dog we had when I was a kid—if he doesn't think it's time to go, he won't budge. I don't want to imply I know better than the Lord what you should do or when you should do it. Let's leave it in his hands, okay? After all, that's where it's always been anyway."

"I appreciate what you've said, and I'll think about it, but I'm not ready to make a decision yet," Casey said. "I would like to go to the Gathering tomorrow though."

"Good. I look forward to it." Lydia shook back her hair, and a small grin lit her features. "I'm sure it will surprise more than a few people when we arrive."

Casey's drawn brows prompted her to continue. "As I said, the Body is very aware of those who come to belong to it. Since they knew I was spending the weekend with you, more than one person said perhaps we'd never see you again once you pulled back like this, and they didn't necessarily believe I'd given you good advice when I told you to stay away from Gatherings all week."

Gray eyes searched Casey's face. "I have the utmost faith in God, however. He answers the heart cries of his children when they ask to be led to where they can be happy, productive, and blessed. Give him the chance to speak to you about where you need to be. I pray you will find your heart's desire there."

Casey recalled her prayers from the previous few days and felt something leap inside at the idea of being where God wanted her. She thanked him silently for sending Lydia to stir that desire yet again. The decision seemed clear-cut, but something inside her still resisted.

9

asey fixed her eyes on the car ahead and saw Lydia's head nodding to the song tape she had popped into the player. After the warm, cozy weekend with Lydia, she hated driving in tandem. The closer they came to the Gathering Place, the more nervous she became. She felt like a returning penitent, not someone who had missed a few Gatherings.

When Lydia's signal blinked for the final turn into the Gathering Place, Casey rolled down her window. The sound of singing drifted into her little car, wrapped itself around her heart, and stirred a longing that took her breath away.

Webster Forsythe watched Audrey as she played. Her fingers strolled across the keyboard, but the people who made up his flock were her real instrument. She was a virtuoso as she worked to shape the group's mood. He depended on her to prepare the surface on which he would carve his message. The carving was easy when the surface of the Body was soft and pliable, as Audrey always made it.

He noticed her eyebrows rise in amazement. He pivoted toward the door. Casey and Lydia entered the room arm in arm, and he saw Casey drag Lydia forward toward the chairs. Even Lydia seemed surprised and delighted by her fervor. Together they moved to the first row behind the Brothers' row, which was the nucleus of the concentric rings.

"Score one for Lydia," he said under his breath. She seemed to have a knack for doing the opposite of what he directed, yet everything always seemed to turn out for the best. Still, he would have to curb her very soon. She set a bad example for the other women. True, she had never challenged him in public before last week, but that dispute could indicate future disobedience. He couldn't get a true grip on her commitment to the Bodylife, and especially to him. Something in her devotion was out of place, and he couldn't pin it down.

Kurt sat transfixed in his chair across from Casey and Lydia. It was clear which way his sympathies lay regarding Lydia's apparent success with Casey. Webster's lip curled slightly at the longing on Kurt's face. Still, a body was a body, and it was his job to cement this latest body into the group. He would take them any way he could get them.

Webster reviewed his outline. People were impressed by the time they assumed he devoted to study each week. They were also impressed when he "let the Spirit lead"—right off the outline. The truth was that he only prepared to speak on the first two points. This week those two points would pull out all the stops.

Casey closed her eyes and sang with all her heart. She had finally learned the words to enough songs so she could concentrate on worship, not reading the words. Sisters flanked her. Brothers sat in front of her, their deep baritone and bass voices blending with the high, sweet altos and sopranos of the Sisters. She was surrounded, she was welcome, and she had been missed. She felt content.

Lydia called for repetitions of verses with abandon. Between songs Brothers and Sisters rose to their feet at a dizzying pace, building the flow of the Gathering. Two broke down in tears when testifying, and the emotional energy accelerated with the outbursts. Casey felt the group's taut anticipation as they waited for Webster to lift them to yet a higher level of worship. When he stood to speak, she felt faint, an unusual and rather exciting sensation for her.

Webster looked into many eyes before beginning to speak. Then he grinned and lifted a white page aloft. "I'd like to ask the Brothers to pass around the outline for today." Laughter tinged with excitement answered him. "I'm going to do my best to get through it this time."

The few who did not share the loud laughter appeared to Casey to be newcomers—a couple in polyester to the right, and two older women and a man whose round eyes showed shock at the volume of the singing. Newcomer couples always stood out like weeds on a golf course, stubbornly sitting together, rather than enjoying the worship time as the others did—the women together, the men circling Webster. Casey and Lydia exchanged glances and giggled. She could feel it was going to be a good message.

"I'm continuing with the subject we've discussed all week—which is why I can hope to complete the outline. I've had three evenings so far to attempt it." Casey hated that she had missed the messages leading to this one, but she would buy the tapes. It would make her drive back to Grovers both productive and bearable. She clicked the top of her pen and wrote the date on a fresh sheet.

"We've been talking, singing, and enjoying the concept of the interconnectedness of the church, the intertwined purposes of God." His complex phrases and precise pronunciation washed over Casey. "The Bible says the very heavens declare the glory of the Lord. I say the very earth we tread declares the glory of our need to be interconnected." A heartfelt amen swelled from hundreds of throats. "We read many stories about animals who seek out their homes season after season, pets who come back to their owners from thousands of miles' distance, and people who seek to reestablish relationships even after decades. We marvel at these stories but don't see the true meaning. They are outstanding examples of our underlying, unshakable, undeniable need to connect on a deep and permanent level.

"Many people come to our Gatherings to look for 'the answer.'" He made quotation marks in the air with his fingers. "I see them come in, sing our songs, listen to our testimonies, buy our tapes and books, and leave. I know that within a day or two all the good the Gathering has done them will wear off. In an effort to recapture the sense of belonging, of being joined to something wonderful, they may come to midweek Gatherings. They may drive long distances to do so, arrive home late at night, and be exhausted on their jobs the next day, all in an effort to be connected—but it doesn't work, does it?"

Heads shook throughout the room. In the second row Casey drank in each word, echoed each emotion, and felt the emptiness inside. She wanted to run. She wanted to stay forever. She could not do both.

"We live as we do, in close contact, with daily Gatherings and constant interaction, but not because it's written in the bylaws of an organizational charter," Webster continued. "We have no bylaws but the Bible. We're organized like the early church, and our hearts are at rest.

"We all once chased the dream of a vibrant, exciting, uncompromising body of believers. When we found it, we had to make a choice: to live entirely *without* it, or to live entirely *within* it. There was no middle ground. To try to straddle the fence would have broken our heart.

"That is the choice that, sooner or later, each person here must make. Which will it be?"

Casey began to sob quietly. She could hardly see his face through her tears, but she knew he was looking directly into her eyes and deeply into her soul.

"I don't know about you, but I can't think of anything more horrible than to glimpse the Bodylife, yet have to mold myself to the world twelve hours a day to survive. If I did that, I might survive physically, but my spirit would wither away. If I gained the whole world but ended up with a spirit as dead as a dried weed, what would I have gained?" His voice dropped to a whisper. "Nothing but the world."

Three hundred people leaned forward to catch his words. "Nothing with which my deepest nature could connect."

He sat down and put his face in his hands.

A thunderous whisper resounded. *Amen!* The silence stretched, punctuated by muffled sniffling. When the tension in the room stretched painfully tight, Casey rose to her feet. She held a tissue and pressed it to her upper lip. She tried in vain to stop the tears that wet her cheeks. As she wavered on her feet she heard the thunderous whisper again. *Amen!*

"I'm so tired of being alone, trying to be an island, living unconnected." She took a deep, shaky breath and wiped her nose. She looked out over the people she had come to love. She was in the wall of fire. It was time to decide whether to go forward or to step back. "I don't want to be alone anymore. I want to be here."

In one motion Carol and Lydia rose and bracketed her, weeping with her. She pulled strength from them.

"I want this more than I've ever wanted anything in my life." With a small, quivering smile, she added, "Does anybody have room for a Sister and her cat?"

Joy exploded from Lydia. She and Carol wrapped their arms around Casey at the same time, which caused a tangle of appendages and lent some much-needed levity.

Lydia shook her head. "I'm afraid we're already fighting over you."

"Amen!" the others roared. "Amen!"

PART II

My people have become lost sheep; their shepherds have led them astray. They have made them turn aside on the mountains; they have gone along from mountain to hill and have forgotten their resting place.

—JEREMIAH 50:6

10

Webster Forsythe reviewed the documents on his desk, his pen poised for the final signature. "Almost no equity. That's good," he murmured to Dominic, "and it's in a pretty nice part of town. We'll hold onto it for a while and sell when the market turns around."

"I've already lined up someone to rent it," Dominic offered. "We don't want it to stand empty."

"Someone from the Body?" Webster did not want to scatter his flock.

"No, an outsider, but someone who can be brought in later. We need to get Casey here and make sure she thinks there's no going back. We used our usual go-between to buy the house the day after it came on the market. She'll take it as confirmation from God that she move."

Webster smiled. "There *is* no going back. Once they've tasted the Bodylife, they're spoiled for anything else. That's our motto, and we deliver every time." He scribbled his signature. "How about those families who left a few months back. Any word of them?"

Dominic frowned. "One settled into a mainline Christian church." He brightened. "But the other two have popped up in congregations all over town. I don't think they can settle."

"Be sure a few families keep in touch with them," Webster said, collecting the papers into a tidy stack, "but pick them with care. We want them to act as a magnet, not as filings that get pulled away."

"I have some couples in mind. They need their first assignment, and it will make them feel more connected to the Body if they think they're helping build it up."

"Good. I'll be sure to tailor the message in that vein." Webster added with a slow smile, "The Spirit willing, of course."

"Of course." Dominic smirked.

"Casey?" the voice on the phone trilled. "I heard you're moving to the Sisters House!"

"I'm sorry I haven't had time to call you." Casey waited for the inevitable Great Gretchen Idea.

"Why don't I pop over and help you out? I'm so excited for you. I want to be part of your move if I can." The offer was too tame, so Casey waited, braced for the rest.

"I'm sure you want to put your best foot forward at the Sisters House. Let's go shopping and get you new bedroom stuff. A new quilt, new sheets, new towels."

"That's sweet, but I don't have to put on airs with the Sisters," Casey said. "I'll go with what I have."

"Didn't you tell me you've had the same bedding since college? It's more than time for something new. Maybe something white and pretty. With lace."

Casey felt impatient. "My bedding is fine. My sheets are fine. My towels are quite respectable. If anything, I need less stuff, not more. I'm going from a house to a single room."

"All the more reason to have nice things—"

"Gretchen!"

Gretchen fell silent, and then said in a tiny voice, "I was trying to help."

Casey repented of her quick temper. She would have to get control of it if she hoped to live successfully in the Sisters House. No one there appeared to have temper problems. "I'm sorry. I'm under a lot of strain. I had no idea how much stuff I had until I tried to pack. Then you suggested I get more."

"I'm sorry too," Gretchen said. "I wasn't thinking. You know me; let the mouth run, and the brain might catch up next week."

The contrition in Gretchen's voice melted Casey's resistance. "Why don't you come over? I could sure use your help. Sisters have been here off and on all week, but I'm alone today, and I want to see you. Bring Jennifer and the little fire horn too, if you want."

"We'll be there in ten minutes." The phone was on its cradle almost before Gretchen finished speaking.

Casey looked at her watch and gave her eight minutes, tops.

Grace Forsythe pulled into the drive of the large, well-kept home known as the Sisters House. She cut the engine and then sat and took in the clean windows, the bright drapes, and the sprinklers watering the lawn. She couldn't find anything out of place, and it irritated her. She would find something.

She opened the car door at the same instant three women rushed out to greet her.

"Sister Grace," Carol cooed. "How nice to have you stop by. We're finishing our chores for the morning."

"We're very excited," another said. "Casey will be moving in this weekend."

"Yes, that's what I'm here about." Grace let an ominous note creep into her voice. "I wanted to check your preparations." She sailed ahead of them into the house, her nose twitching and her eyes darting to seek out the first infraction.

She was pleased to find a plant in the window languishing for lack of water. There were three crumbs on a kitchen counter. The Sisters had not yet vacuumed the room where Casey would be installed. The cleaner was in the hallway, but her visit had caught them unprepared. She addressed each problem with an appropriate Scripture regarding cleanliness and diligence. At last she settled in the living room to address the three nervous women.

"When is she being moved?"

"This S-Saturday," Amy, the youngest, stuttered. Her pale eyelashes quivered with agitation.

"The trucks are all ready, the Brothers organized?"

"Yes, Grace, we've seen to all that," Lydia said, her voice still calm despite the rigorous inspection. Grace knew Lydia did not like her. She was always polite, but the older woman sensed that she forced herself to speak in measured tones whenever Grace was in earshot. It would be fun to break down that composure.

"I hear she has a cat. We can't have that." Grace sniffed as though she smelled the unsavory odor of an untended cat box.

"What?" Lydia had been trapped into speaking.

Grace purred. "We don't want to be attached to anything or anybody outside the Body."

"Casey is very new to the Bodylife." Lydia said. "She was reluctant to commit herself in the first place. If we now make a rule that her cat isn't allowed, she could walk away from us for good. He's quiet and well behaved." Grace sensed Lydia's protectiveness of Casey and knew she would fight to the end on this point.

"You were right once before about Casey. We'll have to wait and see, won't we, dear?" Lydia blanched at the implied threat. Grace would be hovering, hoping to see her make a mistake worthy of discipline.

Grace snapped her handbag closed, and the other women jumped. She stood, and they scrambled to their feet. "I leave Casey in your hands, for the time being. After awhile I'll want to see her and begin to work with her. There's a lot to learn in the Body to make each member fit in."

She turned on her heel. It left a black smudge on the wood floor. "Oh, I'm sorry about that." She examined the heel mark with satisfaction. "Lydia, you can get that off, can't you?" Lydia's pocket bulged slightly, and Grace realized with satisfying amusement that she had closed her hand into a small, tight fist.

"Of course. Don't give it another thought." The tightness in Lydia's voice played like music in Grace's ear. She moseyed out to her car to delay her departure as long as possible. When the door finally swung shut behind her, she knew the three people on the other side took their first deep breaths in more than an hour. She smirked halfway down the block.

11

asey stood in her small room and set the cat carrier on the floor. Boxes were piled high, but a passage was clear from the door to the bed. The Sisters had put fresh sheets and blankets on the bed earlier. She had arrived with Lydia, after one last dust and vacuum of her beloved Jewel. Thinking of it nearly broke her heart.

Andrew yowled, and Casey knelt. She sprang the catch on the carrier door and swung it open. The cat put a tentative foot on the unfamiliar carpet.

"It's okay, sweetheart," Casey soothed. "This is our new home. You and I are going to live here together. It's like home, but smaller." She eased herself to the floor with her back against a heavy box. Large tears trailed down her cheeks. Andrew apparently saw no immediate danger and emerged in a businesslike way, padded to Casey's side, and put a paw on her folded leg. With a stifled sob she gathered the cat into her arms and rocked with him. Andrew began to wash her salty hands to comfort her.

After a few minutes Casey chided herself for falling apart now that she was where she had longed to be. She straightened her glasses, ran a quick hand through her hair, and patted Andrew. He wriggled free to explore the room, poking his nose in every crevice between boxes, under furniture, or behind curtains. His activities brought a smile to Casey's face and a soft glimmer to her eyes.

The last place Andrew explored was the top of the bed. He jumped to the coverlet and proceeded to sniff the entire quilt.

Satisfied that it smelled familiar, he curled up in his accustomed place next to the pillow. Then he looked at Casey, still huddled on the floor, and blinked. As she started to rise, she heard a knock at the door. She called to the visitor to come in, and Lydia peeped around the door, her eyes searching the sea of boxes.

"Down here," Casey waved tiredly.

Lydia eased into the crowded room, closed the door behind her, and perched on a box of books. "I came to see how you were doing. I know it's quite an upheaval. I'd be happy to help."

Casey shook her head, lifted her glasses from her nose, and rubbed her eyes. "It's more than an upheaval." She hesitated. As she had so many times, Lydia seemed to sense her thoughts.

"You're thinking it's a mistake, aren't you?"

Casey's shoulders drooped.

"I thought the same thing on my first night." Casey looked up with surprise. "In fact, the only person I've known who didn't was Carol. She came in and threw down her bags, walked into the kitchen where we were making dinner, and asked which knife was hers."

"I suppose they think I'm a washout right about now." Casey knew her refusal to eat dinner had not gone over well with her new housemates.

"Right now, you're not hungry for anything." Lydia's voice was kind. "Not for dinner, not for us, not for putting your things away, not for thinking too much about what's happened. As I said, I felt the same way when I first arrived. I know tomorrow morning this door will pop open," she pointed to the door behind her, "and out you'll bounce, eager to explore the Bodylife from the inside. And we'll all be there to welcome you."

Lydia rose from her box and moved to the door. "I'm right on the other side of the wall if you need me. Just knock." A small grin teased the corners of her mouth. "Or throw something. I'll be over in a flash."

Casey nodded with bleary eyes and gave a small wave of thanks as Lydia left. She raised herself from the floor with a muttered exclamation as her tired muscles reminded her of the last few days. She crawled onto the bed and wrapped one arm around the cat. She fell into an exhausted sleep almost before she kicked off her second shoe.

12

asey ventured to the company break room. The room appeared empty as she approached, and she was relieved. Her relief evaporated when she saw Jessie poking half-heartedly at a salad, alone in the midst of the tables and chairs. Her friend's isolation compounded Casey's feelings of guilt, and she would have continued down the hall if Jessie hadn't caught sight of her.

"Casey." Jessie laid aside her napkin and fork, and rose. "Come sit with me while I finish lunch."

Casey advanced, coffee cup in hand, and turned on the faucet. She swished her cup clean and grabbed a paper towel.

"I've got lots of proofing to do. Maybe tomorrow—"

"Hey, everybody needs a break. Only a few minutes. Please."

Despite Jessie's soft tone, Casey's heart accelerated. She experienced something akin to fear whenever she encountered Jessie now. With reluctance she slid into the chair across from her.

"That looks good," she said to break the silence.

"I haven't been hungry for days, but I have to eat something."

"You, not hungry?" A corner of Casey's mouth lifted. Jessie put down her fork.

"My appetite vanishes when I'm worried. Casey, I'm more worried about you now than I've ever been in my life." Casey's eyes widened with alarm, and she put her hand on the table to rise. Jessie reached across the table. "Don't run, and don't shut me out." Casey felt her hand go clammy under Jessie's warm grasp.

There were tiny lines around Jessie's eyes. Her makeup was flawless, but the lines were new, and she hadn't learned how to conceal them yet. It flashed through Casey's mind that she was responsible for those lines. Concern for her had left an imprint on Jessie's face.

"I'm fine." Casey surprised herself with the normal tone of her voice. "I know I haven't spent much time with you lately, and I'm sorry, but I've been so busy. I don't seem to have a minute to myself anymore."

"Do you remember the story from the New Testament that tells about a struggle between an angel and the Devil over Moses' body? I've been waging my own battle every night for the past week over the body of a sister in Christ—only she's not dead." The lines around Jessie's eyes grew more pronounced. "I feel like I've got hold of your feet, Casey, and the Devil has hold of your head. I know from Scripture that I'm going to win, but I wonder if you'll survive the tugging."

Casey began to sputter. "Who asked you to battle over me? I'm *fine*. Why would you think otherwise?"

"I called you at home three days ago." Jessie tried unsuccessfully to hold her gaze. "The number has been disconnected. What's going on?"

"Oh, that." Casey gave a nervous titter. "I moved, and my number didn't go with me." She knew etiquette dictated that she immediately give her friend the new number. She couldn't bring herself to do it. The silence stretched. The coffeemaker on the counter growled like a caged beast.

"Where did you move?"

"To Crescent Hills. I'm living with other women in a lovely old house on a beautiful street." She tried a smile, but Jessie didn't return it. "Andrew just loves all the attention he gets in a houseful of women."

"Why would you give up your Jewel and move so far away from work?"

"There's more to life than work."

"What 'more' draws you to Crescent Hills?"

Casey felt the world turn right side up at last with a question she could answer without evasion. "Oh, there's real life there. Real worship. Real fellowship. I'm part of the Body now, and I feel so connected. When I'm here at work, I feel like a plant that's been ripped from the soil. The closer I get to Crescent Hills, the more I feel the Body reach out and embrace me. I roll down the windows so I can enjoy the sweet smell of it and be engulfed in the warmth of being part of it." Casey locked her eyes on Jessie's and willed her to understand.

Jessie rocked back in her chair in the face of Casey's vehement reply. She swallowed before she spoke again. "What you're saying doesn't make sense. Isn't the body of Christ everywhere Christians are?"

"That's true, but some parts of God's family are better for me than others. I've sought and found a place where I can grow and be loved like never before. We still graze in the same pasture, Jessie," Casey reassured her. "I moved to another part of the field, but the Shepherd is the same."

"Is he? Are you following the Shepherd or the sheep?"

"Of course I'm following the Shepherd. Do you think I would have sold my home, moved in with other people, and given up so much if I hadn't sought to get closer to the Lord? And I *have* gotten closer, closer than I've ever been. I've found people who are as serious about him as I am. I'm happy," Casey insisted. "Can't you understand that? Or are you jealous that I'm growing?"

Jessie looked skeptical. "If you're so happy, why do you look like a ghost? Have you looked in the mirror lately? The clothes you wear these days! I doubt that a denim smock ever lived in your wardrobe before, and certainly not anklets and sneakers. You don't have a speck of makeup on either. You don't look happy; you look miserable. Don't you see what's happening?"

"I see a lot happening here, and I don't like it a bit." Casey rose to her feet. "I see you trying to throw roadblocks in my path to happiness and spiritual fulfillment. I see the friendship we had in the past dragging me backward instead of encouraging me on in the Lord. I see I'm on the right track, or else this opposition wouldn't spring up. Thanks for confirming my direction." She pivoted on her rubber-soled heel. "Enjoy your lunch!"

Casey did her best to lose herself in the Gathering, but the words she and Jessie had hurled at each other days before still bothered her. She looked at the other Sisters, and she saw them as Jessie would see them—no makeup, matching denim smocks, and tennis shoes. It startled her to realize how much she had come to accept what had at first seemed foreign. She tried hard to fit in, and she felt part of herself die each time she did what the Body wanted, as opposed to what she wanted. Webster talked all the time about the struggle to put aside one's own preferences for the surpassing beauty of accepting the Body's preferences.

She tried to picture Jessie as she had seen her that day—bright floral skirt, orange and deep-blue blouse, orange lipstick, dark eye shadow, breezy blue scarf around her head—in a Gathering. No, Jessie wasn't Bodylife material.

Casey frowned. It bothered her more than she cared to admit that Jessie, whom she had always looked up to as her spiritual elder sister, wouldn't fit into the Body. She never considered herself so different that the two of them couldn't belong to the same church. She had always treasured Jessie's spiritual insights, yet now she chafed at them and tried to avoid her.

She did her best to put her usual enthusiasm into the song they were singing. It was one of her favorites, an old tune with new and better words. When the song ended, Darren, the Brother who wrote the song numbers on the erasable board, rose to his feet. Casey looked at him with interest. She found herself drawn to the big, silent man and hoped she would get to know him better now that she lived at the Sisters House.

Darren opened his Bible. With no preamble, he read, "'When I was a child, I used to speak like a child, think like a child, reason like a child; when I became a man, I did away with childish ways.'" He stared at the words as though he saw them for the first time. Then he looked at the group.

"I've struggled so hard the past two weeks, and it's drained me." His voice cracked. Casey leaned forward. "I find myself at odds with counselors I once valued, turning away from people who once led me, and it hurts. It has caused me to question my certainty that I should be here in the Bodylife." Darren dashed tears from his cheeks, and his voice became stronger. Casey was riveted by his words.

"All through Scripture I see admonitions to heed the words of those older than I am in the faith. So why do I want to run from the very men who led me to the Lord?" A rustle of anticipation fluttered through the Gathering. Casey, tense, yearned for Darren to answer his own question—and hers.

"I felt pulled in two directions. I felt my soul tearing as I tried to be true to old teachers and to follow the Bodylife at the same time." Darren looked around at the people whose faces craned toward him like flowers to the sun.

"When I was in the third grade, I had a wonderful teacher. I loved Mr. Murphy; he taught me a lot." Darren paused. "Then I went on to the fourth grade, and I had a new teacher. It never crossed my mind to go back to Mr. Murphy's class. I was in the fourth grade now, and we learned new material. Mr. Murphy was the keeper of third-grade material."

He shook his head. "With that thought in mind, I realized the Lord has been asking me, *'Why do you want to go back to your old teachers when I've given you new ones?'* He led me to the passage I read to you from First Corinthians about growing from child to adult. I don't think like those old teachers anymore, because they taught me when I was a child. Now I need to find 'adult education' teachers, and I have—right here." Darren sat down, and an emotion-charged amen washed over the group.

Casey took a luxurious breath, smiled, and turned to Lydia. "Amen!" she said, her eyes dancing. Her gaze fastened on Darren's bent head.

"Amen," she whispered again.

13

C asey stood uneasily on the Forsythes' unfamiliar doorstep. The immaculately groomed yard was the product of untold hours of work by the Brothers, she knew. Though curious about the inside of the house, she had always been reluctant to visit—it meant she would have to be around Grace. The woman made her uncomfortable.

However, when Grace called, all the Sisters jumped, as Casey had when summoned this morning. She wondered if she had done something wrong. The door opened, and Grace stood framed in the rich wood entryway.

"Casey, do come in." Grace gestured. "I thought we'd have lemonade and a little chat on the patio. How does that sound?"

"Great." Casey watched Grace's eyes travel over her plastic headband, denim smock, and cotton blouse. They paused at her shoelaces, which were imprinted with cats chasing balls of yarn along their length. She could not have felt more chastened if Grace had told her to step outside and remove them.

Grace silently turned and walked through the house. Casey focused her attention on her hostess's rigid back and tried not to snoop. Outside, they settled into cushioned patio chairs. Grace poured lemonade from a frosted pitcher into two tall glasses and handed one to Casey.

"You look tired. Is everything all right at the Sisters House?"

"The house is great. I love living there. Everyone's wonderful. I'm tired from work, that's all. My boss has aggressively recruited authors to turn in their projects, and my desk at work is always overflowing." Casey forced herself to stop babbling.

"Your work is in Grovers, isn't it?" Grace took a sip from her glass. When Casey nodded, she made a sympathetic sound. "Such a long way—then so much work."

"It's not so bad. I listen to Brother Webster all the way there in the morning and singing tapes from the Gatherings on the way home. By the time I get back to the Sisters House, I'm refreshed."

"I hear you fall asleep standing at the sink doing dishes sometimes." Grace's lips formed a mirthless slash.

"Not quite, but almost." Casey laughed to cover her nervousness. "Some days are worse than others. You know how it is." She felt a chill. What if Grace made her leave because of her job? Where would she go?

"I do know how it is, and I know it doesn't have to be that way." Grace adjusted her skirt over her knees and looked sharply at Casey. "How long have you worked in publishing?"

"Five years."

"You're a good editor and proofreader?" Grace looked at the sky and leaned back in her chair. "You know how to put together a publication?"

"Yes. Why?"

Grace leaned forward suddenly, which startled Casey. "We need you, Casey. Not just the Body, but Webster and I." She held Casey's eyes in an unbreakable grip.

"I don't understand."

"You know Brother Webster works very hard for the Body."

"I never see him rest."

Grace pounced. "Exactly." Then she glanced over her shoulder. The beautiful yard was empty. "I have to tell you something, and you must never repeat it to anyone."

Casey took in the tense line of Grace's shoulders, her earnest expression. She nodded twice.

"Webster has a weak heart. One part of it is paper thin, and we could lose him at anytime." Grace paused for this revelation to sink in. She bit her lower lip. "I'm frightened. I try to do anything I can to help him, but I can't do it all."

"We can't lose Brother Webster!" Rising dread engulfed Casey.

"I'm so glad to hear you care about him as I do." Grace's shoulders sagged. "There's something only you can do that will take a great deal of strain off him."

"Tell me." Casey took Grace's hand. For the first time she felt a sense of communion with the woman.

"Brother Webster speaks almost daily, and we record what he says. All the pamphlets and books in our bookstore are distillations of those talks," Grace said. "He stays up all hours working over those manuscripts before they go to press. He needs an assistant to relieve the burden."

"I'm not old enough in the Body to be an assistant to Brother Webster." Casey gulped.

Grace's sharp voice cut through the still air. "You want to keep your talents to yourself and watch him collapse with a fatal heart attack during a Gathering?" Her voice turned soft and coaxing. "I'm asking you to put aside your own ambitions and to build the Body instead."

"You want me to do this in the evenings after I come home from work?" Casey shook her head as the enormous task loomed over her.

"No, I'm asking you to give up your job in Grovers and work for Brother Webster full time. He needs that much help, you know."

"Does he know you're asking me to do this?"

"Now you've put your finger on the rough spot." Grace sighed. "He doesn't know, and he'd be upset if he did. He doesn't want anyone to know about his physical weakness, not even so the Body can pray for him. So, we'd have to engage in a little charade for his benefit, as so many saints did in the Old Testament."

"I don't like to lie. It would have to be aboveboard, all the way." Casey felt her jaw set. On this point she would not budge.

"If Queen Esther had insisted on being honest to the core, the Jews might not have survived to bring the Messiah to life," Grace argued. "If David hadn't been crafty and wily, King Saul might have captured him."

"I know Old Testament heroes sometimes weren't honest, but didn't they encounter discipline as a result?" Casey frowned and tried to understand what Grace wanted.

"And so will you—discipline of your will—and you'll be a better Sister for it." Grace drained her glass and stood up. "If you don't care enough about Webster to try, I'll have to wait for someone else to come along with your unique combination of skills. I hope he or she doesn't take too long. I don't know how long Webster has."

"That's not fair." Casey reached up, gripped Grace's arm, and pulled her back into her chair again. "Of course I want to help. But I won't lie to Brother Webster."

"Perhaps 'lie' is too strong a word. Tell Webster you want to help with his publications. Step in and take over. There's nothing deceitful about that."

"But, I need to pay bills. I can't live without a paying job."

"Webster wants people to work for the Body out of love for the Lord, not love for money. However, you and I can make an arrangement to take care of all that. I will see to it that your bills are paid from a fund I have at my disposal. In effect you'll be an independent contractor—but under contract to me, not to Webster. I'll give you twenty-five dollars a week for pocket money, and in return you'll handle all his publishing efforts." Grace looked at Casey. "What do you think?"

"I was thinking twenty-five dollars a week is nothing. Then I realized I haven't spent money on anything but gasoline and books from our bookstore in a month—and if I worked at the Gathering Place for Brother Webster, I could walk there in good weather." Casey's mind worked.

"If you ever need additional money, I'll be here." Grace took both of Casey's hands in hers. "I need you, Webster needs you, and the Body needs you. Think of this as the Lord's call on your life."

Casey felt her heart leap. How long had she wanted the Lord to call her and give her a task? Here it had opened up before her, and she had fought it. She started to reply, but Grace forestalled her.

"I don't want your answer right now. Think about it; perhaps talk to other Sisters, leaving out Webster's physical problems, of course. Tell me in a week." Relieved, Casey nodded. Grace squeezed her hands, then they both rose.

"Thank you for coming over. I'll look forward to your answer soon."

Grace closed the carved wooden door and turned her back to it. She listened to the tread on the thickly carpeted stairs and looked up to meet her husband's eyes as he descended.

"You played that very well, my dear," he said. "My heart feels weaker already."

Grace laughed. "I've told you for years you need to let me do some reeling in. Maybe now you'll believe me." The acid edge to her voice ate into her smile.

"She isn't landed yet."

"Oh, Webster, don't be stupid. This one is so eager to be hauled in I could have had her drinking lemonade from my shoe out there. It's so entertaining to let her squirm for a week and think she has a choice whether to take the bait or spit out the hook."

"You take this 'fishers of men' thing too seriously." He smiled.

Grace began to hum as she walked away. She needed to make an appointment—perhaps grant an audience was more accurate—with the Sister who cut the Bodylife women's hair. She intended to make the women change to a short bob, up over the ears, like Casey used to wear hers before she let it grow to accommodate one of the requisite headbands. Those headbands were going to be out, starting this afternoon.

A soft tap sounded on Casey's door. The quiet tinkle of the bell on Andrew's collar mingled with her quiet response. Lydia entered with a tray in one hand and her Bible under her arm. Casey sat with her own Bible open across her knees.

"I thought we might talk a little if you want to." Lydia gestured with her chin at the tray. "I always talk better with something to drink in my hand. Isn't that how we first became friends?"

Casey remembered the coffee shop, a lifetime ago. "I don't think I'm good company tonight, but come on in. I don't think I want to be alone either."

Lydia addressed the cat with mock outrage, "Alone? And what are you, window dressing?" The cat blinked with apparent pleasure at her tone.

Casey stroked the purring body next to her and nuzzled his head. His purring increased in volume, and his front paws clenched in pleasure.

After she set down the tray, Lydia sank into the overstuffed chair. It was all that remained of Casey's comfortable living room furniture. A chocolate aroma drew both women to the mugs. Casey looked over the small room as she reviewed the changes in her life in less than a year—from her Jewel to a single room, from being independent and lonely to living and working with four other women. A loud sigh escaped her as she acknowledged that much of the loneliness was still with her though the independence had almost totally disappeared.

"That sigh was far too deep to be borne by one set of shoulders," Lydia said. "What's wrong? Something has been eating at you for days."

"You've always been one to go right to the heart of a matter." Casey breathed in more of the chocolate aroma from her cup and took a quick sip.

"I find beating around the bush exhausting, don't you?" Concerned gray eyes measured Casey's unsmiling countenance.

"You're right, and I'm far too tired for games. I'm too tired for lots of things, including thinking, yet I sit here by the hour straining to do so anyway. I need to move to praying and deciding, yet I can't even get the puffy thought balloons to hover over my head." Casey batted her hand in the air above her, exasperated.

"'My burden is light.'"

"What?"

"That's what Jesus said about the responsibilities the believer could expect to deal with. He didn't say they would be meaningless or easy, but he did say there would be joy in the doing of them that makes for light work." Lydia paused. "Sometimes, if a burden is too heavy, it's best shared." When Casey shook her head, she added, "Or a friend can help to get the load balanced before the bearer heads off carrying it alone again." Her eyes searched Casey's weary-looking face. "Won't you trust me?"

"It's not a matter of trust. It's a confidence that can't be divulged that's weighing on me." Casey closed her eyes, exhausted.

"If the secret's not yours, why is it so heavy?"

"Because I seem to be the one who can help take the burden off another person. But there are too many things that would have to change, and I'm at the top of the list." Casey folded her hands in defeat.

"I've faced many difficult decisions in my life," Lydia said. "The ones that counted were the most painful. They were also the most clear-cut." Casey's eyebrows rose. "I knew what had to be done. It was a matter of my 'want-to' getting in line with my 'know-what.'"

"So, how do you get a stubborn 'want-to' to be obedient to a Spirit-led 'know-what'?" Casey grinned for the first time in days.

"It gets easier all the time. Every time I make the leap of obedience, I feel such relief and joy. The burden gets lighter immediately, and remembering the release has helped me to make the leap faster as the years have gone by."

Casey remembered her own decision to move to the Bodylife. She had expected things to go better after that act of obedience, yet the wall of fire was in her path again.

"Being part of the Body doesn't solve anything," Lydia said. Casey gaped at her. "If you expect it to simplify your life, you'd best buckle your seatbelt. Being in the Body, in constant contact with the saints and in Gatherings day after day, is like rubbing sandpaper on your spirit. The tough skin the world allowed you to grow over your spirit gets worn off, and there are nerves underneath." Lydia chuckled. "Making big decisions over big issues is one of the quickest ways to abrade it."

"I wish I were strong like you."

"I'm one of the weakest people you'll ever meet," Lydia said. "My strength comes from yielding, and I fight every day to be weak enough for God to overwhelm me with his love, guide me with his Spirit, and deafen me to the world's clamor with his still, small voice. That's the heart of whatever you're struggling with. I don't need to know the actual details. I can sense the conflict raging within you, and I'm here to come alongside you, to be Jonathan to your David, and to help you win this battle."

Casey's hands gripped one another as though each one could pull the other out of a pit.

"Don't fight it," Lydia urged. "Let yourself express the fear and the longing and the crazy hope inside you. Don't put up the wall of isolation. My nose is skinned raw from running into it. Take my hand before the bricks get too high, and let's go to the Father about this one. He's been waiting all week."

Without a word Casey reached out her hand. Lydia captured it in a confident grip, then dropped her head and began to speak to God for her friend.

14

Jessie Barlow walked toward the building that had been her professional home for ten years. No matter how much she relished her job, it was always difficult to return after two blissful weeks of vacation with Claude. They did not have to go anywhere special or do anything unique. Being together was enough for them. She thanked God for such a man, such a marriage.

The stack on her desk was every bit as intimidating as she feared it would be. She had come in early to deal with it before the phones started clamoring. She picked up her coffee cup and stifled a groan. A multicolored crust coated the bottom. She fished in her huge purse, found a plastic bag she kept for miscellaneous emergencies, dropped the cup in it, and sealed the bag. The cup could wait until she could sanitize it in the dishwasher at home.

She moved through the dim maze of cubicles, entered the kitchen, pulled a foam coffee cup from the dispenser, and filled it with steaming liquid. She inhaled the aroma and blessed the cleaning staff, whose final task each morning was to start the coffeepots brewing. She made a mental note to drop a thank-you card in their box.

For the next two hours Jessie sorted, tossed, and prioritized her mail. By then the office bustled. She looked at her empty coffee cup and decided to get a refill before she opened the phone line. She exchanged greetings and answered stock questions about her vacation. Something was in the air, however. People avoided her eyes. She shrugged and moved down the corridor. She would ask Casey what was going on.

Her fashion sense took in Casey's new outfit when she saw her in her cubicle from behind. After the dull colors and drab styles her friend had worn since attending her mysterious church, this outfit was a breath of warm spring air. Bright fabric spilled off the sides of the chair. Jessie wondered if more than her wardrobe had changed.

"Casey, stand up and let me see that dress!" Jessie saw Casey freeze, as did everyone else in the corridor. The woman turned to face her, and she saw with shock that it wasn't Casey at all. The hair was similar, but the face was not the one she looked forward to seeing. Her eye caught the nameplate at the side of the cubicle: *Mary Scott.*

"Oh, I'm sorry," she said. "I guess people have moved around while I was gone. Are you new here, Mary?"

Mary looked around at the other people who had paused when Jessie's cry first rang out. "I started two weeks ago. I took Casey's place."

Jessie went cold. She looked around, half sure she would find Casey in the crowd, giggling at the joke she had played.

"Jessie, will you come to my office for a moment?" A deep voice rumbled behind her.

She turned and looked into the blue eyes of her boss, Bob Murphy. His crisp salt-and-pepper hair fell over his forehead, which was wrinkled in concern. They entered his office, and he shut the door behind her and forwarded his phone calls to voicemail so they wouldn't be disturbed.

"Sit down."

"I thought this was a trick Casey was playing. What's going on?" Jessie sat at the edge of a chair.

"I knew you'd be upset. Didn't you get my voice message to come see me right away this morning?"

"No, I decided to go through the mail first, then voice messages."

"I had hoped to spare you that little scene. I know you were close to Casey, and that this would upset you."

"What's happened?" Jessie jumped from her chair and gripped the front of his desk.

He waved his hands. "Nothing. I'm sorry; I know the way I said that made it sound dire. Casey's left the company. I've replaced her with Mary." He looked at Jessie with pity. "She didn't tell you, did she?"

Jessie sank back into the chair. "Mary said she started her job two weeks ago—the day I left for vacation. Didn't Casey give you any notice? How did you find someone this fast?"

"She gave me two full weeks. I spent it finding Mary. When Casey gave me her notice she asked me to keep it to myself. Now, can you tell me what's going on?"

Jessie sagged in her chair, stunned. "Didn't her request sound odd? Why didn't you come to me?"

"When an employee asks me to keep something confidential, I do. You know that." Bob's integrity was legendary.

Jessie apologized. "I didn't mean to jump all over you. Did she give you a phone number and address to reach her?"

"She said she would if she left any unfinished projects, but she finished every single thing she had on her desk—even manuscripts that aren't due for months. She didn't leave a number. Don't you have one?" He shifted in his chair as worry lined his forehead.

Jessie studied her clenched hands. The misery in her voice filled the small office. "Casey hasn't been sharing confidences with me lately."

"Did you two have a disagreement? You used to be like two peas in a pod."

Jessie mulled over her answer, then reached a decision.

"Do you go to church, Bob?" His eyebrows shot up at the unexpected question.

"I used to." His voice was quiet. "When Ellen was alive, and when our kids were young, we went all the time." He looked sheepish. "I haven't been lately though. Why?"

"Casey and I are both Christians." She saw him nod. "We aren't Sunday Christians; we're seven-days-a-week Christians who have a vital and living relationship with God." Again he nodded, and a wistful look crossed his face. Jessie saw the longing and recognized it for what it was. She tucked the thought away for another time. Right now she had to focus on her friend. "Nine months ago, Casey started attending this church in Crescent Hills. Once she became involved there, she started to change."

"How do you mean?"

"At first there were little things. She was tired all the time, because she would drive to Crescent Hills every evening. She began to dress plainly and stopped wearing makeup. Then the changes became more significant. Her opinions and theology changed. She said things that weren't biblical."

Jessie saw she had begun to lose him. She leaned forward. "Then she sold the house—the house for which she'd saved every dime she earned for three years to make a down payment. She put everything she had into that house to make it her special place."

Bob's eyes narrowed. Jessie knew he was remembering when Casey bought the house. Her face had glowed for months.

"She sold it so she could move into a house in Crescent Hills with a bunch of other women who are all involved in this church."

Bob frowned. "You mean like a commune?"

"Sort of. I think this group now controls her. I listened to how she described these 'Gatherings,' as they call them, and I'll tell you, the hair on the back of my neck still hasn't gone down. Now you tell me she left here in total secrecy and didn't tell the one person who would have tried to talk her out of it." Jessie gripped the edge of his desk again. "The more I think about it, the more worried I become."

"Well, when you spell it out like that, I'm worried too, but what can we do?" He held up his hand as she opened her mouth to speak. "She's an adult and can make her own choices. We have no claim on her, no ability to change her direction. What can we do but watch and wait?"

Jessie sank back, defeated, and her eyes blurred. Bob shifted in his chair.

"I know you're upset, but we need to be realistic and practical here."

"You're right, and you're wrong," Jessie argued. "Legally there's nothing I can do, but spiritually I think there's a great deal I can and must do. It all comes down to one word—*pray*."

She rose and looked at Bob. Her tears had dried, and her heart blazed with determination. "I plan to do all I can to bring her back to reality, and I'll bypass the legal system on my knees to do it." She held his gaze. "And I think you'll be doing the same."

She left in a swirl of turquoise and gold and closed the door behind her with a determined snap.

Casey pounced on the typographical error in the manuscript and marked the correction in a firm hand. Her foot moved back to the floor pedal to rewind the tape a few seconds.

Webster's voice filled the tight earphones. As his fiery oratory soared through her mind, her eyes tracked across the page.

Casey felt alive as never before, humming under her breath as she worked. She felt honored to be the person who handled this delicate task. It was important to eliminate every grammatical and typographical error. People noticed things like that, and it influenced their acceptance of the material.

The transition from volunteer to full-time assistant had been easy. She first showed up on a Saturday to volunteer her time. Webster had asked her what she would like to do, and she had told him her background. His eyes had lit up, and she was gratified. Webster had given her a few short chapters to edit and proofread, along with several tapes containing messages from recent Gatherings. She quickly acquired the knack of editing while listening and finished in record time. He looked so relieved; she knew the plan that she and Grace had worked out would be successful. She could help prolong his life by doing what she did best.

After the first weekend she stopped in a few evenings for a week, then every evening the next week. She had given two weeks' notice at work, and had shown up at the Bodylife office at 8:00 a.m. the next Monday and had worked full time ever since. No one asked what had happened to her job. At first she feared they would, but everyone took it in stride that another Sister had given her whole life to the Body.

The book she now edited was the second since she started working for Webster. It was easy to fill volume after volume if he stayed on one theme for several Gatherings. She doubted that anyone but Webster was as bathed in the Gathering messages as she was. She heard them when he uttered them the first time; she input the original transcription from the tape into the computer; she listened again to the tape as she edited the final copy; she took home a copy of each book when it was done and browsed through it for the sheer joy of editing work such as this. It filled every pore of her soul, and she reveled in it.

She also felt closer to the other members in the Body now that she wasn't torn between two worlds. She could give herself to every conversation, since almost every one revolved around the Body. When the Gathering Place needed to be cleaned, she could stay and help instead of being at work an hour away.

She could be there when the office phone rang, and she was always free to respond to a Sister in need. She was there when a Brother looked for another Brother he had heard was at the Gathering Place. She was available when a lost soul responded to a newspaper ad and wanted information about the Gatherings. She was at the hub. She was connected. She felt more involved than she had ever felt in her life.

She also felt alone in a new way. Despite so many barriers having dropped between her and the others in the Body, she still felt they were more connected to each other than to her. Maybe it took time and familiarity. She was sure she'd feel different in a year.

She heard the bell that indicated someone had entered. She set aside the headphones, rose, and stepped into the hall. Darren looked up from a paper in his hand and smiled.

"Morning, Sister Casey." His eyes twinkled. "I hope I'm not interrupting your work."

"Oh, no." She felt shy. "I just finished a project, and I need a break. What can I do for you?"

Darren looked at her, and Casey felt the telltale red flush as it crept up her neck, and she hated herself for it. She thought in exasperation that she might as well pull out a white handkerchief and wave it at him in surrender. The embarrassed flush quickly turned into an angry one.

"I was at the Gathering Place trimming the bushes and remembered I need to make a copy," Darren said. "Before I drove all the way down to the copy center, I thought I'd try the office." He must have sensed her irritation. He took a step backward. "I'm sorry to bother you."

"Of course you can make a copy here." Casey fought to control her roller-coaster emotions. "Make ten if you like. Let me show you." She turned and gestured to the copier in the corner of the room she called Machine Heaven. Every possible laborsaving business machine was crammed into the central room. The copier was her favorite. She raised the lid, placed Darren's document face down, and showed him where to align it on the glass.

"You sure you only want one copy? Not ten, not collated, not stacks of pages all stapled in one corner? You can choose whether the staple is straight up and down or at an angle." She grinned at him.

"Yikes, I didn't expect to launch the space shuttle. I just want a copy. No staples, no folding, spindling, or mutilating." He grinned back at her and watched as she made the appropriate selection. A clean copy spat from the side of the machine, and she retrieved his original.

"Come in anytime. We've got enough equipment here to turn your one-page document into a multivolume manuscript." She stole a look at him as he held the two pages.

"I appreciate the service." His eyes held hers a second longer than she anticipated.

She felt the red begin at her collarbone again. To cover it, she turned and snagged a large envelope from the worktable. "If you

plan to keep that copy nice and flat, you'd better put it in here."
She heard the higher note in her voice and tried to control it.

He slid the pages into the envelope and saluted her with a
touch to his brow. "Again, thanks for the service." He turned and
threaded his path among the humming machines. With a glance
back, he opened the door and left. Casey expelled a long breath.
She heard some Sisters greet Darren in the driveway and returned
to her office. By the time they entered and passed her desk, she was
deep into editing a new manuscript.

15

Lydia gave Casey a discreet signal. Casey saw it and responded with a tiny nod. She silently counted to five, then turned to Darren and excused herself. Lydia had exited by a different door. To anyone watching, it would have looked coincidental, but Casey had learned there was little coincidence in the Body.

"Over here!" Lydia's hiss drew Casey's eyes to the door from the kitchen out to the patio. She stepped out.

"For heaven's sake, you can't even tell me in the kitchen?"

Lydia drew her farther from the door until the two stood in the darkness beyond the light that spilled from the windows.

"I was afraid Carol would kill you in another minute or two."

"What are you talking about?" Several men had come from the Brothers House for Visiting Night. All visiting was done in groups, and Casey found it quaint and exasperating by turns. She had the opportunity to talk to Darren but not in any depth with six or eight other people nearby.

"You're spending too much time with Darren and not enough with the other Brothers."

Casey frowned. "And?" She let the question hang in the soft spring evening air.

"Carol is ready to have a fit."

"What does Carol have to do with me?" Casey heard the piano swell again and relaxed. She didn't want Darren to leave before she could say good night.

"It's not what Carol has to do with you." Lydia looked full into Casey's eyes. "It's what she has to do with Darren."

"Are you going to get to the point?" Casey asked, hands on her hips in exasperation.

"Darren and Carol will be married by the end of the year."

"Since when? Carol has never said a word." Her disbelief rattled in her voice. "Neither has Darren."

"When a couple has been approved by the Brothers, there's nothing more to say. The Brothers felt the end of the year would be the best time for them to marry. Everyone in the Body knows."

"So they're engaged, but they never talk about each other." Casey's voice rose and her words were clipped. "Come to think of it, I've never even seen them talk *to* each other. What kind of engagement is that?" She crossed her arms and looked at Lydia.

"You know the Bodylife is different than what we've all come from," Lydia said. "Carol and Darren will be married—and you mustn't spend time with him."

"It sounds medieval!" Lydia shushed her and looked over her shoulder. Casey lowered her voice. "How am I to know who I can talk to and who I can't if people don't admit they're engaged or wear engagement rings or even have pictures on their dressers? What kind of a minefield is this anyway? Why invite engaged people to Visiting Night at all?"

Lydia's gentle reply didn't stop Casey's agitation. "Until they're married, Visiting Night is almost the only contact Carol and Darren will have, for their own good, to build up their spirits, and for the health of the Body as a whole. I wanted to let you know before you became attached to Darren."

Casey knew it was too late for that. She took a deep breath to steady herself.

"I see. Well, thank you for telling me, Sister Lydia. I appreciate your advice." It was her pain that brought her claws out to rake across her friend's heart. She looked back toward the lights, her eyes hollow. "I think I feel a headache coming on. It will probably leave if I go straight to bed. Could you make my excuses for me?"

"Of course," Lydia said. "Why don't you go around to the side door? It's unlocked. Lock it when you shut it, and I won't have to when I make the rounds later tonight."

Casey nodded and escaped deeper into the darkness, following the line of the house until she reached the door. After she slipped through, she turned the bolt noiselessly. Farther down the hall, the light and music from the living room spilled out, and Carol's beautiful voice soared. Casey was sure she heard Darren harmonizing.

She hadn't seen the signs because they were subtle in the Body. Now that it had been spelled out to her, her face burned in shame. Darren no doubt thought she was throwing herself at him. How awkward he must have felt when she didn't get it. She would watch her step in the future.

When she heard Lydia also join in the singing, she assumed that no one had noticed she had not returned. She moved to her room, shut the door behind her, and picked up Andrew. His sleepy "meow" comforted her as she began to cry. Andrew dragged a raspy tongue across the back of her hand.

It would be a long night.

Another Gathering. The power and volume of singing erupting from hundreds of throats assaulted Casey. Wave after wave of notes and words washed against her fragile composure and made her want to run away for the first time since she came to the Body. To her left Amy sang with a fierce alto that seemed to rattle the bones in Casey's chest. On her right Lydia's sweet soprano made Casey's head ache.

Her mind wandered through the past two months and evaluated experiences as quick snapshots of them jostled in her mind. The move from her Jewel. The struggle to compress her life into a single room. Quitting her job and leaving Jessie without a word. Quick, sympathetic rasping caresses from Andrew's tongue during her frequent crying sessions. The work at the Bodylife office and the growing pile of publications in her room at home. Lydia's incomprehensible words about Darren and Carol's future as the two women stood in secrecy on the moonlit patio. The sinking sense she felt when she caught sight of Darren. The perceptible chilling of her heart that was crippling her ability to be the Bodylifer she was desperate to be.

Casey tried to focus on the Gathering and realized someone had risen and stepped into the center of the group. She was surprised to see it was not Webster, but Dominic. The beauty of his face caused women's eyes all around the room to soften. Many a hand unconsciously tugged a wandering lock into place or straightened a neckline.

"Amen!" Dominic said, with force and a touch of defiance.

"Amen," people echoed, though not with the usual vigor they accorded to Webster.

"When Brother Webster called me and asked me to let the Spirit lead me to your hearts during this Gathering, I admit I was taken aback." A blush softened Dominic's chiseled features. "I asked him why he couldn't speak today, and he said, 'The Spirit has his hand over my mouth.'"

Casey imagined a huge hand over Webster's mouth and wondered when it would be removed. However, she joined everyone else as they opened notebooks and clicked pens to the ready. She prayed that the message would dispel the dark clouds that troubled her spirit.

"It's a heavy burden to carry a message you've dreaded for months to hear from Webster, relieved each Gathering when you didn't."

The crowd stilled. Casey knew she wasn't alone in wondering what message she would dread to hear preached. She guessed they all wondered if light would be shed on a secret sin, weakness, or failing.

"What I want to talk to you about today is four-letter words." After a pause and a brief smile, he added, "No, I'm not talking about the kinds of four-letter words we're all bombarded by, slapped with, insulted by, and can't escape from in our culture today."

Casey was pleasantly surprised by Dominic's presentation. He knew the secret of the pause, and wasn't afraid of dead air. When he resumed speaking, however, she transcended her objective study of him and opened her heart to his message.

"I want to talk to you about only one word today. It's a lonesome, ungodly word." Dominic looked over the group, focusing on several different members briefly. "The word is *self.* It's the word the Devil loves best, and it wounds God the worst. It's a word I've hidden behind for years and that persists in trying to wrap itself around me like a flag around a flagpole. I'm sick of it, and I'm certain you're all sick of its stench on me." Dominic wiped his temple with his thumb.

"The word *self* is quite gregarious; it tends to attract lots of company. It bonds with all kinds of words or word fragments that worm their way into our hearts and cripple us. Let me give you some examples." From between the pages of his Bible he pulled out a paper slip. He took a deep breath and read in a slow, measured voice, pausing after each word.

"Self-assertion. Self-appointed. Self-complacent. Self-conscious. Self-control. Self-deception. Self-defense." The handsome face twisted in pain as the litany continued. As if flashlights shone on the secret corners of their souls, his audience seemed to cringe with each battering word.

"Self-esteem. Self-help." He gave a small snort of disbelief. "Self-indulgence." He paused. "Self-preservation." His voice softened and broke. "Self-reliance." He looked over the group and singled out a very young, very competent Sister. Her eyes filled, and she sobbed.

"Self-respect." He dropped his voice to a whisper, and Casey leaned forward to catch his words. "Self-seeking. Self-styled. And, worst of all, self-sufficient." A tear shone on his smoothly planed cheek. Quiet sniffles could be heard throughout the crowd.

His cadence had been perfect for Casey to make note of all the words, and they sank into her heart and rose up again as malodorous, ugly things. She bit her lip and wished she could take back the prayer for a message that would touch her heart. She had wanted something reassuring, not this unrelenting assault.

"Every word I have listed—and there are many more, as we all know—is a powerful denial of who God is in our lives and what the Bodylife means to each of us. I've dreaded hearing Brother Webster read a list like I just read, because I know this list has my face, my heart, my soul all over it.

"I'm not alone, Brothers and Sisters, am I?" This time the amen lacked nothing of the response Webster would have received.

"Coming to the Bodylife is like moving to a foreign country. The hardest thing to pick up in this new country, for me anyway, has been the language. Not the words. Those have come easily to me. Words like *Gathering, Brother, Sister, Body*. But I have clung to my old language, preferring to use the new when I'm with you, but in my head I speak the old one. I let my language build a barrier around me, and I keep you, my beloved Brothers and Sisters, at a distance." Casey felt the fire and magnetism of his glance.

"I'm here today to learn a new vocabulary, and I want to help you learn it too, if you don't know it already. I don't intend to continue the duplicity of my soul any longer, and I hope you don't want to either. We need to absorb these new vocabulary words, learn them by heart, and by spirit too." The men and women before him leaned forward in anticipation.

"Here we go," he said. "Body-assertion." He paused. "Body-appointed." As he continued his slow, measured delivery, Casey saw something so powerful it moved her to tears. After the second phrase, someone whispered, "Amen." When he said "Body-control," a Brother rose to his feet and stood, head bowed, his eyes wet. "Amen," his lips formed. As the list went on, more people stood as a term touched upon the dark places of their souls.

"Body-esteem," Dominic intoned. Eight people rose. The amens grew.

"Body-help," he said. Amy grasped the back of the chair in front of her and stood. Casey remembered the self-help books Amy collected like small boys collect marbles.

"Body-indulgence." A rustling rose all around Casey.

"Body-preservation." Casey felt a sob clutch in her throat as Darren rose, to be greeted by a Brother's arm around his big shoulders.

"Body-reliance." From nowhere Casey could remember seeing, Webster stood, out of character in a polo shirt and dark slacks. She did not know when he had arrived. His silent confession brought forth sobs all around the room.

"Body-respect. Body-seeking." Dominic whispered, his voice choked with emotion. "Body-styled. Body-sufficient." Casey stood, her heart smitten by her determination to rely only on her own abilities, not call on the Body when she was in need. By the time Dominic finished his list, not a single person was still seated. The final amen reverberated, fanned the flame in Casey's soul, and found its expression in her tearful acknowledgment.

16

C asey sat with her hands in her lap and let the excited voices around the table wash over her. The Sisters had invited the usual quota of guests home from a Sunday Gathering, and all had settled into their chairs to enjoy the delicious meal. Conversation centered, as always, on the message Webster had delivered. For weeks he had built on Dominic's pivotal and passionate message. Those who hadn't attended that Gathering said they felt cheated. Casey wished she could recapture the joyful abandon she had felt that day. Steam from the ubiquitous lasagna tempted her, but she ignored it as she wrestled once again with a vague sense of dissatisfaction.

As the meal commenced, and before the conversation moved to deeper matters, one of the new women mentioned a cooking class she had been attending. "I'm in a class that's working its way around the world through different cuisines. I think my favorite so far has been Chinese cooking," Iris said. "It's so versatile and good for feeding a crowd. Plus it's very healthy."

Casey sat up straighter in her chair. "I used to cook with a wok," she said. It seemed like a lifetime ago. "I got a book on Chinese cooking, and I'd take it with me to the grocery store so I could get the right ingredients." Casey laughed at the picture she must have presented. "They got to know me pretty well in the produce department."

"Do you mean we've got a Chinese cook under our roof, and we didn't even know it?" The sparkle in Lydia's eyes belied her mock anger. Casey joined in the fun at her own expense.

"When you all sleep at night I come out to the kitchen and practice my knife work."

Amy giggled. "So that's what I heard the other night. You're lucky I didn't call 911 when you yelled out, 'Hi-yah!'"

Carol rolled her eyes. "That's Japanese, not Chinese."

They all grinned and attended their plates. Iris smiled at Casey, who thought she might have made a friend. She toyed with the idea of joining the class Iris attended. The thought made her happier than she could have imagined.

"I don't think you believe me." Casey looked up and down the table. "I'll have to prove it to you. You pick the date, and I'll prepare a Chinese feast for you, Sisters. Then you won't kid me."

"I believe you're on cooking detail next Thursday," said Carol, who wasn't fond of cooking and kept a close watch on whose duty it was on any particular day. "So we'll anticipate gastronomic ecstasy," she said.

The laughter dissolved into a general discussion of the way the Sisters House operated—who did what chores, how they handled disputes, and many of the other things newcomers liked to hear about.

Casey contributed a few insights, absorbed as she was in planning her special dinner. She felt a warm glow as she pictured her triumph in the kitchen and the positive impact it could have on the whole Body. Maybe she could teach her Sisters how to cook something other than lasagna. For the first time in a while, she had something special to contribute. It felt great.

"Is that all that's going on at your house, Sister Lydia?" Grace asked, her voice sharp and probing.

Lydia dreaded these interrogations. As a Sister she was under Grace's authority, and so she tried to suppress her irritation and the small knot in her midriff that felt like fear. These verbal games with Grace always drained her. This morning, with the beginning of a fever and chills, her stamina was lower than usual.

"I can't think of another thing, can you, Grace?" Part of her was elated by the smell of freedom her boldness brought.

Grace's lips were a wintry slash across her face. "I understand there's to be a special dinner party tonight. I thought you'd like to tell me about it. Sister to Sister."

"I try not to waste your time with unimportant things, Sister Grace," Lydia said. Her heart thumped; her mind whirled. This was going to be bad for Casey, and she was going to be made to cause the pain, she was sure.

"I happen to think this is very significant. The fact you don't says a good deal about your progress in the Bodylife."

That remark stung. After the years she had sought nothing more than to mold herself to the will of the Body, to make her every effort, gesture, and thought revolve around what she was taught, this was what Grace thought of her. She swallowed a retort and lowered her eyes. It didn't matter that the woman was wrong. God had placed Grace in authority over her. The problem was Lydia, not Grace.

"Forgive me, Sister Grace. I'm not as old in the faith as you, nor as wise. Please tell me what you need to know, and direct my path in this matter. I'm confused about it."

"I happened to hear from another Sister in passing that Casey is going to make a spectacle of herself this evening. I am amazed you encouraged her in it."

"Spectacle?" Lydia's head shot up. "She's making us dinner, that's all. She has been despondent, and I thought it would be good for her to have a project to serve the Body."

"There's that phrase again—'I thought.'" Grace turned toward Lydia, and her voice took on an artificial mellowness. "It isn't the dinner, it's the motive. That always gives them away."

"Casey wants to give us a treat. She wants to introduce us to a different kind of cooking. I think that's a fine motive." Lydia clenched her hand inside her smock pocket. Her house key bit into the soft flesh of her finger. The pain steadied her.

"Motives are like artichoke leaves. There are lots of them on each artichoke. You pull them off one by one, and get past the showy ones on the outside to the softer ones in the middle. Then at last you reach the heart of the matter, and it's covered with spines that have to be scraped away before you can get a good look at it." Grace's eyes moved to Lydia's pocket, and Lydia forced her hand to relax.

"Beneath Casey's obvious motive is a hidden motive that reeks of self." Grace mimicked a young girl's voice, nothing at all like Casey's. "I want to make a special dinner. I want to impress you. I want you to pet me and make much of me. I want to be known as different from the rest of you." She sighed. "Don't you see, Lydia? She's crying out to be different, not seeking to blend into the Body. It's her nature, and we have to curb it. This dinner is a good place to start."

Alarmed, Lydia stared at Grace. "You don't mean you want me to tell her not to do it, do you?" she whispered. "She's worked so hard on the menu, done all her shopping. She's looking forward to it." A tiny note of defiance crept into her voice. "And so am I."

"Oh, I considered that, but there's another way. I'm certain her meal will be excellent. Therefore, you must all exercise discipline when it's served. Remember, this is for Casey's good—for her future in the Bodylife."

"I don't understand." Lydia's voice was flat.

"I've already explained it to the other Sisters. Now I'll explain it to you," Grace said. And she did.

Casey stood at the cutting board, relaxed in the kitchen of the Sisters House for the first time since she joined the household months earlier. In part this was because she was cooking something she loved and was doing it as a treat for others. It was also, more than she dared admit to herself, the fact that she was alone.

A dozen bowls of various sizes were lined up on the counter. She knew from experience that wok cooking was fast, with no time to stop and chop while stir-frying. She peeked into the oven to check the egg rolls she had made before beginning her final preparations for the stir-fry. They were warm and crisp to the touch.

She lifted the top off the simmering pot of soup. She would stir in the eggs immediately before she served it, for perfect egg-drop soup. The golden broth and the swirling vegetables and exotic mushrooms made her inhale deeply before she put the lid back on the pot. She turned to the assembled bowls and her ingredients. A quick glance at the clock made her jump. She hefted the bowl of chicken that had marinated all afternoon and dumped it quickly into the hot oil.

From beyond the closed kitchen door she heard the clatter of cutlery and plates being put on the table. There were definitely some advantages to living with other women. With a light and eager heart she hurried to finish her preparations.

The glorious food stuck in Casey's throat as she chewed and swallowed. Her misery and total bafflement made her want to stand up and demand to know what was wrong. Instead she held her silence and tried to keep from gagging on a savory bit of egg roll. The five housemates sat in their accustomed places, but there was no conversation this night. Instead, over their heads floated Dominic's recorded voice as he intoned the damning list of words that had so castigated the entire congregation.

When Casey had entered the dining room in triumph, the bowls of fragrant food displayed on a large serving tray, she anticipated the excited voices of her Sisters. Instead serious faces greeted her, as did the sound of the tape of Dominic's sermon. It had continued to grind onward to its inevitable conclusion all through the meal. Not one comment of praise or thanks was sent down the table to Casey, where she sat rigid with surprise and hurt. Her one attempt to ask if everything was to their liking was hushed by Carol.

"Yes, everything's fine. Oh, do you remember this part? This is where I fell apart, and so did almost everyone else at the Gathering." She pointed her fork at the tape recorder playing on the counter. They all attended to the words; no other conversation was attempted.

Since she had come to the Bodylife, Casey had seen many incidents she didn't understand. She knew she was supposed to get some message from this shaming, but what? It hurt more than she could say. If they'd had a message to deliver, why didn't they come out in the kitchen and tell her, so they could all enjoy the meal together as usual. Why the subtle humiliation? Why hurt her when she was vulnerable and least expected it?

Casey tried several times to catch Lydia's eye. She had their emergency signal ready to use the instant she got her attention. She and Lydia had used it rarely, most notably the night Lydia had told her about Darren and Carol. That she could not get Lydia to look at her drew together the two humiliating incidents like the sides of a drawstring to form a constricting ring around her heart.

When the tape ended, not one scrap of the wonderful meal was left on the table. At least there would be no leftovers to remind her of this tragic night. She knew she could not have faced the food again, even if she had to skip meals to avoid it. As the women around her echoed the final amens of the taped congregation, Casey felt panic rise. She could not face them in the kitchen with her as they cleaned up, not speaking of the meal, shaming her further. In all honesty she wanted to take the debris outside and bury it in the backyard. Instead she took the offensive.

"When I was little, we had a rule in my house." She forced a smile as she fought back tears. "If someone made as big a mess in the kitchen as I did tonight, they also had to clean it up. Please, leave your plates and dishes. I'll take care of it."

"Thank you, Casey." Carol folded her napkin, put it on the table next to her clean plate, and rose. "That would be very nice." The other women stood with her and scattered to their respective rooms. The dreadful meal was over at last.

As she worked in the kitchen for the next hour, Casey felt her anger mount. She cleaned until the kitchen sparkled. When she returned to her room, her fingers were wrinkled from the dishwater, her face a mask of misery. She collapsed on the bed. Andrew curled against her, cradled in the arc of her body as she lay on her side and pulled her knees toward her chest. She stroked his fur for comfort, and the cat purred and rubbed his face several times over the waterlogged skin on the back of her hands.

When Casey's hands stopped stroking, Andrew ceased to caress them, and neither moved until morning.

17

Casey awoke from her deep, depressed sleep, yawned, and stretched, feeling just as devastated as she had the night before. The fiasco of the previous evening engulfed her in a fresh wave of misery. Though sleep had blunted the memory, she felt cold anger rise anew. Determined to pursue the issue, she vaulted off the bed and headed for the door.

In the hallway Rita almost dropped the tray she carried when Casey's door flew open. Casey, equally surprised, came to a sudden stop.

"My goodness, you startled me!" Rita clutched the tray. "Where are you off to in such a hurry?" She tried to lighten her tone with a smile.

"I have to talk to Lydia." Casey's eyes moved in the direction her feet were already moving.

"Well, you'll have to wait, I'm afraid." Rita's voice held a note of warning. She lifted the tray to capture Casey's attention. "Lydia's sick. Brother Eric has been here already this morning and left to get some things for her. He says it's the flu."

Casey stood frozen in the hallway, unsure what to do with her momentum. The news that the physician had visited Lydia surprised her.

"He said she should have fluids and to try to get this oatmeal down. I hope it stays down longer than the last batch we tried."

"When did this happen? She seemed fine last—I mean, I didn't hear her get up in the night or anything." Casey had pushed aside the look of Lydia's stricken face from the disastrous dinner party and assumed her pain had been empathy. Perhaps there had been more to it, if she had been in any kind of condition to notice.

"She was running a fever yesterday, and when she went to bed it got worse. Her temperature is a hundred and three, and Eric said she's not to be disturbed." This last phrase was delivered with finality and authority.

Casey turned back to Rita and put out her hands toward the tray. "Let me take it in, then. I'll see that she eats it." Her eyes clouded, and she whispered. "I've got to talk to her."

"I'm afraid that's out too." Rita's voice was less officious, but still firm. "I've already had the flu this season, remember? Eric said no one should go in or out who hasn't had it. She's quarantined for the moment. It's amazing how something like this can spread like crabgrass throughout the Body if we're not careful." With a last look at Casey, Rita eased past her and balanced the tray in one hand so she could turn the knob with the other. The door shut with a soft click behind her.

Her mission thwarted, Casey was not sure what to do next. She heard Carol and Amy in the kitchen but did not feel up to facing them. It was Lydia she wanted to talk to, and Lydia was off-limits. She decided she had better pull herself together for the day. She hoped Lydia would be well enough by evening to need company.

She was halfway to the Bodylife office when she felt the first heavy drops of rain on the back of her neck and the top of her head. She had been so deep in thought when she left the Sisters House she hadn't even looked at the sky. She stopped and looked up now. Heavy gray clouds hung down with impending menace. As she studied them, she felt the sloppy sting of big drops on the backs of her hands, her cheeks, and more in her hair. Her glasses quickly became streaked.

She turned to look back the way she had come and estimated the distance. It was the worst possible spot on her journey for this to happen. If she turned back for her car, she would get wet on the way home and be late as well. She decided she wouldn't be much more miserable if she went on than if she retraced her steps. She plodded forward again and tried to ignore the rain as she ruminated about why the Sisters decided to turn her special treat into an indecipherable lesson the previous night. If they'd had something to correct her about, why hadn't they come right out and said it? They certainly hadn't been reluctant to do so in the past. There were times when she felt more alone in a house full of women than she had when she lived alone. On this soggy morning she couldn't determine whether she was becoming a more integral part of the Body or playing a game.

If it was a game, the price was high. She had given up her home, her job, her friends—everything familiar except Andrew and a few possessions—to come here. It had felt right to do so at the time. Was it still right? Not for the first time she wished her parents were still alive to provide a safety net in her life. The accident that killed them both when she was twenty had done much to form her independent mind-set, but she'd trade it in a heartbeat to have them back.

A cracking finger of lightning flashed across the sky. She stopped and felt hot tears slide down her face and realized they were the only part of her that was warm.

Once she halted in the wild, wet weather, she could not make herself move forward or backward. She had almost decided to sit down on the curb and have a good cry when a pair of headlights gleamed, and she shielded her eyes. The vehicle slowed, turned into the driveway she was about to cross, and stopped. The passenger door was pushed open, and a voice called out to her.

"Casey, get in, quick!" Her glasses were so blurred with rain that she could barely see, but she dove for the shelter of the pickup's cab without hesitation and slammed the door shut behind her. "What on earth are you doing out here on a day like this?"

As she adjusted to the muffled sound the rain made on the roof of the truck, she was slow to recognize the voice. When she did, she was glad her glasses had fogged in the warmth of the cab.

"Good morning, Darren." She tried for levity. "Lovely weather we're having today." She reached in her pocket for a tissue to wipe her glasses and found only sodden wads of moist lint.

"Didn't you listen to the news? This is a major storm, and you're out walking around in it and making jokes." He sounded like a parent scolding a child who'd run into traffic. "Where's your car?"

"I walk to work to save money." She shivered and tried to fight the tremors. The more she clenched her muscles, the more she trembled.

He turned the heat up all the way and reached behind the seat for a towel. "Here. Wipe your glasses and your face, and try to blot up as much water from your hair as you can. You're losing a lot of heat through your head." He nestled the towel in her trembling hands.

As Casey removed her glasses, Darren backed the truck into the street, then put it in gear again and stepped on the gas. After driving less than a minute, he turned right, coasted down a small hill, and rolled to a stop in the lot of a neighborhood park. He left the engine running to keep the heat on.

Casey watched from the corners of her eyes as shining silver globes of rain slid down her hair and hung suspended from the ends. She knew she looked dreadful, but she didn't care. She finished wiping the lenses on the towel, rubbed it over her face, then began on her hair, her eyes closed in weariness. Minutes passed in silence as she blotted and rubbed and ran her hands through her hair to straighten out the wild spikes the towel had raised. Then, with an enormous sigh, she let her hands and the towel collapse in her lap.

"I'm your friend." Darren's voice was gentle. "At least I'd like to be. I may not be able to help, but I've got pretty broad shoulders, and they can carry quite a load. Won't you let me try?"

Casey adjusted her mind to the incredible fact that she was out of the rain, becoming drier and warmer by the minute, and sitting in total privacy with him. At last, with a small cough, she glanced at his face before looking away again.

"I feel—" She stopped, unsure whether to continue or retreat.

"What do you feel? Tell me. I won't tell anyone."

"I feel about like those clouds out there. I'm full of stuff that needs to come out, but I know when it does, it's going to burst over everybody around me. I've held it in too long, and there's no way to keep it back anymore. Do you understand?"

"Yes. Well, maybe not. Tell me."

"I could spiritualize it and say my self is at war with my spirit, that I have to adjust to fit into the Bodylife like everyone before me has had to do, and I'll be fine. But I'm not so sure about that. I'm tired of pretending. I'm full of expectations everyone else has for me, but the real me is locked away in a little dark room deep inside and can't be let out for even a second, or I'll be asked to leave the Body." She twisted in her seat so she could face him. Her hands clenched and unclenched on the sodden towel.

"And if they put me out, where would I go? What do I have left?" She heard her voice rising, but there was no volume control this morning. "I've walked away from everything to be part of the Bodylife. I packed everything I could into a storage locker and sold or gave away things I'd had all my life, and now," the panic increased in her chest and her voice strained, "I begin to wonder if I've done the right thing, or whether I've wrecked my whole life." A sob caught in her final words, and she dropped her eyes.

"Well, another myth bites the dust."

"What?" Casey's head shot up.

"I thought you were the perfect Bodylifer, and I envied your ability to do all those things and never look back. Now I find you're human after all." He shrugged. "I must say it's a bit of a relief."

"How could you not know I've been all torn up inside? Everyone in our house knows, and they let me know they can see it, with great regularity."

"Maybe you let your hair down more at home. When I see you, the Bodylife mask is in place."

She rocked back in her seat. It was the last thing she expected from him. He also appeared to be the perfect Bodylifer-in-training, yet he spoke in an irreverent tone about the duplicity she had carried on for the better part of a year.

She felt a small smile move through her cold cheek muscles. "Well, I guess we're even then. I thought the same about you, until about sixty seconds ago."

To her delight Darren threw back his head and laughed. His entire face lit with it, and his posture exuded relief. "I guess one lesson we all learn when we come to the Body is how to 'keep up appearances.'"

Casey's eyebrows drew together. "On the surface that's funny, but inside," she thumped her chest with her fist, "it hurts. It's tearing me apart." The tears that had stopped rose up like twin tsunamis and threatened to inundate her cheeks yet again. Darren reached out his hand, caught hers, and squeezed it. Her heart contracted with it.

"You said it would be spiritualizing the whole thing to say your spirit was fighting your self, but isn't that what's really going on? You're learning to be part of the Body. You're learning to let go of the *me* part of you and retraining everything in yourself—mind, body, will, and spirit—to think in the language of *we*. That's a huge undertaking. That's why we do it together." His voice provoked a pleasant rumbling somewhere deep down inside her. She put aside the nice sensation and focused on his words.

"Together? But we don't do anything together here." He looked surprised. "Sure, we go to Gatherings together, we live together, we eat together, we read things together, we sing together." She stopped and panted for a moment. "But we never *are* together." She raised their clasped hands to eye level so the union was fixed in their eyes. She squeezed his hand. "We're never together, like this, inside." She let her hand fall back to the seat and was surprised when he did not withdraw his.

"I have never felt so alone," she said. "I've never felt less able to talk to people or more compelled to weigh every word as I do here, never feared condemnation for a stray thought as I do here. There is no one here for me to turn to." Her hand slipped from his, and she began her slow kneading of the towel again. The rain,

tossed by gusting winds, tried to break into the truck from different directions in turn. The warm bubble where they sat billowed
with steam from Casey's wet hair and clothes.

"I'll admit I've felt the same things you feel since I moved into
the Brothers House," he said. "I thought it was guys not being
open like women are. I never had brothers, so I don't know what
kind of relationship I expected, but it was overly optimistic." His
seat belt strained across his chest as he sat turned in his seat and he
released the catch, using the time it took to recoil onto its roller to
take a deep breath. "I said it was a relief to hear you say you felt as
you do, and I meant it. Now I don't feel so alone." He looked into
her eyes. "How about you?"

"I feel a little better." Her eyes dropped. She felt her heart beat
faster, as if he were about to ask her for a date. She scolded herself
for her foolishness. He was pledged to someone else.

"Maybe we could help each other. I think we both have the
same goals, but we need to get over the rough parts here at the
beginning. Why not do it together?" He touched her hand, then
withdrew.

"How can you say that?" She was stunned.

"What do you mean? I asked if we could be friends." He looked
confused.

"I don't think it would be appropriate under the circumstances,
do you?" She waited for a retraction. It didn't come.

"Sorry, you lost me." He frowned, bewildered.

"Carol."

"What's Carol got to do with anything?"

"Do I have to go through the embarrassment of spelling it
out?" The challenge in his voice angered her. Her cheeks burned;
the tears that had watered her eyes were gone.

"I don't have any idea what you're talking about. We were having a nice conversation, meeting each other for the first time on a
decent level, and *boom*, you froze up on me. What's going on?"

The tension in his body looked like guilt to her. She considered
getting out of the truck, but realized as she squinted through the

windshield, she had no real idea where they were. The rising moan of the wind and the clatter of huge raindrops held her in her seat.

"Okay, I give up." She turned back to him. "What's one more humiliation in a long line of them in the past few days?" She slapped the crumpled towel down onto the seat between them, scattering droplets. "I'm hurting like I've never hurt before, and you offer to be my friend, knowing it's impossible for someone who's engaged to become the kind of friend you're talking about."

Darren's eyes had darted to her left hand as she spoke, and the pucker of his brow deepened.

"Look, where I come from, when a girl's engaged, she does the men around her a favor by wearing a ring so they know to stay clear. I'm sorry if I overstepped a boundary, but the signs seem to be down." His eyes darkened beneath his brows. "I initially thought you and Kurt were something of an item—at least he seemed to act like it. But since I never saw much coming back from you, I assumed you were unattached."

"I'm not the one who's engaged." Casey said.

Darren's eyes widened in surprise, then his shoulders slumped in apparent relief.

"This is a total misunderstanding. I'm not engaged either." He lifted his hands toward her, palms up, in apology. "Is that why you've been so standoffish? You thought I was engaged?"

She let her eyes roam over his face. He appeared disingenuous. She shook her head in disbelief. "You're going to marry Carol later this year. The Brothers approved it. Lydia told me to back off." She paused, shrugging. "It seems to be common knowledge, except to you."

There was no mistaking the confusion in Darren's expression.

"They told you this? I don't understand. I mean, I like Carol all right for a Sister, but she's not my type. We've never had much contact, other than at Visiting Night." He thought about it. "She's been friendly, even a bit possessive, now that you mention it. Maybe she hopes I'll ... I mean, that we'll ..." He turned back to the steering wheel. "Let's go back to your house. I have some questions to ask."

"No! Oh, please, don't make me go there with you to talk to Carol. She's been gloating over this. I can't sit there and watch her say it's true one more time. Not with you there."

"But it *isn't* true!"

"All the same, that discussion should be between you and Carol. I don't want this whole conversation dragged into it and have to explain when and where it happened. Please, drop me off at work. Ask your questions after that."

"We haven't finished this discussion, but for now I'll take you to work." He looked at her hair and clothes. "You're almost dry. You won't be much later than if you'd walked the whole way."

Casey's thoughts tumbled as he put the truck in gear and drove out of the lot. She wondered what the rest of the day would bring. It would be one that would shake up both the Brothers House *and* the Sisters House, she was certain. She wondered what else it would shake up in the process.

18

Casey spent the next three days in a maelstrom of worry. The uneasiness she felt about her conversation with Darren grew and chilled her as if she'd wrapped herself in a wet tarp. The worst part was the utter loneliness she felt as she grappled with it. She'd never realized how much she depended on Lydia to be a sane, calm sounding board for her confusion until she was denied her company.

In her darkened room Lydia tossed in fevered dreams, waking with a cry from time to time. Each movement in her room reverberated in Casey's adjacent one. When she at last began a weak recovery, Casey heard the change in timbre of the voices in the next room. When Eric and Carol emerged from the room, she was planted on the carpet outside the door, determined to see Lydia.

"She's better, isn't she?" Casey searched their faces and found confirmation there. "It's too soon to tell how long she'll need to stay in bed," Brother Eric cautioned, "but she's out of danger at last."

The exhaustion in his voice touched Casey's heart. It had to be terrible to be responsible for the health of all the people who made up the Body. What if someone didn't recover? What would that do to the faith of the Bodylifers? Or that of their resident physician? Casey saw the shadows on his face.

"You need to take a break, or you'll end up in the same condition." She smiled at him, able at last to see past his obstructive protectiveness to the man inside. "There's warm apple pie and hot coffee in the kitchen. Why don't you and Carol go sit for a moment? I'll stay with Lydia." Eric turned his face toward the enticing waft of cinnamon from the kitchen.

"We have ice cream too," Carol wheedled.

The ice cream decided it for him. As he left, he held a warning finger under Casey's nose. "You can see her, but don't talk her ears off. She's worn out. Let her rest." A soft smile took the sting from his words. "Thanks for sitting with her. I think it will do both of you good."

For the first time in two minutes, Casey's heart beat with a regular rhythm. She waited until they had gone down the hall and disappeared before she turned the knob on Lydia's door and glided inside. It was so dark and stuffy that she left the door open several inches to let in some fresh air and enough light to navigate. She sank into a chair that appeared to have grown roots next to the bed. A small night-light near the head of the bed cast a feeble glow.

Casey studied her friend's face in the dimness. The change a few days had wrought in Lydia's countenance made her heart clench. Despite the lack of illumination, dark circles were obvious beneath her eyes, their half-moon shapes cupping her feathery eyelashes. Her hair, always gleaming and straight, was scrunched up behind her head to let cool areas on the pillow touch her neck. Casey took in the changes, and her heart ached for the difficult time her friend had been through.

A soft exhale caught her attention, and she was startled to see half-opened lids reveal knowing eyes. Lydia licked ravaged lips as she sought to speak. "I must be better or they wouldn't have let you in here."

"Don't be so sure." Casey tried to lighten the mood as she reached for a cup of water with a straw on the bedside table. "Maybe this is my last chance to say good-bye." She offered the straw to Lydia, who took a sip. After she put the glass down, Casey leaned forward, her elbows on her knees, and grinned down at her.

"What a way to go!" Lydia grinned back as best she could. Warmth invaded the room that had nothing to do with the temperature. "Oh, how I've missed you. I feel like there's been a wall between us, and I don't mean this one." She reached out and put the palm of her small hand on the divider between their two rooms. In a curious, gentle movement, she stroked the wall.

"Even in my illness I knew you were on the other side, and I'd touch the wall to be close to your spark and brightness." The white hand brushed back and forth on the wall one final time and then fell to the bedcover. "But even if there'd been a window in this wall, and the window had been wide open, I still would have felt a wall."

"It's my fault. I was stupid, and I've been waiting for days to tell you so." Casey picked up Lydia's hand and pressed it. The hand that gripped hers surprised her with its sudden strength.

"Nonsense. You were hurt. You were upset and had questions to ask me. I would have kicked down the door if I were you."

"I tried, but they tied me up and locked me in the broom closet." Casey gave her a wan smile.

"I'm sorry." Lydia used her grip on Casey's hand to help her rise onto one thin elbow, her eyes bright with the need to communicate. "We haven't been fair to you, and I have a lot to explain." Without warning her cheeks flamed with a sickly color, and she lay back gasping.

Casey half arose from the chair. "Do you want me to call Eric?"

Lydia forestalled her friend with a raised hand until the weakness passed. "I have a lot to explain, and I will in a day or two. I don't have the strength right now." She shook her head, in obvious irritation at her own weakness. "What I need right now is special healing so I can sit and talk to you as I've longed to do since you came to this house." Lydia brushed her fingers across her forehead and removed the light mist of sweat that had formed there. She was about to say more when a flash of movement and the soft tinkle of a bell accompanied Andrew as he rose from the floor at the foot of the bed and surprised them both.

"Andrew," Casey whispered. "What are you doing here?" She reached for the cat to remove him from the bed before he could disturb Lydia.

"No, let him be. I've missed him almost as much as I've missed you." She watched as the rumbling cat stepped over her legs and marched with purpose along her side next to the wall until he reached her face. He purred as if he had discovered catnip and gazed down at her. She smiled up into his enormous eyes. "Hello, old darling."

Andrew gave a soft yowl and put a paw to Lydia's face. Casey watched, poised to lift him away, her eyes darting from the cat to the woman and back again. Andrew brought his whiskered face close to Lydia's and sniffed. He licked several times at the hair above Lydia's forehead and purred louder. After it stood straight up, he sat down beside her and looked over at Casey for approval. Both women laughed.

"Now I *will* get better. That's my special healing touch." Lydia's eyes began to droop.

Casey reached across her and lifted the heavy cat into her arms. She nuzzled his neck and gave him a quick, grateful kiss. The cat struggled, and she put him down and watched him trot out the door again, his tail held high, his mission accomplished. At the same time, she heard sounds far down the hall as Carol and Eric returned from the kitchen.

She turned to Lydia and placed a soft kiss of her own on her friend's forehead. "Good night. We'll talk when you're better. For now, sleep and dream of charming Prince Andrew come to wake Princess Lydia from her long slumber."

When Eric and Carol opened the door, they found Casey sitting in the straight-backed chair, keeping watch over their patient and humming one of the songs they'd learned together in the preceding weeks at a Gathering.

By the next day Lydia could tolerate strong broth and sit up for almost an hour before tiring. Two days later she got out of bed and sat in the bright, cheerful living room swathed in a bathrobe that had become too large for her emaciated body. The Sisters were busy with chores but took the opportunity to pass through the living room every chance they got. Andrew was given special dispensation to roam the house when Lydia requested he join her and warm her lap. He gloried in the duty and amazed Casey when he stayed for hours rumbling and snoozing as Lydia stroked his striped fur.

By the weekend Lydia was able to get dressed in casual clothes that hung on her thin frame and take a turn around the backyard with Casey as she leaned on her arm. They stopped at the patio, and Casey lowered her into the lounge chair. She pulled up a second chair for herself and sat down. Brother Webster had promised important messages, and extra Gatherings always meant guests, and guests meant additional cooking and entertaining at the Sisters House. Because she was helping Lydia, Casey was exempt from the whirlwind of activity, and she was glad. She still felt fragile and unsure where the Bodylife was concerned.

Lydia straightened in her chair and looked into her friend's face. "I hear the clatter of questions rattling around in your head, and I wish you'd spit them out. We might not get a chance like this again."

"They've battered at me for so long it might take me awhile to get them all out," Casey said. "I was frantic when you were ill. I realized how much I've come to depend on you to guide me through the Bodylife. It scared me."

"What frightened you about it?" Lydia watched a bird hop across the grass. "Paul had his Barnabas, didn't he? We all need someone to escort us into the Body, and to help us adjust to it once we're there."

"It's like I can't 'do' the Body without you. I feel so inadequate."

Lydia leaned forward and tapped Casey's knee. "You're quite correct. You can't 'do' the Body without me. You can't 'do' it without all of us." Lydia let the thought hang for a moment, then went on. "Do you expect your thumb to go to the office and perform your job each day without the rest of you? It goes, but it takes the rest of your body along with it. It can't perform alone. That's what a body is all about—interconnectedness and interdependence, as Paul wrote in his first letter to the Corinthians. You're as knit to us as a thumb to a hand, and we're as much a part of you now as your hand is to your arm. The Bodylife is not a game of solitaire, Casey. It's a team sport, plain and simple."

"But even on a team, some plays can be made by a single player. Sometimes I feel it's my time to make a play like that; but when I do, I'm left on the sidelines by everyone else."

"The dinner." Lydia's face clouded.

"Yes." Casey was careful to keep a belligerent tone from her voice, but inside, her heart beat faster. She wanted to get all her hurt out in the open at last. Still, she watched Lydia to see if she tired, prepared to break off the conversation for later discussion. "What was so wrong about trying to give you Sisters a treat? I know the food was good. I ate it. I've learned to make it well. It wasn't the quality of the offering—so what was it?"

"I'm glad you put it in terms of an offering. It makes what I must say easier," Lydia gathered her words. Casey sat unmoving and waited for the explanation that had eluded her.

"You remember when we discussed offerings at the Gathering a month ago? Webster talked about the Spirit's view of offerings." Lydia looked at Casey, who nodded. "In the Spirit's realm it's immaterial whether the offering is a sack of gold or the tiniest coin of a poor widow. What's important is the heart of the giver."

For once Casey felt impatient at one of Lydia's explanations, but she held her tongue.

"Your dinner was superb. I've never tasted better. Your effort could not have been any greater, nor your intentions any better." She measured her words as her eyes measured Casey's face. "But tell me from your heart, wasn't there the smallest spicing of your offering with the sharp herb of pride? Pride in your originality, in the fact that everyone else in the Sisters House prepares Italian dishes, but here you could prepare a full Chinese dinner for us?"

Casey considered the words, searching her mind for their truth or fiction. "I'm glad I'm able to bring talents to the Sisters House.

I don't think that's wrong though. As your analogy suggests, the thumb is *supposed* to do different things than the little finger does. It's made for different tasks. I don't see a problem with that." She fought an urge to cross her arms over her chest.

"Different tasks, but in tandem. If the thumb began to do jobs alone, and the little finger had no way to assist, the little finger would soon atrophy. That's the danger of what you described. The Body needs to function together, or it won't function at all."

"But that's so ..." Casey stopped herself, wary to show her hurt.

"Say it, Casey, it needs to come out."

"That's so *crushing!*" She was surprised by her own rage. "Why bother to learn or try anything but the same old tired things? Most of you have been together for years, even decades. How can you expect—or even want—newcomers to the Body to be identical to you? Don't you feel stagnant? Don't you feel like the whole world has passed you by? Don't you think stifling people is wrong? I feel like I'm suffocating, and I'm letting you all do it to me. That's the sick part!" When the words stopped, she covered her mouth, her eyes large behind her lenses. "I didn't mean all that!" Her hoarse voice croaked with regret.

"You meant every single word. I'm glad you let it out. Maybe now we can make progress." Lydia's gray eyes sparkled as she squeezed her arm.

"No, I was frustrated and hurt. I didn't mean to sound so harsh and condemning." Her eyes pleaded for understanding.

"You meant it. Your perspective is still shifting from one frame of reference to another. You're right that we allow the world to pass us by; that's what we're trying to do. We want it to slip away, to loosen its grip on us, to take its tentacles out of our souls and let us blend into the Body for God's purposes, not ours. How very difficult this must be for you right now."

Exhausted, Casey sat back and watched Lydia, hoping she wouldn't be thrown out. Anything but that.

"Settling into the Body is the stress of moving into a new house, learning a new job, and marrying into a new family all rolled into one." Lydia shifted on the chair. "Everything the world teaches opposes what we try to achieve in the Body. We've given up everything to make the attempt, and so have you. How awful that you feel so alone in the process, but how normal. Everyone who has come to the Body has gone through the same thing."

"Not you. You were born for this life. You move through it like a swan on a still pond."

"Is that what you think?" Lydia laughed. "Oh, my friend, you couldn't be more wrong. I rage against the injustice of putting myself aside. I'm incredibly frustrated when I let others do a so-so job of something I can do superbly. I rattle the bars, I batter my wings against them, I scream inside. Haven't you heard it?"

Casey leaned forward in her chair and put the back of her hand across Lydia's forehead. "You're delusional. You're feverish or something. Maybe you need to go back to bed."

"I'm fine, and I'm speaking the truth. Yes, I rage, but I offer my anger and frustration back to my Lord and ask him to weld me tighter into the Body, because I know that what I'm suffering is withdrawal symptoms from the world and all its charms. What are these when compared to the all-surpassing richness of what I've found in the Body? Nothing! I stomp on them!" She ground her heel into the flagstone. "There's nothing in the world I'll let come between me and my Body." Her eyes blazed with an inner light. The air between them crackled with her vehemence.

"But you're talking in the realm of the Spirit." Casey let an edge creep into her voice. "I live in a physical world. I'm a person, with feelings and desires and fears, and I can be hurt. I don't reside in the realm of the Spirit where everything is clear. You, my Sisters, turned your backs on me, scoffed at my offering, and left it like a piece of moldy bread in the back of the refrigerator."

"That wasn't the way it was meant to be left." Lydia dropped her hands to her lap, exhausted. "If I hadn't become ill, this wouldn't have festered in you all these days." Her eyes pleaded for understanding. "I hope you know I would never hurt you that way."

"I'm sorry for blowing my top." Casey said. "I know you didn't mean to hurt me. The timing was messed up, and I let things get all twisted in my head. You've given me good things to think about. Don't shut me out or think I'm a total idiot. I'm struggling, that's all." Casey let the boiling pot of her heart begin to cool and still.

"I don't mean to discourage you, but you will go on struggling as long as you're in the Body," Lydia said. "That's the value of the Bodylife. Like rough stones in a lapidary drum, we grind the sharp bits off each other and come out, after much time and bumping, as semiprecious stones fit for the Master Jeweler to use to adorn his kingdom. That's what we're after here, nothing less."

When Casey at last reeled in her thoughts and took stock of her companion, she was chagrined to realize what the exchange had cost Lydia. Her pale face and slack expression were eloquent reminders of her still fragile state. She jumped to her feet and bent over her.

"I'm so sorry. I've tired you, and you look terrible."

"Why, thank you, my dear, you look ravishing yourself." Lydia rolled her eyes and crossed them comically.

Casey helped her up, her haste apparent in her less-than-gentle treatment. "Don't joke with me. If you have a relapse, it will be all my fault, and I don't need that guilt trip right now. You're going back to bed and taking a nap the rest of the afternoon." She steered Lydia toward the kitchen door.

"Whatever you say, nurse."

Something significant had happened in their exchange, however. When Lydia's health improved, and she regained her strength, Casey hoped they could explore the new territory together.

19

Webster's office was cozy, with book-lined walls, leather chairs and sofas, and a state-of-the-art computer on the massive desk. He wheeled his executive chair from behind his array of equipment and joined the circle of men. Dominic sat to his right, as always. Several other Brothers filled out the group.

As they prayed, Webster kept an eye on Darren from beneath lowered lids. He had heard that Darren had tried to stop what he obviously assumed to be a false rumor about him and Carol. Webster could almost see the tension in his soul. It drove a wedge between Darren and these men, who emulated all he should ever want to be or have. He knew action was needed to pull him back into line.

Silence fell, other than the ticking of the wall clock. When the sobbing began, he saw Darren jerk. His eyes snapped up and swept the room, and Webster carefully avoided locking eyes with him, uncertain he could control his own expression. The other men all glanced away, looking as if they'd crawl under the plush oriental rug if they could. Wrenching sobs contorted Dominic's handsome face. Great round tears slid down his chiseled cheeks and splashed on his folded hands. No one moved. At last Webster broke the silence. He pivoted his chair and put his hand on Dominic's back.

"Brother, what is it? What breaks your heart in this way? Do you have a message for us?" He turned to the group and included them in his questions, despite their obvious discomfort with the emotional outburst.

"Oh, my. Such a vision. Such a feeling of helplessness." Dominic took several ragged breaths and looked around the circle as tears sheeted his eyes. "I've never felt the sorrow of the Spirit so strongly in all my life." He sobbed again.

"Can you tell us what you saw?" Webster asked at last.

"It was frightening. I saw danger so clearly, yet I was powerless to stop it."

"Who was in danger?" Webster leaned closer, his body tense.

"I saw him walking with his eyes shut, and there was a high cliff. Every step he took, he moved closer to the edge. There was no way for me to stop him." Dominic sucked in a shuddering breath and closed his eyes briefly. "When a strong tree grew up in his path, he went around it. He was determined to throw himself over the cliff—and there was intense sadness all around him as others mourned his loss before he even got to the edge." Fresh tears pooled in Dominic's eyes and slipped down his cheeks.

The men exchanged glances, fidgeting as their uneasiness filled the room. "I saw the trees interlace their branches to try to capture and hold the man, but he would duck and go under their branches or climb over them as he fought to get to the edge of the world. That's what it looked like—the edge of everything. I couldn't see the bottom of the cliff. I was afraid it didn't have a bottom, and the man might fall and fall forever." Dominic shivered.

"Did the man get to the cliff? Did you see his face?" Webster asked.

"In the beginning he was too far away, but there was something familiar in his walk." Dominic's face clouded, and he frowned. "It didn't seem important who he was at first, only that he had to be stopped. Then I saw that he didn't just climb over the branches or wiggle under them. He uprooted trees altogether and dragged them behind him. I knew he would throw himself over the edge and drag them over with him."

Dominic's penetrating eyes completed a circuit of the room, then returned to Darren. "It was you."

"Me?" Darren half rose from his seat on the couch, then settled on the edge. Sweat appeared on his brow, and his fingers dug into the gap between the cushions as though he could hide himself in the small darkness. The shoulders of the other men relaxed visibly as the spotlight turned to Darren, not one of them.

"I think Brother Dominic has been given a word from the Lord for you." Webster studied the man perched on the couch with inward satisfaction. "The Lord often spoke in parables, even to his followers, but he told them he would reveal the meanings of the stories. With his help and guidance, let's see if we can't put this one together." Webster turned to the other men. "It could be Darren himself we are to think of, or he may represent a group like the younger Brothers." He let the statement hang and waited for a response.

"I think if it were a group, there would be a group of men in the vision," said one of the older Brothers, his voice carrying relief as the discussion moved from emotion to logic. "I think this is specific." Webster nodded and turned to Dominic.

"Does that feel right to your spirit, Dom?"

With sorrowful eyes fixed on Darren, Dominic nodded. The fabric beneath Darren's arms darkened with clammy perspiration.

"Maybe the trees were prayers people were praying," Kurt suggested.

Webster cut him off firmly. "I think we need to look at the use of trees in the Bible to know what the Lord meant. I don't think he'd switch symbolism." Kurt looked at the floor, chastened. "How were trees used in the Bible? Do you remember?" Webster gave the smaller man a chance to redeem himself.

Kurt raised his head, his eyes hopeful. He frowned and thought quickly. "Well, in the New Testament, Jesus called himself the vine and us the branches."

"Exactly," Webster said. "I think the trees were members of the Body, trying to stop Darren." He turned to Dominic. "How would you describe the trees you saw?"

"Full grown, with lots of leaves."

"So, mature members of the Body tried to keep Darren from throwing himself off a tremendous cliff, and he was determined to destroy more than himself there. He dragged these mature trees with him as well." Webster looked soberly at Darren, as did the rest of the group. The pendulum clock regulated their heartbeats to one united pulse as they stared at him. Darren swallowed nervously and looked from Webster to Dominic, who nodded his agreement with the interpretation.

"So, the question is," another brother said, "what is Darren involved in that has the potential to destroy him and us as well?" Webster winced, as did Dominic beside him.

"Succinctly, if a bit rudely stated," he acknowledged. He turned again to Darren, one eyebrow raised. "Son, I don't want to put you on the spot, but the picture Dominic paints is pretty frightening. If this is indeed a warning from the Lord, we need to take it seriously." His hooded eyes, overshadowed by massive, shaggy eyebrows, swept the group quickly and returned to Darren. "I won't ask you to bare your soul right here in front of us." He watched as Darren's tense shoulders fell in clear relief. "But I do want you to meditate on what has been said here this morning."

"We'll cut off our prayer time early today," he told the others. "I want Darren to spend today meditating, praying, and thinking. Then tomorrow morning I want to meet with him privately to discuss this situation."

All Darren could do was nod in acquiescence. The other men rose quietly and moved toward the door. Darren rose to leave, his eyes haunted. Dominic stopped him, tears still bright in his eyes, to give him a pat on the back. Darren's own eyes welled, and he moved blindly to the exit as if something was snapping at his heels.

Dominic and Webster listened to the sound of Darren's flight. Dominic closed the door and turned to face the older man, whose face transformed itself from pensive to pleased in a heartbeat.

"I don't think there's any doubt the seed's been planted, my boy." Webster rolled his chair back behind the desk and dropped into it. "Unless I miss my guess, that Academy Award–caliber performance of yours will pay dividends for years to come."

Dominic bowed deeply and grinned. "And you thought those acting classes I took at the university were a waste of time. I'd say they've done us far more good than all the math and science courses put together." He crossed his arms and leaned against a bookcase.

Chuckling, Webster rubbed his ear and then dropped his hand to the desk blotter to toy with a letter opener. "I only hope my performance tomorrow lives up to yours today."

"Oh, it will." Dominic turned to grasp the doorknob. "I've never seen it fail."

"Your confidence is inspiring, like your visions." Webster grinned. Dominic saluted and hummed as he went through the doorway.

20

Casey was surprised to see only Webster's shiny Lexus in the parking area when she arrived at work. On a normal day the men who met to pray with Webster in the morning were still at it when she arrived, or on their way out. Since her talk with Darren in the truck, despite her lingering confusion about the relationship between him and Carol, she looked forward to a glimpse of him as he left to begin his day. She found his dedication to prayer and Gathering with the other Brothers very attractive. Missing the men had one upside: She didn't have to duck and weave to avoid Kurt's hopeful eyes and fiery blushes this morning. As awkward as it had been talking to Darren about Carol, it was even more uncomfortable for her when she realized a similar assumption had been made about her and Kurt. She was glad none of the rumors about her or Darren had any truth behind them.

She opened the door and passed through the machine room, down the hall to her small office with its endless stack of tape recordings and transcripts. She decided to get coffee first. The ritual from her days at the publishing house died hard. As she picked up her mug and went to the kitchen to fill the pot and start the coffee brewing, she couldn't help thinking of Jessie.

Her former coworker had made no effort to contact her since she quit. As she washed out her cup, Casey admitted she hadn't exactly blazed a trail for her to follow. Now loneliness and longing for the friendship they'd shared swept over her, and she had to grip the edge of the sink for support. She straightened and turned, setting down her cup with a thud.

She tried to remember whether anyone had actually told her she couldn't have a friend who wasn't part of the Body. Nothing came to mind. As she walked back down the hall, she glanced at her watch and calculated that Jessie would be at her desk having her first cup of coffee and planning her day. There couldn't be a better time.

Casey didn't bother to sit down at her desk but reached for the phone and punched the buttons from memory. The phone rang, and she clutched the receiver. Her heart leaped when the phone was picked up, and Jessie's early-morning voice came on the line.

"Jessie Barlow, may I help you?"

Casey was sure she heard a discreet sip from a coffee cup follow the greeting, as well as a small click, and she smiled. "Let me guess. You're wearing those incredible parrots in your ears today." Her eyes shone as she looked out the window but saw only her friend's face. The silence on the other end of the line stretched several seconds.

"Casey?" Jessie said. "Is that you, honey?"

"Yes, it's me. So, am I right about the earrings?" In her mind she and Jessie continued their relationship right where they had left off.

"Oh, I'm so glad to hear from you! Where are you?"

"I'm in my office. I was making coffee down the hall, thought of you, and couldn't resist giving you a call. So answer the question."

"Question? Oh, the earrings." Jessie sighed with exasperation. "Yes, you're right. How did you know?"

"They click their little claws against the telephone when you wear them. I recognized them right off."

"I can't believe you called. I'd almost given up hope. What have you been up to?"

"Proofreading, transcript checking, and manuscript coordination. Sound familiar?"

"I thought you hated this job." Jessie laughed for the first time. The sound poured over Casey's heart like honey over warm toast.

"Well, I guess it's what you edit and proof, not where you do it that counts." She sobered. "I didn't realize how unfulfilled I felt until I started working on Brother Webster's publication staff." She knew she trod on dangerous ground. She bit her lip and wondered how Jessie would respond.

"Well, I must admit I've run across more edifying verbiage in my life than *Aluminum Plant Safety Procedures,* which I've been working on for a week." Jessie giggled.

"Oh, that sounds like a real page-turner." Casey relaxed.

"It's bad enough I have to proof this stuff, but without my little buddy to share breaks and lunch with, it's mind-numbing. Do you ever do lunch anymore?"

Casey turned from the window, half sat on the edge of her desk, and struck a dramatic pose. "On occasion I permit myself sustenance." She switched back to her own voice. "What did you have in mind?"

"Well, tomorrow I have to be up your way for a meeting that will end by eleven thirty, and you know what time that is ..."

"Hungry time!" They said it in unison. The joke was an old one, but it never ceased to make them laugh. They did so now. There was a click on the line, and then another.

"Jess? You still there?" Casey started to reach for the phone to redial.

"I'm here. What was that?"

"Who knows? Squirrels on the telephone poles or something."

"So how about a girls' lunch out? You tell me where, and I'll be there," Jessie's tone was warm.

Casey pursed her lips and thought. "Well, there's a great little Mediterranean place I've been to a few times at the south edge of Crescent Hills. I think you'd like it. Nice atmosphere, reasonable prices, big portions."

"Well, as long as it has atmosphere, that's all I care about." The portion size had always been the key to their dining decisions. It felt good to Casey to kid with Jessie again.

"Then let's call it a date. How about eleven forty-five? That way we'll beat at least part of the crowd." She twirled the receiver cord around her finger and gave Jessie directions to the restaurant.

"Sounds great. I can't wait."

"See you tomorrow." Casey stood and turned toward the phone cradle.

"Oh, Casey—"

"Yes?"

"Give me your number real quick, in case anything goes wrong. You know how meetings can go." Casey heard the sound of Jessie slapping her desk several times. "Now where's my pencil gotten to again?"

"Check your right ear," Casey said, as she had so many times in the past when her friend forgot she had lodged her pencil in her wiry hair so it jutted out like an antenna.

Jessie chuckled. "Yeah, yeah, I know. If it was a snake … So give me your number."

Casey gave her office number and replaced the receiver in its cradle. She stood for a moment and enjoyed the warm glow that hovered around her and the feeling of anticipation the lunch date produced in her spirit. It would be wonderful to see Jessie again, and it sounded as if she wouldn't badger her about the Bodylife. Maybe she could again invite Jessie to a Gathering so she could see for herself. She sang under her breath and moved toward the door as she remembered the coffee that had started this incredible chain of events.

The shrill ring of the telephone echoed in the big house. Grace stood beside the table on which the phone sat. Only one person had this particular number, and she enjoyed toying with him and letting it ring awhile before she lifted the handset.

"Yes?"

"She called someone outside and made a lunch date for tomorrow." He spoke in a hushed voice. "You'd better do something about that."

"Who did she call? Not that dreadful Gretchen woman. Did you get the details?"

"It was someone she used to work with."

Grace came alert. "Are you certain? Let me hear it." She could hear him fumble with the apparatus. He'd never been comfortable with machinery—that's why she'd had it made automatic. When he played it back to her, she didn't care for the tone of the banter. She didn't care for it at all.

"What are you going to do?"

Grace frowned and held her response for several seconds. "I'm going to think, dear husband. Then I'll act, and not before. Now go back to your computer and leave me in peace." She put down the telephone without a good-bye.

21

arren arrived at Webster's office early in the morning while the ink of night still coated the sky. He sat across from him, huddled on the edge of the couch in misery, his shoulders hunched as he stared at the floor. He had been optimistic about this meeting. He wasn't able to find anything in the Word that explained the vision Dominic had reported the day before. He had imagined facing Webster with a clean heart, as an equal. That fantasy evaporated at the door.

Webster cleared his throat, and the sound drew Darren's eyes from the floor. The older man, his silver head bent, kneaded his hands together then tore them apart and placed one on each knee. He raised his eyes to Darren's face.

"Brother, I am most disturbed to hear that an entire day of seeking the Lord has left you as much in the dark as you were yesterday. I, too, have sought the Lord, and He has revealed the meaning of the vision, but I had hoped it would be confirmed in your heart." He shook his head and again stared at the floor.

"Brother Webster, I've never prayed as hard or as long as I did yesterday," Darren protested. "I read, I prayed, I cried, I fasted the whole day. I don't know what else I could have done." His tone changed from defeat to slight belligerence.

"Yes, you were pretty busy. Perhaps that was the problem. You were so busy being someone seeking the Lord you didn't have any time left to do the seeking." Webster's lips curved upward. He waved his hand at Darren as he began to argue. "Don't take it as a criticism. It's an easy trap to fall into." He studied the younger man. "Let's review the vision again and see if we can make sense of it, shall we? I think when we're done, we'll both understand."

Darren slid farther forward on the couch. He was at a disadvantage on it, since he was several inches below Webster's height in his tall desk chair. The position annoyed him; he rose and moved to a straight-backed chair. A white outline of irritation wreathed Webster's pursed lips.

"Dominic said you were persistently moving toward a precipice. He said you were oblivious to any interference, even when trees sprang up to block your path. In fact you uprooted those trees and dragged them with you toward the cliff. Isn't that right?"

"That's what Dominic said." Darren kept his voice light and earned a frown from Webster.

"Do you like it here, Brother Darren?" His tone mixed irritation and anger.

"You mean living with the Brothers?"

Webster nodded.

"I think it's where I need to be."

"That's not what I asked you. I asked if you liked it here."

"If you mean, is it fun one hundred percent of the time, no." Darren took his time before he continued to answer the question. He rubbed his bearded chin and looked at Webster. "If you mean, do I always feel comfortable, do I always feel like I made the right choice in coming here, no again." Webster rubbed his hands together in a washing motion, about to speak again. Darren cut him off. "But I never came to the Body based on my feelings. I knew when I came here that I'd have to sacrifice and endure discomfort and a change in my routine. I knew it would require a change of whose will I followed and whose good I looked out for." His voice became stronger with each phrase. "Despite everything, I still believe I'm in the right place for me."

Webster studied him. "You speak as though what you mean is, you believe you are in the right place for you *for now*. I hear the words quite loudly in my spirit."

Darren's eyes widened as he thought about Webster's words. Then he looked away so he didn't have to face him. "I never thought about it, but it's possible you're right. Maybe I'm still sitting on the fence." He looked at Webster, and his eyes pleaded. "Is that what you think this whole vision was about? My potential indecision about remaining in the Body?"

"I think that's part of the problem." Webster removed a large cloth handkerchief from his pocket and polished his glasses. "As long as you stand with one foot planted in the Bodylife and one foot planted in the world, you're a danger to yourself and to the rest of us, because you're vulnerable." He shrugged and then seemed to change the subject.

"I grew up in a rural area, and there was a stream running through one part of our property." Webster's eyes softened in memory. "As a boy I spent a great deal of time playing around the stream. When you're a child and there's a swift-flowing stream nearby, there's always something fun to do. One of my favorite things was to toss sticks into the stream, then run ahead along the bank and wait until they flowed past me. I'd do it over and over again." A warm, reminiscent smile flickered across his face. "Every once in a while a stick would get lodged in the bank, like it was trying to escape the current and get up on shore. It couldn't, of course, and it also could no longer continue downstream—but the damage didn't stop there. Pretty soon a few leaves or long strands of grass would lodge against the stick. Then more stuff would get hung up. Sticks, leaves, an old paper bag someone had thrown in upstream. The longer that stick held on to the bank, the larger the pile of debris it accumulated. After awhile everything going by was either caught in the dam or had to divert around it and run the risk of getting hung up on the opposite bank."

Darren pictured the scene Webster had painted for him and blinked several times. "Are you saying I'm the stick? I'm hanging up the whole Body?"

Webster surprised Darren when he laughed aloud. "Oh, I don't think you're a big enough stick yet to affect the entire Body." He chuckled, then sobered. "However, you do seem to have a grip on the bank, and the smaller sticks, the ones on the very top of the water, can become entangled with you." The old pendulum clock filled the room with chimes as it struck six o'clock. They had been talking for an hour already.

Darren shook himself. "I understand your analogy about the stick in the stream, but I don't see how it relates to Dominic's vision."

"If you understood the stick, you'd understand the vision. The analogies are two sides of the same coin." He spoke clearly, as if to a slow child. "In both illustrations someone who is head-strong chooses a course that will, if not corrected, affect and harm others around him. In this case, around *you.*" The two men stared into each other's eyes. "Shall I be plain?" Webster leaned forward in his chair and rested his weight on his elbows on the armrests.

"I wish you would."

"You've moved into the Bodylife. You've joined us in the most practical ways. Your behavior is exemplary. You have joined us with your body, and perhaps even with your mind, but you have not yet joined us with your heart. Not all of it, at least. Even as we speak here today, you are in the process of giving away part of your heart, letting it become a snag in the river to an unsuspecting Sister who will become entangled on it and perhaps be crippled in her ability to proceed in the Body."

Darren knew in his gut what was coming, but he forced himself to remain statuelike and wait for it.

"It's natural that a young man would be drawn to a girl like Casey Ellis. You're not the only one in the Body she's had that effect on. However, in the Body we put aside what is natural, and we take on what is better. In a worldly group your relationship with Miss Ellis would be your own business, but this is not a worldly group, is it?"

Darren knew the question was more than rhetorical, but he held his tongue. He felt sweat break out under his shirt.

"What sets the Body apart and makes people do crazy things like leave families, jobs, homes, and dreams in order to join us? It's that we don't follow the world. We follow the Lord, and him only." Webster studied Darren. "You are new to the Body. Casey is even newer. Both of you still have at least one foot and part of your heart in the world. You're both still thinking you can take what you like, leave what you don't, and walk away if you disagree with the Body, but that's not true."

"What do you mean by that?"

"You can't walk away from here, because you aren't the same person who came in. There is no going back. After this you are unfit for anything else, because you've tasted the best. It's like trying to go back to a dry packaged mix after your first bowl of homemade soup. There's no comparison."

"I don't plan to leave."

"Not today, you don't." Webster observed him from beneath his unruly brows. "But you still let the thought cross your mind. You cling to the bank. You're walking toward the edge of the cliff, and God help anyone who gets in your way. You still think leaving is an option, despite what you know in your heart to be true. There's no turning back once a man has put his hand to the plow— not even to bury his old life."

Darren pondered in silence. All his life he had wanted to belong somewhere, with people who were serious about the Lord and who moved ahead with him. Here he had found that place. His heart sank at the thought that he had endangered the Body with his self-will.

"What must I do to get out of the bank and back in the current? What must I do to turn and walk away from the cliff? How can I mend what I've already broken in the Body?" The honest questions tumbled out of him as he clasped his hands and his gaze bored into Webster's deep-set blue eyes.

"I think you've started turning from the cliff this morning, but the cliff will always be there. You have to do more than walk away from it. You have to anchor yourself to something farther from the edge so you can't get to the cliff no matter how hard you try."

"More than anything in my heart, I want to be part of the Body," Darren said. "I gave up a job, left my family, broke my lease, and sold most of my possessions. I have nothing left but myself to give—and I don't want to be halfhearted in the giving. Please tell me what I must do."

"Again, let me be plain. The apostle Paul acknowledged the difficulty for young men to be alone and single-minded as he wished them to be. Because that's the case, I want you to take that great heart of yours and settle it on a Sister." He put up his hands as though to keep Darren from racing from the room. "Not a Sister new to the faith or one new to the Body, for neither could be the anchor you need. A Sister who has learned to submit herself to the Body, to the sovereignty of God, to the destiny mapped out for her when the foundations of the world were laid. A Sister, in short, who has left the world behind and entwined her heart with the Body."

Darren suspected what was to come but moved forward nonetheless. "Do you have a particular Sister in mind?"

"I could let you choose a Sister on your own, but I fear that would be a repetition of what you have left behind in the world." Webster rubbed his hands together as if they were cold. "I want you to let your spirit learn discipline and submission, and to take joy in the learning. Yes, I have a Sister in mind." He drew out the tension. "Carol Martin."

The name dropped into Darren's mind and found its fit within the questions and fears he had struggled with for weeks. In a way it was a relief to hear it voiced. Rebellion rose in him at the presumption of this man telling him whom he should love. At the same time he felt the breathtaking exhilaration of standing at a great fork in his spiritual road. In an instant he saw his future roll out before him. There were two divergent paths—one of obedience and submission, the other of selfishness and pride. The choice appeared clear-cut. A pang went through him when he saw Carol standing on one path and Casey on the other—especially seeing a shadowy figure next to her, that might well be Kurt. However, he now knew one path led to light and life, the other to increasing darkness and cold, despite its allure. Darren's shoulders sagged, then straightened as he struggled with the turmoil within.

"Let us pray together," Webster urged. "It isn't often I am privileged to see a soul join in the fight and head off on the right track toward glory and joy."

Darren felt a tear roll onto his cheek, and he dashed it away. As the clock chimed the half hour, they prayed. Relief surged in him as he gave in and was engulfed in the current of the Body. He relaxed and let it carry him along.

22

asey stood in a bay window nook and looked out into the restaurant parking lot. Too excited to sit and wait, she stood with her feet warmed from sunlight that streamed through the window and across the carpet. When she saw Jessie pull into the parking lot fifteen minutes late, she breathed a sigh of relief, and her eyes welled up at the impending reunion. Jessie came through the door, a swirl of pink, green, and striking black. Casey took one look at her and raced into her friend's welcoming embrace. She wasn't alone in having wet eyes, she noted.

"Oh, girl, it's so good to see you!" Jessie hugged Casey hard. After one more squeeze she pushed her away. "Now, where's that atmosphere you told me about?" Both women burst into giggles that held a hint of nervousness and the warmth of remembered camaraderie.

"Right this way, madam." Casey led the way past tables that sprouted like mushrooms from a rich tile floor. The room was overhung with baskets of live ferns, and soft light filtered down from a vast skylight. The restaurant was busy, but Casey had put her jacket on the back of a chair when she arrived. She was glad to see that no one had moved the jacket to a less desirable table and taken the one she wanted.

Jessie settled herself, looked around, and nodded. "You get ten points for atmosphere. Now where's the menu? I want to see these big portions you bragged about." She affected a stern tone, but her eyes danced as she drank in the pretty room.

"I'm glad you like it, because I'm too hungry to go somewhere else. What took you so long?"

Jessie rolled her eyes. "Franklin."

Casey feigned a horrified expression. "Oh, no! They let Franklin into your meeting? Say no more!" They both went into gales of laughter over remembered encounters with a man who asked endless questions about nothing. It felt very good to be together. They studied the menu and placed an order when a harried but pleasant waitress paused at their table. Jessie took up the conversational ball.

"Well, I'm doing the same old thing, so there's no need to talk about me. Tell me more about what you're doing." She smiled. "Do you have an office with a window?"

The light question eased Casey's fear of an awkward meeting. She grinned. "A window, four walls, and a door, if you can believe it."

"To think I'd lose a coffee-drinking buddy over architecture."

"It's not the Ritz by any means, but I don't have to share the office, and I'm left alone to do my work. It suits me." Hesitantly, Casey told Jessie what her day was like, from the time she rose early and arrived at the office, to when she turned on her beloved machines. A small blush crept up her cheeks, and Jessie pounced.

"I know how you love machines, but the look on your face isn't for any machine I ever heard of. What's up?" She leaned across the table to hear the details.

"I don't know what you mean." Casey teased, then relented. "Okay, I'll tell you." Her eyes fastened on the table. As she opened her mouth to speak, the waitress slid two salads in front of them. Casey busied herself with hers as she spoke. "There are Brothers—men from the church—who meet in Webster's office every morning for prayer. They're usually leaving as I come in." Casey took a bite of salad. Jessie left hers untouched.

"They? What's this 'they' stuff? I think you mean *he!*"

Casey knew that her blush confirmed Jessie's suspicions. "Well, he's one of them." She reached for a warm, fragrant breadstick. "Anyway, I start the coffeepot when I get there, and that's what I was doing yesterday when I thought of you and couldn't resist calling."

Jessie still had not touched her salad. "Not so fast, coffee lady. Back up to the part between getting out of your car and starting the coffee. That's the stuff I want to hear." Jessie picked up her fork and speared an artichoke heart, but her eyes returned to her friend's face.

Casey decided to tease her further. "Well, I park in my usual spot, unlock the door, and go and put down my purse. That's when I think of coffee." As she watched Jessie swallow and prepare to launch another volley of questions, she held up her hand and stopped her. "Okay. His name is Darren, and he's new to the Body like I am. I think he's pretty special, but I don't want to go on and on about him. You know what will happen if I do."

"I feel like a camel that's been shown where the oasis is, then given a paper cup with a few drops of water. But yes, I know what will happen if you talk about him. He'll evaporate like morning fog and slip away. At least I know his name though. That's more than you've given me the last three times you were interested in a man."

"Yes, and all three times the minute I told you about a man, he disappeared," Casey nibbled at the soft breadstick. "You're a jinx on my relationships, Jessie Barlow!"

"Oh, now it's a *relationship*, is it? That's even better." Jessie grinned.

"Eat your salad." Casey applied herself to her own plate. The noise volume in the restaurant rose in waves and made it difficult to converse until diners applied themselves to the salads and steaming breadsticks that appeared on their tables.

"If the entrée lives up to the salad, then we're in for a treat."

"I've been here three or four times and never been disappointed."

"Do you come with friends?"

"I stop in when I have errands to run in this part of town, like picking up supplies for the office." Memory of her solitary lunches made her voice catch, and she knew Jessie saw through her brave front.

"I didn't come here today to pry." Jessie held up two fingers to stop Casey from cutting in. "And I'm not going to—but if you need a lunch partner, you know where to find one." The offer was simple and clear.

"Thanks for being a friend. I'm doing what I think is best, what fulfills me most."

"I just don't want to be cut off from someone as special as you because we choose different lives. Promise you won't avoid me, and I promise I won't bring a rolling pin. Deal?"

"Deal." Casey reached out and squeezed Jessie's hand.

As Casey tucked her hand back in her lap, a shadow fell across the table. She looked up, expecting the waitress with their heaping plates. She was stunned to find Grace Forsythe at her elbow. She felt the hairs on the back of her neck rise up in alarm. Without a thought she scrambled to her feet.

"Grace! What are you doing here?" Casey felt a cold, clammy hand grip her heart. Her face drained of the happiness she had felt.

"Why, what a coincidence." Grace said with a smile. "I had no idea you knew about this restaurant. This is one of my favorites." She looked at Jessie and extended her hand. "You must be a friend of our dear Casey. I'm Grace Forsythe." Jessie slowly raised her hand to shake Grace's, and Casey babbled introductions.

"I'm sorry. This is Jessie Barlow, a friend from the publishing house where I used to work. We met for lunch, that's all." Casey felt compelled to explain herself. She felt salad churn in her stomach.

"May I?" Grace placed her hand on a chair and pulled it out an inch or so. She looked over the top of her glasses. They could not, with good manners, say no. With wooden movements Jessie moved her purse to the floor at her feet, but kept her eyes trained on Grace as she slid into the seat.

"I'm very glad to find you here." Grace gestured to the full tables around them. "I would never have gotten a seat if I hadn't seen someone I knew." She snagged a waitress as she squeezed between chairs. "I'd like an iced tea, please." She looked away before the waitress could acknowledge the order. "Don't let me interrupt you. This looks like a reunion. Pretend I'm not here."

She placed a vertical finger across her lips and looked at both women. "I'll be as quiet as a mouse."

"We were discussing how different our lives are, now that I'm part of the Body." Casey fiddled with her silverware. "Jessie and I worked together for years, doing what I do now but without the meaning Brother Webster's words have for me." Grace settled back in her chair. Casey realized that her free talk with Jessie was over. Grace would not leave the restaurant one moment before they did.

Jessie studied Grace with ill-disguised uneasiness. Then she seemed to reach a decision. Casey was relieved when, with a shake of her head that set her earrings dancing, she smiled and spoke at last. "Yes, we used to have many arguments over lunch, debating Bible passages, dissecting our lives, learning about friendship from each other. We spent a lot of time at lunch, didn't we?"

Casey nodded and wondered where Jessie was going. She sensed something different in her, a hard edge to her glittering smile. Something was up.

"We have lots of characters in our office." Jessie emptied a packet of sugar into her iced tea. "There's Florence, the cleaning lady, who leaves notes on our garbage cans when we put things in them she doesn't like to empty." Jessie's eyes held Casey's for an instant. "Remember her?"

"I remember her telling me not to chew gum anymore, even though I always wrapped it in paper before I tossed it out."

"Now the notes are Day-Glo orange, in case we're tempted to overlook them." Jessie chuckled, then turned to Grace and continued. "We also have a guy named Franklin who can never get the point the first time around. Whenever we wanted to stretch a meeting, we'd invite Franklin to attend. That would double the length of the meeting without any effort."

Grace flashed a tight smile at Jessie, and Casey knew she didn't like all this talk about something outside the Body. Perversely, Casey decided to prolong the discussion.

"And how's Bob?" She turned to Grace. "Bob Murphy is Jessie's boss. He yells and shouts and waves his arms a lot. Then he relents and lets everybody do things as they think best. He has to posture a bit first though." The smile that tugged at Casey's mouth was warm with affection.

Jessie gave a quick bark of laughter. "Do you remember the time we had Franklin and Bob almost at each other's throats? The editorial meeting for the geology textbook series, wasn't it?" Casey nodded, her eyes shiny with remembered humor. "Franklin kept asking questions, and Bob's arms started pinwheeling, he was so frustrated. Then four pagers went off in succession!"

Casey then turned to Grace. "But the best part was that only one page was real. After Cathy left to answer hers, she paged one of us still in the room. We each did the favor for someone else after we escaped. One by one, we all left the room, and pretty soon Franklin and Bob were left alone—but their meeting went on another forty minutes." Jessie and Casey howled over the trick.

In the midst of the laughter Casey felt a sharp nudge on her foot. At first she thought Jessie had kicked her by accident, but when the nudge came twice again, she knew it was a signal. When their eyes met, she thought she knew why Jessie had taken them down memory lane. She picked up her iced-tea spoon, stirred the tea in her glass and struck the side of the glass three times to mimic the three kicks. Jessie relaxed.

Grace's iced tea arrived with the meals Jessie and Casey had ordered. She ordered a salad; as Casey feared, she was camped at their table. After a few minutes during which they sampled and complimented the food, Casey laid aside her fork and squirmed in her chair.

"Excuse me." She got up. "I have to visit the ladies' room." She scooped up her purse as she went. Passing behind Grace's chair, her eyes caught Jessie's for a brief second.

"Where's Jessie?" Casey asked as she sat down and picked up her napkin.

"She got paged by the big boss. Urgent." Grace wound an anchovy around her fork and popped it into her mouth. "Didn't you see her over by the restrooms?"

Casey frowned in surprise and looked back in the direction from which she had come. "No, but the phones are at the end of the hall, and the bathroom is halfway down. I didn't even look down there when I came out." She shrugged and picked up her knife and fork. "This manicotti is wonderful, Grace." Casey gestured toward her plate. "Are you sure you don't want some?"

"No, thank you, I've had it before. I'm hungry for salad today." Grace attacked the defenseless lettuce in her bowl.

Ten minutes passed before Jessie returned to the table. She looked flustered and mumbled to herself. When she dropped her purse on the floor under the table, car keys fell out with a loud jangle. Casey leaned under the table, picked up the keys and slid them into her own purse. "I tucked them in the outside pocket," she lied and gestured toward Jessie's purse. Jessie nodded and looked pleased with herself. "What was your urgent page?"

"Bob's all crazy about our current project because it goes to press on Friday. You know the drill." She sipped her tea.

The rest of lunch passed with small talk. Grace told Jessie bits of the history of the Body. Casey felt a burning compulsion to revisit the ladies' room but restrained herself. She didn't need to use the facilities. She hadn't needed them the first time.

At last, the check paid and their purses gathered, the three women left the pleasant restaurant and stepped into the bright outdoors. Casey and Jessie shared a quick embrace. Jessie shook Grace's hand. As Casey approached her car, she tingled with anticipation. She slipped the key into the lock, twisted it, and watched the lock button pop up. She settled herself behind the wheel and placed her purse on the passenger seat on top of her sweater, which had been in the back seat when she went into the restaurant. The purse sat lopsided, riding a bulge in the sleeve.

She maneuvered through the crowded parking lot. As she reached the entrance, Grace's elegant car rolled up behind her. She was glad she hadn't stopped to examine the sweater. She signaled a right turn and pulled into traffic. Grace turned right as well but turned left at the next light.

At a large shopping center, Casey headed for the service driveway. She slipped behind the shopping center and into a secluded lot. She checked her rearview mirror. No shiny sedan. She took a deep breath, moved her purse, and lifted the sweater as she inserted her hand into the sleeve. When she pulled her hand out, she held a compact cellular phone and charger. A piece of paper torn from the yellow pages was wrapped around it. Scribbled in its margin was Jessie's home phone number.

Despite the awkwardness of Grace's presence at her lunch with Jessie, Casey savored the warmth of conversation with her friend as she opened the door to the office on Monday. She moved through the room, flipped on power switches, and listened to the various beeps and whirs that indicated the machines were coming to life. When she retrieved her coffee cup and headed for the kitchen, she couldn't resist her impulse. She went back to her office, picked up the phone, and dialed. The receiver was lifted on the fifth ring.

"Jessie Barlow," came her friend's precoffee voice.

"Hey, girlfriend. I can tell you haven't had your coffee yet."

"Why do you think the phone rang so many times? I was halfway to the coffeepot when you called. Some friend!"

"Sorry. I'll have to remember to call later, so you can have your java first."

"That would be much more civilized." Jessie's mock anger warmed her heart. "So, how goes it with you this Monday morning?"

"Oh, fine." Casey sank into her chair. "I was remembering our lunch."

"It was so nice to see you. I hope we can make a habit of it."

"That would be fun, wouldn't it? Maybe once a month or something."

"Maybe next time we can go someplace where we can talk and not be interrupted."

"I'm sorry about Grace. I had no idea she'd be there." Something fluttered in Casey's stomach as she thought about that aspect of the lunch, and she didn't like it.

"I have to say, I've never met anyone I had such a negative gut reaction toward. It's because I care that I say this." Jessie took a deep breath. "I've been worried about you ever since you got involved in that group—but now that I've met this Grace person, I'm alarmed. Couldn't you feel the spiritual darkness in her?"

Casey bristled, hearing the echoes of all the discussions they'd had about the Bodylife prior to her move to the Sisters House. The accumulated debris blasted from her in an instant. "Are you saying I've lost all ability to discern? I'm stupid? I'm lost, and you see the true way?" Casey heard the anger in her voice but couldn't stop it.

"I'm talking about Grace, not you. I sensed a real spiritual void in her, and it frightened me."

"I think we've had this discussion before. I think you're jealous I've found something to build my life around, and you're still doing the same old things." She heard Jessie begin to sputter. "I hoped you would be happy for a friend who has found what she's been looking for. Sure Grace is a little weird, but I'm not following Grace, I'm following Jesus. Who are you following?"

"Don't you think it's odd the only way I could think to communicate with you was to slip you a phone? Isn't it a little out of line when you can't even go to lunch without someone shadowing you and intruding on your special time out?"

Casey was silent. She'd mulled over the same thoughts for two days. However, it was one thing for her to question them and quite another for Jessie to point them out. Her uneasiness made her lash out.

"I see nothing wrong if a friend stops at our table in a crowded restaurant and sits with us. As for the other, that was your idea, and you'll notice I haven't felt the need to use it. You can expect it back in the mail in a day or two. I think we've said enough." She started to pull the phone from her ear but she heard Jessie's pleading voice.

"Casey! Please, I know you're angry, and I'm sorry, but keep the phone and the number. I'll always be just a call away." Without responding, Casey hung up the phone.

It took her twice the usual time to prepare the coffee, her mind in turmoil as she replayed the conversation. When she finally got her coffee, she searched the office for a small box to mail the phone and its charger back. Every one she found was either far too big or a little too small to send it safely. In the end she dropped the search but determined to return the phone at the first opportunity.

23

asey's hands closed convulsively over the heavy book as it slipped from her lap. Her eyes flew open, and she jerked to wakefulness. Her room swam into clarity, and she discovered Lydia kneeling beside her as she tried to ease the book from her grip.

"It's okay, I'll save your page." Lydia slipped a tissue into the book and closed it, then set it on the floor beside the chair. She studied Casey's sleep-blurred eyes. "You look as if you could have slept there all night. Why don't you go to bed? I found Andrew in the hall most indignant you'd forgotten him. I guess the door closed behind him."

Casey woke fully and looked around the room with large eyes until they fell on the cat as he moved purposefully toward his favorite spot on the bed. She sank back into her chair. "I'm sorry, I didn't mean for him to be a bother. I fell asleep for a minute."

"Andrew is never a bother, and you know it." Lydia sank to sit cross-legged on the floor beside Casey's chair. "You, on the other hand, are beginning to bother me quite a bit. Why are you so exhausted? It's not like you not to know where Andrew is."

Casey passed both hands over her face in a scrubbing motion and raked her fingers through her hair. She gestured to the book Lydia had taken from her. "I was trying to proof this before it goes to the final press stage tomorrow, but even then the pressure won't let up, because there's another book of outlines to prepare and print before next weekend's special Gatherings." Exhaustion hissed out in a sigh.

"I'm beginning to think this job wasn't such a good idea if it wears you out this way."

Casey rubbed the tense muscles in her neck and shoulders. She had given up doing anything more than glancing in the mirror these days, unhappy with the shadows under her eyes that seemed to become more pronounced each time she looked. Weariness prompted honesty. "I feel like it's been years since I've been able to pull my head out of a book or my eyes off a page, but it's all work that has to be done right away, so the special Gatherings we've all been working so hard to prepare for go right. Webster's new book has to be done before then, and the outline has to be ready for people to pick up when they come to the Gatherings. Usually I know when big jobs are coming and can work around them. All this came up so fast, it blindsided me." Casey's fingers traced the geometric pattern of the fabric on the chair arm. She let her head fall against its curved back.

"Is there anything I can do to help?" As Casey shook her head, Lydia pressed on. "Don't say no. There has to be something mere mortals can do to assist Superwoman." A small smile crept across Casey's face. "I'm not leaving without an assignment."

"I could use another pair of eyes to run over the text to look for typos. I get so I can't see them anymore—at least until I see the outline in print and hold it in my hands in a Gathering. Then I see every mistake. And so does Grace."

"Don't worry about what Grace says. She's not your boss."

"Oh, yes, she is." Horror froze Casey's face, and she swiveled to look first at Lydia, then at the open bedroom door.

"What do you mean?" Lydia glanced over her shoulder, apparently having caught Casey's fear of eavesdroppers.

Casey moaned. "Just forget I ever said that."

"You did say it, but what did you mean by it?" Lines appeared in Lydia's forehead.

Casey closed her eyes as her need to confide warred with her fear and weariness. The ramifications of getting on Grace's bad side had stilled her tongue until now, but in her fatigue she didn't care.

She needed a friend more than she needed safety. She rose and tip-toed to the door, looked both ways in the hall, and closed it. She returned to her chair and leaned forward to put her face near Lydia's. "This must never go further than us." Lydia's eyes widened as she nodded.

"I don't work for Webster; I work for Grace." She studied Lydia's face. Her silence demanded explanation more loudly than words would have. "She told me something about Webster's health that made it imperative for him to have someone help him with his publications. That's how I came to work for him, but he doesn't like people to be paid to work for the ministry, so Grace gives me money, and Webster thinks I'm a volunteer."

"What's wrong with Webster?" Lydia frowned.

"I can't tell you." Casey shook her head.

"All right, if it's a confidence you must maintain, that's fine. However, I don't like the underhanded way you came to work for Webster. I thought you got a regular paycheck for all the work you do. How are your bills paid? I know they are, or Carol would have a fit."

"Grace pays my part here each month and gives me a little bit for pocket money." Casey had gotten used to the arrangement over the past several months.

"It's almost as if you're a dependent child on an allowance, not a respected employee on a salary. How much does Grace give you? I'll bet it's not much." Lydia struck her fist on her folded knee. "I feel responsible for all this. I never intended for you to be tied to a job that doesn't even support you."

"It's not your fault. How can you even think that? I'm the one who took the job."

"Yes, but I remember our talks before you made this decision, and now that I know what you had to choose between, I'm sorry I wasn't a better counselor for you." Lydia shook her head, indigna-tion plain on her face.

Casey squeezed her hand. "Thank you for your concern, but I'm all right. I made the choice, and I don't regret it. Right now things are hectic, and I can't seem to get my head above water, that's all."

"Of course you're drowning. How stupid of me not to see it before. Tomorrow morning I want you to give me some pages to proof." Casey felt weak with relief at the offer. "And we'll talk no further on the subject unless you want to."

Before tears could further betray her exhaustion and stress, Casey leaned forward and hugged Lydia hard. Even in her emotional state, she felt Lydia stiffen and heard the quick intake of breath caused by her tight grip and wondered about it. As she pulled away to question Lydia, Andrew gave a massive yawn from the bed. He stood up and stretched with his back arched and toes sunk into the blanket, then lay down again. The women laughed softly at him.

"I think that, as usual, Mr. Andrew has had the last word on the subject for today." Lydia looked at Casey with mock severity. "To bed, young lady, and no arguments!"

"Yes, ma'am," Casey said in a small voice, relieved to have another set of shoulders to bear her burden, even if those shoulders looked frail to Casey's newly appraising eye. Lydia rose from the floor stiffly. Casey felt exhaustion wash over her, but made a mental note to keep a more watchful eye on Lydia.

24

Casey considered the emptiness inside her as she sat in the hubbub of the final Gathering of a monumental weekend. Despite being surrounded by hundreds of enthusiastic and noisy people, she felt alone. She had made the deadline; the book had sold well all weekend, and people were quoting from it already.

Casey ignored the noise around her and lifted her heart to God in silent pleading. She was so lonely. She wondered how that could be true in such a crowd. The feeling of being connected that she had anticipated when she moved in had not materialized. Hope had risen anew when she went to work for Webster, yet here she sat, tired, alone, and sad. Casey compared her feelings with the biblical "fruit of the Spirit" listed in the book of Galatians, and they came up far short. What was she doing wrong?

Her turmoil was compounded because Lydia was ill again. Casey remembered how awful Lydia had looked a few days earlier when she had semi-collapsed during a meeting to finalize details for this special Gathering. She had not rallied since then, and Casey longed to leave the Gathering and go sit with her. If she weren't trapped in the middle of a row, she would have gotten up and gone. Instead she fought to focus on the celebrating people around her.

"I have to say something!" cried an overweight woman with a florid face and bright, formfitting clothes as she jumped to her feet. "This is my first time here, and I have to say I have never heard anything like this before. I'm thrilled to my shoes!" She squealed and jumped up and down on tiny feet for emphasis. Happy amens greeted her statement. "I feel like I've been dying of thirst, and I didn't even know it," she continued. "Now I'm face down in the water, and you just try to drag me away!" She sat down, and affirmations rose like a tidal wave.

Casey found it hard to keep her mind on the woman long enough to register what she said. The joy, the life, the expectation had all bled out of her and left her flat and discouraged. Her eyes fell on her open Bible, and she read a verse three times before it sank in. She read it again and shook her head at the words of Jesus recorded there.

"Come to Me, all who are weary and heavy-laden, and I will give you rest. Take My yoke upon you, and learn from Me, for I am gentle and humble in heart; and you will find rest for your souls. For My yoke is easy and My burden is light." Contrary to the verse, her life was filled with burdens that dragged at her like heavy bags of sand tied to her legs and arms. She couldn't remember how it felt to be light and happy and free.

She began to pray fervently for a special blessing from God to remind her why she was here. She longed to be on the path to joy again. Desperate for the support her friend gave her, she prayed that God would make Lydia healthy and strong again.

She was startled to see Webster on his feet again and realized that another ten minutes had passed while she was reading and thinking.

"We know this is true from experience," he said.

She wondered what she'd missed.

"We have seen the Spirit's leading in individual lives and watched him carve a path through our midst to begin something new among us." Casey glanced at the women around her. All craned their necks to see Webster, smiles teasing their faces.

"This time the Spirit has led two people to our Body, then built them into it as strong, viable members. Now he is leading them to build themselves up together as a family, and we will all be part of the celebration and joy of their new beginning." He smiled broadly, swept the room with his eyes, and flung out his left hand, like a magician introducing his beautiful assistant.

"Carol, come here for a moment, my dear." Carol rose from where she sat three seats to the left of Casey, a bright glow creeping across her cheeks. She stepped out from the row, advanced to Webster, and took his outstretched hand.

"For those who are new to our Body, let me tell you about Carol. She has been part of the Body for several years. The first day she came to a Gathering, she said she found what she'd been looking for all her life, much like this lady over here." He gestured to the chubby woman, who bobbed in her seat. "But Carol came and joined us at once and became one of the first women in the Sisters House. She's been a mainstay ever since." He looked at Carol, who seemed pleased and embarrassed by the attention. "Many times Carol and I have talked about what God had in store for her here. I have to tell you she was prepared to pour out her life for this Body as a single woman, if that was God's will." The smile wreathed his features. "I'm happy to report, however, that it isn't."

A joyful amen broke from the group. Webster continued to hold Carol's hand, then reached and pulled Darren to his feet from his place in the center circle. The deep scarlet that raced from his collar to his hairline was like a beacon in the room. Many women snickered with delight at his discomfort.

Casey sat as still as a stone, her heart pounding. It was true, after all.

"In a few weeks," Webster's voice boomed, "we'll celebrate the wedding of Carol and Darren right here with every member of the Body present. How else can a union be blessed, other than from the bosom of the Body?"

Although the crowd shouted agreement, all she heard was the pounding of the pulse in her head. She stared at Darren and willed him to look at her, to explain with a glance what was happening. His eyes remained fixed on Webster.

"I can think of no better way to conclude this special series than with an announcement of a marvelous wedding Gathering to come." There was a burst of applause from the seated assembly. As one they were all on their feet, the women hugging Carol, the men shaking Darren's hand and slapping him on the back, with Kurt first in line with congratulations. Casey stood as well, mostly in self-defense. If she hadn't risen, the other women in her row would have trampled her as they fought to join the happy throng swirling around the couple. Casey felt a dead calm in her chest. She moved backward slowly. When she found herself free of the crowd, she turned and went out the back door. Without a thought she began the walk home. Her head whirled with the scene she had just witnessed, and she put together pieces that had puzzled her for weeks.

She was glad, for once, that the walk from the Gathering Place to the Sisters House was a mile. She would need every step to work through her thoughts. In fact she needed more. She turned right at the next street so she could circle the block before proceeding. The change from busy street to quiet residential area was immediate. Trees cast shadows on the sidewalk and made a gentle tunnel that broke the monotonous sunlight. Her head, which had ached before the Gathering, began to clear. Her mental and emotional anguish was far greater than any headache.

Casey cast her mind back and tried to sort out the clues she had missed. When Lydia told her about Carol's attachment to Darren and implied it was mutual, she had pulled back from her attraction for him. Then she recalled their conversation on the dreadful rainy morning after the Chinese dinner debacle. He had told her there was nothing between him and Carol. He could not have spoken more plainly.

She had been busy learning her new job, getting used to living in the Sisters House, and trying to fit in. She had not seen Darren, other than quick glimpses in the morning as he left Webster's office, and at regular Gatherings. Still, something had been bothering him a month ago; he had looked haunted, with dark circles under his eyes for many days. Then he started to use the back door to leave Webster's office. She remembered her unique moment of connection to him when they talked during the rainstorm and felt a bitter laugh rise up at the will-o'-the-wisp she'd chased. He'd not spoken privately to her since that day. Now it all made sense.

Her stride was steady when she left the Gathering Place, and she looked up to realize she had covered a lot of ground. She was at the entrance to a small park, and realized it must have been where Darren had driven her the morning he found her floundering in the rain. On impulse she headed down the steep drive. There were a few cars in the lot and a volleyball game in session on a sandy court. She walked to a picnic table tucked under the trees away from the game.

She brushed away a few stray twigs and sat on the table with her feet on the bench, her elbows on her knees and her face in her hands. Frustration escaped through her clenched teeth like noisy steam. It had been a long time since she misread a situation as badly as she had the one with Darren. What a dope she'd been.

A truck rolled into the parking lot and slowed to a stop. Casey hoped the person in it would drive on. Her heart sank when a figure stepped from the truck and moved in her direction. She kept her eyes on the ground and hoped her body language would convey her desire to be left alone.

"So you've found my thinking place." Casey's eyes snapped up to find Darren ten feet away. She jumped as if she were guilty of an embarrassing public act and blushed.

"It's okay. I don't have a lease on the bench or anything." He chuckled, then frowned, puzzled by her behavior. "What are you doing here?" he asked.

The thought crossed her mind that he was schizophrenic. Her puzzlement and hurt made her bold.

"Me? I'm sitting here thinking of things like life, marriage, lies...." She did not attempt to soften her voice. She wanted to hurt him.

"Oh." He looked down at his shoes, then back at Casey. He gestured to the table next to her. "May I?"

"It's a public park. I guess you can sit where you please." She slid farther from the place he indicated.

He sat on the table, then stared at his hands. "I bet you think I'm a real jerk, don't you?"

"I'm surprised, that's for sure. Wasn't it in this very park you told me clearly you weren't marrying Carol?" She did not pull her punches. She had to know.

"Yes, I did."

"You lied?"

"At the time there was nothing between us." He looked from his hands to her eyes and held them with sincerity.

"So this new romance blossomed in the last few months, and now you're getting married?"

"That's not quite the way it is."

"Are you marrying Carol in a few weeks or not?"

"Yes, I am." Darren rubbed his hands on his thighs. Casey wanted to shake him. She faced him more directly.

"Darren, I thought we might have been something. If that's not the case, I'll live. But I also thought we could be friends, regardless of whether it went any further." She looked at him, and he raised his eyes to hers. "As a friend I'm asking you, what on earth are you doing?"

"Have you ever wondered what it was like for Enoch?" Darren looked off into the distance and spoke in a quiet voice. She frowned and started in surprise. "It says in the Bible that Enoch walked so close to God that one day God took him. Have you ever wondered what it must have been like to hear him so clearly there was little difference between being here and being there?" He shook his head in wonder. "All my life I've wanted to be close to God like that. I've wanted to hear him and talk to him and have him direct my life." Darren's eyes became a deeper shade of blue as he spoke.

Casey watched him, listened to the sound of his gentle voice, and knew he would get to the point eventually.

"When I found the Body, I think I went a little crazy. I was excited to find people who were a bit like Enoch." He smiled. "Nobody disappeared from one day to the next, of course, but they appeared to walk a lot closer to God than I did. So I made some heavy decisions and put my life into the hands of the Body." He gave her a sharp look. "You did too."

She nodded, and he turned his gaze back to the trees across the park. Casey slid off one shoe to ease a blister her hasty walk had raised.

"When I came here, I was told I would be attempting the impossible. I thought they were joking," he said, "but I came to see they were right. It's impossible to live the life I must live while encased in this flesh." He lifted his arms, looked at them, and let them fall back into his lap. "So I had to die to this flesh from the very first day. It's been the hardest, ugliest, and most wonderful thing I've ever tried to do."

"How does this relate to—"

He raised one hand and dropped it to his knee again. "I have to lay out the background for you to understand. You see, I'm not marrying Carol because I've fallen in love with her. I'm doing it because it's the Body's will—and I've put myself under the Body's will in all things."

"You don't love her? How can you marry her then?"

"I feel God has told me clearly that this is what I should do." For once his deep voice didn't move her. "He spoke to me through the Brothers and Webster, and I saw it clearly then." He gazed off and seemed to see something she could not.

"What did they tell you? How could anybody talk you into this, when you know it's wrong?"

"What's wrong is that it took me so long to see it," he said. "But others saw it, and they took the time to tell me what they saw. One of the brothers actually had a vision one morning when we were praying. It was extraordinary." He turned to her with solemn intensity, and she was powerless to stop his words. Part of her hoped he could help her see it as clearly as he did.

As he described the vision, Casey watched his hands betray his agitation as they made endless circles around his knees. "Webster told me to go and think about the vision and try to make sense of it." He shook his head and looked around him, then gestured to another table under the trees. "I sat over there the whole day, read my Bible, and tried to figure it out. I couldn't find anything to hang the images on and gave up in defeat."

"But what did it mean? It was just a dream somebody had. You can't base your life on that."

"The next morning, I had to meet privately with Webster." Darren continued as if she'd never interrupted. "He explained the meaning God had given him for the vision, and although I didn't like it, I saw the logic, and I felt the conviction." He looked at Casey. "He said I wanted my own way in having a relationship with you, even though it wouldn't be good for the Body. He said I didn't want to bend my will to the Spirit and accept God's direction for my life."

"How did he know we were thinking about a relationship at all?" Casey felt fear and irritation that she'd been the subject of such a discussion.

"He knew. He said the whole Body knew, and it trembled."

"How could it have any impact on the Body at all?" Casey leaned toward Darren to see his expression more clearly.

His eyes avoided hers. "We were going to put what we wanted ahead of what the Body needed. We're both new to the Body; it makes us vulnerable. We need people to guide us into the deeper experience of the Body, people who've experienced it for a longer time than we have." He shook his head. "When I talked with Webster, he showed me I've reached a point in my life where I have to advance or retreat. I can retreat into myself, or I can advance and pick up my responsibilities in the Body. I chose to go with the direction of the Brothers. I feel it's a matter of spiritual life or death for me." He turned and faced Casey, his eyes dark in their concentration.

She shuddered. "Listen to what you're saying. You're going to marry someone you don't love because somebody else told you a story and then interpreted it to mean they think you should."

"I'm choosing to follow life, even if I don't understand it, even if I don't agree with it. I want to follow the Body and the Spirit."

"This isn't the Spirit—it's craziness. These are decisions that will affect the rest of your life, and you're letting other people make them." Despair rose up like fog around her. She leaned forward to say more, but his dreamy expression took her off guard.

"Decisions that will affect the rest of my life? I hope so. I hope I've reached the point where I can make choices the Spirit leads me to make for no more reason or logic than that the Spirit has asked it." He rose from the table and dusted off the seat of his slacks.

"This is modern America, not Europe in the Middle Ages! We don't arrange marriages here."

He faced her and held his hands out in supplication. "I'm not talking about America. I'm talking about the kingdom of God. I'm moving into the next phase in my spiritual growth. I can see you don't understand. I hope you will some day."

He turned to go, but her voice held him in place. "Before they decide who *I* am to marry? Is that what you're implying? How many families here got started this way?"

Darren turned back to her. "This Body has many strong, godly marriages that have stood the test of time. I've yet to talk to a couple that didn't come about as a result of a Brother's vision. I think you have to admit that what frightens you is the loss of control." He looked into her eyes and nodded as though he had verified something he expected to see there. "Maybe someday, when you're ready to deny your will and take on the Body's will, the Brothers will have a vision for you that will be perfect for your life." His voice dropped to a whisper. "I hope and pray that's the case."

His departing footsteps made soft swishing sounds through the grass, then louder thuds as he walked across the asphalt to his truck and got in. Casey felt her world rock and crack open as she watched the truck's taillights disappear from sight.

PART III

I have gone astray like a lost sheep; seek Your servant, for I do not forget Your commandments.

—PSALM 119:176

25

The sound of plates and cutlery carried down the hallway to Casey's room, but it stirred no hunger. She sat on the bed with her back against the wall, her knees drawn to her chest. Andrew leaned against her in warm comfort. She stroked him and let her eyes roam the room.

Everything she owned had taken on a new personality when she moved it from her home to this small room. Things accustomed to breathing space now sat together in tight formation. She could almost feel their claustrophobia, and it echoed her own. She shook her head and wondered how this had happened. It was wonderful when it started, yet now she hid in her room in misery and felt an urgent need to escape the Body altogether.

She wished she could talk to Lydia, but her illness made it impossible. Casey glanced at the wall that divided their rooms and wondered for the hundredth time what was wrong with her friend. Casey needed someone well and strong right now.

When she thought of strength and solidarity, Jessie Barlow's dark, smile-creased face, warm eyes, and deep, chuckling voice came to mind. She took a deep breath and remembered their last conversation. She had hung up on Jessie. There could be no comfort there. Or could there?

With growing hope, Casey reached across the bed and lifted her purse. She rummaged through it until she found the compact phone. It had worked its way to the bottom in the weeks since she made a mental note to mail it back. Now it rested in her palm like an oversized black bug.

Casey looked at the door and verified that the lock was pushed in. She unfolded the phone. She had never owned a cellular phone, so she examined it closely. She assumed if she pressed the power button, then the number and the "Send" button, the phone would work.

To keep any beeps from escaping, she placed her thumb over the grille on the earpiece and touched a few buttons. The sound was absorbed. Heartened, she punched in the number written on the paper that had been wrapped around the phone and hit "Send." Halfway through the third ring, Claude's deep voice filled her ear. Casey was startled to hear him and would have hung up, but she wasn't sure how with the cellular phone. She did the only thing she could think of on the spur of the moment.

"May I speak to Jessie?" She spoke quietly, and again sneaked a look at the door. There was a pause on the other end of the line.

"I'm sorry, I can barely hear you. Did you ask for Jessie? Can I say who's calling?" Claude's liquid, confident voice gave Casey courage.

"Tell her Casey." She whispered as loud as she dared.

Claude lowered his own voice. "Hold on. I'll get her right away."

The phone was muffled, then Jessie's voice came on the line. "Casey? Where are you?"

"I have to talk quietly. Can you hear me okay?" Casey heard the sound of dishes rattling and appliances running.

"I can't hear you. Hold on a second, honey." There were ten seconds of silence before Jessie's voice came through clear and unaccompanied by household sounds. "Say something again, and let me try here."

"What did you do?"

"I came outside. It's a lot quieter. I can hear you fine. Now what's up?" Jessie's voice was careful and measured. It wrapped Casey's sore heart with peace.

"I'm so sorry. I was such an idiot the other day," Casey said in a rush. "I have a lot to say to you right now, but first I need to know you forgive me."

"There's nothing to forgive, sweetie. I'm glad you called." Casey heard her settle onto a chair on the patio, and its iron legs made a telltale shriek on the concrete.

"I may have to hang up in a hurry. If I do, how do I turn off the phone?"

"You press *End*, then *Power*. Why would you have to hang up?"

Casey pulled the telephone from her ear, located the two buttons she would need, and then returned it to her cheek. "I need to tell you some things, and I don't want you to interrupt. Is that all right?"

"I'm all ears."

"I told you when we had lunch there was someone I was interested in here. I have to say, the way they do things here is a bit old-fashioned. No one dates. We get together as a group on Visiting Night. Someone here told me Darren was engaged to a girl in the house where I live. It's called the Sisters House, because single women live here." Casey took another deep breath and realized she had a lot of ground to cover for Jessie to get the full picture. It made her tired to think of it. "Anyway, I had a chance to talk to Darren about it one day when he picked me up while I was walking to work in the rain. He said it wasn't true and made it pretty clear he'd like to get to know me." Casey shook her head. "I'm not telling this well. That's not the point at all."

"Case, take your time. I'll listen all night if you need me to. Tell it any way you want. I'll sort it out in my head later."

The warmth in Jessie's voice melted her heart. She reached for a tissue from the box at the head of her bed. She caught a tear as it slid down her face, and bit her lip. "Thanks," she whispered. "You're the best." She was too choked up to speak. At last her throat opened, and she took a shuddering breath. "I'm sorry to blubber. I'll try to get through this." She stretched her legs to ease the cramps she felt in her thighs. "We had a special series of Gatherings this weekend. At the end Webster announced that Darren was indeed going to marry my housemate, Carol."

"Oh, honey, I'm sorry. He sounded nice when you talked about him at lunch."

"I didn't lose him to Carol. He doesn't love her at all. He told me so."

"But he must, if he's going to marry her."

"He's marrying her because the Brothers told him to." Casey's voice was flat.

"Just who are these Brothers who are telling people what to do?"

"The Brothers tell everyone in the Body what the Spirit reveals to them." She put up her hand as if she could stop Jessie's objections. "Now isn't the time to debate the rightness or wrongness. I agree with you, or I wouldn't be calling. Darren told me all the long-term couples in the Body got started this way." She paused. "Jessie, that's *dozens* of couples who were told to get married." Casey let her words sink in for a moment and then pressed on. "When I came here, I was so sure I'd found something beyond anything on earth, but now I see ugly and ungodly things going on below the surface. It scares me."

"It scares me too. What can I do to help you? Do you want me to drive up there right now and bring you home?"

"I'm not sure what I want or why I called." Casey rubbed her temple.

"I know why you called. The Spirit told you to reach out to somebody who could grab you as you fell. I'm honored you chose me." Casey sniffled and reached for a tissue. "I think you know there are things in the group you don't want to be associated with and can't condone. Give serious thought to getting away from there. Tell me what and where and when and how. I'll be there."

"You don't know how I've tied myself to the Body." Misery saturated Casey's voice.

"When I was a little girl," Jessie said, "I had a very wonderful grandmother. I used to spend a few weeks each summer with her. I remember one time she found me crying over a little necklace. It was twisted into a terrible knot. I cried and carried on and said it was ruined. She sat down beside me on the stoop, patted me on the back, then took the chain and began the intricate work of untangling it. 'Jessie, girl,' she said, 'whatever is tied can be untied.' Then she got the knot out for me. It took her awhile, but she did it, and I never forgot it."

Casey blotted another tear and slid down farther on the bed as she listened.

"I say the same to you. I don't care how you're tied to the group. Whatever is tied can be untied, and I'm willing to help you do it. You know, Claude and I have been praying our way around this Jericho for months. We love you very much. So if you hear the trumpet blow and the walls start to crack, don't try to hold them up. Climb over the rubble and come home."

"Thanks," Casey whispered. "I've got to go now. I'll call you again soon, I promise. I need to think."

"Be sure to plug the charger in the wall and hook the phone to it so it's ready when you need it. Call any time. We'll always be here for you."

Casey ended the call, then slipped her hand down the wall next to her bed until she found the outlet she recalled seeing and had never needed. She plugged in the charger and settled the phone behind a pillow, deep under the bed to charge. Somehow, doing so was like keeping hold of Jessie's hand, and she fell asleep with a smile.

26

From her seat at the breakfast table, Casey watched Amy set the wicker meal tray on the kitchen counter.

Carol glanced up as she scrubbed a heavy pot in the sink. "Is that going out or coming back?"

"Coming back." Amy frowned. "The way she's eating, it's hard to tell, isn't it?"

"You mean the way she's *not* eating. Brother Eric said he'd be by this morning. We'd better leave the tray and ask him if we should change what we give her." Carol returned to her pot scrubbing.

Casey rose out of habit and picked up a towel from the rack suspended below the cabinets. She started to dry the items Carol had already washed and rinsed. "Has he said what he thinks is wrong? I mean she doesn't get better, no matter what he tries. Maybe she should go to the hospital." Lydia's increased weakness frightened her, and she was desperate to find a way to help her.

"The Brothers talked after the Gathering last night," Carol said. "They told Brother Eric to do whatever he felt was necessary."

"The Brothers?" Casey felt her blood pressure rise. "What have they got to do with Lydia's treatment? They aren't doctors. Why were they even talking about it?" She set down the cup she'd been drying, fearful she would drop it or throw it.

"The Brothers are consulted about everything. You know that," Carol smirked. "That's their function in the Body."

"I know they're consulted!" Casey's voice rose. "But I ask you again, what do they have to do with Lydia's treatment? I realize you're pleased with what they've decided for you, but Lydia's very life may hang in the balance here!" Her eyes blazed, and Amy took a step forward as if to block her if she lashed out at Carol. Casey didn't intend to do so, but the anguish on Amy's face helped her to cool down.

"Yes, I do think the Brothers know what they're doing." Carol smiled smugly. "You'd better put a little effort into getting on their good side or you could find yourself not liking their choices for your life."

It was more than Casey could stand. "I'm not likely to allow myself to become as mindlessly obedient as all of you seem to have become." Her hands contracted into fists. "If that's the admission price to this little group, I hope I never manage to pay it!" She turned and left the kitchen, letting the louvered doors swing wildly behind her.

She knew her words and attitude would shortly be conveyed to Grace and the Brothers. There would be repercussions. She didn't care. Carol gloating over her victory was more than Casey could stomach. If she weren't so concerned about Lydia, she'd pack her bags right then. She slowed her stomping to quiet steps so as not to disturb her any more than she probably already had.

What on earth was wrong with Lydia, she wondered.

"She said that?" Webster's eyebrows crept farther up his forehead as he listened to Carol's recital of her confrontation with Casey the previous morning. He turned to Grace, who sat in the small circle of people assembled in the Gathering Place. "I think you have a problem here, my dear."

"I think we've had a problem with her since she first came to a small group in Grovers." Stephanie's cool voice cut off whatever Grace had planned to say to defend herself. "She's never given herself to the Body. She never will. She's one of those who come, then go—and good riddance."

"No!" The exclamation from Kurt was anguished. "She's not

like that." He turned on Carol. "You must have misunderstood what she meant."

"I understood, Kurt. It's you who has lost the ability to see." She tapped his glasses where the frame bridged his nose.

He jerked away from her and turned to Webster. "She'll be all right, wait and see. She needs the right member of the Body to bring her along."

"And you're the right member, Kurt?" Stephanie's mocking tone turned serious as she leaned forward in her chair. "If she's going to be salvaged, now's the time. If not, it's best to cut our losses and move on." Tension overshadowed them all.

"I think Stephanie is right." Grace said. They looked to Grace and avoided Kurt's frantic eyes. "At least partly. This is the time to salvage the effort we've put into Casey. I think it can be done, and if it doesn't work, the sooner we know, the better."

"Why bother?" Stephanie crossed her long, thin arms and leaned back. "We've cut people loose who were better candidates than she is."

Grace headed Kurt off with a glance before he could reply. "They weren't as useful to us as Casey is." She held the thin woman's eyes, then shifted her gaze to Webster. "Have you found her work satisfactory, dear?"

"She's got real skill when it comes to the books and other materials." He stretched his long legs into the small circle they made. "I think she's worth an effort."

"Then what do you want us to do?" Carol asked.

"What I have in mind will take more than the women in your house to accomplish. It will take the whole Body." Grace turned her cold eyes to Kurt. "I think nothing but death will save her." Her voice was low and husky.

Kurt blanched. His head dropped, and his breathing quickened.

Dominic spoke up for the first time. "That's a bit drastic, don't you think? And it's labor intensive. Can we manage it with the wedding to take care of?"

"I've thought about that," Grace said. "I don't think we can do both unless we do them at the same time. That will make the additional activity less noticeable as well, since Carol lives at the Sisters House too."

"So we let her stew for a month?" Stephanie's eyes bulged in disbelief. "Her attitude will spread to others by then, or she'll be gone on her own steam. A month is a long time."

"That's why we're moving the wedding up to the weekend after this one." Grace dropped her bombshell.

Webster eyed Carol and saw a slight jolt go through her. He knew she liked the idea of marrying Darren but hadn't accustomed herself to the reality yet. The change in date would get everyone moving a little faster in the Body, and Grace was clearly enjoying their discomfort. Webster leaned forward and put his hands on his knees, prepared to rise. "So, are we in agreement?" It was clear he expected no opposition to Grace's plan, and he got none. "Good." His mouth was a thin line. "I think we all have work to do, so let's be about it."

The others rose as he did. Within ninety seconds the room was left empty and silent.

"What day is this?" Lydia asked, though her eyes didn't open.

Casey leaned closer from her post in the chair beside the bed.

"Hey, I didn't know you were awake," she whispered. "You've been holding out on me." When she saw a small grin cross Lydia's face, she patted her arm. "To answer your question, this is Saturday."

"Morning, afternoon, or night?" Lydia kept her eyes closed. The curtains in the room were drawn.

"Half and half," Casey replied. "It's almost noon, so not morning, but not afternoon either. Why? Do you have a pressing appointment I should know about?" She was delighted to see the grin break all the way across Lydia's face.

"Didn't I tell you? Today is my debut appearance with the symphony ballet. I'm dancing the lead in *The Nutcracker*."

Casey snickered. "You have that right, my friend. You're the biggest nut I've ever met." She gently squeezed Lydia's frail hand as it lay atop a patchwork quilt that swallowed her in the bed. Lydia smiled.

"Am I to take it you're feeling better today? I don't recall dancing being on the agenda for the last few weeks."

A small frown crossed Lydia's smooth forehead. "Has it been so long? I'm sorry."

"Sorry you got sick? I never saw you stand on the corner with a sign saying, 'Want to be sick. Please expose me to something.'"

"I'm such a bother. I never intended to be."

"No one ever does, and you're not."

"Well, at least it won't be for long," she said.

Casey studied her face and saw peace there. "Then you're beginning to feel better at last." A small bubble of optimism tickled her heart. "I've missed you so."

Lydia opened her eyes to small slits to see her friend's face. "How could you miss me? You've sat here for hours at a time. What's to miss?"

"I knew you'd been holding out on me. Have you also hidden chocolate bars in this bed to tide you over between the meals you refuse to eat?" She made a show of conducting a search for evidence and was rewarded with a quiet chuckle.

"Would you eat oatmeal and Jell-O and mashed bananas if you knew you had stashed Heath bars and Butterfingers nearby?" She lifted one hand as though to point out her alleged storage place, but the effort was too much, and her hand fell back to the coverlet.

"It's a funny way to get attention," Casey teased to hide her dismay.

With no warning Andrew leaped from the floor and paced along the far side of the bed. He began to purr as soon as his feet touched the blankets, and his happy noise became louder the closer he got to Lydia's face.

"Andrew! Not again." Casey half rose, intent on shooing him out the door. The cat sat down next to Lydia's pillow, his tail a neat curl over his front feet, and purred even louder. Casey could not grab him without the risk of falling onto the sick woman, so she gave Andrew her special *I-am-not-pleased* look. It had its usual effect—none.

Lydia rolled her head in Andrew's direction. "Hello, sweetheart," she breathed. "Have you come to be my knight in shining fur again?" She looked at Casey. "He comes in here every time you let him out, you know. Except when Carol sits with me. I think he knows she'd report him. He's very bright."

"I'm sorry. I'll keep him in my room. I don't want him to disturb you."

"I like his company. There's nothing like a nice cat purr when you feel lonely. I enjoy him." Casey settled back into her chair.

"It's strange that he doesn't trust Carol."

"I think he's a good judge of character." Casey snorted. Lydia forced her eyes open again. "I need to talk to you about things, and I need you to adjust my pillows so I can sit up a bit. I don't want to fall asleep before I'm done talking."

"Maybe more sleep is what you need. We can talk when you're better."

"No, we need to talk now." Casey relented and lifted Lydia's head and shoulders with one arm and adjusted her pillows with the other, then settled her back.

After several deep breaths Lydia reached out a feather-light hand and stroked Andrew as he sat beside her. He ran his tongue over her wrist and hand to reward her. After a gentle rub against her arm, he blinked at her and paced with soft steps back to the foot of the bed. He jumped down to the carpeted floor and wiggled out the door, his tail and head high.

"He always knows how much I can stand, then he goes away. He's remarkable." Lydia looked after the disappearing cat with tender eyes. Soft blonde hair fanned out from her head on the pillow and made her face look smaller. Her eyes looked enormous, now that they were open. "I've had time to think while I lay here. I wasn't holding out on you. I was too tired to talk."

"I was teasing. I knew you couldn't talk. I was surprised to find you were conscious at all." Casey reached for Lydia's hand and stroked the long, thin fingers.

"When you lie still and your eyes are closed, people think you can't tell who's in the room, and they think you're deaf, too. I heard all kinds of things I wasn't supposed to hear." The small smile dashed across Lydia's lips. "Much of what I heard was about you, though it doesn't take eavesdropping to realize you're unhappy. In many ways I feel your unhappiness is my fault, and it worries me."

"You have been nothing but a steadfast friend to me. How could you think you have any part in my unhappiness?"

"So, you *are* unhappy." Lydia's statement allowed no argument. "And I am the one who brought you to it."

"I made my own choices, start to finish."

"Yes, but you had nudging, and I was the one who did it." After several seconds of silence, Lydia's weak voice continued. "I think it's time you leave."

"I've tired you. I'm sorry." Casey looked at her watch and braced her hands on the arms of the chair to stand up.

"No, I mean leave this place. This house. The Body." Lydia's words stopped Casey in midmotion.

"Leave? And go where?"

"This Body is a very small universe, my friend. There's a whole big world out there within the body of Christ. You need to go. This place will not nurture your spirit as it needs to be nurtured." Lydia shook her head. "I've been even more foolish than you. I've been taken in too, but for much longer, and I drew you and others in."

"What do you mean?" Casey was rocked by Lydia's confession.

"It's like the old Wild West towns in the movies—all facade and no substance. The Body doesn't deliver on its promises. It doesn't free; it imprisons. It doesn't produce growth; it stunts it. It doesn't bring us closer to God; it makes us more like each other. It's all a facade."

Casey bit her lower lip and met Lydia's eyes. "I've had the same thought but pushed it down. I never expected to hear it from you."

Lydia struggled to sit up and leaned toward Casey, bracing herself on one thin arm. "You must go soon. Your unhappiness is read as rebellion, and it can't be tolerated. Very soon life here will become extremely unpleasant for you. You must go before then. Promise me."

"Come with me, and we'll both start fresh." Casey felt a spark of hope. "I'll take care of you until you're on your feet, and we'll help each other put our lives back together."

Lydia eased herself back onto the pillows and shook her head. "I can't go with you."

"Why? You see the same things I do. How can you stay? What hold can they have on you to make you stay?"

"I won't be here long. Then I'll be free."

"Then come with me now. Don't delay, since you plan to leave anyway."

Lydia's smile was the saddest Casey had ever seen. "I will be free, but not like you. I won't get better. I'm going to get worse soon, then I'll die."

Casey's heart lurched. Her ears roared.

"No."

"I'm afraid there's no doubt. Brother Eric has come and gone innumerable times and run all the tests he needs to run. There's no mistake. I've known for some time, but he confirmed it a few days ago."

"What is it?"

"Cancer. That's the cause of the pain, and the weakness."

"I'll take you to a hospital." Casey thought through how she would carry Lydia to the car. "We'll get treatment. No one has the right to deny you treatment. Who are these Brothers anyway?" She heard hysteria in her own voice.

"No one is denying me treatment," Lydia reassured her. "There's no point in starting treatment that won't make me well, and will make me a good deal sicker before I die. I choose not to take that route. There's no point."

"Oh, Lydia! You can't die!" Casey's throat closed.

"If I didn't know I was leaving you in the capable hands of Jesus, I'd refuse to go. I meant what I said. You must leave as soon as you can. They have plans to bring you into line. It's not something you want to go through. I've seen it happen to others."

"What do you mean? What can they do?"

Lydia shook her head. "Take Andrew and go. There's nothing in this house you can't replace. Don't think twice, just go."

"And leave you here like this?"

"Yes."

"I won't."

"I've lived in the Bodylife too long. I don't want to die alone. I want to have people around me."

"I'll be there with you." Casey felt the tears dampen her cheeks. She tried to blink them away as they hid her view of Lydia.

"I plan to spend my last weeks repenting my part in bringing several people—especially you—into the Bodylife and all its deception. Who knows? I might be able to send a few more out before I'm done."

"Lydia, you can't martyr yourself like this. I'll find a way to get you out, and we'll get treatment for you. You might be wrong about this. People with cancer go into remission all the time."

"I've been in remission for ten years. I know all about it." Casey was startled. "I had cancer when I was in my early thirties. Then I got lucky, but I knew within weeks when it came back, and I also know there's no third chance for me."

It explained a great deal, Casey thought—Lydia's profound silences, her deep warmth that sometimes drifted into melancholy. If she had thought about it, she would have realized that Lydia had all the traits she had come to recognize in people who had danced with death.

"I want you to make plans today," Lydia urged. "Don't put it off. Things will come to a head soon, and you need to be gone before they do."

"You'll have to pray for me, because I can't just leave you. If I'm to go, God will have to give me the strength."

Casey saw lines of worry on Lydia's forehead fade as exhaustion took over. She lifted Lydia's head and shoulders again, removed the second pillow, eased her down, and pulled up the blanket. Lydia was fast asleep and did not feel her ministrations.

Casey moved silently to the door, then turned back to watch Lydia as tears dropped unheeded from her watery eyes.

"What am I going to do?" she whispered hoarsely.

27

Casey stood in the doorway of her room and tried to make sense of what she saw. Boxes were everywhere, but they were unfamiliar in shape and marking.

Amy's dark-framed pixie face popped up from behind a large box, and she jumped when she saw Casey. Her small hand flew to her chest and pressed against her rumpled blouse.

"I think I'm more startled than you are. What happened?" Casey's eyes roamed the room in sudden concern.

Amy read her almost as well as Lydia did. "Andrew's fine. He's in your room."

"This is my room, or it was when I left this morning."

Amy collapsed onto the top of a box and pulled off the bandanna tied around her hair. She mopped the back of her neck and blotted her face with it as she spoke. "Grace surprised us with an inspection this morning right after you left for work. It seems we weren't as obedient to the teaching about getting attached to things of the world as we should be, so she told us to move to different rooms." Amy stretched and winced. "We've been at it all day."

"What's a room got to do with attachment to things?"

"We get settled into one place, and pretty soon we begin to call it 'my room' or 'my space.' That's bad. It shows a pride of possession."

Casey looked at Amy's earnest face and realized that at least part of her believed what she had been told. She decided not to fight it and took a light tone to get beyond her anger. "So, which space do I now occupy, without getting attached to it?" She forced a smile despite her seething frustration.

Amy looked relieved by her response. "You came out pretty well. You have the room at the end, the one with its own bathroom."

Casey decided a bathroom made up for the inconvenience of the ridiculous situation. She stepped out the door, eager to verify that Andrew was safe. If her old room was chaotic, it was nothing compared to her new one. Amy had spent all day putting her own things to rights. Although others had moved Casey's possessions, no one had put anything away. Andrew crouched on top of bed linens piled in a chair. He meowed when she appeared.

"Oh, sweetheart." She closed the door and picked him up. She held him close, tucked his head under her chin, and stroked him as she comforted him. She surveyed the disarray, then sat on the bed, still holding the cat. She gave her full attention to rubbing and scratching his favorite spots and was rewarded moments later with the first distant rumbles of a purr.

"That's better, old boy." She kissed the top of his head. "I know it's been a tough day for you, and I'm sorry I wasn't here. It'll be all right, you'll see. It's only for a while. I promise."

The cat blinked as he enjoyed her touch and voice and settled in to lick her hands as she stroked him. Casey knew they drew strength from each other, and clearly both felt a great deal better when at last she rose from the bed. Andrew began to explore.

The room did indeed have a tiny bathroom. While it didn't have a tub, it had a shower. In a house full of women with one bathroom in the hallway, it was an unimaginable luxury to have even a small bathroom. Casey shoved Andrew's litter box under the sink and ran fresh water in his bowl. She poked about, found his food bag, and poured a bit of the dry cat food he loved into his decorative ceramic bowl. When he settled in to munch, her spirits lifted.

She decided she would enjoy the room while she could, and mused that her movers had done her a favor by packing up all her belongings. She would leave soon enough, and it would save her the trouble. If only she could figure out what to do about Lydia.

Thoughts of her friend drove Casey to the door once more. She waved quickly to Andrew, who was busy washing his paws and rubbing them over his face. She went out into the hall and headed for Lydia's room.

Everyone in the house except Lydia, who was too sick to move, was jumpy and out of sorts. Casey assumed it was the upheaval of the household after Grace's order and did her best to stay out of their way. She knew her disillusionment with the Bodylife clung to her like a scent, and she stayed in Lydia's room all evening to avoid snapping at the others.

With each moment Casey spent in the bedside chair, more of Lydia slipped away from her and from life. She longed to see the blush of good health back on her friend's cheek, but instead saw a rough, unhealthy ruddiness that accented her overall pallor.

She looked around the room that so expressed Lydia's personality. There were the rows of books of Bible exposition; dried flowers and simple fabric accents that made the room cozy and welcoming; and her closet, filled with simple, no-frills jumpers and shirts. When she looked back to the bed, she was surprised to find Lydia's eyes studying her as she had studied the room.

"Hey, sleepyhead," she whispered. "I was about to go get Prince Andrew to come and awaken Sleeping Beauty again. How are you feeling?"

A grimace flitted across Lydia's face and was gone. In its place appeared an unearthly peace.

"I feel fine." She smiled. "Never better."

It broke Casey's heart that Lydia made light of her illness. She pressed Lydia's hand with care. The bones in her fingers seemed to shift around in their skin glove.

"You don't have to pretend for me. If you want to scream, go ahead. I won't think less of you."

"I think I'm past the screaming stage. The Lord has given me the blessing of numbness. I know it's only a matter of time before the gnawing beast returns."

"I hope all the bumping and banging today didn't keep you from resting."

"What was all that anyway? No one told me." Lydia looked puzzled.

"You're not the only one." Casey let her exasperation surface. "Grace decided today was the ideal day for a round of musical chairs—or rooms." Lydia was still uncomprehending. "She told Amy and Rita to move everyone's stuff from one room to another—everyone but you, thank goodness."

"Then who is in the room next to mine?" Lydia looked at the wall between her room and what had been Casey's room. It appeared to upset her more than Casey had anticipated.

"Amy. Andrew and I are in Carol's old room, but we've got our own bathroom, so it's not all bad."

"You have to leave here!" Lydia's eyes flashed to her friend's face. She appeared panicked. "Don't settle into that room. Make your plans, pack up Andrew, and *go.*"

"Now don't get all upset." Casey made soothing sounds as she would to a child or a small animal. "I'm making my plans. They did all my packing for me." She attempted a levity she didn't feel.

"This weekend is the wedding, isn't it?" Lydia closed her eyes and let her head sink into the pillow.

"Yes, Sunday, right after the Gathering. I figure it will keep them occupied for a few days. I'll go before they have time to get their feet back under them." Casey said it though she knew she couldn't leave her dying friend while she stole away.

"I think you're right. They'll be too busy to bother with you for a few days." Her eyes opened halfway, which Casey thought was as far as she could manage. "Remember, you said you'd go. I am holding you to your promise." The thought that Lydia could hold her to anything was ludicrous. She could get out of bed only with great effort.

"I think it's time for both of us to get some sleep." Casey didn't want to debate the issue again. She yawned and looked at her watch.

"No, we have to have this clear first. I want your word you'll go." Lydia's eyes burned bright with illness and determination.

Casey dropped her eyes and tried to think of a way to avoid what Lydia demanded. "We'll talk more tomor—"

"I won't sleep until I have your promise."

Casey ran her fingers through her hair in frustration as she heard the resolve in Lydia's voice. They locked eyes and the silence stretched between them. She couldn't stand the pleading in Lydia's eyes. "I promise," she whispered miserably.

Lydia nodded, then her eyes closed and she moved her index finger in an abbreviated wave before she lapsed into sleep.

Casey sat and watched Lydia's chest rise and fall for another ten minutes. Her silent tears fell while she considered scenario after scenario to remove Lydia from the house with the least fuss for all concerned. None of the plans she played out in her head were without snags. At last, confused and depressed, she dimmed the light next to Lydia's bed and tiptoed out to return to her new room and continue her thoughts in restless sleep.

Casey awoke with a headache she knew would be with her all day. She squinted to shut out the morning sunlight and rolled over to look at the clock. It wasn't there.

Puzzled, she opened her eyes further and saw chaos all around her. For an instant she was confused. Then, with the rush of remembrance, her anger returned like a white flame. The clock wasn't where it was supposed to be because she wasn't where she was supposed to be.

Andrew raised his head from the neat round bundle his body made in its curled space next to her pillow. He made a desultory effort to drag his tongue over his furry side a few times, then returned to sleep.

Casey pushed back the light blanket that covered her and moved toward the bathroom. The novelty of her own bathroom pleased her. She ran water over her hands and patted them across her eyes; the cool refreshment brought instant alertness. After she toweled her face dry, she drifted back into the bedroom and began to dress for the day. Even though it was Friday, all work at the office was halted by preparations for the wedding scheduled for Sunday. Every spare pair of hands would be called on to prepare food or help with other tasks. She delayed as long as possible, since she hated the idea of helping prepare for a wedding she didn't believe should take place.

Stalling, she sat on the bed to pet Andrew. She heard a babble of voices. She frowned, listened, and tried to sort out who was in the house. A cold finger of dismay crossed her shoulder blades when she heard one particular voice in the hall. Knuckles rapped sharply on her door, and it opened to frame Grace. She stepped in without asking permission and shut the door behind her. She wiped her hands against each other as if the doorknob had been dirty and turned to survey the disorganized room. Casey decided to take the offensive.

"Good morning, Grace. Why, yes, do come in." She let her displeasure crackle in her voice. Grace took the rude tone in stride.

"I see you haven't made much of a dent in putting this stuff away yet. You know, Amy had all her things put away before she went to bed last night."

"Well I guess I'm not as used to moving as Amy no doubt is by now." Anger grew within her, and she tried to master it. Grace narrowed her eyes and moved to the chair near Casey's bed. She lifted off a box, set it on the floor, and settled herself.

"I think it's time you and I had a little talk. Your behavior is something of an embarrassment to the whole Body, and it must stop."

"Just what behavior is that?" Casey seethed, her voice acidic. "Thinking for myself? Expressing my own thoughts? Disagreeing with something you or Webster has said? Which is it?"

"All of those things are divisive in the Body." Grace's staccato speech echoed in the box-filled room. "The Body functions because its members all go in the same direction, but right now this Body has a twitch in one finger that is driving the rest of the Body crazy."

"Perhaps it's the twitch being driven crazy by the Body."

"Do you think you are the first person to ever come to this Body and have a rebellious thought like that?" Red crept up Grace's neck, and the expression on her face turned cruel and ugly. Her eyes flashed over Casey. "You are nothing more than that," she snapped her fingers, "in the history of this Body. Many have come and gone who thought they were smarter than the rest of us. They were wrong. Many who left crawled back later."

"I can't refute that." Casey tried again to get her anger under control. "All I know is, things are happening in this group that aren't good for all of us." She had said it. She blinked in surprise at her own audacity.

"I think it's time you learn what is good for you, as you put it, and what is not." Grace's voice was low, frightening. "You need to get past this, for your own good and the good of the Body. You must die to yourself, utterly."

"Maybe a month ago I could have gone for that. Now I have a better idea—" Grace jumped to her feet and cut off Casey's words as if she had hit her.

"I don't want to hear your ideas. All I want to hear is your acceptance of the headship of the Body and the right of the Brothers to direct your life." She moved quickly to the door and then turned with her hand on the knob. "It's time for you to die, Casey, and now is when you get started."

Casey stared, wide-eyed. She didn't know what Grace meant, and she didn't like her cruel tone.

"This room will be your tomb. Like Jesus you need to pass through the grave to come out the other side. Three days from now we'll open this door, and you will confess that what I have told you is true about the Body and your place in it." With a swift motion

Grace lifted a plastic grocery bag from the hall and deposited it in the room. Casey felt strength flood back into her legs, and she quickly stood.

"This is ridiculous. I'm not going to stay in my room for three days like a bad girl."

Grace's thin smile never made it to her cheeks, much less to her eyes. Without another word she stepped from the room and closed the door behind her with a thud. There was a small click, then her footsteps receded down the hallway.

With the click Casey looked at the door. Unlike every other door in the house, the knobs had been reversed on this one; the lock was on the outside.

28

Casey marched to the door and grabbed the doorknob. It wouldn't turn. She tried to shake the door in its frame, but it was solid. With a final jerk, she turned and put her back to the door as her heart pounded. Claustrophobia gripped her for the first time in her life. The loss of freedom choked her and left her gasping. She pushed away from the door and stumbled across the box-strewn room to the window, intent on raising it so she could take in great gulps of air. She brushed aside the curtains and was reaching for the lock on the window when she looked outside.

Five Brothers trimmed bushes, raked the lawn, and carried buckets of plants for transplanting into the yard. She froze, watched their activity, and assessed what their reaction would be if she opened the window and climbed out. She had no doubt the pretense of yard work would be abandoned. After she had watched them for a minute, her thoughts began to clear.

She pondered what they could really do to her. Kill her in broad daylight in a suburban neighborhood without anyone noticing? She snorted and had almost made up her mind to open the window when a movement from the bed drew her attention.

"Andrew! Oh, my goodness, what am I thinking?" She dropped onto the bed. "I might be able to outrun them, but I can't leave you behind." She ruffled the cat's fur as the reality of her situation hit her, both Andrew and Lydia large in her mind. She leaned down and kissed the cat on the top of the head. A quiet buzz grew in his throat as he fell asleep once more.

Casey noticed the grocery bag near the door and got up to investigate. She put it on top of a box and withdrew the items—a box of saltine crackers, a jar of peanut butter, a nonserrated plastic knife, and one shiny, foil-wrapped Hershey's Kiss. Her eyes filled at the sight of the candy. It must have been Amy who decided to try to send a message to her in this simple way. She carefully lifted out the chocolate and set it aside.

As she turned back to look at the boxes filling her room, it all became clear in a blazing instant. This was the only room with a bathroom, therefore the only one someone could be shut into. The reversed doorknob was the final detail. Her possessions had no doubt been examined as they were moved, and anything useful for escape had been removed. She was immensely glad she'd been compulsive about putting the phone and charger into her big shoulder bag and taking them with her wherever she went.

Like Lydia she had known something was coming, but neither of them had expected it to happen until after the wedding. Their miscalculation had made the entire plan work for Grace. Casey felt weak at the idea of such concerted effort to imprison her and bring her to the Body's way of thinking. She stretched out on the bed, and her nauseated stomach settled. She lay there a long time, thinking through the events that had led to this incredible situation and wondering how she had missed the signs.

There had to be something she could do to get out without a direct confrontation in the yard with the Brothers. Grace was thorough, but not infallible. There must be a crack in the four walls that surrounded and menaced her. When she ran out of even the most fanciful ideas she could come up with, she sighed and did what she'd known she would have to do eventually.

"Jessie Barlow."

Casey's heart leaped when she heard the contralto voice at the other end of the line. "Thank God, you're there!"

There was a pause. "Casey? Is that you?"

"Yes, it's me. I have to whisper." She heard Jessie get up from her desk and close the door to her small office.

"Why do you have to whisper?"

"You won't believe this. I'm not sure I do." Casey took a deep breath. "Grace locked me in my room this morning. She says I have to stay here for three days until I've died to myself and accepted the way things are done here as the right way."

"You're a prisoner? Hang up right now. I'm calling 911."

"No!" Casey whispered desperately. "No, don't do that. Please."

"You can't seriously think I'll do otherwise."

"I want your help. Please don't fight me on this. Let me tell you—" She broke off as something appeared under the door, shoved through from the other side. "Hold on." She set down the phone and retrieved the index card from the floor. She frowned as she looked at the handwritten message on it. "Sorry," she said. "Someone stuck a note under the door, and I needed to see what it said."

"Well, what does it say? Are they going to let you out?"

"I'm not sure what it means. It's a verse reference." Casey was puzzled.

"I have my Bible here on my desk. What's the verse?"

"Romans 11:23." Casey heard the rapid swish of pages as Jessie located the verse, then waited to hear her read it aloud.

"I don't like this. I think we need to call the police."

Alarmed, Casey almost forgot to whisper. "What does the verse say?"

"'And they also, if they do not continue in their unbelief, will be grafted in, for God is able to graft them in again.'"

"I don't understand. What's the context?"

"Oh, I don't think the context is what they're after. It's lifted wholesale from its bed in the midst of other verses and turned on its ear to warn you that you're expected to come around to their way of thinking, or else."

"Yes, I guess you're right. Oh, what a mess."

"You're getting out of there *now*, and I will call the police to be sure that happens."

"Don't do that, please!" Casey looked at the door to be sure the knob wasn't turning. She had no control over who came and went. "It's not as simple as you think. I have Andrew to think about. Then there's Lydia. If you call the police, they'll come in here with sirens blaring. All the noise and excitement could literally kill her. Please. Let's think of another plan." Casey sensed that Jessie was ready to fight her all the way until she mentioned Lydia. She had wept her pain into the phone the night she learned that Lydia was dying, and Jessie had wept with her. Now there was hesitation in her voice.

"What do you suggest?"

"I'm not sure yet. I need to think. They're all at lunch, and there are people in the yard. I bet someone will be there all night to watch the window." Casey worked the situation through in her mind. "I need to plan. Will you promise me you won't call the police until we've tried to work this out?"

Jessie's voice was steely. "I will not call the police on one condition. No discussion on this condition, either. You must call me without fail every two hours to tell me you're okay. I mean right through the night if necessary, no excuses. If I don't hear from you, I call. Clear?"

"But what if—"

"No discussion. Deal or no deal?"

"Okay, deal." Casey felt a smile as small as a Hershey's Kiss creep across her face.

"I'll be waiting. If I don't hear from you, we stop playing this game, and we get you out of there."

"Thanks. I'll call you in a few hours with the details."

"Two hours." Jessie's voice was firm and insistent. "I shouldn't even give you that long, but I will, for Lydia."

"Aye, aye, Captain." Casey made a mock salute with her hand to her forehead. "Thanks for being there. I love you more than I can say."

"I'll be praying. Now get off the phone and get to planning."

Casey drew courage from the sternness in Jessie's voice. She turned off the phone and slid it under her pillow.

If Casey had any doubt the crackers and peanut butter were to be her entire diet for the three prescribed days, it was dispelled by the sound of people leaving the dinner table later to go about their evening chores. She sat in the dark so she could see into the well-lit backyard. To her dismay three Brothers returned to the patio and looked as if they planned to remain. There could be no escape using that route.

Casey called Jessie again at eight o'clock and told her about the situation. They talked for a few minutes and agreed to talk again at ten. Jessie again pushed to call the authorities, but Casey pleaded for more time. She knew Lydia would be even more upset by a visit from the police after sundown.

After she talked to Jessie, Casey turned on the light in her room and closed the curtains. To get out the window, she needed a diversion. She lay on her bed and tried to think of a workable solution to get her and Andrew out unnoticed. At eight thirty another card made its appearance under her door. Angered by the ridiculous method of communication, she snatched it up. It was another verse reference. She looked up 2 Corinthians 10:5–6. It alarmed her far more than the previous verses.

"We are destroying speculations and every lofty thing raised up against the knowledge of God, and we are taking every thought captive to the obedience of Christ, and we are ready to punish all disobedience, whenever your obedience is complete."

She pored over the text and read extra nuances into every word. The basic meaning seemed clear enough; this punishment was not the end of the road, but the beginning. She redoubled her efforts to devise a workable plan. An hour later another card was slid under the door.

"Why don't you come in and tell me?" Casey shouted. "Just open the door, for crying out loud!"

She heard feet retreat hastily down the hall. She tried to ignore the card, but curiosity got the better of her. She picked it up. She thumbed through her Bible as she sought the book of Hebrews. There, in the fifth chapter, she read verse eight, "Although He was a Son, He learned obedience from the things which He suffered."

"Same story," she said aloud. She wondered if the verses were preselected for an occasion like this. If she understood Lydia's warning, this wasn't the first time someone had been locked up to die to herself. She wondered if they kept a set of cards on hand for emergency use, or if Carol, Rita, Amy, and the Brothers were scanning their concordances to find verses to impress her with the importance of obedience. She sensed Grace's hand behind it all, and it made her shiver.

Just before she called Jessie at 10:00 p.m., another card appeared under the door. A verse from the fourth chapter of Ephesians joined a growing pile in front of her.

With a sigh, she pushed the obnoxious cards away from her and flipped open the small telephone. She glanced at the door to see if any shadows moved beneath it. As she had at eight o'clock, Jessie answered on the first ring.

"Are you okay?"

"I'm fine. No change, other than a bunch of verses under the door. There are still Brothers in the yard, but everyone is settling down for the evening."

"So when do you get out?"

"I'm still not sure *how*, much less *when*."

"I can't stand this. It's crazy. Claude and I will drive up, knock on the door, demand to see you, and if they won't let us in, we'll go bring a police officer back with us."

As comforting as the mental image of Jessie and Claude storming the drawbridge was, Casey knew it wasn't the right thing to do. "I appreciate that, and I know I'll need you to help me. Please let me figure it out. I've been praying for wisdom and a clear head. I'm confident a way will open up." There was silence at the other end of the phone, and then Jessie sighed.

"As much as I hate to say it, I have the same conviction in my heart. But I want to get in the car and start driving. I'm frantic."

"I know. I'm in no danger though, and I'll be waiting for God's plan to materialize. Will you wait with me?"

"I'll wait all night if I have to, but I don't have to like it."

"I've got to go. I'll call you in two hours."

She shut off the phone, then used the bathroom and turned off the light in her room. After her eyes had adjusted to the gloom, she peered from behind the curtains to survey the backyard. Her heart skipped a beat. No one was in view. Then she caught a movement on the patio. A lone Brother sat in a chair several yards from her window. Her hopes plummeted. She crept across the room and curled up on the bed, Andrew at her back.

Before she drifted off, she saw a small square of paper glowing on the floor inside the door. In her exhaustion she resolved to simply ignore it.

29

Casey woke with a start from a deep sleep. Andrew gazed down at her and withdrew his whiskered face from hers to avoid her hand as she rubbed the cheek he had tickled. She lay for a moment, disoriented by the room and the break in her sleep. Then her heart jumped, and she grabbed at the buttons on her watch to light up its face.

Relief washed through her. She hadn't missed her call with Jessie. She knew her friend wouldn't hesitate to call the police if Casey neglected to check in. She stood and stretched so she wouldn't drift back to sleep. For good measure she went into the bathroom, ran cold water on a washcloth, and rubbed her face vigorously. She came out refreshed and saw Andrew at the door, staring at the floor.

"I'm sorry, old boy, but no nocturnal roaming for you for a few nights. I can't open the door." At her first words the cat turned and studied her with his big owlish eyes. Then he returned to his stance. Casey sat on the bed and patted the blanket next to her. "Come here, sweetie."

Andrew did not move. She decided to make her call, but he began to play with the card on the floor. She wanted to get the upper hand by not picking this one up. Andrew continued to play, his activity becoming louder and more insistent. He banged up against the door with his body as he sought to get a paw under the card. Afraid he'd awaken others in the house, Casey set down the telephone in exasperation and padded over to scoop him up. She left the card on the floor. He squirmed in her arms, and she realized he'd go right back to it. She bent and picked it up, then tossed both the cat and the card on the bed before she dialed Jessie's number.

As she waited, Casey watched Andrew pounce upon the card. Jessie's voice chirped in her ear.

"Casey?"

"I'd like to know who else calls you at this hour." Even though she had to whisper, Casey felt better just hearing her friend's voice.

"You're forty-five seconds late. I was about to pick up the phone and call the police. I meant what I said."

"I know you did. I had to get Andrew. Somebody shoved another card under the door, and he won't stop playing with it."

"What does this one say?" Either Jessie was downstairs or Claude had also not gone to bed. Jessie certainly wasn't whispering.

"I don't know. I didn't even look. I'm sick of these things. They frustrate me, since I haven't thought of a workable plan yet." Casey expected a new barrage, but it didn't come.

"Any change since we talked last?"

"Nothing, other than the cards under the door." She moved across the dark room and used one slim finger to move the drape at the window. "There's still one guy on the patio." She looked at the crack under the door. "But it looks and sounds like everyone else is asleep—except me and Andrew, who thinks it's time to play."

"And you tried the doorknob again?"

Casey crossed the room, gripped the knob, and quietly rotated it clockwise, then counterclockwise.

"It's still locked." Andrew swatted the white card and made a small mock growl as he pounced on it. To quiet him, Casey put her hand over the card. He wormed a paw under her outstretched palm, which tickled her. She snickered.

"Are you crying? We'll think of something, honey."

"No, I'm laughing." She suppressed a giggle.

"Well, I wish you'd share the joke. This is no time to be—"

"It's Andrew. He won't leave this card alone, and he's tickling me to try to get it away."

"Well, if he's curious about it, I am too. Why don't you tell me the verse reference? I want to know what it says so I can better gauge the situation there and help you decide what to do next."

To appease both her friends, feminine and furry, Casey picked up the card and turned it over. A shock jolted her when she recognized the handwriting. "This one is in Lydia's writing." She rubbed the card with her thumb. "I don't understand. Has she joined with the rest of them on this?" Her heart sank as she contemplated the ramifications of that possibility.

"It's hard to tell unless you give me the verse," Jessie's patience sounded frayed. "What is it?"

"There are two references this time." Casey couldn't make out the tiny writing. She pulled a small flashlight from her purse. "The first one is Old Testament, and it's a long passage, Judges 7:16–22." She listened while Jessie found her place, and then waited for her to read the passage. "What does it say?"

A puzzled response came back. "Maybe she wrote down the wrong thing. This is a story about a battle. A small army went up against a much larger one, and they defeated the larger one when they attacked at night, blew trumpets, broke pitchers, and waved torches to confuse the other army."

"It doesn't make any sense." Casey confirmed the verse reference.

"You know, I can't see Lydia betraying you. Let's take it at face value. Maybe she's trying to encourage you. After all, you are one against a much larger force."

"But I'm not just one. I've got you and Claude, Andrew, and Lydia. Most of all, I've got Jesus. I'm quite an army, all on my own."

"Good girl! Now, what's the other verse reference?"

"It's in the New Testament." Casey squinted at the card. "Just one verse this time. Acts 9:25." Again the sound of pages flipping.

"I think this is what we've been praying for! It's about Paul's escape from Damascus after his conversion, when the Jews there wanted to kill him because they didn't trust him. It says, 'But his disciples took him by night and let him down through an opening in the wall, lowering him in a large basket.'"

"An escape plan!"

Jessie's voice rose in timbre as her enthusiasm built. "If you put the two verses together, it sounds like somebody is going to stage a diversion, and you're to go out through the wall—the window."

Casey absorbed the words and felt a surge of hope. "Why didn't Lydia write that down?"

"She did, as clearly as she dared. If she's as ill as you described, it was a struggle for her to write as much as she did. She had to be careful in case the note was found. It had to look like the others. You must bring it with you when you leave. Lydia will be blamed otherwise."

"But I don't know what I'm supposed to do!" Casey panicked. "And Andrew! What do I do about him?"

"Hmmm. You have a cat carrier, don't you?"

"Yes."

"Get it out and be ready to put Andrew into it. Watch for your opportunity. Stay awake. Be ready. It's hard to tell what form the diversion will take."

Casey turned the flashlight on the index card a final time and scrutinized every inch of its surface. She gasped and held it closer to her eyes.

"Wait a minute." She peered at the back. "There's another note on the card. It's hard to make it out in the dark...." She struggled to make sense of the soft figures that had been breathed as much as written on the paper. "It says three a.m." Casey guessed they were both studying their watches.

"Here's what you're to do. I want you to sleep from now until two thirty. Do you have a way to make yourself wake up?"

"Oh, I'm sure I can't sleep. I'm too keyed up."

"You might need the rest. Can you do it?"

"My watch has an alarm on it. I can put it under my pillow to muffle it."

"Okay. At two thirty you need to get up, put Andrew in his carrier, and pull together whatever you can't live without. The bare minimum, Case."

"All right. My purse, my keys, a few clothes."

THE GATHERING PLACE 217

"Clothes we can replace, and books and everything else, but not you and Andrew. Keep it light."

"Then what?" Casey closed her eyes as she rehearsed the motions.

"Then get over to the window and wait for deliverance, my friend. I don't know what form it will take, but it will come." The steadiness in Jessie's voice helped Casey to slow her own racing heart.

"While you do that, I'll be driving to Crescent Hills."

The thought of Jessie riding to the rescue warmed her heart. She gave her the address and described the neighborhood to her.

"I'll park in the next street north of your house, then. Come through backyards. Stay away from sidewalks and lighted areas."

"If I'm not out by four, I'll call you again. Can you take the phone with you?"

"You've got my cell phone in your hand." Casey felt stupid. "My other phone is wireless, but it can't go far from the house. If you can't get out, page me at four. You remember my pager number?"

"Remember the restaurant?"

"Yeah." There was a giggle in Jessie's voice, then she sobered. "If you want me to wait longer—and I will, as long as it takes—then page me once. If it looks like there's no way tonight and we have to try again tomorrow, then page me twice in succession." They prayed briefly and ended the call.

Casey unwrapped the chocolate Hershey's Kiss and let it dissolve on her tongue, absorbing the gentle comfort as she programmed her watch to wake her and slid it under her pillow. Despite her concern to the contrary, she fell into a deep sleep. Woven into her dreams, red numerals flicked forward at a steady pace and lit up the chaotic thoughts that tumbled there.

30

Muffled electronic chirps confused Casey when they broke into her sleep. She listened for several seconds before realizing it was her watch alarm. She almost pulled the watch from under the pillow before reality froze her hand clamped around the beeping timepiece. As she fingered the buttons and turned off the alarm, she watched the crack beneath the door to see if the noise had been heard.

Seeing there was no sign of movement outside the door, she got up and moved to the window. Her finger shifted the curtain only far enough for a one-eyed look into the backyard. A man still sat on the patio, looking droopy and bored but awake.

She went into the bathroom and repeated her earlier performance with the washcloth and cold water to awaken her. Despite the darkness she peered into the mirror and saw that the outline of her hair was ragged and uneven. She ran the damp washcloth over her hair, and then combed it into place with her fingers.

Back in the bedroom she turned on the tiny flashlight and cupped it as she examined various items in the room to see what she would take. Things that had not been important the day before took on new significance and meaning. She didn't want to leave anything behind but knew she must. With a sensuous stretch, Andrew rose from the blanket and yawned. He jumped to the floor and rubbed against Casey's legs as she stood in indecision. She felt the usual tenderness wash over her at the sight of him. She scooped him up and held him close.

"You're right, as usual," she whispered. "You're the only thing in this room I can't replace." She hugged the cat and felt him begin to purr. He rubbed his face on her hand, his eyes closed to slits in his enjoyment. Casey put him on the bed and checked her watch. Quarter to three. She slipped it on and moved through the boxes to the closet.

She grasped the cat carrier and took it to the bed, worried it would be the usual ordeal to get Andrew into it. To her astonishment, the instant the door was opened and she had spread one of her T-shirts on the bottom, Andrew marched in, turned around, and lay down. As she closed the door, she breathed a prayer of thanks. The last thing she needed right now was to try to catch a cat in the dark without making any noise. She stuck her fingers in through the grille on the front door, and he rubbed his face against them. For the first time she felt they might get away.

After she had placed the cat carrier next to the window, she took a last look around her. Her eyes fell on her Bible. She knew that even though the actual Scriptures could be replaced, her association with this particular Bible could not. She had ten more minutes to endure before three o'clock; she made a quick decision to upgrade her luggage. She rummaged until she found a large shoulder bag and put her purse, her Bible, her notebooks, the cellular phone, and the index card with Lydia's message into the bag.

Looking at the small pile of index cards that had been pushed under the door in the last day, a thought came to her. Casey could not resist. She retrieved her Bible from the bag, flipped to the small concordance in the back, located the verse she wanted, and wrote across the back of one card in large letters: *John 8:32.* She smoothed the bedcovers and placed the card in the center of the bed. Back at the window, she looked around the edge of the curtain again. It was two minutes to three.

A slice of yellow light streamed as the kitchen door opened. From her watch post, Casey could see the light but not the door. The man rose quickly and turned toward it. She recognized Kurt's outline. She knew from his longing glances at Gatherings and his attention at Visiting Nights that he had a crush on her and wasn't surprised he was the one left on guard. He moved in the direction of the kitchen door, and Casey silently undid the latches on her window. She opened it a few inches. Refreshing cool air streamed in, and subdued night sounds surrounded her.

Casey lowered herself to her knees next to Andrew's carrier to peek around the drape. Kurt returned to the chairs on the flagstone patio, moving slowly. Someone was with him.

"Thank you." Lydia's voice floated to her ears, and Casey saw her lower herself gently into one of the chairs. "I needed the night air. I'm sorry you have to find out my little secret." She gave a quiet laugh.

"What secret, Sister Lydia?" Kurt asked. Lydia had maneuvered it so she sat in the chair facing the window; Kurt was forced to sit in the one facing away.

"Oh, my nighttime wanderings in search of coolness." She waved a fragile hand toward the darkened yard.

"I was thinking it would be nice to go inside and warm up."

"I'm cooking at a higher temperature than other people these days." Lydia fanned herself with her hand.

Curiosity seemed to overcome the young man, and he leaned forward, clasping his hands before him. "Does it hurt?"

"Yes, it hurts to be in my body right now." He nodded, and Casey wondered that he'd asked such an awkward question. "Other than Brother Eric and Casey, you're the first one to ask me that question. I think cancer scares people so much they can't even talk about it."

"Well, it's a frightening disease. I don't want to end up like ..." He stammered to a halt.

"Of course you don't want to end up like me. I don't want to end up like me either. Believe me, I've wrestled with the Lord over my fate many times, but it always comes back to one thing."

"What's that?"

"Am I closer to Jesus this evening than I was this morning? And if I am, would I be if I didn't have this disease gnawing at my insides?" She coughed into her curled fist. "When I look at it in perspective, I can see tremendous growth I might never have achieved any other way. Some people are able to grow closer to God when times are good. I seem to grow best when things are rough. He didn't give me this to make me grow, but he did give me peace in the midst of it...."

"But don't you feel cheated?"

"Because I don't get to do all the things I had planned and dreamed about?" Lydia stopped fanning herself and looked into his eyes. "I feel privileged."

"I'd be so angry I couldn't even talk."

"I learned something most people don't. I learned *my* plans, *my* dreams weren't what God had planned for me at all. If I believe he is the Creator and Master of the universe, with everything under control, then I also have to believe his plans are better for me. His ultimate plan for me is to grow closer to him. That's what he wants for me for all eternity. He can make use of any situation—good or bad—to bring that about."

"But can his plans mean you have to be sick and die young?" The puzzlement in Kurt's voice struck Casey to the heart; she longed for Lydia's answer as much as he did.

"My Brother died young too," she said. Casey felt her eyes widen with surprise.

"Your brother? I don't think I knew that you had a brother."

"My Brother Jesus. He had the potential to be the greatest healer and preacher the world has ever seen. His followers wanted him to rule the world, but the Father had a better plan. I would be a most ungrateful and unfaithful woman if I didn't do as he did in the face of impending destiny. He was honest with his Father and said he'd prefer not to die an ugly death. I've done the same thing. But he went a step further and said he'd rather have the Father's will than anything. It's my turn to do the same thing.

"Don't you want to yell at God sometimes?" Casey's fingers gripped the bottom of the window as she moved to ease it up further. She was wasting the time Lydia was buying her.

"No, that would be a bad idea." Lydia's voice was louder than it had been. Casey froze when she saw that Lydia's gaze was fastened on her fingers protruding below the window.

"What do you mean? I think it would be a normal thing to do." Kurt tipped his head in puzzlement.

Casey withdrew her hands, and Lydia relaxed in relief. "What I mean," she said as she waved a hand before her face as though to clear the thoughts from her muddled mind, "is that it's a bad idea to try to impose our will on God. Look through the Old Testament; you'll see examples of that principle. Eve in the garden of Eden. Abraham and Sarah and Hagar. Joseph's brothers when they sold him and told his father he'd died." She sat for a moment and breathed in the night air. "In every case God is able to turn what we do into good, but how much better would it be for us if we moved with his hand in the first place?"

In a gesture that touched Casey's heart, Kurt took one of Lydia's hands and squeezed it.

"You're right. I never thought of it that way. But when you want something so bad, it's easy to think God put the thought into your heart, and so it has to come true." Casey dropped her eyes in shame and knew he spoke of her.

"Those are the times we have to be most willing to hear what he has to say. When we are taken up with our own dreams, his voice can get lost in the roar of our desires." Lydia gasped and put both hands to her face, rocking.

"What's wrong?" Kurt jumped and moved to her, panic in his voice.

"I need to take my medication. The pills taste really bad, so could you get me a glass of juice?" He moved immediately toward the door. "And put a few ice cubes in it, if you would."

The moment the door swung shut, Lydia stood stiffly from her chair and staggered to the window. Casey raised it quickly. The old screen pushed out easily. She handed the cat carrier to Lydia, who lowered it to the ground as if even this weight were too much for her. Casey slid out the window, then reached up and lowered it again. She pressed the screen back into its place.

"Go with God, my dear sister." Lydia clasped Casey and pushed her away at the same time.

Casey's eyes filled as she hefted the cat carrier and shoulder bag and backed away. Though she longed to run back and hug her one more time, Lydia's eyes implored her to hurry. As she rounded the corner, she saw Lydia stumble back and resume her seat. The door to the kitchen opened. Casey looked at Lydia, frail and small in the darkness as she fought to give her a chance to escape. She raised a quick hand and melted back into the shadows, determined that Lydia's effort not be in vain.

31

As soon as Casey reached the shadows under a large tree in the side yard, she set down the cat carrier, stood still, and let her eyes adjust to the darkness. She crept toward the front of the house thinking of her car parked out front. She couldn't leave it there. She pictured herself driving up to Jessie's car, lowering the window, and giving her a thumbs-up.

Her car was parked where she always parked it, under a streetlight. She wanted to kick herself for this bit of foresight. From the darkness she examined the windows along the front of the house. No curtains stirred. No lights blazed. She turned back toward the street and took her first step.

The breath stopped in her chest. Among the four other parked cars, one had an occupant. In the tricky light it was difficult for her to tell the true color of the car, but the driver's shape was unmistakable. Stephanie had felt it necessary to watch her car. It was a trap.

She moved backward to where she had left Andrew. She lifted the carrier, settled her bag on her shoulder, and moved to the hedge dividing the Sisters House from the home next door. She had watched young children crawl back and forth through the hedge. She found their well-worn pathway and eased through it. She felt much better once she was safely on the other side. Following the hedge to the back of the property, she encountered another hedge perpendicular to the first, dividing it from another yard. Suspecting the children would have carved out a similar pathway through this hedge, she moved along it. Halfway along she found the opening and bent double to get through. The cat carrier snagged on a branch. She forced herself to gently untangle it, not tug on it until the branch broke. Her pulse roared in her ears, but at last she was free of the bushes.

She examined the yard into which she had crossed. She looked at the back porch and saw a shiny silver bowl gleaming in the subdued light of a half moon. Her nostrils detected a doggy smell endemic to yards with large dogs. The fact the dog hadn't barked yet didn't give her much encouragement. Depending on its breed, it might wait for her to get closer before it attacked. Any sound from the dog would betray her.

She raised the carrier to eye level and looked in at Andrew. He peered out, his head swiveling, his eyes taking in details she couldn't hope to see. When he crouched back down comfortably, she let out a breath. Her hand was slick on the handle as she began to work a path around unfamiliar landmarks. When she rounded the side of the house, she stopped again in deep shadow.

Her heart leaped when she saw Jessie's car in the distance. She watched her in the driver's seat as her head swiveled every few seconds to look out the front, rear, and side of the car. Casey wanted to race to the car but recalled the chilling discovery of Stephanie outside the Sisters House and checked every vehicle in sight. None appeared to have anyone inside.

"Okay, sweetheart, let's go," she whispered to Andrew, more to give herself courage than him.

Casey hopscotched from shadow to shadow and arrived at the passenger door without Jessie knowing she was there. When she tapped on the glass, Jessie jumped, her hand flying to her mouth to stop her cry of alarm. Casey eased open the door, slid inside, and settled Andrew's carrier on her lap.

"Go," she said.

Jessie locked the doors, turned the key in the ignition, and pulled onto the street. Halfway down the block, she turned on the headlights. Neither spoke until they were several blocks from the Sisters House.

"I hope you have the phone in your bag charged up enough for one more call, because Claude will be going crazy by now."

Casey felt a wide smile crease her face, and her eyes became shiny with released tension.

"Lydia! What on earth are you up to?" Rita moved to Lydia's side as the sick woman swayed and braced herself on the hallway wall.

"Bathroom." Perspiration beaded her forehead.

Rita took her arm and felt Lydia rest her fragile weight on her. Lydia's eyes were more sunken this morning than the previous day, as if she hadn't slept. "I'll wait and help you back to bed," she offered as Lydia disappeared from view.

Rita leaned against the wall and waited. As she did, her eyes roamed the hallway and took in the familiar framed photos. To pass the time, she studied the group photos in detail and picked out familiar faces from the Body. She drifted down the hallway until she reached Casey's room. Rita glanced over her shoulder, then put her ear to the door. She heard nothing. Perhaps Casey was still asleep.

She heard running water in the bathroom and turned to hurry back to Lydia when something caught her eye. She saw an index card half protruding under Casey's door. Curious, she bent and picked it up. The card had a verse reference heavily crossed out in ink, and another written below it. The card must have come from inside the room. She took the card and went back to the bathroom as the door opened and Lydia swayed out. Rita caught her housemate's arm and guided her to her room, making maternal noises. When Lydia was back in bed, Rita pulled the card from her smock pocket.

"I found this outside Casey's door. What do you think it means?" The two of them took turns looking at both sides of the card.

"I'm not sure of the reference. Why don't you look it up? My Bible is right there." Lydia waved a weak hand toward the small round table next to her bed.

Rita turned to 1 Timothy 1:15 and read aloud. "'It is a trust-worthy statement, deserving full acceptance, that Christ Jesus came into the world to save sinners, among whom I am foremost of all.'" Rita looked up. "What do you think it means?"

"I think Casey is doing better with her three days than we expected she would." Lydia's eyes glowed with fever.

"I'd better tell Carol," Rita said. "And Grace."

Lydia watched her go. Inside she felt her last reserves crumble. It had taken hours to gather the strength to look up the reference, write out the card, carry it to Casey's door, and drop it on the floor, making sure it was visible from the outside. She had been on her way back to her room when Rita found her in the hall.

She knew she had bought her young friend time, and gathered Casey mentally in her arms and put her into the hands of God.

32

Another ceiling. Another bed. Another window. Another life.

The litany swirled through Casey's mind as she studied the newest ceiling in her life. Typical of his adaptable nature, Andrew had curled up for a well-deserved nap. She drew his tail between her fingers as she reflected on her sudden break with the Body.

After they had called Claude and reassured him, she and Jessie had driven home with few comments. Both were drained by the experiences of the previous twenty-four hours and needed to absorb what had happened. When they reached Jessie's home, she and Claude showed Casey to the guest room, saw to her needs, hugged her, and left her alone.

Although her body craved sleep, Casey's mind whirled. She felt disconnected in a profound way and knew she was on the edge of a mental collapse. Eventually her eyelids became heavier than her thoughts, and she drifted into a deep, troubled sleep. She continually roused herself with sharp cries and fought her way back to sleep again. After a particularly frightful awakening, she was childishly relieved when a soft light fanned under her door, which opened to two worried faces. Casey sat up at once so they would come in.

"I'm so sorry to keep you awake." She fidgeted with the sheet. Jessie and Claude moved in unison to her bed.

"Don't worry about us," Claude said. "We wanted to be sure you weren't fighting off an army of home invaders." His eyes twinkled, but his hand was firm on hers, and it gave her courage.

"I should be relieved," Casey said. "I mean, we spent the last twelve hours trying to get me away from the Sisters House, but all I can do is thrash around and question whether I've done the right thing."

Jessie rubbed her forearm with smooth, gentle motions. "I think you're in shock," she said. "After all, you completely gave yourself to these people. In the end they locked you up. Yet despite that, you still have feelings for them—especially Lydia—and it's very possible you'll never see her again. Of course you're torn up inside."

Casey fought tears at the mention of Lydia's name.

"You have to be realistic, my dear." Casey moved her eyes to Claude's gently creased face and the gray tufts at his temples. "It will take time to come to terms with your experience." He traded a glance with Jessie and turned back to Casey and squeezed her hand. "We're both here to help you. You'll have to start again with baby steps until you learn how to walk strongly on your own, and we'll hold your hands as you do."

This time when the tears welled up, Casey couldn't stop them, nor did she try. "What planet did you find this man on, Jessie?" she finally managed. "How many men would allow their wives to go tearing off into the night to rescue a friend and then bring her into their home? He surely can't be human."

Jessie gazed lovingly at Claude before she answered. "Yes, he's pretty special." Her eyes lit. "And everything he's said tonight is absolutely true. We want to help you in any way we can. However, we're not sure what needs doing. So will you promise to let us know what's happening inside you? It's the only way we can be effective prayer warriors for you."

"It's a deal," Casey whispered. She reached out to embrace them both. For the moment the shadows in her mind receded.

Darren lay stretched on his small bed, his final evening as a single man. His strong hands were clasped behind his head, and he stared at the lines in the white stucco ceiling without seeing them.

Heavy tread moved past his door as household members went to dinner.

A married couple from the Body oversaw the house, the wife handling the cooking, organizing the shopping, and making lists of chores for them all to do. She was a plump, cheerful woman who loved to watch the men devour her excellent cooking. It was an ideal arrangement for all of them. Darren was hungry, but his mind was in turmoil. He decided to forgo dinner to finish thinking through what nagged him.

He had heard by accident that Casey had been given the ultimate treatment to bring her back into obedience. It was a relief to know she wouldn't be at the wedding. Darren wasn't certain he could stand with Carol and look into Casey's eyes without being torn in two. The thoughts that had nagged him for the past weeks returned. The words that had passed between him and Casey in the park still bothered him. On reflection he had sounded arrogant and self-righteous. Neither was a trait he equated with himself.

A sense of superiority had swept over him when he first heard of her confinement. He had caught himself thinking it was justified. Now he was appalled. He tried to put the Body first, to live the life of a Body member. Nevertheless, something in him stirred at the thought of someone he knew, admired, and respected confined against her will to change her behavior. Despite all the rhetoric to the contrary, it wasn't right.

Something about Casey seemed to rile people. When she first came, she appeared to be the ideal person needed to round out the Body. She had moved in among them, sacrificing her previous lifestyle, home, job, and ambitions. She was enthusiastic in the Gatherings, cheerful on Visiting Night, and a good hostess when newcomers lingered at the Sisters House after a Gathering.

However, under all the obedience ran a thin current of discontent. Darren had sensed it strongly when he picked her up on the day of the storm, and it had grown over time. He would have liked to help her, to be her friend. He sighed deeply. He knew Carol well enough to realize she would be possessive of his time and attention.

After tomorrow there would be no more friendships with women. He remembered the richness such relationships had brought to his life and felt a tug of disappointment and regret.

As his thoughts turned to Carol and being a married man, Darren could no longer push down the uneasy feeling he was about to make a big mistake. Even so, he would be steady and firm tomorrow. The decision to marry Carol had been a watershed in his Bodylife experience. He couldn't go back now.

Knuckles sounded against his door.

"Darren? Telephone," Felicity called, which caused his brows to draw together in surprise.

"Who is it? Do you know?" He rolled to a sitting position on the edge of the bed.

"The man didn't say."

Darren crossed the room and swung the door open. Felicity smiled at him and finished drying her hands on a towel she carried.

"Thanks," he said as he followed her to the kitchen and the telephone.

Her new life began to fall into an easy routine. After a weekend of restorative sleep, she had risen on Monday when she heard Claude and Jessie get ready for work. She joined them for breakfast and then insisted on cleaning up the kitchen, freeing them to leave at a more leisurely pace. Jessie kept her home beautifully, but throughout the day Casey found small things she could do to save her friend effort later.

When she was not doing chores, Casey sat in the backyard on the porch swing and thought. She reviewed the last year and a half, painful as it was, because she could not yet find where everything had gone wrong. She wondered if it would have worked out if she had tried harder. Perhaps she was not spiritual enough for the Bodylife. The thoughts punched through her mental fog, and eventually she grew weary. Then she rose, retired to her room, and slept the afternoon away. She knew this was indicative of depression, but the escape felt so good. To make up for it, she tried to have dinner ready when Jessie and Claude came home.

As she dusted around the living room telephone, she sat down and let the rag settle in her lap. She replayed in her mind the phone call she had made. It hadn't done any good, but she had felt it imperative to make the attempt. Claude had taken the receiver from her after she had dialed.

"May I speak to Darren, please?" he asked whoever had answered at the Brothers House. "Oh, my name won't mean any-thing to him." There had been a long, tense pause as Claude listened for Darren to come to the phone. At last he tightened his grip on the phone. "Is this Darren?" he asked, and listened to a reply. "Hold on, please." He handed the phone to Casey and left the room. She took a deep breath and had a hard time letting it out again.

"It's me, Darren." There was a profound silence at the other end, and then his voice came back light and chatty.

"Oh, how nice to hear from you." There was another pause.

"Are other people right there with you?"

"Yes. Yes, that's right. I remember when we met." She heard the tightness in his throat as he fought to maintain a normal conversa-tion. After all, she was supposedly still in confinement.

"I understand." She was one of the few people on earth who would. "I called to say only one thing."

"Yes?"

"You don't have to go through with this marriage tomorrow." She bit her lip.

"I think I do." There was a quiet sadness in his voice.

"Jesus says his yoke is light, his burden is easy to carry." Casey's reply was steady and firm. "He tells us to come to him when we are heavily laden." She paused. "Lydia told me that when I feel like I am carrying the weight of the world, I'm picking up and hauling burdens that were never mine to carry in the first place." She let him absorb her words, pacing herself carefully. "You can walk away," she said.

"Well, I'm not sure we agree on that particular text, Brother, but maybe we can talk about it at a Gathering when you come."

She wanted to groan in frustration. She could say anything she wished, but his carefully couched replies were driving her crazy.

"I'm afraid I won't be in any more Gatherings. God bless you and keep you." She hung up the phone and wondered if it had been worth the effort. Now she sat beside the instrument again and longed to dial the Sisters House. She had to know how Lydia was. She had to hear the voices to which she was so accustomed.

But after the unsatisfying conversation she'd had with Darren, she turned her eyes away from the telephone and forced herself to continue dusting.

Hours later the receiver was slick in Casey's hand as she listened to a third ring. It would all depend on who answered.

"Hello?" It sounded like Amy. Relief swept Casey, and she put on her best chipper voice.

"Hi. What's going on?"

"Oh, they're on their way." Amy sounded frazzled.

"Oh, good. What about you?"

"No, I promised to sit with Lydia this morning," Amy said. "It takes me almost all morning to get her to eat enough breakfast to carry her through the day."

"How is Lydia today, anyway?"

"About the same. Since the weekend, she's not been able to leave her bed. I think she overtaxed herself."

"What does Brother Eric say?" There was a long pause.

"Who is this?" Amy's voice held a whisper of fear.

"It's me, Amy. Please don't hang up." Casey took a deep breath and waited to hear the click and the dial tone. It didn't come.

"What do you want?"

"I need to know how Lydia is." A longer pause.

"I shouldn't talk to you."

"But you already are, so we might as well go on." Casey tried a light laugh before getting serious again. "I didn't mean to trick you. I was so afraid you wouldn't talk to me."

"If I'd known it was you, I would have hung up." Another pause. "But no one else is here. So this conversation is not happening, okay?"

"I'll never tell." Casey was wild with relief.

"Lydia doesn't have long." Amy's voice wavered. Casey clung to the phone. "Brother Eric said it could be a few days or a few weeks."

"Is she in pain?" Casey didn't care that her heart showed in her voice.

"Not physical pain, but she misses you terribly." Casey's heart turned over in her chest. "She's also worried about all of us. We've had a few really good conversations."

"About what?" Casey was surprised.

"Well, it's funny because it's all Grace's fault." Amy snickered. "When you disappeared, Grace was the one who discovered it. She assumed you'd find a way to take Lydia with you, and she stormed into her room to check. But Lydia was there."

"Believe me, if Lydia had let me, I would have."

"I know. Anyway, she started in on Lydia. She told her she was totally useless except for causing trouble, and she was going to do the worst possible thing—die and leave everybody else to clean up the mess."

"She said that to Lydia?" Casey gasped.

"Yeah. Then she told Lydia she had twenty-four hours to find another place to die."

"No! Where is she now?" Panic engulfed her.

"Let me finish." Amy's voice warmed to the tale. "When she said that, Kurt stepped between them and said that Lydia didn't have to leave. Since he had the guts, I stepped up beside him. Grace turned to Stephanie for support, and Stephanie surprised everybody. She folded her arms and said, 'The horse is out of the barn, Grace. No point whipping the stable boys now.'" Amy giggled.

"Of all the people to stand up for Lydia."

"Grace knew she'd lost; Stephanie has always backed her up. So, Lydia stays. She'd taken care of all the arrangements. Brother Eric said it would only take one phone call to handle everything, despite what Grace implied."

The thought of what needed to be "handled" brought a lump to Casey's throat. "Is she safe there? If she's not, I'll come and get her."

"She's fine," Amy soothed. "Somehow she seems to think she has work to do, and she won't be moved for anything." That remark brought softness to Casey's face.

"Lydia has always been remarkable."

"Oh, while I have you on the phone, what about your stuff?"

"It's yours. Take whatever you want, and toss the rest," she said.

"Your car disappeared. Did you come get it, or was it stolen?"

"Neither. A friend came and got it for me." Casey was again grateful to Jessie and Claude for their unending assistance. She and Amy fell silent, and Casey realized the conversation was nearly over. "May I call you again to find out how she is?"

"I don't think that would be a good idea. If I get caught, it won't be pleasant. There might be repercussions for Lydia. Why don't you give me your number, and I can call you if ... anything changes."

"I'm sorry, Amy. I hope you'll understand if I say I'm not comfortable with that. It's all a little raw right now, you know?"

"I'll let Lydia know you're all right though, okay?"

"Oh, do tell her that." Casey longed to drive to Crescent Hills and sit by Lydia's bed. "Tell her I'll always love her and remember her." Her voice broke. She heard the soft click as Amy hung up.

33

Kurt marveled at how quiet a hundred people could be if they wanted to be. Every chair in the first eight rows was filled. The group looked like a bull's-eye in the midst of hundreds of empty chairs. Kurt had no wish to converse with anyone; he slipped into a seat in a rear row and opened his Bible. He knew no one would interrupt him if he appeared to be engrossed in it. His mind had whirled since word of this Gathering had passed from house to house Monday and Tuesday. Kurt looked around surreptitiously. The familiar faces had a solemn cast. Audrey sat with the women, since there would be no need for the piano. The space Casey would normally have occupied seemed to have closed up like water in a bucket when a hand is withdrawn from it. Kurt sighed, turning his eyes back to his Bible. The heavy atmosphere oppressed everyone.

Neither Webster nor Darren was present yet. When Webster entered alone, a fist formed in Kurt's stomach. Webster moved with pantherlike stealth through the crowd and materialized in the center circle, drawing gasps from several people. His expression was hard, and his shaggy white brows met over his intense blue eyes.

He began without preamble. "I hoped this would take a different turn. However, there appears to be no alternative open to us." His eyes traveled over the group and lingered on different individuals. Carol, her eyes hollow, looked away from him. The corners of Dominic's mouth turned down. Grace appeared lost in thought, her eyes unfocused and her hands slack in her lap. Stephanie hooded her eyes with her lids and drew her thin lips into a tight line. Her services were also not needed tonight; there would be no recording of this Gathering.

"I've spent two hours with Brother Darren this evening regarding his refusal to follow the Brothers' direction." Webster pulled his handkerchief from his back pocket and began to polish his glasses. "I regret to tell you it was not a productive meeting."

A small breath escaped the group. They waited with dreadful anticipation. Webster, drained, looked not to have the energy to draw out the moment and play its drama. Kurt knew he'd expected to be victorious.

"In the New Testament the apostles set up a church infrastructure to administer the Body in each locale." Webster replaced his glasses before he stowed the handkerchief in his jacket pocket. "They did this because they knew that disputes and disruptions would arise, and it was wise to have a final authority to deal with those difficulties."

Kurt stirred uneasily. He had always endorsed the idea, but tonight he felt uncomfortable.

"We have the Brothers to guide us, because God has poured himself into these men in a mighty way." A low amen broke from the group. Kurt heard himself respond by reflex. "Brothers don't make directions for us to follow. They pray together, seek God, and bring us what they have learned with humility and tenderness." Again the chorus endorsed Webster's words. Kurt held back. "Humility and tenderness." The words startled him; he had never applied them to the Brothers.

"Darren was a member of a tight circle of men who met in my office every morning for prayer. He was part of our hearts and involved in our petitions." Webster shook his head sadly. "For this reason it is so difficult to have him turn against direction at this critical time."

Kurt saw Carol slip out and walk quickly to the back door. He knew she would not return. Webster waited while she exited.

"We're united. We're not unconnected people who live our lives in isolation from one another. We're joined into one Body, and when one of us refuses to cooperate, the whole Body hurts. This is what Darren's refusal to cooperate with the Spirit has brought about."

Kurt's heart went out to Carol. He was in the best position to empathize with her. Her feeling of rejection when Darren backed out of the wedding had to be deep and cutting. It echoed his own feelings when he discovered that Casey was gone. Yet since her departure, his rational mind had taken over.

It was Casey's independent spirit that had drawn him to her. She would not have meekly submitted if the Brothers had told her she was to marry him. If she had, he saw now, it would have destroyed who she was. The verse reference she had left behind, "You will know the truth, and the truth will make you free," echoed through his mind as he mulled over the situation. He licked his lips, as if tasting the first freedom of waking from his unrealistic dream, then turned his attention back to Webster.

"The Word is very clear on the issue of rebuking sin in our midst," Webster said. "It is sin to actively refuse to maintain the peace of the Body." The amen was stronger as the group gathered steam for what was to come. "Darren has had the error of his ways pointed out to him." Webster held up one finger. "He has been asked to repent and reconsider his decisions." He raised a second finger. "He has refused to do so." A third finger. "He has been confronted again, and again refused." Another finger went up, and wearily Webster dropped his hand. "There is only one further step for us."

The ensuing silence took on a life of its own, became a presence in the room. Kurt found he was holding his breath and let it out silently. Webster looked at his watch.

"Darren is removing his belongings from the Brothers House and will depart within the hour. We agreed this was essential to maintain the unity of the Body and the stability of the Brothers House." Webster's eyes traveled over the group. "From this point forward there will be no contact with him, unless he first comes to the Brothers and repents." His eyes turned from blue to steely gray. The line of his jaw hardened. "I ask you all to join me in prayer to stem the tide of evil swirling around the edges of the Body, threatening to overtake us and rip us apart." Webster sank into his chair, his eyes already closed, his hands clasped.

Dominic immediately began to beseech God for protection of the Body and its unity. Others joined in, and the chorus became fevered. Webster slid to his knees. Many others followed suit.

The painful fist tightened in Kurt's stomach as he listened to the prayers and watched Webster and the others. The finality of the pronouncement chilled him. For the first time he found it impossible to join his spirit to theirs. The feeling frightened him, but the pain cleared his mind. He wondered if there was something in the way the situation had been handled that had caused Darren to balk at following the Brothers. Suddenly he had to know. He raised his eyes and looked around carefully. Every head was bowed, every eye closed. It was not difficult for him to rise, walk to the door, and step through it without being observed.

The bed of Darren's truck was filled with dark plastic garbage bags. He had not had time to gather boxes and pack properly; the bags would have to do. He hefted two more and reached to close the tailgate, but decided to take a last look to be sure he had not missed anything. He turned from the truck toward the house.

Kurt stepped from the shadows, startling him. He approached to within fifteen feet of Darren and stopped. The two young men stared at each other. Darren wondered if the group had changed its mind and sent Kurt to tell him not to go. The expression on Kurt's face told him otherwise.

"Webster said I had until eight thirty." He glanced at his watch and saw that it was not even eight yet.

Kurt glanced quickly over his shoulder toward the Gathering Place. The lights could barely be seen through the hedge that separated the two properties.

"They're praying right now, so don't worry. No one else is coming."

Darren studied Kurt and saw the tension in his body. He had not gotten to know him well, even though they both lived at the Brothers House, because he'd sensed the other man's interest in Casey from the day she first appeared. Now his curiosity was piqued.

"Why are you here?"

"I had to ask you something."

"I assumed no one would be allowed to talk to me."

"I'm stretching it a bit by deciding the shunning doesn't go into effect until they finish praying."

Darren liked his candor. "Well, then, before I turn into a pumpkin, you'd better ask your question."

"Did you refuse the Brothers' counsel because of the way they handled it, or was it something else?"

Darren sat down on the edge of the tailgate and swung one leg as he braced himself with the other.

"What did Webster say?"

"He didn't say anything except you refused to do what the Brothers asked."

"Well, he's right about that." Darren paused to collect his words. "I want you to understand one thing. This has nothing to do with Carol." Pain and remorse shot through him. "I hope she knows that. Webster wouldn't let me talk to her. This is a matter of what is and isn't right in the Body."

"What do you mean?"

"There are a lot of tremendously good things happening here. The unity among people is astonishing. The dedication to Scripture and the closeness that develops among people are wonderful." He felt the ripping inside that would immobilize him shortly when he realized what he had lost. "But there are also things here that aren't right, and I can't go along with them."

"Such as?"

"Such as unity at the price of integrity. Asking people to go along with things they don't believe in so there's a surface appearance of unity and agreement."

Kurt shifted from one foot to the other.

"The idea that any one group of human beings is more enlight-ened *than* others—and better able to hear the will of God *for* others—is just flat wrong," Darren continued. "I know it from my study of the Word, and I know it here." He tapped his chest with his fingers. "To be told who I am to marry and spend the rest of my life with, that's beyond the authority of anyone in any capacity in the church. Even if I was wildly in love with Carol, the Brothers still wouldn't have the right to approve or disapprove the union."

"What are the Brothers for, then, if not to give us direction?"

"That's a very good question." Darren looked again at his watch and stood. "I've got to get moving."

"Where will you go?"

"I think I'll find myself a nice little motel room for the night and think things through."

"And after tonight?"

"I don't know, but I'm sure it will come to me."

Kurt stepped back as Darren moved to pass him. He turned and moved toward the lights of the Gathering Place.

Darren made a final round of the house, got in the truck, and pulled away, his thoughts as scattered as the stars that punctuated the dark bowl of the sky.

34

Like a tireless rodent digging its subterranean burrow, the pain bore into Lydia. She no longer remembered what it was like to be free of pain.

Eric brought her tablets to take when the pain was at its worst, but they also made her feel detached from her body and unable to control her thoughts. The relief was welcome, and she hoped it was a foretaste of what it would be like to finally be rid of her body and ascend to the Lord; but the price she paid in confusion and letting precious time slip by in oblivion was higher than she was willing to pay.

In the month since Casey's departure, Lydia had not left her bed. Sisters had taken shifts to nurse her. They were gentle with her but did not share their hearts. The wall between the healthy and the dying grew taller each day as she sank closer to the end.

Only in Amy did she find a spirit strong enough to take Casey's place in small measure. With her she could talk—or be silent. Amy did not require her to be upbeat or heroic. It was a relief when Amy took over from the other Sisters, as she usually did for the evening shift. A small smile crossed her face as Amy quietly stepped in, a tray balanced on one arm. Lydia knew she would spend hours trying to coax nourishment into her, and because of her growing affection for Amy, she would do her best to take it.

"No dawdling over dinner tonight. You have a gentleman caller arriving in half an hour."

Lydia gaped at Amy in surprise. "Who? I'm in no shape to have visitors. Look at me!" She raised a thin hand to her hair.

"I can't believe you'd give up an hour of conversation because your hair needs combing, but we can take care of that."

Amy lifted Lydia's shoulders and adjusted her pillows. She held a mug of warm broth to her lips and encouraged her to drink. Lydia raised a hand to steady the mug, but she was not strong enough to hold it. Amy, as usual, gave her a quick update on news of the Body.

"The new volunteer doesn't have very good spelling skills, and she apparently let Webster's book go to press with a bunch of errors in it." She shook her head. "I think they're going to reprint the whole run. What a mess!"

Lydia used a toothpick to spear a slice of banana from a small plate Amy held out. As the soft, flavorful fruit dissolved in her mouth, she listened to Amy ramble on. She managed to get down more food than she thought she could but less than Amy wanted her to. It was a compromise they always made.

Amy put aside the tray, picked up the hairbrush, and carefully ran it through the thinning hair that covered Lydia's sensitive scalp. She slipped a jeweled clip into her hair to dress it up a bit.

A soft knock sounded on the door, and Amy moved to open it. When Kurt stepped into the room, Lydia could not have been more surprised. She had not seen him since he defended her to Grace. He moved to the bed and pulled up the visitor chair. Amy sat carefully on the edge of the bed. The soft light from the bedside table fell across them as they all took stock of each other.

"How do you feel today, Sister Lydia?"

"If you've got a limo out front, I'll put on my dancing shoes." She smiled.

"If renting a limo is all it takes to get you back on your feet, I'll be right back."

Amy enjoyed their banter. When the slow blush crept up Kurt's neck to his cheeks, they both knew he was working up the nerve to say what he had come to say.

"I don't want to take a lot of your time or tire you out."

Lydia waved a small, dismissive hand.

"I've wanted to come for a while. I know you had something to do with Casey getting out of the house, but I really don't care how it was done." Kurt looked steadily into Lydia's eyes. "I came over tonight to tell you that you did the right thing."

Surprise flooded Lydia.

"I didn't think so at the time, but my opinion is changing on a few issues, and I wanted you to know I don't hold anything against you for that night."

Even though Lydia felt no guilt for assisting Casey, she had experienced twinges of remorse for the way she had used Kurt as her cover. She did not realize how much it had bothered her until she was forgiven. "Thank you, Kurt."

"Has Amy told you what happened in the last day or so?" He looked at Amy, who shook her head.

"Is it about Casey?" A rush of fear swept over her.

Kurt immediately put a hand on her thin arm. "No, nothing to do with Casey. It's Darren." Lydia's arm jerked under his hand. "He left the Body last night. There was a special Gathering."

"I wasn't sure whether to tell you, Lydia," Amy said. Her eyes pleaded. "I didn't want to worry you."

"Why was he asked to leave?"

"He refused the Brothers' counsel to marry Carol," Kurt said.

"But he refused weeks ago."

"The Brothers and Webster tried to talk him back around. Webster finally gave up. He was removed from the Body last night."

"No, he wasn't." Lydia shook her head firmly. "He was asked to leave this particular group, but no one on this earth has the power to remove him from the body of Christ." Lydia's voice vibrated in her thin chest. "The same goes for Casey. She is no longer part of the Bodylife experience, but she is still very much part of the body of Christ, and always will be."

Amy and Kurt straightened as the strength of her words washed over them. Both took deep breaths as if they had been stifled for hours.

"I would have been happier if I had died while I still believed what the Bodylife teaches." Lydia coughed and lay back. "It hurts to lie here day after day and recount to myself the mistakes I've made and the people I've misled."

"What mistakes?" Kurt's tone told her he genuinely wanted to know.

"The mistake of putting more stock in the words of people than in the Word of God." She closed her eyes and gathered her strength. "The error of giving up the mind God gave me in exchange for security, uniformity, and not having to think—and most of all the mistake of drawing others into the same errors." Her eyes opened halfway, and she watched Kurt. "I thought I'd get closer to God when in reality I only became more acceptable to a select group of people. For that I sold my integrity. I'm very glad it didn't cost me my soul. Thank God!"

"If I'd heard you say this even a week ago, I would have felt compelled to report it." Kurt leaned forward and took Lydia's hand. He smiled down into her eyes. "But I've done a great deal of thinking, especially since last night."

"I'm so glad, Kurt." Lydia gripped his hand once, then let her gaze move to Amy. She'd forgotten briefly she was there. Amy ducked her head shyly.

"It's a relief to hear someone else say that," she confessed. "Darren came several times for Visiting Night. He was always firm in his faith and a joy to be around. To have him cut off from us like that didn't feel right."

"I asked him why he wouldn't go along with the Brothers," Kurt told them. "He said there are good things happening in the Body and bad things—and having spouses chosen for Bodylife members is one of the bad things." Both women looked at him.

"When did you ask him that?" Amy asked. Kurt's face reflected chagrin at his slip.

"I left the Gathering and went to talk to him last night before he left."

"Good for you." Lydia was filled with warmth for Kurt. "Thank you for doing that. It would have been awful for him to leave without a single person brave enough to say good-bye."

"It wasn't an urge to be nice that drove me. I had a question."

"What was it?" Lydia prompted.

"I asked if the Brothers aren't more direct channels of God's will than we are, what are they for?"

"What did Darren say?" Amy asked.

"He didn't say anything, and the more I thought about it, I realized that was his answer." The three sat for a thoughtful moment. Finally Lydia turned to Amy.

"I think I can handle a little more banana now."

Amy rose eagerly and went to the tray she had set on the dresser. She retrieved the plate and came back to the bed.

"You're good for her." She grinned at Kurt. "Maybe we should have you come every evening."

"I'd like that." Kurt smiled at both of them, shy but pleased.

"So would I." Lydia speared a slice of banana and winked at him. She remembered her promise to Casey. She thought she might have enough strength left for the task.

35

Kurt slouched comfortably in the chair near Lydia's bed. The bedside lamp cast a warm glow over her dozing face. Her frail chest rose and fell slowly as she relaxed and escaped the pain for a time. She had finally given in and taken half a pain tablet from Amy.

In the beginning Kurt had come because he felt he should, and because he noted that very few others in the Body did, other than caregivers. As the days passed into a week, then two, his admiration for her grew, as did his need to spend as much time with her as possible before she was gone.

His eyes took in Amy's soft motions, and he felt the dawning awareness that she was also a reason he came and spent his evenings in this chair. Her careful tending of the dying woman touched him deeply, and her ability to sense what Lydia needed before she asked for it showed her heart as nothing else could. The three of them talked or sat in silence. It did not matter. A bond was forged in the evening hours that would have taken years in normal circumstances.

This night found Lydia particularly weak. She did her best to rally when he arrived, but he knew it cost her a great deal and immediately insisted she sleep. She had dropped into unconsciousness. He marveled at her stamina to last this long, and realized the end was rapidly approaching. Tears stung his eyes as he looked at the tiny woman Lydia had become, and he saw Amy's eyes glisten as well.

He hastily rubbed his eyes as he heard a soft knock on the door. It opened to admit Eric. As a doctor, he had a much better idea how Lydia fared. He had told them the breathing that had begun to rattle was a sign of approaching death. Her new habit of falling asleep, sleeping deeply, and coming only partially awake spoke volumes about the struggle occurring in her body.

With a nod to Kurt and Amy, Eric removed his stethoscope from his bag. He felt her pulse. He touched her icy hands. She did not notice him as he checked her for signs of distress and pain.

"Has she had any medication tonight?"

"Just half a pill," Amy whispered.

Eric shook his head. "Half a pill isn't enough to put anybody out. It's her body making her rest for the final battle."

Kurt turned sad eyes to Eric. "Then is the final battle at hand?"

"It's already begun." Eric tucked Lydia's hand under the quilt and moved to the second chair that had been squeezed into the room. Amy sank to her usual post on the edge of the bed, and together they silently watched each breath.

When Lydia opened dreamy eyes, a small smile played across her lips, and a sigh escaped her. "So beautiful," she murmured. "I want to stay longer and longer each time."

"What did you dream?" Amy asked.

"Oh, not what. *Who.*" Her lips parted to show tiny white teeth, and bright spots glowed on her cheeks. "I saw a whole new realm, and in the midst of it there Jesus was, dancing like David in the Old Testament. He put out his hands to dance with me as well. There were scars in those hands, and I wept to see them, knowing it was for my sake he had received them, but he swept me into an embrace and said, 'Little sister, you were worth it all. Stay with me forever the next time you come.'" Lydia closed her eyes, still smiling. "I think next time I shall."

A small cry escaped Amy, and she rested her hand on Lydia's arm. "I'll miss you so." Tears cascaded down her cheeks.

Lydia shook her head. "How can you miss someone who's at home, knowing you'll be headed home yourself eventually?"

Suddenly, Lydia's eyes opened wide. Her arm struggled to free itself from the blanket, but she was not strong enough to accomplish it. In an instant Amy leaned over her, her hand soothing Lydia's shoulder.

"Everything's okay," she crooned.

Lydia shook her head. "Letter," she whispered. Her eyes searched the bedside table, then locked on Amy's gaze. "Can you find my letter?"

"What does she want?" Eric half rose from his chair.

Amy turned to look over her shoulder at him and Kurt. "Something about a letter. She hasn't gotten mail in months, so I'm not sure what she means."

"My letter." Lydia struggled to form the words. "Pillow?"

Amy carefully slid her hand under the pillow, and Kurt heard the soft crackle of paper there. She slowly extracted folded sheets. Relief flooded the sick woman's face. She lifted her hand and brushed against the paper with a touch as light as a butterfly's wing.

"You must take it," she panted. "Get it to Casey."

Kurt stood behind Amy. He saw she had been drained by the frantic seconds of not knowing where the mysterious pages were.

"We'll take care of it," he whispered. Amy cast him a grateful look and slipped the letter into the pocket of her jumper. Kurt stepped aside as Eric put a hand on his shoulder, then bent over Lydia. He looked at Amy, then at Kurt, and shook his head.

They resumed their seats and watched Lydia struggle for breath, again drifting into unconsciousness. Kurt lifted Lydia's translucent hand and warmed it carefully between his own. He savored the touch of a woman he had come to cherish deeply. The living room clock chimed the hour twice before Lydia stirred again. The others in the room had hardly moved. When her eyes opened, her face was radiant, and her smile warmed the room.

"I want to stay this time," she whispered, and the joy in her face told them her wish was to be granted at last. She exhaled, inhaled, exhaled. Then they realized it was over. With no more fuss than she had made in life, Lydia slipped from the world into the arms of God in the space of two heartbeats.

Kurt held Lydia's hand even as he felt the remaining warmth leave it. He found he could not take his eyes from the smile that graced her face. He marveled at how utterly still a body became when its spirit no longer lived within it.

Somehow Eric found the strength to stand. He put a hand on Kurt's shoulder and squeezed it. He turned to Amy and hugged her. At last he turned to the door. "I'll go make that phone call," he said quietly.

PART IV

For thus says the Lord God, "Behold, I Myself will search for My sheep and seek them out. As a shepherd cares for his herd in the day when he is among his scattered sheep, so I will care for My sheep and will deliver them from all the places to which they were scattered on a cloudy and gloomy day."

—EZEKIEL 34:11–12

36

essie rested her hands on the sill and breathed deeply. The intoxicating scent of orange blossoms filled the room behind her, heavy and moist, heralding the beginning of spring. Behind her Claude stirred from his newspaper.

"My, that smells wonderful. I never tire of it." He rose and crossed the room to stand at her side.

"I remember the first spring we were here." Her eyes swept the large backyard. "It took me awhile to figure out what smelled so good."

"Yes, and once you did, I had to go out and buy three trees." Claude's arm hugged her shoulders.

She slapped at his chest playfully. "You haven't had to buy oranges or lemons in years." They were still enjoying the view and the scent when Casey rose quietly from the couch, not wanting to break in on their pleasant interlude. Claude heard her and turned, his arm still around Jessie.

"Casey, come smell this." He softened the command with a smile. "We're standing here like a pair of old dogs with our heads out the window."

Claude and Jessie continually tried to interest her in her surroundings. She had shut down on every level since she'd left the group in Crescent Hills, and it clearly worried them. To please them both, she stepped to the window and inhaled. The orange blossoms worked their magic on her, and she breathed deeply and smiled. "Oh, lovely." She closed her eyes as she enjoyed the scent. "It's almost like magnolias but not as heavy."

Andrew jumped up from the floor and walked daintily along the windowsill in front of them.

"Andrew, you are a cat of excellent taste," Jessie said as they watched him. A bird landed in the yard, and he immediately sank to a hunting posture and made soft clicking sounds with his mouth to lure the bird closer. He gave them all a disgusted look when their mirth frightened the bird away.

Casey began to withdraw into herself again. Claude put a hand on her shoulder. "Come talk with us for a while." He turned both Casey and Jessie back toward the living room. Though there was a momentary pause, Casey followed willingly enough. Andrew crouched again on the windowsill, ready for the next bird to land. Jessie and Casey settled into the soft couch, and Claude lowered himself contentedly into his favorite chair. Jessie turned toward Casey, one leg folded beneath her. Casey toyed with the fringe on a pillow.

"How are you doing?"

Casey exhaled through her nose. "I'm sorry to be a burden on you." Her eyes fastened on her lap.

"You're not, and you know it. We only want to help." Jessie reached out and brushed a stray lock of hair from Casey's forehead. When Casey didn't reply, she looked to Claude.

"We're as new to this situation as you are," he said candidly. "We know you've gone through something that has you doubting your own shadow." Casey gathered the pillow to her chest and hugged it as she rested her chin on it. "We've not pried into what's happening inside. We want you to feel comfortable telling us."

"I find myself stumped by the simplest things." Casey shook her head. "I don't like to be by myself because I'm not used to it anymore, but that means following you both around like a puppy."

Claude studied her. "We never had any children. We really don't mind having you underfoot, because it's more than a bit of a delight to us."

"Thank you," she whispered. One tear splashed onto the pillow.

"We want you to know you can tell us anything—or nothing," Claude said. "As we said when you first arrived, you can ask us for help, live here as long as you like, and take as long as you need to feel confident again." Casey kept her eyes on Claude's wide brown ones as if they were her only lifeline. "We'll pray for you every day, every hour, every minute if need be."

"There's nothing you've been through that our Father can't bring about to good. Nothing." Jessie was emphatic.

Casey began to cry in earnest. Jessie enfolded and held her as she wept. Claude moved quietly to the couch and sat on Casey's other side. He rested his broad, dark hand on her hair and was silent. She eventually ran out of tears and sat in their embrace, hiccupping like a child. Without her awareness, Andrew had climbed into her lap, and she gripped him absently.

"Thank you," she whispered again. They both patted her.

"That's what family is for," Jessie said.

With a final shudder, Casey sat upright. She melted when she saw Andrew gazing up at her with his big, concerned eyes.

"My sweetheart." She rubbed his ears. "You know, Andrew has always been my greatest comfort when I'm upset." She looked from Jessie to Claude and back to the cat. "I think God sent him to me for that purpose."

"God puts comforters and helpers all around us," Jessie said, "but sometimes we take them for granted. I hope I never learn to do that." Her eyes shone as she looked at Claude.

He winked at her. and his eyes affirmed the same feeling. He turned to Casey. "Why don't we pray right now?"

She stiffened. "I'm not so good in that department right now."

"You won't object if we pray, will you?" She shook her head and dropped her eyes. Claude reached to take Jessie's hand, and they each kept a free hand on her.

"Father, we've got a wounded sister who needs your special bandaging and emergency care. Only you know how to put her back together after the experience she's had. We trust you to do that. Use us in any way necessary. Fill Casey with your peace. Let this be a time of growth that solidifies her faith in you. Bring beauty from ashes, as you promise in your Word to do. Thank you that she's come to us, so we can watch the miracle of her recovery and be participants in it. A cord of three strands is very hard to break, Father, so make us three intertwined strands to help each other be strong. In the name of Jesus."

"Amen," both women said.

Casey marveled as she heard Claude thank God for her and her problems. She hugged him, then Jessie. When Andrew let out a yowl, she grinned and hugged him too.

"Do you think he can really do that, Claude?" she asked.

"I've always found God to be a man of his word, Casey." Claude reached over and picked up his well-worn Bible. He flipped pages. "If anybody but Jesus was in charge of all this, I'd be worried. But he's given us a guarantee we can take to the very gates of hell, if necessary."

He began to read Romans 8:28–30, "'And we know that God causes all things to work together for good to those who love God, to those who are called according to His purpose. For those whom He foreknew, He also predestined to become conformed to the image of His Son, so that He would be the firstborn among many brethren; and these whom He predestined, He also called; and these whom He called, He also justified; and these whom He justified, He also glorified.'"

Casey let herself fall into the embrace of the comforting words as he continued to read. At last he concluded with verse 31, "'What then shall we say to these things? If God is for us, who is against us?'" Peace fell over her like a satin sheet. All three drank in the words.

"I like all those times it says 'God,' 'He,' or 'His' in that passage," Jessie said in a dreamy tone. "*God* causes ... *His* purpose ... *He* foreknew ... *He* predestined ... *He* called ... *He* justified ... *He* glorified ... *God* is for us." She smiled. "It doesn't sound like he left much for us to do, so what are we worrying about? We just have to get out of the way and let him do it."

"Doesn't she look beautiful when she thinks about Scripture?" Claude asked, his warm eyes on her. "Mrs. Barlow, if you weren't already my wife, I'd ask you to marry me right now."

"Oh, a girl likes to be asked." Jessie giggled, her face alight. Casey watched her friends with affection.

"Jessie, will you be my wife as long as I live?"

"It's going to take more than death to get away from me, Claude Barlow. I've already asked Jesus to put my mansion across the golden street from yours so I can keep an eye on you."

"I can't think of anything more delightful." He grinned.

"Oh, you two." Casey rolled her eyes.

Claude looked at his watch, refolded the paper, and picked up his coffee cup. Jessie took another sip of juice and began to stack her dishes and silverware. Casey felt tension, as she did every workday morning.

"What are your plans for today?" Jessie asked as she folded her napkin.

Casey felt a knot in her stomach. "I'm not sure. Do you have anything you need me to do?"

"If you felt like it, you could mow the grass."

"Sure, I can do that. No problem."

"You don't have to if you don't want to." Claude stopped as he prepared to push away from the table.

"No, I want to do it."

"You're not ready to go to work yet, you know," he said gently. When she jerked, it was clear he had struck a nerve. "Think of this as a time of rebuilding, and don't feel bad if you aren't able to charge out the door with us."

"I do feel guilty." Casey leaned back in her chair. "I see you both off each day and wonder if you're thinking what a lazy slob I am."

"We haven't given it a second thought," Jessie said. "Claude's right; you're not ready yet." Casey began to relax. "He's also right in saying you don't have to cut the grass. You don't have to be busy from morning to night to justify yourself."

"I don't want to be a burden." Casey said sheepishly. She saw the storm about to break on her from both directions and grinned. "I'm teasing. I like to be outside."

Jessie looked thoughtful, and then her face brightened. "Well, why don't you look around and find a nice spot for my garden?" She grinned at Claude. "We have a running joke each spring that I'm going to have a vegetable garden, but neither of us has time to plant it, so it never happens."

"This year will be different," Casey vowed.

The project stirred something in her, and she scarcely noticed when Jessie and Claude rose and hurried to complete their morning preparations. She sat at the table and poured herself another cup of coffee, then turned in her seat to gaze out over the backyard and note where the patterns of sunlight and shadow fell.

A small plot of ground took shape under Casey's careful hands. She decided to start small and see what she could do. As she turned the soil, she thought of the last year and felt again the pain the Bodylife had inflicted. Often she dodged the thoughts and focused on the soil, but inevitably her mind roamed back to questions that plagued her.

How could she have gone so wrong? Why hadn't God stopped her before she made wrong choices? Where was he now, and why did he let the Bodylife group continue to deceive and mislead vulnerable, unsuspecting people like her? After that terrible experience, how could she ever trust her own judgment again?

Ever since she had left the group, she had become increasingly angry with God. Her heart burned with the thought that he could have stopped her from becoming involved in the Bodylife at all. From there it was an easy jump to believe that he *should* have done so. So intense was her resentment that she found it nearly impossible to pray, and when she tried, she waited for amens to second her comments. She felt bereft and isolated without the affirmation. She found it hard to discipline herself to read the Bible, since others had directed her study for so long. It frightened her badly.

When Jessie suggested a garden, Casey jumped at the opportunity. She was sure it would keep her busy enough to make her too tired to think, but the more she labored, the louder her thoughts raged. She wondered if she would always feel this way, or if God would find a way to break through again. In her mind they stood at opposite edges of a vast crevasse, and she could see no way to cross it.

She braced her foot on the shovel, leaned her weight on it, and watched the blade slide into the damp earth she had soaked earlier in the day to soften it. As the blade disappeared, she felt a lurch in her chest and stood still. It was as if God had called her name quietly and said, *"This is your heart, child."*

She stared at the ground and began to work the shovel again as she pondered. The ground was poor soil for growing anything other than weeds, and she could not turn it over initially. Only when she soaked it was it soft enough to work at all. Did her heart require a flood of tears to soften it enough to be turned over?

She broke up the chunks of dirt. Many had stubborn patches of crabgrass attached to them. She picked up each clump and slapped it against the back of the shovel to save the dirt and tossed aside the weeds. With shame she realized that attitudes had grown up in her heart that weren't supposed to be there either. How many times had God had to bang her against his shovel and shake her free of clinging weeds?

She continued to enlarge the little garden patch until it covered a square of ground ten feet by ten feet. She raked and hoed the soil, then dragged out heavy bags of manure. As she slit open the first bag, the acrid odor engulfed her. She went in search of a pair of garden gloves. Gradually she worked five bags of manure into the soil, grimacing as she did at the new analogy that sprang to mind. If the last year had been manure to her life, it was sure to enrich her for many years to come. She wrinkled her nose as she worked the manure deeper into the earth and reflected on the patience of God as he had worked the same in her life.

She used a seed spreader to broadcast nutrients across the rich soil mixture and went over it again with the shovel and rake. Her back ached and sweat ran freely as she worked, but the continual unfolding of revelation made the chore a joy to her. How often had God had to enrich her life with experiences that smelled bad to her but were designed to make her soil capable of supporting his growth?

After a full day of labor, exhausted yet triumphant, Casey dragged a lawn chair over to the garden and uncoiled the hose. She turned it on herself first and then watered the tilled ground to send the nutrients deeper. If she put plants into the earth too soon, the fertilizer would scorch them and kill them immediately. It reminded her of the rush she had been in to grow in the Lord. In the end it had led her to put down her roots in soil that damaged her.

When Jessie rounded the corner of the house and saw a neat new garden patch, she stopped and applauded. Casey turned off the nozzle on the hose, stood, and bowed theatrically. Because she felt so good after her day of exertion and the things she had learned about herself, she gave the nozzle another twist and playfully sprayed her friend as well. They heard Claude's rich laughter from the patio door and turned.

"I'm almost afraid to ask what's going on out here." He grinned.

"We're returning to nature and giving up indoor plumbing," Jessie replied playfully.

"I hope this is an optional exercise." Claude shook his head, a fond look in his eyes that encompassed them both.

Casey turned the hose in his direction, but he dodged back inside. Wet and squelching in their shoes, she and Jessie went in to prepare dinner. Casey could not wait to share her thoughts from the day with the two people who were most eager to hear them. She cast a glance over her shoulder.

"Thanks, Lord," she whispered. "I'll be back for more."

37

re you sure about this?" Jessie asked as she and Casey stood near the front door and waited for Claude to come downstairs for church. "You can come with us if you'd like. You know you're welcome."

"I have to do this." Casey shifted her Bible and purse from one arm to the other. "I started out there, and I have to go back to see if I was wrong."

"Something in your church made you hungry for more," Jessie reasoned. "You went after something that turned out not to be what you thought it would be, but is the place you started more right for you now?"

"I have to go back so I can either open or close that particular door." Casey set her jaw.

Claude came down the stairs, and he and Jessie swept out the door. She followed slowly and got into her car for a solitary drive to church for the first time since she'd left Crescent Hills. She felt dread, curiosity, and a strange lethargy. Her gradual thawing toward God had continued all week as she planted the new garden, and she felt a need to go to church at last. She wondered what state of mind she would be in when she returned.

"Casey, it's good to see you back," Pastor Sternbridge reached to shake her hand on her way out the door after the service.

The sights and smells of the church had instantly transported her back to the last time she attended. She had selected a seat near the back, not surprised to see regular attendees in their accustomed seats.

The singing seemed subdued after what she had experienced in the Body. She heard her own voice far louder than any others and immediately reduced its volume. Each successive song called for a conscious effort so she would blend in. No amens rang out, there was no spontaneous sharing, and the sermon was one the pastor had preached before.

The experience reaffirmed the feeling that she had been right to look for more. It lifted her spirits to have the confirmation. As she faced Pastor Sternbridge, she wondered how to respond to his welcome since she had no intention of returning.

"Thank you, Pastor." She shook his hand and prepared to step out into the bright sunshine.

"I'm glad you came to your senses." He was almost casual.

"What do you mean?" She stopped as a chill crossed her heart.

"That group you joined." He looked smug. "I'd heard a lot of things about them, and I was afraid you'd be hurt."

Casey was thunderstruck. A small flame of rage flickered in her heart. "You knew I was walking into a bad situation, and you didn't say anything?"

"Would you have listened?"

Before she could reply, she was nudged from behind. The pastor turned to greet his largest and most devoted follower, a wide woman in a flowered dress, sporting a chaotic floral hat, and toting a handbag large enough to accommodate a small car. Her heavy perfume made Casey sneeze.

"Better look after your cold, dear," the woman said as she turned to monopolize the pastor's attention.

"It was a fair question," Claude said as he sliced mushrooms on the cutting board.

Jessie bustled behind him, reaching for the pots and pans she needed to prepare one of her famous Italian feasts. Casey leaned against the island countertop and watched Claude's deft hands reduce the fat mushrooms to elegant, paper-thin sheets.

"I seem to recall," he said, "that a certain close friend of yours had several conversations aimed to make you stop and think, but you didn't hear her." To her credit, Jessie kept silent.

"I'd like to think that if the pastor had tried to stop me, I might have turned around at a crucial moment." Casey propped her elbows on the counter and put her chin in her hands.

Jessie turned from heating olive oil in a large skillet and reached around Claude for the mushroom-laden cutting board. She transferred the slices into the fragrant hot oil and began to stir them with a slotted spoon.

"The only way to get through this thing is to be brutally honest with yourself. No dodging responsibility." Jessie looked at Casey. When she didn't react defensively, she continued. "I know you're afraid you might make another error in judgment down the road. You have to be honest about why you made *this* one before you can be confident enough to make your next decision without fear."

"Think back to when you decided to get involved in the Bodylife." Claude wiped his hands. "How would you have reacted if the pastor had spoken against it?"

Casey stared into space for a moment, and then looked back at Claude.

"I would have thought he was protecting his membership roster."

Jessie turned back to the stove and concentrated on the skillet. Casey worried. "Am I really trying to put the blame for this on someone else?"

Claude leaned a hip against the island and studied her for a moment. "It's natural to want to have another reason—any other reason—for the things we do, other than being unwise at a critical moment. That's gone on as long as people have been around. Look at Adam and Eve in the garden. She ate the apple but blamed the serpent that talked her into it. Adam ate the apple too but blamed Eve for bringing it to his attention. Then he went a step further and said, 'It was the woman you gave me,' and implied that God was to blame." Casey was still.

"Do you think God is to blame for your situation, Casey?"

She mulled over his question. Claude and Jessie waited.

"He could have done a lot to stop me, and he didn't," she said. "What's the point of being his child if he doesn't keep me from running out to play in traffic? Would it have been so hard for God to have stopped me from making such a horrible mistake?"

Jessie added linguine noodles to boiling water and moved her exquisite sauce to a back burner to simmer. She joined her husband and friend as they clustered around the kitchen island. Casey's cheeks burned with small red spots of anger.

"I think you're mature enough to know that God doesn't always speak to us in an audible voice or physically restrain us when we start to do something outside of what he intends," Claude said, "but I think he did everything he could to stop you."

"But I didn't stop. That's the point!"

"Yes, that's exactly the point," Jessie said. "He told you in his Word how to test those who would want to lead us. He warned you about pride and outward shows of piety. He told you he loves you and wants what's best for you, in his timing." She reached across and brushed a finger against Casey's arm. "He did all that, then let you make the choice, and he has lived with—and suffered with—the choice as much as you have."

"There were warning signs along the road," Casey admitted as conviction flooded her. "I guess I was too caught up in the scenery to read them."

"Be honest; you threw the map out the window," Jessie said. As the pasta water boiled over, Casey felt the scalding truth of her words.

Jessie passed another clean plate to Casey for rinsing. Claude turned from the cupboard where he'd deposited the last one to receive it, dripping, from her hands.

"I had an interesting conversation with Bob Murphy today." Jessie's face was thoughtful in the bright light over the sink. Casey looked at her sharply and wondered what he had said to stay on Jessie's mind so long.

"I'm up to my ears in projects, and I told him I could sure use some help."

"Let me guess," Casey snorted. "First he turned red, then he turned white, and then he fainted at the very idea, right?"

"I think there was blue in there too. You know what a patriotic guy he is." Jessie grinned. Casey laughed. "But I didn't put up with his chameleon act. I told him he could continue to bring projects into my office until doomsday, but they wouldn't get done any faster than this old pair of eyes could do them."

"Whose eyes you calling 'old,' woman?" Claude took a playful swipe at her with his towel, and she winked at him.

"I got him to agree that I could bring a few projects for you to work on here at home, if you'd like to." She lifted one gloved hand from the water and held it up in caution. "He doesn't have a position open right now, but it's a start."

"It might be nice to be able to work part-time from here," Casey mused, taking the next pot, rinsing the soap off, and handing it to Claude. She turned to Jessie, more animated than she expected to feel. "You know I'd like to help in any way I can. He doesn't even have to pay me."

"I offered to pay you from my check, and he refused." Jessie let the water drain from the sink and turned to Casey. "That was the truly remarkable part of the conversation. Bob said, 'The laborer is worthy of his wages.' I asked him where on earth he came up with a line like that, and he said—as casual as you please—'Oh, my pastor talked about it on Sunday.'"

"His what?" Casey's eyes popped. "Since when does Bob Murphy have a pastor?"

"I think my face looked about like yours does, and I asked him that before I had time to think. He said he's been attending church since all this trouble came up about you." Jessie looked down.

"When I returned from vacation to find you'd left the company without telling me, I went over the edge."

"That's putting it mildly." Claude folded his towel and led the way to the living room. "She was as frantic as I've ever seen her." They settled into their favorite spots, Claude in his chair, Casey and Jessie on the couch. Claude's words sliced through Casey, and her conscience stirred.

"I told him I was scared to death about what was happening and demanded to know why he hadn't told me what you planned while there was still time to stop it."

"I'm surprised he didn't, actually," Casey said.

"Well, you know Bob. When you told him it was between you and him, it stayed right there. I told him we had to do something immediately. He reminded me you were free to make your choices. We had no legal right to interfere." Jessie smiled. "I told him I would bypass the judicial system on my knees."

"Oh, Jess. It seemed so right at the time," Casey sank into the couch and pictured the confrontation. Claude's voice brought her back to the present.

"Sounds to me like 'beauty for ashes' has begun. Imagine, Bob Murphy going to church." He shrugged sheepishly. "Of course, why should we be surprised? After all, we prayed that the Lord would turn this situation for good. I'm only surprised at how he's doing it."

Some of the weight pressing Casey into the couch lifted as she considered his words. What else would God do to redeem the mess she had made? She was sure she wouldn't have to wait long to find out.

38

Piped music played unobtrusively over Casey's head as she flipped languidly through the clothing rack. The sign above it proclaimed it to be final closeout merchandise. She could see why. She wondered who wore avocado any more. It had been ugly in pictures she'd seen of the seventies and had not improved with age as far as she was concerned. She drifted to an adjacent rack. Her mind automatically calculated how she would look in the plaid smock her hands spread beneath the hangar. All it needed was a T-shirt and matching anklets.... She froze, realizing she had been drawn to a Bodylife outfit from hem to shoulder despite more than a month away from the group. Sweat broke out on her forehead as she looked frantically for a different style of clothing. Suddenly a familiar voice broke upon her.

"Casey!" Gretchen crowed as she flung her arms around her. "Praise the Lord! Oh, amen! I can't believe I ran into you here. None of the Sisters seem to shop here. I think the bargains are great though." It had been months since Casey had seen Gretchen at a Gathering, and a quick glance told her all she needed to know.

"Gretchen. Pregnant again?"

"I know, I said the last one was the last one, but amen! Here we go again." She laughed sheepishly. Casey shook her head, baffled by Gretchen's maternal drive.

"Where's the baby?"

"Cedric? He's with Gerry's mom. She loves to babysit."

Casey doubted it. As Jennie darted between display racks, Gretchen pounced on the smocks Casey had been studying.

"Oh, amen. I've been looking for a sale on these. This is too sweet. I've got a T-shirt that would go perfectly with this. I need anklets though. Help me find a pair to match."

Casey noted that Gretchen was not wearing Bodylife-approved clothes today, since she had not expected to run into anyone from the group. Her stretchy midcalf pants and oversized shirt showed her real inclination. The smocks would be for Sundays when she wanted to blend in. Casey was plotting an escape from Gretchen's flow of words when a cold breeze chilled her heart.

"I thought it was funny, that's all," Gretchen said. "I mean it didn't feel normal."

"What did you say?"

"I asked what you thought about the skimpy memorial service we had for Lydia. I mean she'd been a part of the Body for a long time. A simple mention tacked on at the end of a Gathering didn't seem enough."

Casey's hand shot out, and she gripped the circular rack to keep from falling. The roar in her ears was as loud as a train in a tunnel.

"Lydia," she whimpered. "Lydia."

Gretchen was oblivious to her distress. "I know we do things in a low-key manner in the Body. I've never been sure why." She shrugged and turned back to the dresses. "But there's low-key, then there's borderline negligent."

"Lydia is dead? Tell me. When?" Casey seized Gretchen's arm in a painfully tight grip. Gretchen studied Casey with a puzzled frown.

"A week ago. You know that. For Pete's sake, you live in the same house." She tipped her head to one side as if to do so would bring Casey into sharper focus.

"A week ago." Casey dropped her hand from Gretchen's arm and slumped onto a small stool a shop assistant had been using.

"Why didn't you know Lydia had died?"

"I don't live in the Sisters House anymore." Casey covered her face with her hands briefly, then looked dully at Gretchen.

"Really? Then where are you living? That's one of the neat things about the Body. You can move around and live with different families whenever you want, and you don't have go through all the hassle of selling a house."

"I don't live with anyone from the Bodylife. I left the group." At last Gretchen was speechless. "I had no choice, Gret. Things happened that I couldn't agree with, and I was in the middle of them. I left a couple of months ago."

"No wonder I haven't seen you. Besides, Gerry had to go to Italy for six weeks for the company. It was his first trip to Europe, and we all went with him. It was marvelous."

Casey stood and placed a hand on Gretchen's arm. "Please tell me about Lydia. What's happened?" Gretchen fell back a step. As she did so, Jennie plowed into her from behind. Gretchen's hand whipped around, caught the girl's wrist, and immobilized her.

"Lydia had cancer. Surely you knew that?" Casey nodded. "Well, she died of it about a week ago. The Bodylife members cleared out her room, and at the next Gathering there was a minute of silence."

Casey waited for her to continue.

"That was it. No wake, no funeral, no burial service, nothing. Kind of spooky how quickly she disappeared from the Body."

"Lydia has never been more part of the body than she is at this moment," Casey said firmly. "She's free. That's what's important."

"Well, amen!" Gretchen turned back to the clothing rack. "Now which of these do you think would look best on me?"

"I've got to go, Gretchen. It was nice to see you. Thanks for filling me in." She turned and headed toward the door.

"I'll see you on the Lord's Day! Amen!" Gretchen called after her.

Casey stopped, as guilt swept her. She turned and went back to Gretchen, the sorrow over Lydia's death heavy in her eyes. "Gret, I haven't been around in a while because I finally realized that the Bodylife isn't what it seems from the outside. There are a lot of things going on within it that are contrary to how we're supposed to behave as Christians." She put her hand on Gretchen's arm, capturing her friend's full attention with her pain-softened voice. "I left the Sisters House, and I left the Bodylife for good."

Gretchen frowned and shifted the garments she had accumulated from one arm to the other. Jennie, for once, was still, delighting in playing with a decorative belt that hung to her eye level. "What do you mean, stuff that's not right?"

"People are abusing authority, twisting the meaning of Scripture, and getting others to do things they would normally never do—in the name of unity. I got burned," Casey said, her gaze gripping Gretchen's eyes. "I don't want to see you hurt, too." Unsure how to continue, she gave Gretchen a hug. "Just keep your eyes open, OK?"

When Gretchen had no reply to her strange outpouring of words, she smiled sadly and left the store. She longed to soak in a hot bubble bath to ease away her tension and to think through how she could convey to Gretchen—and others—the truth about the Bodylife. She also needed space to weep, to mourn for her friend, to talk to God about heaven's newest resident.

Casey emerged from the tub much later, her fingers and toes wrinkled. She had stayed in the tub, letting out water from time to time and running fresh hot water again until her tears were exhausted. She mentally reviewed every memory she had of Lydia and honored her in prayer to their mutual Father. Only then did she feel released from the grief that had assaulted her when Gretchen spoke so casually about Lydia and the skimpy memorial. She realized it would take study and preparation before she was ready to help anyone else in the Bodylife, but she was willing to make the effort.

She dressed in fresh clothes and toweled her hair briskly. She put on her glasses and slipped her feet into sandals. With a determined stride, she collected her Bible, a notebook, and a pen. She carried them to the backyard and dumped them out on the picnic table Claude had brought home two days earlier as a surprise for Jessie. She spread out the implements like a surgeon preparing to excise diseased tissue. In many ways the comparison was appropriate; she intended to cut away the last remnants of the Bodylife from her mind and spirit, since that had to be done before she could ever hope to reach out to others.

Before she plunged into the task she had set for herself, she went into the house and returned with tea in a tall glass tinkling with ice cubes. She put the glass within easy reach and opened her notebook to the first page. She read through the notes she had taken at various Gatherings. For each Bible reference she had jotted down, she turned to the Scriptures and looked it up. She had never had time to do so before. Sometimes she was startled to discover what the other half of a verse said. Several times when she put the verse back into its proper context it changed the implied meaning entirely. Other times the verses stood up to her scrutiny. After she had studied several verses she sat back, confused about what to do next.

"Lord, here I am trying to sift the wheat from the chaff, and I didn't even come to you first. Please open my eyes and help me understand what you are saying. I want to be free from any error I've allowed to creep into my mind." She rubbed her eyes and resumed her study. In each case what she had been taught was either confirmed or refuted by deeper study of the passage.

She picked up her pen and drew a vertical line down the page. Over one column she wrote *Truth* and over the other *Error*. She set out to dissect, sift, and review until she was satisfied she had found the good and identified the bad, working through the afternoon. The ice in her tea melted, condensation beaded and ran down the outside of the glass and made a puddle around its base.

When she began to feel chilled, she looked around and judged by the lengthening shadows that she had sat unmoving for hours. She had filled sheets with her findings. Again and again she trembled with joy when she discovered that something that had thrilled her heart when she heard it in a Gathering was really true. She was also struck to the soul with the realization of how careless she had been to unquestioningly absorb dangerous attitudes and untruths. Pride lurked at the core of believing she'd found something others had missed. She repented of her pride as she discovered it repeatedly in her own handwriting.

Casey stretched, stood stiffly, and gathered up her materials. Her mind spun with all the things she would share with Claude and Jessie over dinner. She was energized to continue her study for the next several days—as long as it took—but this first day had given her a glimpse of freedom and hope. To celebrate her productive afternoon, and as a special remembrance of Lydia, she decided to whip up a modified Chinese dinner, and hoped it would erase the sting of the last one. She spent the next hour in happy preparation and was rewarded with her friends' delighted smiles when they came home from work. Her study had begun the process of rewriting the mistruths that had crippled her spirit, and the dinner brought closure to the wound within her heart that had never quite healed.

Two nights later, as cricket songs filled the air, Casey jumped when a big hand closed on her shoulder. There was concern in every line of Claude's body as he bent to look at her face. Jessie crowded behind him.

"You worried us. Are you all right?"

"Claude?" Casey blinked and looked into his face. She took in Jessie's frantic expression and the dark yard. Her eyes widened, and she checked her watch. "Oh, my, look at the time!" She attempted to rise, but Claude stopped her as he slid onto the bench beside her.

"No, sit a moment." He reassured Jessie with his eyes, and she sank onto the opposite bench. "We didn't know where you were when we came home, that's all."

"I'm sorry. I didn't mean to upset you. I've been sitting here thinking." Her voice was soft and dreamy.

"How long?" Jessie ventured.

"It seems like a second or two, but it's been a couple of hours, I guess. I had to think it all through. I know you both think I was pretty stupid to get involved in the Bodylife, and you're right."

"It's never stupid to seek after God," Claude said. "That's what you set out to do. This particular group turned out to be the wrong way to go, but you made the attempt. That's commendable." She gave him a grateful look.

"I thought I had found perfection, people who were as serious about God as I was." She wrapped her arms around herself. "Instead what I had found was deception. Calculated, deliberate, coordinated deception."

"I know you were disillusioned by this group, but they're only misguided. It's not a plot," Jessie chided gently. Casey shook her head slowly.

"That's what I thought, but it's not true." She picked up a notebook from the table. "You know I've been reading through all my notes from when I was there. I've worked at it all week. I wanted to clear this from my head. Like I told you at dinner the other night, God has been wonderfully healing in it all. He confirms some things, refutes others, and has helped my mind to stabilize again.

"But today it all came together, mostly because of two lists." She flipped open the notebook and displayed a page with two columns of words. "There was a morning when we had a powerful sermon. It was by someone other than Webster, but it struck everyone in the room with real force," she explained as she traced the columns. "He drew a comparison between the way most people are—selfish—and the way we should be—centered on the body of Christ. The way he illustrated it was to list a bunch of words or phrases containing the word *self*."

She gestured to the notebook, and they followed her finger to the first list.

"Words like *self-reliance, self-esteem, self-control*. Then he turned the congregation on its ear when he listed the words again, this time substituting the word *Body* for *self*." She ran a finger down the second column. "*Body-reliance. Body-esteem. Body-control.* Do you see?"

"I can see why people were captured by the message," Claude mused. "There's some truth in it, isn't there?"

"That's what I've found. It isn't all a waste. But in this case I saw something I hadn't seen and was never meant to see." Again they bent over the notebook. "There are not as many words in the second column as in the first. There's one left out." Jessie and Claude compared the lists.

"The only one missing is ... self-deception," Jessie said at last. "It's listed, but its counterpart isn't." She looked up at Casey. "I don't see the point."

"The point is, it was a deliberate omission, yet it was the truest word there. Every other word was repeated, and in the same order as the first time. There's no way Dominic could have missed the word accidentally. He deliberately avoided it."

"This is significant?" Claude asked. "Maybe it didn't fit the sermon message."

"Oh, it didn't fit all right, but he could have left it out of the first list too. Body-deceit. It ran like a current under everything there."

"You've drawn a conclusion from one second in one sermon?" Jessie asked.

"Oh, no, I'm not that quick to judge." Casey gathered her papers together and tapped them on the table to bring the edges into alignment. "But I've sat here for hours, reviewed every conversation I could remember, every action, every Gathering, everything I can recall. Under it all, the deceit is clear when I look at it objectively. The way I was carefully drawn in, the increased responsibility I was given, the tests of my loyalty, the reinforcements when I needed to be reassured—every step was calculated, planned, and orchestrated. I learned the subtle signals Bodylife members pass back and forth in a Gathering. I participated in it like the others." She hung her head.

"And Lydia?" Jessie asked in a quiet voice.

A flash of pain shot through her. "At first I thought she was part of it too, but she admitted she had been deceived herself, and I believe her. I think any role she played was with good intentions." Casey said. "Her earnest desire the last time I saw her was for me to leave the Bodylife, and she wanted to send out any others she could. I'll never know if she succeeded." Her voice caught. "Perhaps she never even had a chance."

"Never is an awfully long time," Claude said. They sat together in the fragrant darkness as moths and other bugs battered against the porch light, then Jessie rose.

"We love you, Casey." She looked down at her. "I know we don't have the full picture of what you went through, but we're glad to take part in your healing."

Claude patted Casey's back again as he stood. "As you said, it wasn't all for nothing. You've gained insights, and you've had your spiritual discernment antibodies stirred up."

"Antibodies?"

"Sure. When you catch a virus, it stirs up all kinds of things in your body to fight it off. Once you've had it, they get stirred up even faster the next time. You got a dose of deception, and I dare say when it rears its head in the future—and it will—your spirit will fight back more vigorously to protect you better from its invasion."

"What a wonderful analogy." A smile broke across Casey's face. "I'll keep it in mind, Dr. Claude." As they moved toward the house, the welcoming light reached out to embrace her. She squeezed her friends' hands as a sense of peace she had never expected to feel again filled her soul.

39

As Darren drove into the neighborhood park, he reflected on the times he had been there—to wrestle with his thoughts, to calm Casey in the storm, to discuss his ill-fated engagement to Carol with her. He found comfort in the familiar surroundings, but at the same time he was haunted by memories.

The sun broke through clouds and illuminated the picnic area, and he saw a slim figure seated at a picnic table well back under the trees. He parked and slowly surveyed the area. A couple played energetic tennis. The volleyball court showed signs of recent activity. A young mother pushed her joyfully squealing daughter on a swing.

Darren slid from the truck and strolled as if he needed to stretch his legs, without a definite destination in mind. He felt silly as he gave in to the need for subterfuge. Nonetheless, he continued his slow advance toward the woman. When he was twenty feet away, he waved as if he had just seen her. Her eyes swept the park before she smiled.

"It's good to see you," Amy said.

"Same here. I'm sorry about this." He gestured to the park, but encompassed the entire situation. He lowered himself to the bench, his larger frame blocking her from the view of any passersby; she relaxed. Awkwardness threatened to engulf them, and Darren knew she could run away any moment. He looked directly into her eyes. "You said on the phone you need my help. What can I do?"

"I was really at a loss, but then you called unexpectedly."

"I was concerned about Carol."

"I was touched by that and decided to take a chance and reach out to you." Her eyes toured the park grounds and returned to him. "I made Lydia a promise before she died, and I don't know how to fulfill it."

A bolt went through Darren at her words.

"I'm sorry. I thought you knew." Impulsively she put a hand out to grip the arm he had on the table.

"I knew she didn't have long, but no, I hadn't heard." He grimaced. "I'm out of the loop these days, as you know."

"It was a gentle and peaceful death. She was longing to go to the Lord. In fact she dreamed she was passing back and forth between this world and the next, and Jesus asked her to stay the next time she came to visit. Not long afterward she went visiting again and didn't return to us."

"I enjoyed being around her, and I know Casey was her special friend," Darren said. "That made her special to me too."

"Before she died, Lydia gave me this letter." Amy reached into her pocket and extracted folded papers. She smoothed a crease. "It's for Casey." She turned it over in her hands. "Kurt and I promised Lydia we'd get it to her." She colored and looked pleadingly at Darren. "It's been three weeks, and I have no idea how to find her." She slid the letter across the table, but kept one hand firmly on it. "I thought you might know how to contact her."

Darren shrugged. "I haven't seen her since before she left the Body. Do you have any idea where she's gone?"

"She left in a hurry and didn't have time to jot down a forwarding address." Amy's expression was wry. "If she'd told anyone where she was going it would have been Lydia, but she didn't know or she would have told us."

"Perhaps not, if Kurt was there."

Amy colored again. "I know what you're thinking, but things have changed a bit for him." She did not meet his eyes. "In the final weeks before her death, Kurt spent a lot of time with Lydia ... and with me." The blush migrated down her neck. "I think you can safely assume that Kurt and I will be leaving the Body shortly, once we've tied up our loose ends."

"Why not leave now?" He regretted her discomfort but was very glad about what she had said. He studied her in the dappled light.

"As Casey discovered, the tentacles of the Body are long. If we're to have any hope of successfully moving out, we'll have to have our feet under us first."

Darren noted her persistent use of the plural. He was afraid to congratulate her for fear he would cause her to close down in embarrassment. Optimism swept him, and he considered the problem of finding Casey.

"I never knew Casey except in the Body," he thought aloud. "I don't know anyone she might have gone to when she left there."

"Well, there was Gretchen," Amy reminded him, "but I haven't seen her much lately."

"Is it possible Casey went to her?"

"I don't think Gretchen could keep quiet about it, and once she said something, the whole Body would know in hours."

They thought for a few minutes, as the couple playing tennis collapsed in exhausted heaps and another mother with a stroller joined the first woman and her daughter at the swings. The birds' shrill cries punctuated the stillness.

"It's really amazing to me how very insulated my life has been. I have a hard time picturing what I'll do without the Body to give my day structure."

"Don't worry. Once you're back in the water, you remember how to swim pretty fast." Darren patted the hand she still held over the letter between them on the table.

"Are you swimming?"

"I treaded water for a few days. Then I started to experiment with different strokes. I'm getting more used to the water and have actually begun to enjoy it again."

Amy fingered the edge of the letter and drew their attention back to the problem at hand. "What we need is to find a place where we're sure to cross paths with her."

"I think you're on to something." Darren pondered. "Regardless of how big the city is, there has to be a place to which we can guarantee she'll return. Then we have to be patient until she does."

He watched a squirrel dash along a branch with something in its mouth. It disappeared into a hole in a tree, then reappeared empty mouthed. When Darren snapped his fingers in triumph, Amy jumped and looked at him expectantly.

"Squirrels!" he exclaimed as he watched them jump from branch to branch.

"Excuse me?"

"Perfect!" He rubbed his hands together briskly. She waited for him to elaborate, and with a grin, he did.

Casey decided to take a break from editing the projects Jessie had brought home. She stretched and got up from her chair. Andrew opened his eyes no farther than necessary to assure himself she was not heading out the door with her usual purposeful stride. He promptly fell asleep again nestled in Claude's favorite chair.

She wandered into the kitchen and peered into the small glass window on the bread machine. It puzzled her that she still had not gotten the first welcome whiff of warm, yeasty bread baking. She opened the lid; the dough lay small and forlorn in the pan. When she put her hand inside the machine, she felt none of the warmth she expected.

"Uh-oh." She twisted the pan, lifted it out, put her hand carefully down into the machine, and groaned. It was obvious the motor had burned out.

She was about to dump the ball of dough into the trash when she thought better of it. She reached for one of Jessie's cookbooks, flipped to the bread section, read the instructions for three loaves, and averaged their cooking temperatures in her head. She set the oven, rummaged in the cupboard, and extracted a loaf pan. After reshaping the dough, she popped it in the oven when it had heated. She set the timer and turned back to the useless bread machine.

She knew how Claude loved fresh bread and resolved to remedy the situation as soon as possible.

With the windows rolled down, the fresh, early summer air redolent with the scent of cut grass rushed through the car. Casey inhaled deeply to calm herself. She was nervous as she approached Crescent Hills for the first time since leaving the Body. At every stoplight she expected to see familiar vehicles. Sweat broke out on her neck, and she tried to reason away her fear. She moved into the left turn lane, and her heart beat faster as she entered the storage facility driveway. Several Bodylife families had taken storage lockers there. Before she approached her locker, she checked all the driveways. She relaxed when she didn't see any cars she recognized.

Casey went to number 118 and saw a small tag hanging on the locker handle, fluttering in the breeze. She caught it and turned it over. *"Please see manager on duty,"* it read. She ran through possible scenarios as to why the manager wanted to see her but could think of nothing. With a shrug she untied the tag and put it in her back pocket.

She unlocked and raised the door and moved in among the boxes and furniture, touching things and inhaling the lingering essence of the life she had given up so thoroughly. Casey thought of her Jewel with a sharp pang. Every item brought a rush of remembrance. She sank into her favorite chair, closed her eyes, and pictured her former home around her.

For the first time since she moved in with Jessie and Claude, Casey longed for a place wholly hers. She let the healthy feeling warm her heart. She had to give the matter thought and talk it over with Jessie. Much as her friends enjoyed her in their home, Casey knew that such a situation caused strain. Jessie and Claude would feel they had succeeded when she was steadily on her feet again.

With a quick last stroke of the chair's soft velour arms, she got up and searched among boxes. At last she found the one housing her bread machine and bore it triumphantly to the car. Since she had burned out Jessie's machine, she would contribute her own.

Her self-imposed task completed, Casey methodically went through other items and extracted enough useful things to tide her over until she moved someplace new. Clothes not suitable in the conformist atmosphere of the Body welcomed her like old friends. Jeans and corduroy slacks, T-shirts and peasant blouses, even constrictive panty hose were appealing and nostalgic. Colorful sweaters, soft, drapey dresses, all reminded her of who she used to be. She took three suitcases full. She also hefted a large box of books.

With a happy cry she retrieved a bag filled with simple toys Andrew enjoyed. The bag held yarn, spongy balls, a Ping-Pong ball, and a pair of balled socks he delighted to carry around like a small kitten. She grinned as she anticipated his pleasure of rediscovery. Only when she closed the door and pulled her keys from her pocket did she remember the tag. She clicked the lock, closed the hatch, and slid behind the wheel.

A new renter was exiting the office with a site map in her hand when Casey pulled up. The manager, a middle-aged, stoop-shouldered man with stringy hair combed across his balding head, stepped out with the customer and pointed to an alley of lockers and then went back inside. The woman waved at her as she passed, and Casey returned the greeting. As she entered the office, a bell tinkled.

"I found this note on my locker, number 118." She handed the tag to the manager across the high desk. He turned to the slots behind him, extracted a small white envelope, and handed it to her. Her name was handwritten on it.

"We won't tell people who has a locker here, but if something comes in and the name matches, we pass it along. I think that's been here about ten days." The phone rang, and he turned to answer it.

"Thanks," she said. He waved as he spoke into the receiver. She left the office, got in her car, and again examined the envelope. The writing was unfamiliar to her. She slipped her thumb under the glued flap and pried it open. A single folded sheet bore a brief message in the same handwriting.

Casey, please call me. I have something for you from Lydia. Darren.

A phone number was jotted below his name. The exchange indicated the number was in Grovers, which puzzled her. She turned the sheet over, but there was nothing more. It took Casey the entire drive home to decide whether she would call. Though curious, she felt uneasy. Only Lydia's name persuaded her.

"Hi. You've found me." His recorded voice sang out. "No matter how good it is, I don't need siding, a new long-distance carrier, or a subscription to the paper. If you're calling about anything else, leave me a message, and I'll call you back." A beep sounded.

"Cute, Darren." Casey chuckled. "What about tickets to the Policeman's Ball?" There was noise as the receiver was picked up.

"Casey!" He was out of breath. "I'm here."

"Oh, screening our calls, are we?"

"All I get are sales calls, and I had my hands full of groceries." She could hear a grin through his voice. "How are you doing?"

"I'm quite fine." She knew he meant more by the question than a casual inquiry. "I'm curious too. This isn't exactly a Crescent Hills number."

"You're pretty sharp for a heretic."

Casey sucked in her breath. "Is that what they're saying?"

"I'm afraid so, but it takes one to know one." There was a long silence on Casey's end. "Are you there?"

"Yes, I'm here." She paused. "So, do you want to tell me about it?"

"I do want to talk to you, but I hate phones. Can we meet somewhere?" Casey's hesitancy must have rung down the line. "I know you've been burned, and you have every right to be suspicious of anyone from the Body," he soothed. She still held back. "You know Lydia is gone?" he said gently.

"Yes." Misery made her voice hollow.

"She left a letter for you."

"With you?"

"No, with Amy. I have it, because she hoped I'd find a way to get it to you."

"Why would Amy think you could find me?" Her guard came up again.

"A special friendship grew between Amy and Lydia after you left, and I think when I left, Lydia probably told Amy I was a safe person to try to reach you through." He laughed as he continued. "It wasn't exactly easy either."

"I don't mean to sound paranoid," she said at last.

"Go ahead. You're entitled."

"Okay." She took a deep breath. "Let's meet in the food court at the mall tomorrow. One o'clock?"

"Great! I'll see you then." They disconnected.

She wondered if she'd made the right choice. She could always skip the rendezvous if she felt uneasy, but she yearned for Lydia's letter. She knew she would go, if only to have this last touch from her.

He dialed the number he had posted on his refrigerator. He was relieved when she picked up the phone.

"It's me. I finally reached her. We're meeting tomorrow at the mall for lunch at one."

"I'm sorry, there's no one here by that name. What number did you dial?"

"I understand."

"No, ours is eight-six-four-two." She hung up.

He turned, put down the receiver, and went back to his groceries.

The ringing phone was finally picked up.

"Hi. It's me. The project is finally going ahead. Tomorrow at one at the mall."

"That sounds like a great offer, but we don't need the driveway resealed. It's gravel," he said and hung up.

She smiled.

40

The food court swarmed with people, but Casey instantly picked Darren out when he entered the dining area. His eyes swept the congested table area, and he looked at his watch. He picked out a table at the rear so he could keep an eye on the various entrances.

From her seat on a bench tucked behind a pillar on the mezzanine level above him, Casey watched Darren watch for her. She looked for any sign he was accompanied by someone else. When she was satisfied, she rose. Her route down from the mezzanine enabled her to descend stairs behind his table, and she appeared unexpectedly.

"Hi," she said.

He jumped and stood to greet her. "Where'd you come from?" She pointed to the upper level, and he shook his head. "That's the one place I didn't look."

"I was counting on that." She sat down as he did, and for a moment they looked at each other, trying to see if the changes they had been through showed in their faces.

"It's good to see you." She knew he meant it. She felt her old red nemesis creep up her cheeks, so she dropped her eyes. She was not sure what to do next.

"Are you hungry?"

"I am, a little. Why don't we get something?" She looked at the different food vendors ranged around the dining area perimeter.

"Do you trust me?" Darren leaned across the table and looked into her eyes. She caught the playfulness in his voice and nodded, and he got up and moved toward the pizza vendor. As soon as she saw where he was going, she realized it was exactly what she craved. Minutes later he returned with plates of pizza slices balanced on top of drink cups. She jumped up to help him navigate the final stretch to the table.

"I realized I didn't know what kind of pizza you liked, so I told them to give me a slice of everything."

She was delighted and inhaled the spicy steam. He grinned at her pleasure, then produced a plastic knife and cut the six pieces in half lengthwise so they could each have a taste of them all. Casey's eyes sparkled as she surveyed the feast.

"May I?" Darren raised his folded hands for her to see.

"Please." She immediately folded her own and bowed her head.

"Father, thanks for enabling me to find Casey. Bless this food and bless our time together. We never want to lose track of who is most important. Be part of our conversation today. In Jesus' name, amen."

"Amen." She echoed him and was aware that the word hit both their nerves.

"Now let's decide which of these is best." Darren shifted pizza from plate to plate. As they ate, she asked him to fill her in. He was animated, but not bitter.

"In the end I couldn't go through with the arranged marriage to Carol. When we were to switch from the Gathering to the wedding ceremony, I knew it was wrong. I hated to hurt Carol," he shook his head, "but I decided it was better to stop the wedding than to hurt her more by marrying her when I didn't love her. I picked up my Bible and went out the back door. It was cowardly but effective."

"That was it?"

"I had a vague idea of standing up and saying what was on my heart. But in the end, I didn't say anything."

"You left the Body right after that?"

"Actually it was weeks after that." He rubbed his hands over his face. "Weeks of browbeating and cajoling and pressure. I should have left immediately. Somehow I wasn't ready to give it up. I hoped the idea of marrying Carol was the problem. Those weeks, however, showed me that it ran much deeper than that."

"I guess you're too big to lock up though." Casey's eyes twinkled. Darren tipped back his head and laughed.

"I don't think it would have worked any better with me than it did with you." He grinned. "Sometime you'll have to tell me how you got out. I decided I would make them throw me out. They held a special Gathering, and I was made *persona non grata*. It's like a dream that I could even have considered doing as the Brothers asked, but it seemed perfectly logical at the time." He looked at her. "How could we have been so wrong?"

"I've been studying a lot these past weeks, and I've come to the conclusion that the same hunger for God that drove me to the Bodylife will drive me all my life." She paused. "And that's okay, but I have to be discerning, not turn off the special radar God gives every believer when it disagrees with what I want."

"The Spirit. I know what you mean. I blew past a lot of caution and stop signs myself on my way into the Bodylife, and it was only later that I saw all the damage my determination had caused." They were silent for a time.

"So, what's the answer?" he asked suddenly.

"Go with God. And check everything with him," she said. Darren nodded seriously, but an instant later a smile broke over his face.

"That's good spiritual advice, but I was asking about the pizza. Which one is best?"

She laughed and realized how much she had missed Darren.

"Well, I'd never had pineapple and Canadian bacon before." She grinned. "I guess I'll vote for that."

"And I'll second your opinion on going with God." Impulsively he stretched out his hand and squeezed hers. "So what's next for you?"

"Eventually I might be able to go back to my old job. I'm doing freelance work for my former boss. Right now there are no positions open, but who knows?" She tilted her head. "How about you?"

"I have a job with a temporary agency, but I'm trying to figure out my next step. I might go back to school and work part-time or move back to Portland and live nearer my brother. I'm not in any rush to decide, and it's great to have a choice again."

She saw his eyes grow large as he looked behind her. Before she could turn to look, two people took chairs at the table in one fluid motion.

"Mind if we share?" Kurt asked.

Casey looked wildly from him to Amy. Then her eyes narrowed and returned to Darren. She remembered her surveillance from the upper level and realized this was exactly what she had feared. He, however, looked equally surprised.

In unison Amy and Kurt each put a restraining hand on one of her arms to prevent her from jumping up.

"Lydia sent us," Amy said.

Her words paralyzed Casey. She shook her head as if to clear it.

"I knew we'd scare her," Amy told Kurt, who looked contrite.

"But if we'd let her see us coming, she would have run," he said. Casey regarded them both suspiciously.

"Kurt and I spent a lot of time with Lydia," Amy explained. "He visited her to the end. The three of us formed a very special bond as her life slipped away. We were both with her when she died." She fell silent for a moment, and then locked her eyes on Casey's. "We wanted you to know your coming into the Body and then leaving was not in vain."

"I don't understand." Casey studied Amy's young face.

"You stirred up the pond," Kurt said. She swiveled her gaze to him. "You came in, bucked the system, and left. For most people it was merely upsetting, but for a few of us," he said and looked at Amy, "it was a catalyst to make us think critically about the Bodylife for the first time." Casey caught the looks passing between Kurt and Amy. She looked at Darren to see if her assessment was correct.

"You see the same things about the Body that drove Darren and me out?" Casey asked. Kurt nodded firmly. "And you and Amy are leaving the group too?" Again the affirming nod. When she turned to Amy, the pink on her cheeks and the radiance in her eyes spoke volumes. "That's wonderful!" Casey hugged Amy, and Darren shook Kurt's hand.

"We also wanted to hear what Lydia had to say. Even though she gave us the letter, we never read it. What was in it?"

Darren and Casey looked at each other, horrified.

"I can't believe I forgot!" Darren slapped himself on the forehead and reached into his shirt pocket.

"We were having such a nice lunch." Casey was equally put out with herself. "How stupid." She reached eagerly for the letter, then turned somber.

"Why don't you read it, then tell us what she said?" Amy suggested. Casey shook her head.

"Even though it's addressed to me, I bet it's for us all. I'll read it aloud." She unfolded the sheets and gulped when she saw Lydia's delicate handwriting. She read in a soft voice, and they all leaned forward as if to embrace each word.

My Dear Casey:

You will receive this after I am gone because someone reaches out to you in love and friendship. Accept the friendship. I know you have a difficult time doing that. Do it for me, and most of all, do it for you.

Casey's voice broke. She took a sip from her drink and resumed.

I wish I could see you smile, visit you now that you are away from the Body, and atone for my part in misleading you. Hindsight has shown me that even though my heart was right, the direction I led you was wrong. I draw great peace in your forgiveness. I wish I could forgive myself as easily.

Tears welled in Casey's eyes, and she could read no further. Gently, Amy took the letter and began to read.

> *Do not grieve now that I have gone (well, all right, you can grieve a little bit!). I am experiencing what men have dreamed about and tried to imagine for centuries: I am in the presence of the living God. I have seen the face of my Brother, my Lord, my Savior, Jesus. Even if there were no feast to come in heaven, if there were no reunion of the saints when I will see you again, one look at the face for which I have longed all my life would be reward enough. As I write, I know it will be a glorious experience.*

Amy bit her lip. Kurt picked up the letter and continued.

> *I ask only that you go on to become the person you were designed to be by the Creator of the universe who hung the stars. You have so much to offer! You were wounded and have grown to mistrust yourself.*
>
> *However, you were never to be trusted in the first place—none of us are. Only Jesus is trustworthy. Only he can heal the wounds inflicted in the house of supposed friends—as he would describe his own scars. Let him heal your wounds and raise you back up.*

Though not as overcome as the women, Kurt wavered in his reading. When Darren reached for the letter he gave it up, indicating where he'd left off.

> *Be good to yourself. Never stop seeking after him. Try every day to open your heart a little more to the people around you who care for you so deeply. Why not start with the person who brings you this letter? I have a deep peace about the messenger, though I have no assurance who it will be. Read these words and picture my smile, touch the paper and feel my hug, wrap yourself in the message I send and connect yourself to life again. With God's help, you can do it.*
>
> *Ever your sister, Lydia*

Amy and Casey wept unashamedly. Kurt and Darren wiped their eyes.

"Isn't it like her?" Casey blew her nose on a napkin. "To encourage, admonish, love, and joke—all in one letter. So like her." She fell silent, and memories flooded her mind.

"She was a wonderful person," Kurt said. "I'm glad I came to know her at the end."

"What did you talk about together?" Casey was hungry for any connection to Lydia.

"We talked about you a lot. And about the Body."

"I called him her 'gentleman caller,'" Amy laughed. "It brightened her whole day to know Kurt would be over in the evening."

"Thank you for doing that," Casey whispered.

"I think I got more from it than she did. I used to ask her how she was, and she always had a funny reply. She'd say she only needed a minute to put on her water wings, or ask me to have them bring the limo around and she'd be out directly to go shopping." They all smiled softly. "The first time I went to see her, it was so I could tell her I understood and I forgave her."

"Forgave her for what?" Darren asked.

"She used me to help Casey get out of the Sisters House. I'm not sure how." He looked at Casey, who looked back sheepishly. "Anyway, I went to tell her she'd done the right thing. It really seemed to make her feel better."

"She would have hated to have you remember her as deceptive," Casey said.

"She was very peaceful at the end," Amy said. "Her only concerns were others she'd drawn into the Body, and she was worried about getting this letter to you. I can see why it was so important to her."

"She knew it would be for more than me," Casey said. "It's amazing she didn't know who would bring it but had faith it would be a friend." She looked around the table. "Friends," she amended. They reached out their hands to each other around the table. Casey was sure she wasn't the only one to feel the presence of a fifth member in their circle.

41

Cold dew clung to Casey's bare feet as she moved around her small garden. The early morning sunlight warmed her back and set fire to the tomatoes peeking between leaves. Each morning she rose early to tend the garden before the day became too warm. After careful tending, she had a veritable thicket of tomato plants and more than a hundred ripening tomatoes. She had finally stopped counting them and worked to restrain herself from harvesting them before they were ripe.

The corn she had planted was a continuous revelation to her. From nothing more than big bits of grass in the beginning, the plants had thickened and shot up. At almost eight feet tall, they towered over the tomatoes, which used the corn as a trellis. Fat ears clung to the stalks, and she anticipated the day when she would break off a few and cook them.

As she worked, she realized it was no accident that God started his special creation in a garden. There was a spiritual dimension to almost everything she did or saw. It stirred her deeply to see the details God had built into even simple plants.

The corn leaves were bordered with a narrow burgundy stripe. The fuzz on them directed moisture so the cup formed by young leaves unrolling was filled with a jewel-like bead of water. The dew, cleverly diverted, provided moisture throughout the hot day.

"God waters me like that," she murmured, stroking the silk protruding from one ear of corn. The peace of the garden washed over her. When she bent to lift the heavy tomato branches, she was delighted to find a huge beefsteak tomato bursting with red vibrancy. She pulled it from the plant. Her first tomato! It filled her hand even as the pungent fragrance from the vines filled her nose. She put the tomato into the small basket she carried for this first harvest morning.

By the time she had completed her circuit of the plants, the basket was filled with glowing red orbs. Even more important, her heart overflowed with gratitude for God's ongoing patience and tending of her life. It had taken a bit of manure for her to blossom, but she felt that the fruit she craved was almost ready for harvest. Like a bead of dew in the crux of a young corn plant, she held the hope of it close to her heart.

"When will you see your friends again?" Claude slid luscious tomato slices onto his plate as the platter circled the table. He almost seemed to regret the steak next to it.

"I'm not sure." Casey accepted the plate from him. "We agreed we'd meet again after Kurt and Amy had left the Bodylife." Her face clouded. "That was three weeks ago. I hope they're okay."

"Why don't you call Amy?" Jessie spread butter on a slice of freshly baked bread and put three tomato slices on it. She took a bite, closing her eyes in delight.

"It's not that simple." Casey reminded them. "You can't call them. You never know who will answer the phone. The Brothers and Sisters aren't free to talk on the phone, make appointments to see people outside the Body without getting into trouble, or to make plans to leave it. You remember what happened when I went to lunch with you. I know it sounds like prison to you, but you get used to it."

"I don't know if I'd want to get used to it," Jessie said.

"It's not healthy, but it's what Kurt and Amy are dealing with right now. I can't call them without causing them a lot of trouble, so I'll wait to hear from them."

"And what about Darren?" Claude examined his forkful of steak with a satisfied air. "I feel a little proprietary about him, since I talked to him on the telephone once." He put down his fork and patted her hand to let her know he was kidding. "Seriously though, I've been praying for him ever since. It's something God has put on my heart."

"That's really sweet, Claude." Casey was surprised. "I'll tell him. I think it will mean a lot to him." She colored. "Or you could tell him yourself next Sunday." Jessie raised an eyebrow. "He's coming to church, and I thought we could have him over for dinner afterward." She tried to sound casual, but her face betrayed her.

"Ah, now I understand," Jessie said. Casey looked baffled. "Cookbooks. Everywhere. Opened to the most incredible recipes. I had a feeling it wasn't just for us." Jessie grinned at Claude.

"I can see him somewhere else if you'd prefer."

"Nonsense." Claude wiped his mouth with his napkin. "I think it's time we both got a good look at this young man and I gave him the third degree. After all, I'm your father stand-in, and I have a vested interest in your happiness. So bring him on."

Casey opened her mouth to protest, but Jessie cut her off. "Don't worry about Claude. He'll be as good as gold." She gave her husband a stern look. "Won't you?"

He adopted a little-boy pout and hung his head. "Yes, ma'am."

Casey burst out laughing at his hangdog look. When he grinned back at her, she knew the special dinner would be all right.

"You tell her," Jessie said.

"Now it's not like she's going to be upset," Claude replied.

"I feel guilty."

"What's to feel guilty about? How could we have known a year ago Casey would be here with us?"

Casey could stand it no longer. She had not intended to

eavesdrop, but she heard their voices as she came down the hall and slowed to a standstill before she realized what she was doing. She stepped into their open bedroom doorway.

"What is it you have to tell me?" Her heart beat quickly. "Have I outstayed my welcome at last?" She kept her voice light but feared their answer. Claude and Jessie turned.

"Honey, no." Jessie rushed to put an arm around her. "We love having you here." She drew Casey into the room and looked at Claude for him to intervene.

"In three weeks we celebrate our twenty-fifth anniversary," he said. Casey felt relief and confusion.

"Congratulations. Do you want me to go away for a few days and give you some space?"

"I'm afraid it's we who are going away. Claude booked a week-long cruise a year ago."

"How fun for you." She looked back and forth between them. Claude looked relieved, Jessie sad. "What is it?"

"Jessie doesn't want to go, because she doesn't want to leave you alone," Claude said.

"Oh, Jessie." Casey hugged her friend fiercely. "I love how you worry about me. Really, I'm a big girl now. I once had my own house, my own life. Remember?"

"But this is for a whole week."

"Think of me as the house sitter. Take a million pictures while you're gone, because I want to see the beautiful turquoise water. Deal?"

"Deal." Claude smiled his gratitude. He turned to Jessie. "Satisfied?"

"Well ..."

"Come on, we've got to get to church." Casey tugged until Jessie surrendered and followed her from the room; Claude brought up the rear. "When do you leave?" Casey asked as they stepped out the front door.

"The twenty-first," he said.

"And we'll be back on the twenty-ninth."

"Stay away as long as you like. I'll be fine. I'll have a nice, dull, uneventful week."

"If you'll take those bulletins you've been fanning yourselves with, we'll run through the announcements," the young assistant pastor joked. "I promise by next week we'll have the air-conditioning working again." A good-natured chuckle rose from the congregation as people opened the folded programs.

"The women's retreat is upon us again," he said. "I know you all remember the moving testimonies we heard last year. This is a life-changing time for many ladies, and I encourage all of you to seriously consider it."

Casey glanced at the bulletin. Jessie dug an elbow into her right side and pointed to the dates. Casey shook her head.

From her left Darren leaned toward her and whispered, "Are you going?" She shook her head again. "It looks like it would be good," he added.

After the congregation rose for a last blessing and farewell, everyone spoke at once. Three women asked Jessie if she would room with them at the retreat.

"Claude is whisking me off to the Caribbean for our anniversary. But maybe Casey ..."

Darren and Casey stood to one side and waited while Jessie and Claude were greeted and hugged by at least half the congregation.

"Is there a reason you don't want to go to the retreat? These seem like really nice women," Darren asked.

She stifled a groan. "I don't do retreats very well. I tend to get all weepy and spend a lot of time by myself thinking. It's exhausting."

"Sounds rough—looking inside your heart, getting closer to God, making new friends—definitely a bad idea." She looked at him and narrowed her eyes. He continued, "I mean, who would want that? You're right. You should steer clear of it."

She saw Darren's smirk and slapped him on the arm. "I think this heat has gone to your head," she said. "We'd best get you out of the sun and feed you, if only to shut you up."

"Where did you learn to cook like that?" Darren asked. He sprawled on a patio chair, the warm glow of the living room lights behind them. Casey basked in his praise.

"Jessie is teaching me. It's like creating an edible painting."

"That it is." He patted his stomach. "I could eat the whole meal again." He slapped his thigh. "Whoops, I just did!"

She joined in his laughter. The fabulous meal of beef wrapped in pastry crust, sautéed garden vegetables, and fresh bread had stretched over two hours as Jessie and Claude got to know Darren. He and Claude had drifted into the living room and talked so long, he was invited to stay for dinner. Fully welcomed to the house, he now sat with Casey while Jessie and Claude finished up in the kitchen, as they insisted on doing. Andrew lounged luxuriously across Darren's legs.

"They're pretty terrific." Darren gestured in the direction of the house.

"They're like parents, friends, and a brother and sister all rolled into one. I lost my parents when I was twenty." She looked up as the first stars appeared in the sky. "In many ways I've been looking for replacements for them ever since. I think that's part of why I was so attracted to the Bodylife. It's very parental, when you think about it."

Darren considered. "Lots of control, plenty of direction, never on your own."

"I beat myself up about it for a while. Then I thought of what Lydia would have said about it." Her voice caught. "She would have told me the hunger for parents is God given. He calls himself our Father. He wants us to be his children. We hunger for that kind of parent-child family relationship with him. I let my hunger lead me to the wrong door, that's all."

"That's an interesting way to look at it. I had many regrets after the Bodylife got done with me too. I'm still struggling to make sense of it." Darren shifted in his chair.

Andrew rose from his supine position, stretched, turned around, and flopped down again.

"I may never truly understand the whole episode," Casey said, "but I'm learning to shake the pan and look for the gleam of gold. When I find some, I slosh the pan harder until the dirt and pebbles have washed out and I can pluck out the gold and keep it." A shooting star streaked across the sky, and they both pointed to it in unison.

"I guess that's the best we can do, try to mine the good from the bad." He sighed and ran his fingers gently under the cat's collar, and was repaid with intense purring appreciation.

"That's true no matter what we go through. I'm finally beginning to see the difference between the journey and the journey's end." The sliding door opened.

"I heard someone quote what a speaker said at a retreat she was on," Jessie said as she stopped behind Casey's chair. "He asked them if they lived a physical life with a spiritual dimension or a spiritual life with a physical dimension. It really shifts the focus."

Claude stepped up next to her and put an arm around her waist. "Was that an insight someone learned at a retreat, did you say? Wouldn't it be wonderful if they had something like that around here?"

His playful voice drew a snort from Casey. She threw her hands up. "Okay, okay! I surrender. I'll go."

"Retreat? What retreat?" Darren asked Claude with a wink. Both men smiled, and Andrew purred loudly.

42

asey changed her mind about attending the retreat. In fact, she changed her mind no less than four times during the first few days after Jessie and Claude left on their trip. By Thursday she had begun to make alternate plans for the weekend.

While Jessie was packing for the cruise, she had given Casey a bag to use for the retreat. She also insisted Casey begin to fill it so she would not back out. The suitcase nagged her conscience each time she saw it. Finally she decided to empty it and put it back into Jessie's closet. As she flipped open the lid she saw a note pinned to the sweatshirt on top.

> *Casey, I'll be praying for you all week. I know you'll have second thoughts about the retreat, but you wouldn't want all those prayers to go to waste, would you? Love, Jessie.*

She smiled weakly. Instead of emptying the suitcase, she added a few more things and at last yielded to the nudging in her spirit. She would be ready in the morning to drive north to the cool pines. Andrew leaped onto the suitcase, startling her. He immediately began to rub his paws on the top of the case as though to sharpen claws he no longer had. She gathered him in her arms and hugged him.

"Don't worry, sweetheart. I'll be back. It's only two days. You'll be fine." She held him away from her and looked into his eyes. "You'll sleep most of the time anyway." She lowered him back to the suitcase, and he immediately sprawled across it, preparing for a nap. "I rest my case." She shrugged.

If she left food, water, and a clean litter box, he would barely notice she was gone. Nevertheless, she did not want to worry about him, so she turned to the phone and dialed a number that had become more familiar to her as the weeks passed.

"Hey, Darren."

"Hey. I'm glad you called. You're not backing out on the retreat, are you?"

"No, it never crossed my mind."

"Right."

"Seriously, I've decided to go, but I want to ask a favor."

"Name it."

"Andrew. I'd feel better if you could look in on him each day."

"No problem. I'd be happy to do it. I like the little guy."

"He likes you too. In fact I get a bit jealous when you two get together." Warm affection flooded her.

"How do you want to work this? I'll need a key."

"I have to go past your place on the way to the retreat tomorrow morning. I could drop it off then."

"Put it in an envelope and slide it under my door. I'll pick it up when I get home and head over to keep Andrew company. It'll make a nice change of pace to sit on a real couch, watch a human-sized television, and enjoy a good talk with a deep conversationalist like Andrew."

Assured that her cat was in good hands, she said good-bye and finished her packing. Knowing that she had made herself accountable to someone else cemented her decision, and for the first time she felt good about the retreat.

Casey remembered her burst of feeling the day before and shook her head. Hands deep in her pockets, she strolled the forest trail, marveling that she had expected anything different from this retreat. As soon as she arrived, the old sense of isolation had descended on her, and she watched the interaction of the other women with envy. Despite their efforts to include her, she felt alien and separate from them. She had already begun her solo walks and thought it might be best to plead a sour stomach or oncoming flu and go home. The idea of facing Darren with her failure, however, was too much. She could always hide upstairs when he came, but he would see her car and come in looking for her.

The peaceful woods soothed her. Sun drifted through the trees and highlighted a flower here, a mossy patch there. Her stomach growled as the bell sounded for lunch, and she turned, putting off the decision of whether to leave or stay at least until she had some food in her.

At lunch the loud chatter of a hundred women filled the room and bounced off the pine rafters over Casey's head. She sat at a table with several other young women. When the subject arose about what church she attended before she came to theirs, she became vague. She was relieved when the retreat organizer called for their attention.

"We've got some great discussion groups planned for this retreat," she said. "That's the good news. The bad news is you'll each have to pick a subject, then commit yourself to one group for the weekend." She held up sheets of paper. "Each group will deal with that subject for the entire retreat, so there's more opportunity to get to know each other and share more deeply. As you leave from lunch, please select your topic and write your name on the sheet."

The noise level increased as women picked up their plates and utensils and carried them to the kitchen pass-through. Then the hubbub around the door began in earnest. Casey waited her turn to sign up. She read through the topics:

Intimacy with God
Developing a Servant Attitude
Revisiting Familiar Verses
Introducing Children to God
Finding Your Spiritual Niche
Discovering Your Spiritual Gifts
Becoming a Prayer Warrior
Accountability in the Body of Christ

She picked up a pen and scrawled her name under the third topic. She felt less threatened by it than any of the others. She would attend one session. Then she would probably leave.

Nothing was scheduled for the early afternoon, and when she stepped into the afternoon sunshine, she headed to her cabin for a nap. Losing herself in sleep was appealing, though she would miss her furry bedfellow and his whiskery wake-up call.

"Our goal for this weekend is to get fresh insights by digging into verses," said Janet, her golden hazel eyes shining as she made eye contact with each woman in turn. "Many will be verses we're all so familiar with we hardly hear them when they're read. But I want us to learn how to get past the familiarity and back to the root meaning behind them."

The group was eclectic. Betty, a bleached blonde in her mid-sixties, had a deep voice and a raspy chuckle. Her vinyl-type jogging suit imprinted with an antique map of the world crackled as she moved. She perpetually fanned herself, her dangling hoop earrings tinkling with each swish of her makeshift fan.

Beside Betty, Angela had already sifted through her Bible to find the verses listed on the sheet Janet handed out. Her long dark hair enveloped her in a silken cocoon in which she and her Bible were alone.

Carlotta grinned, and her widely spaced eyes glinted with pleasure. She had a long, gangly body and shoulder-length hair liberally sprinkled with gray. When she spoke, her arms flailed like branches in a high wind.

Casey, accustomed to the calm presence of Jessie and Claude, found that being so close to these unfamiliar women almost overloaded her senses.

"It's easy for us to become comfortable with prominent verses," Janet continued. "But my heart keeps asking how many other women have sat in this little room, read verses, and nodded their heads with no real understanding, then left here unchanged?

This is the Word of God! It should be fundamentally life changing whenever we open it. I want to seek renewed urgency and dynamic interaction with the Word here this weekend."

"I think the discussion will be a real challenge. I'm ready!" Carlotta flexed her biceps like a daredevil about to attempt a life-threatening stunt instead of a working mother embarking on a weekend of Bible study.

"I get all stirred up when you talk about it. It's an intriguing project." Angela cleared her throat and dodged one of Carlotta's arms.

As Janet called out the first verse, Casey quickly flipped through the pages of her Bible. Her sure fingers deftly turned the last crackly page, and her eyes ran down it to the verse and stopped.

"Here it is," she said. "Colossians 2:8. 'See to it that no one takes you captive through philosophy and empty deception, according to the tradition of men, according to the elementary principles of the world, rather than according to Christ.'" The women, their hair in hues of shining gold, copper, obsidian, or pewter in the sunlight slanting through the cabin window, nodded as though on cue.

Casey sat riveted to her chair in shock. She silently read and reread the verse she had spoken aloud. "Why did we have to start with this one?" she whispered hoarsely. The four women looked at her with a mixture of curiosity and compassion.

No one spoke as Janet dropped quietly to her knees in front of Casey and put her hand on her arm. "What do you mean?" she asked. "What's troubling you?"

Something in the soft touch gave Casey strength and courage. "I'm sorry, I was stupid to sign up for this class," she said. "I thought it would be the easiest group and I could escape unscathed."

Janet squeezed Casey's arm. "What does the verse mean to you? Will you share it with us?"

Casey wanted to pull back, close the book, and walk out immediately. Another voice seemed to whisper, *This is what you came here for. Let go. Let them care. Heal.* She let the second voice win the argument.

"I use my Bible as a combination study Bible and diary," she said. "If something really strikes me, I underline and highlight it and maybe even write a date and a comment in the margin. For instance, the date I accepted Jesus is written next to John 3:16, with a great big 'Hallelujah!' This Bible has been through a lot with me." She stopped, and Carlotta jumped in.

"That sounds neat. I wish I'd done that. I forget things almost as soon as I learn them sometimes—"

"But sometimes what we go through isn't what we want to be reminded of when we open the Bible." Quiet Angela cut Carlotta off. She rested her hand on Casey's back. "Some things are better left buried, aren't they?"

Casey started to nod, then frowned and shook her head.

"You don't know where I've come from. You don't know how stupid I've been." Her gaze encompassed Janet's hand on her knee, Angela's soft eyes, Carlotta's fingers knotted in her lap, and Betty's confused expression. Strangely it was to Betty she turned. "I'm sorry. I didn't mean to dump all this stuff like this. I don't mean to make you feel uncomfortable."

Betty leaned down and picked up the tissue box next to her chair. "Don't you worry, honey. Here, let's each have a tissue, then you can tell us all about it. I know I speak for all of us when I say nothing you tell us will leave this cabin unless you take it out." Angela reached for a tissue and passed the box.

"We're here to listen and discuss whatever you want." Janet had not moved from the floor. "If the verse comes into it, that's great, but don't feel confined by that."

Weary relief flooded Casey. The other women sat back. Their chairs creaked ominously with age and the past accommodation of campers of varying sizes.

Janet got up from the floor and hugged Casey. "Before we get started, let's all get something to drink, so we won't interrupt you. What would you like?"

"Is there any more diet soda—without caffeine?" Janet opened a picnic cooler and rummaged through the cans until she found one, then pulled it out. She wiped the lid with a tissue, opened it, and handed it to Casey. Angela pulled out other cans, offering them in turn to Betty and Carlotta. At last the sound of popping can tops and first slurps died away.

"Do you remember the verses about how in the end times Satan will try to deceive even those who know Jesus?" Casey flipped the pages of her Bible rapidly as she spoke. There were a few nods. "This Bible is a diary of a time when I chased what I thought was of God, only to find out it was nothing of the kind."

"Were you a Christian then?" Janet asked.

"Yes, I was."

Angela looked surprised, and so Casey explained. "Deception is nondenominational and equal opportunity." Her smile was sad. "You know, if you and I stand here together and walk across the room side by side, if I turn even a few degrees away from you, we'll be several feet apart by the time we get across the room. Deception starts out so subtly you don't think the difference matters much. However, every step takes you further from the truth until you can't even see it anymore. It's way over the horizon and out of sight." She frowned and shook her head. "So you begin to think you really have the truth, because the truth is too far away for you to compare notes with it." She stopped turning the pages in her Bible and shut it with her finger between pages.

"I don't care what you've been through," Betty said. "We're going to love you out of this thing. Tell us your story."

"I'm not sure a dedicated Christian can misstep into error like that," Angela said.

"If it weren't possible for Christians to be deceived, then why did Paul talk about it? Why did Jesus tell his disciples to watch for it?" Casey let them think for a moment.

"The verse I read speaks about not letting someone take you captive—which implies you have to give them permission to do it. If I had imprinted that verse on my heart as I should have, I might not have come to such grief." She realized that recounting her story would be harder than she'd expected. An idea came to her.

"Jesus told stories to illustrate his points, and I want to do the same. This is a true story, and it will hurt a lot to tell it because I have to open wounds and show you the mistakes I've made." She opened her Bible.

"All through the Bible, believers are referred to as sheep or lambs that need a shepherd to keep them safe. One of the first Scriptures most people memorize is Psalm 23, which begins, 'The Lord is my shepherd, I shall not want.'"

"Once there was a lamb so hungry for God's pastures she gave up everything to follow him. But it turned out she wasn't following him at all, and she was left in the wilderness, craning her neck for a sight of him...."

Through the long afternoon, Casey marched resolutely along the last steep road back to her Father. Her four new friends walked with her. They didn't flinch when she told them how gullible she'd been. They didn't criticize when she described her doubts and struggles with God. Instead they cheered her on and grew with her as she plucked treasures from among the heaps of gravel that had come to represent her spiritual life.

Somewhere along the way, she forgot her plan to leave the retreat early.

EPILOGUE

Despite her weariness and emotional exhaustion after the weekend retreat, Casey could hardly wait to step into the church Sunday evening. She was not in the habit of attending the evening service, but since this one would be devoted to testimonies from the women on the retreat, she felt energized to go. Women rose to speak about the movement of God in their hearts, and Casey sensed the word *amen* rise to the tip of her tongue repeatedly. At first shocked by the response, she grew to enjoy it as she realized that God had cleansed even this memory for her and she was free to respond.

An hour after the service began, Casey could contain herself no longer and moved forward. She missed Jessie and Claude and wished they were here for this special time, but she would have plenty to tell them when they returned. Right now she needed to focus on what the Lord wanted her to say.

"I decided not to go on the retreat." She saw confused frowns. "Several times." She grinned, and people chuckled with her. "And once I got there, I decided to leave. But I got my heart caught in the Bible and couldn't tear myself away." There were many nods of understanding, and Janet winked encouragement. Carlotta gave her a thumbs-up gesture and her infectious grin.

"God used this retreat like the first shower a homeless person gets when he finally comes in off the street," she said. "I had a lot of filth from my recent past. It's taken many months to crawl back out of the hole I had jumped into, and I don't think I could have done it without a chain of caring people who linked hands and pulled me out. This retreat added more loving people to my human chain of mercy, and I can't say enough about the experience."

Casey's vision blurred as her four new friends stepped out from where they sat together and came forward. They each hugged her in turn, and a soft, whispered amen filled the church. When Casey returned to her seat, she felt her heart open to the warmth surrounding her, and realized she was following Lydia's advice to the letter. The congregation broke into a chorus she had learned at the retreat, and she gave full voice to her joy.

There were still times when she questioned God's role in allowing her to be deceived as long as she had been. She knew the wrestling match in her heart would begin afresh as soon as the glow from the retreat wore off. It was inevitable she would try to take over control again in the future. However, she also felt sure that God would be as available to guide her as he always had been; she would just have to listen better.

The day was bright, and clouds skittered across an azure sky. The old man took it as a hopeful omen and pulled into a parking space in the freshly striped lot. The manicured lawn was achingly green, and he was amazed at the well-behaved children who ran and cavorted on the sidewalks, carefully keeping their feet from touching any grass.

"Good morning," a young woman with wiry red hair said. She reached for his hand and drew him into the building. "We're so glad to have you join us today." Her sincerity made the older man smile. He ran a quick hand through his unruly gray hair and hefted his thick Bible.

Inside, a young man who reminded him of his grandson approached with welcome printed across his handsome face. "Hi, my name's Dominic. I don't think I've met you before. Why don't you come sit by me, so we can get to know each other a little before the Gathering begins."

Amazed and pleased by the warm reception, he followed his new acquaintance, hoping the service would live up to the special glow he already felt.

"Oh, Lord, have I finally found what I've been looking for so long?" His whisper floated up and lodged among the microphones to await later harvesting.

Across town Casey quietly closed her notebook and slid her pen into an outside pocket of her purse. The sermon continued, but she lost herself in thumbing through her Bible, searching for truth to combat the automatic Bodylife twist her mind had given to one of the phrases the pastor had used. It had happened repeatedly in the months she'd been working to retrain her thoughts and unlearn the errors she'd so carelessly taken in. She sighed, realizing the damage of the Bodylife was deeper than she'd expected. She again asked God to temper her reactions and bring her overactive discernment back into balance.

"Save me from myself, Lord." Her lips twitched with ironic understanding at last.

Be on guard for yourselves and for all the flock, among which the Holy Spirit has made you overseers, to shepherd the church of God which He purchased with His own blood....

And now I commend you to God and to the word of His grace, which is able to build you up and to give you the inheritance among all those who are sanctified.

—ACTS 20:28, 32

Author's Note

It would be encouraging to imagine that groups like the Bodylife dissolve and fade away as those recovering from them reclaim their lives. In reality, for every person who leaves a spiritually destructive group, others are pulled in to take his or her place. For those who have been touched by the tentacles of deceit, this could lead to despair—were it not for the mercy and faithfulness of the Lord.

I rest my faith in the ultimate victory of Jesus, who shepherds us to the good grass and binds our wounds when we stray.

—BECCA ANDERSON

READERS' GUIDE

For Personal Reflection or
Group Discussion

READERS' GUIDE

I n *The Gathering Place*, Casey Ellis is a strong Christian who wants to be closer to God. Ironically her desire to know God more deeply starts her on a journey that takes her further from God and into a vortex of spiritual abuse that takes nearly everything she has. With *The Gathering Place* still fresh in your memory, take a few moments to answer the following questions to help you consider your own journey of faith.

1. The Gatherings are very different in style and content from what Casey had experienced at her own church in the past. How would you have reacted to an atmosphere like the enthusiastic one Casey encounters?

2. When Casey tells Jessie more about the Gatherings, she says, "It's so refreshing—but kind of intimidating too, because I seem to have such a long way to go to catch up." This alarms Jessie. If you were in Jessie's place, how would you have reacted? Why?

3. What were some of the warning signs that Casey ignored in her desire to belong and be involved in more vital Christianity? How did she rationalize each one?

4. Have you ever visited a group that raised red flags in your mind? What were they?

5. How would you determine if a group is crossing the line into spiritual abuse? What situations or behaviors might raise a red flag for you?

6. What Bible verses can help you discern a good church from a potentially abusive group?

7. Why would an experience like Casey's cause a believer to doubt herself and God?

8. Many people who experience spiritual abuse take a number of years to recover. Why do you think that is the case? What could other Christians do to help with this recovery?

9. What was the responsibility of Bodylife members once it became clear that Webster Forsythe and his wife were deviating from biblical truth?

10. The Bodylife group based its acceptance of members on their conformity to and performance of its rules. Why does this system cause such anguish? How do orthodox Christians sometimes do the same thing to one another?

11. Casey was a committed Christian hungry for a deeper relationship with God. How did this make her vulnerable to deception? How might spiritual pride push a person to join a group like The Bodylife?

12. Complacent Christians are not generally the ones that fall into deception—they stay in a comfortable church. How can a Christian seeking more fulfilling spiritual life protect himself or herself from being deceived? How can accountability to other believers keep Christians from falling into deception? What is the difference between legitimate accountability to other believers and the all-encompassing giving over of control that Casey fell into?

13. Jessie Barlow planned to attend a Bodylife gathering but was never able to do so. How do you think her ministry to Casey might have been different had she known firsthand what Casey was experiencing?

14. Is it a good idea to attend a group that you believe is abusive in order to try to win members away from it? Why or why not?

15. Do you know someone who is involved in an abusive group? What can you do to keep the lines of communication open, as Jessie did with Casey?

16. People who leave an abusive group are at risk to return to it—or to a similar type of group. Why do you think this is so?

17. There are many Internet resources that can help you or someone you know to learn about the doctrine and practices of abusive groups. How would you go about locating them?

18. Some abusive groups come to recognize the error in their methods or doctrine and reform themselves. What would the Bodylife group have to do to achieve this?

19. Kurt and Amy desired to leave the Bodylife group but had to wait until they felt they could make it on their own. In what ways had they given over control of their lives to the group, and what steps were needed in order to take back that control?

20. Lydia played a pivotal role in coaxing Casey into the Bodylife, as well as getting her out of it. Have you ever done something that hurt another Christian and then tried to correct the situation? Explain.

21. Despite her mistakes, Lydia was at peace when she died. Why?

22. What challenges would a young person who was raised in a group like the Bodylife face when he or she went out into the world and was exposed to biblically accurate churches?

23. The love and acceptance of other people were vital to Casey in her recovery. What concrete steps can you take to evidence the same kind of compassion and concern to someone struggling with spiritual deception?

24. Despite the information available about various abusive groups, people still join them. Why do you think this is?

25. Is there someone you know who is struggling with whether to leave a questionable group who could benefit from reading this story? What specific steps will you take to get it into his or her hands?

More Riveting Fiction from RiverOak . . .

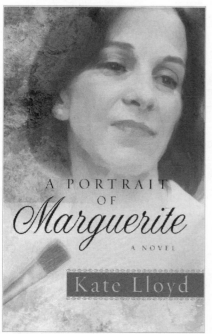

A Portrait of Marguerite

When single mom Marguerite Carr's son leaves for college, she feels as though her life has lost its purpose. After a friend drags Marguerite to a drawing class—her first since college—she rediscovers her long-lost passion for painting, finds unexpected love, and a relationship with God.

A Portrait of Marguerite is a real-life contemporary novel that isn't afraid to lift the corner of the rug to expose secrets and regret, while also offering hope of spiritual, personal, and creative growth. Readers will identify with Marguerite's internal struggles, which are relevant to almost all women today.

ISBN-13: 978-1-56919-056-6
ISBN-10: 1-58919-056-4 • Item#: 104522
320 Pages • Paperback • $13.99

Additional copies of *THE GATHERING PLACE*
and other RiverOak titles are available
wherever good books are sold.

If you have enjoyed this book,
or if it has had an impact on your life,
we would like to hear from you.

Please contact us at:

RIVEROAK BOOKS
Cook Communications Ministries, Dept. 201
4050 Lee Vance View
Colorado Springs, CO 80918

Or visit our Web site:
www.cookministries.com